Jonathan Dee is the author of five no
New York Times Magazine, a frequent
former senior editor of *The Paris Revie*
writing programmes at Columbia Univ.   The New School.
Palladio is also published by Corsair.

Praise for *The Privileges*

'A deliciously sophisticated engine of literary darkness.'

Guardian

'Lucidly written and with a pitch-perfect ear both for contemporary mores and dialogue, *The Privileges* is entertaining - and morally ambiguous.'

The Economist

'Mr Dee has given us a cunning, seductive novel about the people we thought we'd all agreed to hate. His case study of American mega-wealth is delicious page by page and masterly in its balancing of sympathy and critical distance.'

Jonathan Franzen, author of *The Corrections*

'Here is an incredibly readable, intelligent, incisive portrait of a particular kind of American family. Dee takes us inside the world of what desire for wealth can do, and cannot do, both for the self, the soul and the family. Told with admirable conciseness and yet with great breadth, the reader is swept along, watching the complications of such desire unfold.'

Elizabeth Strout, Pulitzer prize-winning author of *Olive Kitteridge*

'*The Privileges* is verbally brilliant, intellectually astute and intricately knowing. It is also very funny and a great, great pleasure to read. Jonathan Dee is a wonderful writer.'

Richard Ford

'*The Privileges* is an intimate portrait of a wealthy family that gradually becomes an indictment of an entire social class and historical moment, while also providing a window onto some recent, and peculiarly American, forms of decadence. Jonathan Dee is at once an acerbic social critic, an elegant stylist, and a shrewd observer of the human comedy.'

Tom Perrotta

'The subjects of money and class are seldom tackled head-on by our best literary minds, which is one of the reasons that Jonathan Dee's *The Privileges* is such an important and compelling work. *The Privileges* is a pitch-perfect evocation of a particular stratum of New York society, as well as a moving meditation on family and romantic love. The tour de force first chapter alone is worth the price of admission.'

Jay McInerney

'Dee is graceful; articulate and perceptive, and often hilariously funny... full of elegance, vitality and complexity.'

New York Times

'Jonathan Dee's scintillating fifth novel, *The Privileges*, tells the story of a golden couple, Adam and Cynthia Morey, who rise swiftly from modest Midwestern circumstances to immense wealth in New York. The book opens at their wedding in Pittsburgh, a scene that's a tour de force of shifting points of view, rendered with artistry and control I haven't seen since Ann Patchett's *Bel Canto*.'

Washington Post

ALSO BY JONATHAN DEE

Palladio
St. Famous
The Liberty Campaign
The Lover of History

The
Privileges
A Novel

Jonathan Dee

corsair

London

Constable & Robinson Ltd
3 The Lanchesters
162 Fulham Palace Road
London W6 9ER
www.constablerobinson.com

First published in the UK by Corsair,
an imprint of Constable & Robinson Ltd, 2010

This edition published by Corsair,
an imprint of Constable & Robinson Ltd, 2011

A copy of the British Library Cataloguing in
Publication Data is available from the British Library

ISBN: 978-1-84901-593-6

Printed and bound in the EU

1 3 5 7 9 10 8 6 4 2

For their inestimable help, the author wishes to thank
Amanda Urban, Ann Patty, Jennifer Smith, Todd Kumble,
the MacDowell Colony, the Corporation of Yaddo,
and the National Endowment for the Arts.

1

A WEDDING! THE FIRST OF a generation; the bride and groom are just twenty-two, young to be married these days. Most of their friends flew in yesterday, and though they are in Pittsburgh, a city of half a million, they affect a good-natured snobbish disorientation, because they come from New York and Chicago but also because it suits their sense of the whole event, the magical disquieting novelty of it, to imagine that they are now in the middle of nowhere. They have all, of course, as children or teenagers, sat through the wedding of some uncle or cousin or in quite a few cases their own mother or father, so they know in that sense what to expect. But this is their first time as actual friends and contemporaries of the betrothed; and the strange, anarchic exuberance they feel is tied to a fear that they are being pulled by surrogates into the world of responsible adulthood, a world whose exit will disappear behind them and for which they feel proudly unready. They are adults pretending to be children pretending to be adults. Last night's rehearsal dinner ended with the overmatched restaurant manager threatening to call the police. The day to come shapes up as an unstable compound of camp and import. Nine hours before they're due at the church, many of them are still sleeping, but already the thick old walls of the Pittsburgh Athletic Club seem to hum with a lordly overenthusiasm.

Mid-September. Since Labor Day, the western half of Pennsylvania has been caught in a late and dispiriting heat-wave. Cynthia wakes up in her mother's house, in a bed she's awakened in only five or six times in her life, and her first thought is for the temperature. She pulls on a T-shirt in case anyone else is awake, passes her burdensome stepsister Deborah (never Debbie) sleeping in flannel pajamas half on and half off the living-room couch, and slides open the door to the deck, from which she can see in the distance a few limp flags on the golf course at Fox Chapel. Cool, tolerably cool anyway, though it's still too early to tell anything for sure. It can't even be seven yet, she thinks. Not that she's worried. The specter of her bridesmaids holding beer bottles to their foreheads to cool off, or of Adam wiping the sweat out of his eyes as he promises himself to her, only makes her smile. She's not the type to fold if things don't go perfectly; what matters most to her is that the day be one that nobody who knows her will ever forget, a day her friends will tell stories about. She turns and heads back indoors, past her own fading footprints in the heavy dew on the cedar planks of the deck.

She never imagined a wedding in Pittsburgh, because she never had any reason to imagine it until her mother remarried and moved out here two years ago. To the extent she'd pictured it at all, Cynthia had always assumed she'd be married back in Joliet Park, but in the middle of her last semester at Colgate she learned that her father had sold their old house there, in which he had not lived for a long time; and when she announced her engagement two months later her mother Ruth went off on one of her unpacifiable jags about Cynthia's stepfather Warren being "a part of this family" and would not stand for any implication that this was less than entirely true. To force-march these outsize personalities back to the scene of the family's dissolution in Joliet Park, to listen to them bitch over the seating chart and over old friends whose post-divorce allegiances were sometimes painfully ambiguous, was out of the question. It would have been a gruesome sort of nostalgia, and pointless at that. A wedding is rightfully about the future if it is about anything at all.

They could have married in New York – where Cynthia and Adam already shared an apartment – and in fact that was the arrangement Adam gently pushed for, on the grounds, typically male, of maximum simplicity. But the truth was that that wouldn't have seemed unusual enough to Cynthia, too little distinct from a typical Saturday night out drinking and dancing with their friends, just with fancier clothes and a worse band. She wasn't completely sure why the idea should appeal to her at all – the big schmaltzy wedding, the sort of wedding for which everyone would have to make travel plans – but she didn't make a habit of questioning her wants. So Pittsburgh it was. Adam shrugged and said he only cared about making her happy; her father sent her a lovely note from wherever he was living now, implying that the whole idea had been his to begin with; and Warren expressed himself by opening up his checkbook, a consequence, to tell the truth, of which Cynthia had not been unmindful.

She tiptoes past the couch to avoid waking Deborah, because waking her might cause her to speak, and on one's wedding day there are some trials one ought to be spared. They don't know each other that well, but little things about Deborah excite Cynthia's derision as though they have lived together for years. The flannel pajamas, for instance: she is two years older than Cynthia but so congenitally chilly that she and Ruth might as well be roommates at the old folks' home. The house was bought with a second life in mind, a life in which the children were grown and gone, which explains why there is only one spare bedroom. Though the couch looks gratifyingly uncomfortable, Cynthia considered a campaign to pack Deborah off to the Athletic Club with all the other guests, so that her maid of honor and best friend, Marietta, could stay at the house instead. But family obligations are perverse. It makes no sense at all that this palpably hostile sexless geek should be one of her brides-maids, and one of Cynthia's many close friends' feelings hurt as a result; yet here she is.

In the kitchen Ruth, Cynthia's mother, whose last name is now Harris, is drinking a cup of tea standing up, in a green ankle-length bathrobe she holds closed at the neck. Cynthia passes her and opens the refrigerator without a word. "Warren's out," Ruth says, in answer to a question it would not occur to Cynthia to ask. "He went to get you some coffee. We only keep decaf in the house, so he went out specially for you."

Cynthia scowls at the effrontery of decaf coffee, a fetish of the old and joyless. Tossing a loaf of bread on the counter, she stands on tiptoe to search the cupboard where she remembers the ancient jams are kept; then, feeling her mother's gaze, she turns her head to look back over her shoulder and says, "What?"

It's the underwear: the fact that she is parading around in it, but also the underwear itself, the unhomeliness of it, the fact that her daughter has grown into a woman whom it pleases to spend a lot of money on underwear. Shameless is the word for it. All Ruth wants is a little gravitas for today of all days, a proper sense of nervousness or even fear, which she might then think of some way to allay. One last moment of reliance. But no: it became clear weeks ago that all this was no rite of passage into womanhood for her daughter – it's a party, a big party for her and all her friends, and she and Warren are just there to pick up the tab. For the last six or eight years, nearly every sight of her daughter has caused a certain look to cross Ruth's face, a look of just-you-wait, though the question "wait for what?" is not one she could answer and thus she keeps her mouth shut. The flatness of

Cynthia's stomach, the strength and narrowness of her hips, more than anything the way she carries herself with such immodesty in a body whose nearness to the modern ideal is bound to provoke an unpredictable range of response; self-satisfied women are often brought low in this world, and for years now, mostly by frowning, Ruth has tried to sneak her insights onto the record.

But she reprimands herself; today, no matter who cares to deny it, is not just any day. She feels the faint echo of her own terror in the hours before her first wedding, a terror that was partly sexual, which counts as a bond between them even though her daughter's sexuality is a subject she has long since lost the fortitude to go near. "So," she says, trying for a conciliatory tone. "This is your special day." And Cynthia turns around, mouth open, and laughs – a laugh Ruth has heard before, the only solace for which is a retreat into memories of when her only child was a baby.

Behind them, the digital clock on the microwave blinks silently to seven-thirty. In the living room, Deborah, having woken herself with her own snoring, makes a little groaning sound that no one hears and pushes her face deeper into the gap between the cushions and the sofa back. At the Athletic Club, the weekend desk clerk consults the computer print-out in her hand and dials the extension for Adam's room. She's seen the Daily Events schedule and recognizes his name as that of the groom; to the scripted wake-up greeting at the top of the printout she adds best wishes of her own, because she saw him last night and he's cute.

"Thanks," Adam says, and hangs up. He too goes straight

to the window to check the weather. His window faces the alley, though; he'll probably get a better sense of the day's prospects from the TV. He turns it on with the sound down but then lies back on the bed, fingers laced behind his head, and forgets to watch.

He hates sleeping alone and maybe for that reason he spent the minutes before the phone rang in an extravagant dream, a dream about driving a car with no steering wheel in it, a car that responded to his slightest weight shifts, like a skateboard or a sled.

One hour until breakfast in the hotel restaurant with his parents and his younger brother and best man, Conrad. Having thought of this, he tries to forget it again so that he can be genuinely blameless if he shows up late. He's a little hungover from the rehearsal dinner, though others, he reflects, will have cause to be a whole lot more hungover than he. Too early to call Cynthia, who's probably still asleep. What would really calm him down is sex with her – as it is he starts most mornings that way; it scatters the vague anxieties with which he wakes – but today that's not going to happen. With sudden inspiration he arches his back and pounds on the wall above his headboard, the wall his room shares with the room where Conrad is staying.

Conrad doesn't hear; up for an hour already, he is standing in the shower practicing his toast. It was the only duty that gave him any pause at all when he accepted the best-man role. He blushes and shakes whenever he has to speak in public; and how relatively easy it would be to pull this off in front of a ballroom full of strangers, as opposed to

7

friends and family with their license for pitiless long-term teasing, people before whom there is no question of pretending even for a few minutes that he is anyone other than who he is.

"They are a charmed couple," he says, because this is a phrase over which he's stumbled in earlier rehearsals; and it's too late now for a rewrite. "They are a charmed chouple. Fuck." And he starts from the beginning.

Waking in the other rooms on the second and third floor of the Athletic Club are friends of the bride and groom – couple friends, friends who have brought especially serious or promising dates – almost all of whom find themselves acting, at that hour, on a sexual impulse that's unsettlingly strong even for the bloom of youth. Some are laughing, and some stare into their partners' eyes with an urgency the memory of which will have them avoiding each other's gaze an hour later. They are not used to the licentiousness of hotel rooms; and the knowledge that on this particular weekend they have not just infiltrated this stuffy club but taken it over gives a subterraneous group sense to each intimate encounter, a sense of orgy that makes them want to offend strangers, to exert themselves until the walls of that place come down.

Indeed there is one couple that knocks the headboard against the wall behind Adam's parents' bed so loudly that his mother just prays she doesn't know them. She even tells her husband to call the front desk and complain, but he's in the bathroom and hears, as a rule, what he chooses to hear.

At eight-thirty Marietta's car rolls into the Harrises' driveway. Inside the kitchen she and the still undressed Cynthia kiss like sisters; "Jesus, it's fucking hot out there," Marietta says. "Oh hi, Mrs. Sikes. I mean Mrs. Harris!" It's more than Ruth can bear; she smiles premonitorily and withdraws from the kitchen.

"So shall we go do the hair thing?" Marietta says, but then all of a sudden Deborah is in the doorway, hair matted, face pebbled from the rough upholstery of the couch, looking at them both with tribal hatred.

"Your phone's ringing," she says to her stepsister, and turns and leaves.

The phone is on the bedroom floor, underneath the jacket Cynthia wore to the rehearsal dinner. Marietta follows her through the living room.

"Thanks for bringing it to me, there, Debski," says Cynthia, though Deborah has disappeared into the bathroom. "So, you didn't bring your dress? Where is it?"

"In the freezer," Marietta says.

"Oh, don't be such a baby. Haven't you heard? It's my Special Day."

"Well, that's my point. You're the bride. Still well within your power to change the whole dress code to, like, beach casual."

"Wear a tank top to your own wedding, slut," Cynthia says. "That's not how we roll here in Pittsburgh."

"I've got that not-so-fresh feeling," Marietta says. "That's all I'm saying."

In his chair watching CNN as they pass behind him,

Warren hears all this and, though he would still like to be a kind of father to this young woman, knows that for the moment the only dignified course is to pretend that he is not even in the room at all.

Cynthia smiles at Marietta and takes the phone out on the deck. "Isn't this bad luck?" she says, sliding the door shut behind her.

"I saw your dad in the lobby last night," Adam says. "I recognized him from his picture. He seemed in pretty good form. Have you called him yet?"

"No," she says, and her heart races a little bit. "I will in a while. Hey, what time is it?"

"Quarter to four."

"Very funny. I mean aren't you supposed to be at breakfast with your parents?"

"Maybe."

"Well don't leave Conrad alone with them, for God's sake. You know how they get. Plus he's got the rings so let's not antagonize him."

Adam smiles, waiting for the elevator in the empty hotel corridor. "Can you believe we're doing this?" he says.

The boards on the deck are already burning her feet. "Not too late to back out," she said, "if that's why you're calling."

"Well, I still have seven hours to think about it, right?"

"Me too. Tell you what, if I'm not there by, let's say, ten of four, you just go ahead and assume I'm not coming, okay?"

"Fair enough. Seeing how everything's paid for and all, if

you don't show I'll just wave one of the bridesmaids up and marry her."

"Which one you have your eye on?"

There is a pause. "I missed you when I woke up this morning," he says.

Her view of the golf course from earlier that morning has now been erased by haze. She closes her eyes. "Me too," she says. "You won't forget pictures, right?"

"Two-fifteen in the Trophy Room. Conrad's carrying around a little schedule."

"Okay," she says. "See you then. Enjoy your last few hours of freedom."

"Gotta go," he says. "The hookers are here."

She hangs up on him, smiling. In the living room, Marietta stands uncomfortably, while Deborah, back on the couch, watches her like a guard dog, like some emissary from the underworld of the socially damned. Marietta can read her hatred only as jealousy, which softens her own attitude a bit.

"So," she says, and remembers that Deborah is a graduate student somewhere, in something. "School is good?"

Adam strolls into the hotel dining room and sees that his parents, sitting with a stricken-looking Conrad, have ordered their breakfast but not touched it. They missed their connection in New York yesterday and arrived too late to make it to the rehearsal dinner, which may have been just as well. He kisses his mother on the top of her head. "How's your room?" he asks. "Everything to your liking?"

Adam's father makes a sarcastic noise, which his mother

recognizes and preemptively talks over. "Very nice," she says. "Very comfortable. You have to point out Cynthia's parents to me so we can say thank you."

The two sets of parents have never met. There didn't seem much point to it. "Marietta made it home okay last night?" Adam asks Conrad. Conrad nods but does not stop eating, because he would very much like to get this breakfast over with. Adam signals the waitress for coffee. He hasn't really looked at either of his parents since he sat down. No one is looking at Mr. Morey, though he seems to be mysteriously gathering himself nonetheless, like a clock about to strike. Two heart attacks have hunched his shoulders in the way of a man much older than he actually is. Up in the room are four portable oxygen tanks, in case he needs them, and in the purse at his wife's feet are various pills and phone numbers. But his short temper and unregulated resentments suggest that his physical failings are a kind of natural outgrowth of his personality, and everyone who knows him, mindful of his angry pride, is unsolicitous toward him. He is tormented by the efflorescence of foolishness and waste of all kinds, everywhere around him. He was a pipe fitter who became a full-time union executive until his disabilities forced him to retire. The Pittsburgh Athletic Club is exactly the kind of place that sets him off. His wife has made him put on a coat and tie for breakfast even though she will now have to hear about it for the next month.

But Adam is not embarrassed by them in this setting, as his brother is, because he doesn't really associate them all that closely with himself anymore. He is amused by their helpless compulsion to be themselves, and will wind them up like a music box at any opportunity. "Hey, you know what I found in my room?" he says. "In the dresser drawer? A list of room rates. Did you guys see that? Do you have any idea what this place *costs*?"

"Oh, Adam, *please*," his mother whispers, "today of all—"

"As it happens, I did," his father says, reddening. "I'm just glad I'm not the sap paying for all this."

"More reason to be glad we never had girls," his mother says, and laughs as if she were being filmed laughing.

"That wouldn't have made a damn bit of difference to me," Mr. Morey says. "I don't have to put on a show for anybody. I don't pretend to be anything I'm not."

Adam abruptly stands up. "Oh look, there's Mr. Sikes," he says. "Excuse me. I'm gonna go practice calling him Dad." And he crosses the room to where the bride's dapper father sits at a table by himself, reading the paper. Conrad watches him leave in disbelief. His parents stare accusingly at each other. A moment later the waitress comes by and fills Adam's coffee cup.

The doors to the hotel ballroom are shut, and behind them, in moments of silence, one can hear the vacuum cleaners run. Teenage girls in stiff black skirts walk from table to table, checking the place settings, counting on their fingers. They work slowly; the air conditioning is turned up all the way, and with the room not yet full of bodies it is exotically cold, the coldest place in the hotel. Only those most desperate for a cigarette pass through the double doors to the infernal kitchen and the steaming alley beyond.

At the hotel bar sits the wedding planner, habitually early, having sent her son and his friend to the florist's in her van, praying they haven't stopped to get high along the way. It's why she doesn't pay them in advance. The bar isn't officially open yet but Masha knows everyone at the Athletic Club; this will be her fourth reception there this year. Though it's before noon, she feels like (as her father used to say) a *drink* drink, and Omar the bartender would certainly comp her one, but while she's on the job alcohol is out of the question. Something like that gets out and your reputation is shot. True, the bride – whose superior attitude Masha doesn't especially care for – isn't even from Pittsburgh and acts as if she might never set foot here again after today; but the stepfather, whose name is on the checks, is some rainmaker at Reed Smith, and the mother, whose superior attitude she doesn't much care for either, is one of those chronically unsatisfied types who love nothing better than to nurse along some scandal, substantiated or otherwise.

But that's the secret to Masha's success: you get invested not in the people, who can let you down, but in the ceremony, which never does. She doesn't say it out loud very often but she thinks of herself as a guardian of some-thing, a finger in the dike holding back total indifference toward the few things that have always mattered, ritual and devotion and commitment. When you thought of it that way, the less you happened to care for the families themselves, the more noble your work became. Her own marriage ended after nine years, but that detracted in no way from the beautiful memory of her wedding day itself; in fact, that's what you were left with, she thinks, that and a beloved if somewhat less than reliable son. Besides, if it were up to her they would all still be together, husband and wife and child, through happy and contentious times alike. But not everything is her decision.

A couple around the bride and groom's age walks into the bar and Omar tells them that he's closed. The boy looks ready to argue the evidence, but the girl says, "Forget it. I need to go upstairs and take another shower anyway." That's what today's going to be, Masha thinks: a pageant of sweat. Eighty-eight already, according to the silent TV screen above Omar's shaved head. That was part of the risk they all assumed when they booked the most beautiful old unmodernized Catholic church in Pittsburgh. That's why she is waiting until the last moment with the flowers. She couldn't book them the weather. Not that that would stop the mother from blaming her for it anyway.

Across town Cynthia and Marietta sit bemused and intimidated, shirtless, their heads poking through holes cut in old bedsheets, as a tight-lipped Polish woman (recommended by Masha) and her young assistant do their hair. They tease each other with stories from their college days; all the stories involve embarrassment or regret but none of them can't be laughed at. Only a few of them are about men because Cynthia and Adam started dating sophomore year. The Polish women, in a kind of secondary theme, speak in unsmiling Polish about God knows what, at least until

Cynthia says something about how badly this whole ordeal makes her want a cigarette.

"Please no," the older one says, her scissors in the air. "Big kiss on altar, your husband think hey, my wife's head smell like fucking ashtray."

Their eyes meet in the mirror, already retelling it.

The doors to the church stand open, for circulation's sake, but the dust hangs motionless on the ramps of light that slope down from the tall windows. Masha watches her red-eyed son and his Mexican friend, whom she secretly calls Señor Detention, try to get the white runner straight atop the sun-bleached carpeting between the pews. She pulls a creased checklist out of her jacket pocket and walks past the kneeling boys to the pulpit; turning to face the rows of empty seats, she solemnly taps her finger on the live microphone.

"Stay out of heat," the Polish woman says hopelessly as Cynthia and Marietta button their shirts back on. "Whole thing fall down."

With the car's air conditioner at full blast, Marietta pulls into the Harrises' driveway again. Standing outside the kitchen door on the tiny landing, flat against the wall in the scant shade of the eaves, Deborah is standing among the rain boots and gardening equipment, smoking a cigarette. She is already wearing her bridesmaid's dress. Eyes barely open, she glowers hatefully at the tinted windshield of the car.

"What is she doing?" Marietta says. She sounds almost scared.

"I don't know," Cynthia says wearily. "There's always some grievance."

"But why is she smoking outside in this heat? Is smoking not allowed in your mom's house or something?"

"Warren smokes. He smokes in the house all the time."

"Then why is she—"

"You know what?" Cynthia says. "Pull out. I can't even deal with going back in there right now. Go on, back out. I know someplace we can go."

Deborah watches them leave and smiles at the prospect of her stepmother's panic. Mother and daughter are so alike. No capacity for seeing themselves through others' eyes, no interest in it. No one ever opens a book in that whole god damned stunted hell-bound house, including her father, whose idea of self-betterment is watching *Unsolved Mysteries*. The aspect of him she's always cared least about is his money, but now that he's letting these two spend it like it's theirs, she resents them as climbers, her nominal stepsister especially. She knows this pains him. Make an effort, he keeps telling her, but no effort is necessary to understand the likes of Cynthia and her friends. One day it will hit them that high school is over.

Adam sits on the bed in his underwear. He's watching the Pirates game on TV. He considers masturbating, out of boredom, but there is too great a likelihood that Conrad or someone else will knock on his door. There is a great sense of bustle in the walls around him but nothing seems to require him right now. It's far too awful outside to go for a run. Why did they schedule the wedding for four in the afternoon, anyway? Solitude and inactivity make him restless. At his bachelor party last weekend – a rafting trip on the Delaware with his six groomsmen – there was never a moment of idleness; gloriously exhausted, they slept in tents, some expensive Scotch but no real drunkenness, the whole thing put together by Conrad, one of the two or three best nights of his life. They'd cheerfully teased him by recounting old hookups, old binges, old mortifications. There was some ritual sarcastic mourning of all the sexual freedom he was waiving, but he could tell – it makes him smile now to remember it – that their hearts weren't in it, because none of them really thinks he is making a mistake. He's slept with other women, before he and Cyn met and, truth be told, for a short time after. What's left to mourn there? Just an adolescent obsession with variety, and he is past that point. They are meant for each other: he feels it so deeply that he's not quite able to say it, not even to her. She's like one of those horse whisperers, he thinks, only it's just him, he's the only one it works on, she's the only one he will let speak to him that way. It would seem juvenile to go back to wanting anything other than what he has. He also has a home, and a job, and he is impatient, in possession of these things, to leave his childish self behind and get the future under way in earnest.

He finds his phone on the dresser and calls her again. "I talked to your dad at breakfast," he says. "You should give him a call."

"I'm going to."

"Where are you?" he says.

"At the airport. Don't try to have me followed."

"No, seriously." He strains to make out the background noise, then realizes it's the same as the background noise in his own room. "Are you at the Pirates game?"

She laughs. "I'm in a bar with Marietta. We've had our hair done, but we're not ready to go back to the House of Pain just yet."

"What bar?"

"In your dreams," she says.

"Well, okay, but just don't show up drunk at the altar, because my last wife did that and, let me tell you, it really lowered the tone."

She smiles. The TV plays on a shelf above the scarred oaken bar, in the wonderful, midday, reptile-house gloom. With her fingers she ruins the circle of condensation that her vodka-and-soda glass keeps leaving on the wood. She knows why he's calling. "So," she says, "you're doing okay?"

When she says it she swears she can hear his breathing slow down. "Sure," he says. "I'm fine. I just don't like all the waiting."

They go over the schedule again and hang up, and Cynthia notices her maid of honor staring at her. "He's nervous, huh," Marietta says. She drinks. "So, are you nervous?"

Cynthia's first reaction, she has to admit, is to deny it without thinking about it, because she knows this is how she and Adam figure in the lives of their friends: as the fearless ones, dismissive of warnings and permissions, the ones who go first. But when she does think about it she realizes that the answer is still no. They are perfect together.

"He makes me laugh, and he makes me come," she says. "And he needs me much too badly to ever fuck things up."

"Well, I'll drink to that," Marietta says, but then she doesn't drink. Her own date is spending the morning in the hotel gym; nothing about this whole weekend will please him as much as the discovery that his daily workout routine doesn't have to be altered. She stares into the cloudy mirror behind the bar, where their elaborately coiffed heads float as if in an aquarium. In this splendid dump they look like extras who have wandered off a movie set. "Hey," she says. "Your head smell like fucking ashtray."

As the heat peaks the city takes on a dirty sheen. Behind the haze the sun can only be approximately located, like the source of a headache; on the sidewalks each citizen moves forward in a kind of cocoon of dampness. The wedding guests have abandoned any half hearted plans to see some more of the city – the church is just a three-minute walk across the park from the Athletic Club and they will wait until the last minute even for that. Unhurriedly they take the tuxedo shirts out of their boxes, recount the studs and the cufflinks, hang the dresses on the bathroom door and turn on the shower to steam the travel wrinkles out of them. With nothing else to do they prop open their doors and turn the place into a dormitory. Someone puts on some music and the first complaint from the front desk arrives. They have begun drinking. Special occasions are marked by feats of excess.

One-forty and no one knows where the bride is. Deborah hasn't said a word; she lies on the couch in her bridesmaid's dress, reading Walter Benjamin and drinking a Diet Coke. Ruth feels as if her brain is going to blow out of her head like a champagne cork. At the same time she feels justified in some way by the threatened emergence into reality of her vision that this whole day would end in disaster. Her daughter left the hairdresser's more than an hour ago. Fine. It upheld Ruth's view of life, her own life at least, to think that the things that mattered to her were, in everyone else's estimation, a joke. Thirty-eight thousand dollars her husband has sunk into this day – more than the old days gave them any right to dream of – and Cynthia has barely acknowledged him; as for Warren, he has been putting on his tuxedo in the bedroom for an hour now, which, since he is a man who knows how to wear a tuxedo, suggests to Ruth that he is avoiding her. What's worst, though, is her full awareness, even at a moment like this, of her daughter's supreme, blithe competence. In another few minutes, with no word from her, they will have no choice but to proceed to the Athletic Club for the photo session as planned, and Ruth knows, in her heart of hearts, that Cynthia will be there. Of course there will be no real disaster: instead there will be the vindication of that refusal to take any of it seriously, to treat respectfully the day that marked the end of motherhood. Till death do us part. Big joke.

The only one who has already braved the walk from hotel to church, several times today in fact, is Masha. Wearing a maroon blazer – a little heavy for a day like this, but the item in her closet that came closest to matching the burgundy of the bridesmaid's dresses – she is losing the battle to maintain a fresh, unruffled appearance throughout the day's events, that projection of capability that's normally a key element of her job; but today, she keeps telling herself, is a special case. She's sent her son to Wal-Mart, even though she knows he's high, to buy every standing fan they have. She's glad the groom is a little late for their meeting before the photo session. She doesn't particularly care anymore how it might look that she's waiting for him in the hotel bar. She drinks club soda after club soda and watches the guys in the band carry their own drums and keyboards and amplifiers into the ballroom, gasping and swearing, while she tries discreetly to check the size of the sweat stains under her arms.

Then the groom enters, black-tied, a very handsome boy with a highly developed sense of charm. "The wedding planner? Oh, she's in the bar," he says as he holds out his hand. It comes back to Masha that he is from New York City and has a way of speaking that's sometimes difficult to follow.

In the Trophy Room they find Ruth and Warren and Warren's mother, who at eighty-seven has lost track of time's more incremental movements and thus is as pleased to wait there indefinitely as her daughter-in-law is perplexed and insulted. They are more or less flattened against the wall by the door in order to avoid inconveniencing the photographer as he testily moves the lights and rearranges the furniture. No one else is there. The photographer, a short man with a neat mustache and a drinking problem whom Masha has worked with many times, is pleased to see her because here at last is someone with whom he may safely lose his temper.

"She has something better to do?" he says, smiling tightly, speaking of the bride. "There's maybe something good on TV?"

With her back to Adam, Masha lifts her eyebrows at the photographer as if to say what can we do, this is what we're working with; and she says, "Allow me to introduce the groom, Adam Morey."

The photographer's mood is softened by Adam's charisma only because he sees that here is a young man obviously not averse to having his picture taken. The groomsmen file in; he can tell, mostly from their adolescent nudging, that a few of them are drunk. Who gives a shit, he reminds himself, and grabs one of them and points to his mark on the floor. He makes a note of the groom's parents (the father has the same strong chin and small mouth, the same convex hairline) standing with their backs to the wall, gazing at their son as if from a great distance, as if crowds were cheering, as if they were standing on an ice floe.

Then the bride walks in, ahead of her own entourage like a prizefighter, in the dress, the makeup, the veil and gloves, the full regalia. Masha and Ruth together make a gasping sound that's as unrehearsed as anything they'll say or feel all day. "No rush," says the photographer, but already his sarcasm is losing its edge – his work bores and harries him but he is not inured to beauty – and he goes to look at her through the camera. Behind Cynthia come the six bridesmaids, Deborah several steps in front of the rest in her eagerness to get out of that awful suite where the beautiful ninnies chattered. The bridesmaids fan out by the door, sharing one of those gigantic bottles of water, picking at the sleeveless wine-colored dresses that are already darkening in spots.

This is why they are late: on her way to the suite set aside for the bridal party's preparations, Cynthia had finally stopped and knocked at the door to her father's room; he had opened the door in his tuxedo, looking like a movie star, though also older and thinner than she remembered him; and then, as she'd known all along she would without quite knowing why, she collapsed in tears. He took her in his arms and shut the door and whispered the little things that only he could get away with and then a few minutes later she reemerged and went to the elevator bank to go get her makeup applied.

He's last to enter the Trophy Room. Life does not seem versatile enough to account for the fact that this man and Cynthia's mother once fell in love and got married. Ruth herself has trouble accepting it as true, not because she has forgotten but because she remembers the strong impression he gave, every day for ten years, that he was late for some amusing engagement somewhere else. Now she watches in horror as Warren crosses the room to shake her ex-husband's hand. It's her fate, she thinks, to end up loyal to men who don't understand loyalty themselves.

There is only one person in the room Conrad's age whom he hasn't known for years, and that's Deborah. It's

her he winds up standing next to after the family photograph; and she doesn't actively ignore him because there's
something in his face that she doesn't see in the Barbie faces
of everyone else in the room.

"I'm actually a little nervous," he finds himself saying.
"I have to give the toast."

That's what it is about him, she thinks, a recognizable
human emotion. Unconsciously she pulls at the neckline of
her bridesmaid's dress to try to keep her tattoo covered. He
looks about eighteen, though she knows he must be older
than that; at some point all these people were in the same
college at the same time, or maybe it just seems that way.
"You'll get through it," she says, not unkindly. "Just be
yourself."

The room grows noisy, and at the center of it, Adam and
Cynthia stand staring at each other, at the odd three-quarter
angle into which the photographer manhandled them when
it became too difficult to explain what he wanted. His arm
around her waist. Something has been missing all day and
this was it. When they are close together no one else can
touch them. Their homes, their families, everything that
made them is behind them now and will remain so from
here on in. Masha pops up with a handful of tissues to wipe
the sweat off Adam's forehead.

"I lost weight while getting married!" Adam says. "Ask
me how!"

"Stop talking!" barks the photographer. "Memory time!"

This is where it starts to become a blur. And now, finally,
as they take orders to turn their heads or change the position

of their fingers – as they stand rooted at the apex of a continually reconfigured V – comes the feeling they didn't quite credit before now, the feeling that the ceremony itself has taken over and begun to bear them along. Everything is dictated from here. They've exchanged themselves for their roles and it is not at all an unpleasant or a violated feeling. In the end not even their memories will have to be relied on; images of the day and night that have been taken out of their hands will arrive in the mail, weeks from now, formally and expensively bound.

The church is a furnace. With the heatwave in its second week, Masha's son was able to find for sale only five standing fans; the breeze they generate falters at about the third row. One young mother with a baby, a cousin of the groom's, stands up from her pew and heads back to the hotel before the ceremony has even begun. But Masha is at home at the intersection of pageantry and crisis; she calls the ushers together to instruct them to seat the eldest guests nearest the doors, regardless of their affiliation to bride or groom, and delivers a quick first-aid course in case of fainting. In the event, though, it's one of the ushers, a blond-haired boy named Sam, who finally passes out, just at the end of the aisle. Too exhausted to be discreet, his friends lay him awkwardly across the rearmost pew. Masha cradles his head in her lap and pulls out the smelling salts she had the foresight to transfer from the home first-aid kit into her purse just that morning.

The rest of them proceed to the altar a man down. What

seemed like such a lightweight job has proved so brutal that it's starting to seem a little funny, all the more so when they stare across the altar at the bridesmaids, who look as if they have just come from a five-mile hike in their red dresses. But then the familiar martial introduction rolls down from the organist's loft, a hundred and twenty people struggle gamely to their feet, and their attention gathers at the point where the light is strongest, at the church door. In the heat and glare the bride and her father shimmer slightly.

Marietta, who unlike most of them has had a few hours to grow used to the sight of her best friend in a wedding dress, keeps thinking about the ceremony itself, how many of its accepted elements seem wrong on symbolic grounds and should be changed. Why would you walk toward the man with whom you wanted to share your life in that halting, infantile gait, slower than you'd walked across any room in your life, as if you were being brought in by the tide? Wouldn't it be more auspicious to slip off your torture shoes and run up there? Then she realizes that what she's having, in effect, is a conversation with Cynthia, who would normally share her subversive interest in the day's many weirdnesses, but who's on the other side of the glass now. They have promised each other over and over that none of what exists between them will be lost, but neither of them has ever had a married friend and so neither of them really knows. She watches Cynthia's father, that charming piece of shit, squeeze his daughter's arm emotively without taking his eyes off their destination; he looks like Washington standing in the boat. Knowing how to behave on grand occasions has never been his problem; it's the ordinary that could never sustain his interest.

When they finally arrive and the last note of the processional fades, he kisses her on the cheek, says something private to her, and withdraws. All eyes turn to the priest, who, in his mountainous bell-shaped surplice, resembles one of those eternally trickling monuments.

"Before we begin," he rumbles into the microphone, "may I suggest that under the circumstances it is permissible for gentlemen to remove their jackets."

For about a year after her husband left her, Ruth took Cynthia to Saint George's in Joliet Park every Sunday, trying to make the best of his absence by mounting a campaign of moral improvement. Then one Sunday Cynthia announced she would never go again, and that was that. So Ruth was surprised when her daughter said she wanted a church wedding. Surprised and a little offended, because a house of worship is not a stage set; but Warren convinced her to let that particular grievance go. Now, as the guests sit in unison and the sound of their sitting throws an echo over the faint buzz of the fans, she's glad to be where she is, if no less mystified.

They have agreed to two short readings. Cynthia's friend Natalie, whose hands she held when Natalie cried after their art history TA called her a cock tease, reads from Rilke's *Letters to a Young Poet*. Bill Stearns, Adam's sophomore-year roommate, who once helped him pop his shoulder back in at a touch football game and then broke a date to wait with him at the emergency room for three hours afterward, soldiers through his unprecedented recital of a poem by Juvenal. The words carry no specific meaning in this context; the hymns and Bible verses, too, are only appurtenances of meaning, but no less heartfelt for that. The trappings of belief are themselves a kind of belief, just as the priest's cassock is his office.

For this reason they are all suddenly united in the expectation that the priest, who does not know them, who won't see them again after today, who has even less experience with intimacy than they do, who has probably said the same thing to thirty other anonymous couples this year, has something crucial to impart to them. With majestic unself-consciousness, he blots the very top of his bald head with what is presumably a handkerchief.

"It is good," he says, "that your life together has begun in conditions that suggest a test." He pauses to appreciate the small laugh that ripples through the pews; the faces right in front of him, those of the bride and groom, are locked in sobriety. "There will be great joys in your life together, of course, but there will also be tests, maybe even severe ones, and the joys and the tests will not always appear in such a way as to seem to offset one another. We may lose sight, at such difficult moments, of the path, the promise, the blessedness of our lives, because we grow too close to ourselves; our purpose here is something that surely we too could begin to make out, if it were given to us to see as God sees. But we do not possess the farsightedness of God. Trust that He sees what you cannot, and that will enable you to go on trusting in each other. And if ever you should doubt

29

yourselves, if ever there comes a time when you doubt your ability to endure hardship, remember that God, on this day and for all time, has given you to each other. He hath made all of us. And He will never ask us to shoulder more of a burden than He knows we have the strength to bear."

The vows they have chosen are the traditional ones. The kiss is more of a relief than anything else; shyly they proceed out the door and down the church steps into the odiferous haze and climb directly into the back of a limo for the one-minute drive around the park to the reception. The guests can see the limo pulling up at the hotel entrance as they trudge back across the park themselves. The bells are ringing, evening is approaching, and though it's still ninety-two degrees, the solemn air has lifted; there's a party at the other end of this walk, and an air-conditioned one at that.

When they reach the end of the receiving line they are at the doorway to the ballroom, where the empty tables glitter and it's as cold as a skating rink. Three idle bartenders smile helpfully. Within minutes they are working like coal stokers, as the younger guests try to recover the buzz they had going in their hotel rooms before the ceremony sweated it out of them. At the head table, a long dais perpendicular to the bandstand, the groom's mother finds that she and her husband have been seated in between their new daughter-in-law's natural parents, perhaps to keep them from killing each other. She tries gamely not to be offended by the idea that the role she has been given to play, on this momentous day in the life of her firstborn son, is that of a human shield. She has an idea who's behind it, even if now is not the time, even if it will never be the time; besides, Sandy feels, the fault is ultimately hers anyway. She went through a rough patch when the boys were little and had to leave home for a while. Literally doctor's orders. Maybe not surprising, then, that her son winds up with a girl who makes every decision, who calls all the shots. Who treats him like a child. But this isn't an appropriate moment for Sandy to start losing herself in the past; for one thing, she needs to remember to count her husband's drinks. Historically, in terms of his capacity for saying the unsayable, five is the magic number.

Scarcely a minute goes by without a knife clinking against a glass somewhere in the ballroom, first one and then a chorus of them: You made us come all the way here to witness your love? Okay, then – let's witness some love. The waitstaff bursts through the double doors like a football team and serves a hundred dinners. Conrad eats his salmon without tasting it and then waits, smiling robotically whenever others at his table laugh at something, until the meal is over and the champagne is poured and the moment is finally upon him.

"I have always looked up to my brother," Conrad says, eyes down, watching with dismay his own spit hitting the microphone. He memorized his toast but now he wishes he hadn't, because holding a piece of paper would at least occupy his right hand, the one not holding the champagne glass, the one floating spastically from his pants pocket to his chin to the back of his head. "When we were kids, everything he set out to achieve he achieved, everything he wanted he worked for until he earned it, everything he did set an example not just for me but for everyone around him. An older brother's distinction, in his little brother's eyes, is pretty much automatic for a long time. But even when I got old enough to get over that feeling and decide for myself, he has never lost any of my esteem. Until today."

The whole ballroom laughs, to intoxicating effect, and when Conrad dares to look up his eye is drawn straight to the bride's stepsister, Deborah, maybe because her red dress is separated from the cluster of other red dresses by the width of the ballroom; she's sitting off in the corner, with her grandmother, or somebody's grandmother anyway. *Just be yourself*: what kind of stupid fucking advice was that? He makes himself look away from her before he loses his train of thought entirely.

"Until today, because here is where his streak as a self-made success ends, and sheer blind dumb luck takes over. Anyone can see that Cynthia is a woman of extraordinary charms" – a whistle from somewhere in the room – "anyone who's ever closed a bar with her or hiked the White Mountains with her or smoked a cigar on the deck of the Staten Island Ferry with her knows that she has a sense of humor and compassion and adventure that's not just rare but matchless. Any man in full possession of his faculties would choose her out of a thousand. But how on earth do we account for *her* choice? What are the odds that such a spectacular girl would be willing to spend her life with a guy who wears those stupid madras shorts he wears; who thinks he's a comedian but lacks the attention span to tell so much as a knock-knock joke from beginning to end; who believes with all his heart that *near* the garbage, ashtray, or hamper is the same thing as *in* the garbage, ashtray . . . That's just a million to one shot, my friends, and frankly my brother deserves about as much credit for marrying this woman as he would for waking up with a winning lottery ticket stuck to his forehead, the lucky bastard."

It is very hard to hold off drinking from the glass of champagne in his hand. He is amazed at how hard everyone is laughing but he still wishes only for the whole thing to be over. Without meaning to he looks up at Deborah again. She's not laughing, but she is leaning forward intently with her elbows on her knees.

"Seriously," he says. "They are a charmed couple. No one who knows them can doubt that they are destined to spend a long, happy, extraordinary life together. And no one who sees that these two wonderful people found their perfect match, and were smart enough to realize it, can help feeling a little more optimistic about our own prospects as we head out into the world. To Cynthia and Adam."

Roars of approval, tapping of crystal. In the parking lot the drummer hears the applause and takes two more quick hits off his pre-gig joint before crushing it under the heel of his shoe.

The moment before the dancing begins, and the principals become hard to find, is the moment when Masha customarily takes her leave. She moves in a kind of crab walk behind the head table, accepting thanks, offering best wishes, smiling at the hundredth joke about the weather as if it were the first one. The money is already in the bank.

You have to give them credit, Masha thinks, taking one last look at the whole spectacle, postponing the opening of the ballroom doors and the blast of heat just beyond. They weren't the most gracious people in the world, but in the end they were willing to spend what needed to be spent.

The first dance: the bride and groom obviously could have practiced more, but their sheepish expressions only make the moment more affecting. They have never danced this way in public before – no one does anymore – and for them to forgo their usual grace, just for the sake of doing it the way it's always been done, is an expression of surprising humility. The song is "The Nearness of You," and before it's half over the parents cut in. Sandy is overwhelmed by her son's mischievous physical power. Mothers generally aren't held in their sons' arms after a certain age and it comes as a genuine shock. The bride's father feels his daughter's cheek on his shoulder, as guilelessly heavy as when she was a child and he carried her sleeping from the car, as he leads her around the floor. There's a man who can dance. Even Ruth doesn't bother trying not to remember. He hands their child off graciously to Warren, and feels the eyes on him as he walks off the floor. This has always been the rhythm of his fatherhood: dazzlement and aftermath. All day long he has endured the look of deep surprise in the eyes of nearly everyone to whom he has been introduced. He knows he has things to be forgiven for, but he considers his daughter's love full vindication, and for those who can't let go of the past he has never had any use.

Then the less ritualized dancing starts. It is the province

of young people fully at home in their bodies, drunk and obscurely tense and in need of release. Only in exorcising them do they feel the demands of this day. The band is bad but honorable, at peace with the fact that, though their ambitions may have sifted down to this, they are still making music for a living in front of an audience. They rarely get a chance anymore to perform for a crowd this young and unrestrained; they don't see anything fearful or destructive in all that energy, but they do understand the role of drunkenness in it and are okay with that. They're even more okay with the attractiveness of the women who join them onstage to arouse the crowd with unskilled go-go routines.

Twenty-two is a zone of privilege, and as the night deepens invisibly behind the heavy drapes, the others are centrifugally driven away, first from the dance floor and then from the ballroom itself. Older couples, couples with children, see where the night is going and finish their cake and politely excuse themselves for the long drive home or just for their beds upstairs. All over the hotel, the urge to transgress is finally breaching its borders. The night bellman goes into the men's room and sees that three tuxedoed wedding guests have pried the mirror off the wall and are hunched over it; he's so afraid of what's expected of him that he decides the prudent course is to go down to the basement and piss in the janitorial sink instead. People flirt with strangers, or even with old friends, in plain sight of their official dates. The desire to do something they know they'll regret is overwhelming. The doors to the ballroom stand open and the smoking and drinking and intense conversational intimacies spill into the lobby – against the rules, but the night staff is intimidated and unsure of protocol and badly outnumbered anyway.

In the midst of all this, still powering it in fact, is utter faith in convention: at eleven-thirty the bride and groom disappear upstairs, and at midnight they return in their "traveling outfits", in which to travel the eight blocks to the gingerbread-style bed and breakfast where they will spend the night. Everyone applauds and then lines up raggedly to say goodbye.

Adam's mother and father are incapable of sharing their sadness with each other. The honeymoon in Mexico is their gift. "You have a safe trip," Mr. Morey says. And then they're in the car and waving. Ruth starts to cry. The band starts playing again, and with the guests of honor gone, decorum gives way once and for all.

Sam, the fair-haired usher who passed out inside the church, is now standing by the door to the kitchen tirelessly hitting on one of the waitresses, who is twenty years old and needs the wages from this evening and therefore tries not to dwell on how very handsome this guy would be if he would just shut up, which she could certainly make him do.

Marietta, drunk and stoic, is downstairs in the hotel gym, allowing her boyfriend to act out a particular fantasy. Who's to say what's creepy? she thinks. In her head is a line from *The Godfather*: someday, she says silently to him as he labors, and that day may never come, I might ask you to do me a service. . .

One of the bartenders leaves his station for a quick trip to the men's room, and when he returns he discovers that the guests have gone behind the bar and taken the bottles back to their tables; he looks around and sees them all smiling at him, not mockingly but with great camaraderie. In the lobby, Bill, the groomsman who recited Juvenal, is trying to talk a married woman ten years his senior into having one drink in his room upstairs. He's actually almost there. He wants to do something he can never tell anyone about. A scared-looking bellhop comes into the ballroom and after one or two inquiries finds Conrad. He tells him there is an urgent message for him, upstairs in his room. The only explanations Conrad can think of are bad ones; he gets off the elevator, opens his door with the key, flips on the light, and standing there two feet in front of him is the antisocial, truth-advocating, tattooed bridesmaid, Deborah.

"Jesus!" Conrad says.

"Close the door," she says.

"How did you get in here?"

"You're not like the rest of them," Deborah says. She's still in her bridesmaid's dress but she's not wearing any shoes. She's very drunk. "I can see you, you know," she says. "You should give up trying to be one of them because you're not."

He's starting to get an inkling of what this is all about. She's not what he usually considers attractive, but on the other hand sometimes life puts something in your path that may never show up there again.

"You deserve something special," she says. Something in him chafes at this self-satisfied Mrs. Robinson routine. But

37

he's in no position to call her bluff; she does know at least that much about me, he thinks. She lifts up her bridesmaid's dress; if she was wearing something underneath it earlier, she's not anymore. She has a piercing that actually makes him wince. He is still young enough to immediately amend a mental checklist of sexual phenomena he has or has not seen.

"Close the door," she says. "Come on. Quickly."

"Aren't we related now?" he asks.

"Get on your knees," she says.

"Jesus Christ!" he says, and he gets on his knees.

In the ballroom an actual fight breaks out. One of the dishwashers has come out of the kitchen and told Sam to leave the young waitress alone; she's reached the end of her shift but is now so afraid to leave the hotel, because she knows he'll follow her outside, that she's in tears. Sam throws the first ridiculous punch, but the real damage is done when he's backing away in self-defense and falls right across the bar, smashing glasses and bottles alike. The women have long since removed their shoes, and so as a safety measure they climb up on the tables and continue dancing there. The band hasn't had this kind of contact high in years. They play until the moment they stop getting paid, and then they play three more songs, and then the night manager comes in and threatens to pull the plug. It would be really punk to tell him to go fuck himself, but they have another job here next month.

So the music stops, and the bar is closed, and the lights are all turned on because the night manager has had all the complaints from upstairs he can take; but there are still twenty or thirty people in and around the ballroom, drunk, tired, euphoric, young, beautiful, sweaty, dressed up and on someone else's nickel, and determined – as who wouldn't be? – to remain all those things forever. When the ballroom is locked they take over the lobby, and when they're chased out of the lobby they take it upstairs to their rooms. Dawn seeps around the drapes. They pass out on one another's floors, across one another's beds, refusing to part, sealing their legend.

At the bed and breakfast eight blocks away Cynthia, in a T-shirt and shorts, is propped up by pillows on the huge four-poster bed, some librarian's idea of a honeymoon bower; she strokes her husband's hair as he sleeps with his head in her lap. He didn't even make it out of his clothes. She's not disappointed. Sex is no novelty; being exhausted together, being each other's safe place – that's what tells you you've found what everybody's always whining about searching for. The air conditioner hums. Tomorrow they will fly to Mexico, and when they fly back to New York Cynthia will be pregnant. When she figures that out, she will wonder again what she is wondering right now: whether it's true what the priest said – that God gives each of us only what He knows we can handle – because, all her life, things have come at her very fast.

2

TIME ADVANCED IN TWO WAYS at once: while the passage of years was profligate and mysterious, flattening their own youth from behind as insensibly as some great flaming wheel, still somehow those years were composed of days that could seem endless in themselves, that dripped capriciously like some torment of the damned. There were two full weeks, for instance, between the end of the children's summer camp and the beginning of school. Cynthia started out full of ideas, but after the zoo, the aquarium, the Children's Museum, the Circle Line, and the other zoo, there was still a week to go. And then came the rain.

Two days since they'd set foot outside the building and April and Jonas, who were six and five, could not find anything to do, separately or together, that didn't devolve into a death match within ten minutes. Cynthia sat at the kitchen table with a magazine and listened to them yelling in their bedroom. An only child herself, she had no experience with this kind of fighting; she took it too much to heart, which was why she was trying her best to stay clear of it now. She had a tendency to lose her own patience and end things by punishing them both indiscriminately in the name of fairness. In spite of which they were now raising their voices on purpose to try to get her to intervene. Then there was some kind of a snapping sound, and Jonas started howling, and Cynthia was out of her chair like a shot and by the time she'd come out of their bedroom again she had told them there'd be no more TV that day, a stupid, spontaneous decision she knew would hurt them but that would really wind up hurting her because it was not even two in the afternoon and they were not going outside and the day would now pass about three times as slowly for all of them.

The kitchen faced back into the building's air shaft, a column of rain. Through the blur she could see the other kitchens in the building, most with their lights off. Cynthia and Adam had hired three nannies in the two years after Jonas was born but they had no luck there at all; one took eighteen sick days in the first two months, and one was so out of it the doors of a city bus once closed with her on the outside and the children on board, though the other passengers had started yelling before the driver could pull away. And when the third one, whom they all loved, quit without notice to return to the Philippines, April was so upset that she'd come into their bed every night for two weeks. So Cynthia, who was down to part-time at work anyway, decided to try it herself for a while, because she just couldn't put them through that anymore. Childhood was not supposed to be about loss. That was three years ago now.

April came out of the kids' bedroom after a while and leaned against her mother's upper arm.

"Still raining?" she said in a weary, grown-up voice. Cynthia nodded and laid her cheek on top of April's head.

"No playground today, sweet potato," she said. "What shall we do instead?"

April sighed thoughtfully. Her face was thinning, where her brother's was still round as a ball, and she had her father's small mouth and sharp eyes. She could read pretty well for her age and so Cynthia closed the *Vogue* she was looking at and laid it face down on the table.

"Want to play Go Fish?" April said.

Jonas got wind of it; April tried to discourage him from joining them by making up complex new rules, which wasn't fair, and Cynthia said "of course he can play" just to forestall that awful whining note in their voices, the note that got in under her defenses and made her own voice turn scary. She could see it in their faces whenever this happened – they were like a mirror at her weakest moments – and then she would end up miserable after they had gone to bed, Adam rubbing her back with a pointlessness that only made things seem worse.

Jonas's hands were small and at one point he dropped his cards on the table. "That's a nine!" April said.

"No it's not," Jonas said as he gathered them up again.

"I asked you if you had any nines and you said go fish!" she said hotly. "Mom!"

"You did not," Jonas said, "and anyway that's a six. And it's cheating to peek at other people's cards, that's what Mom said. Cheater."

"You dropped them right in front of me! And that *is* a nine, you're looking at it upside down, here give it to me—"

"No!"

"Jesus, you're an idiot!"

That was two words she would get punished for, and Jonas looked eagerly at his mother, but a strange thing had happened: his mother was crying. The children withdrew into themselves, frightened, and Cynthia tried hard to stop frightening them, but it was not so easy.

"Sorry," she said to them.

"It's okay," April said reflexively.

"Yeah," Jonas said – and then, fishing up from his kindergarten experience a sentence he'd been taught for the purpose of conflict resolution, but had never actually used, he said, "What game would *you* like to play?"

When they were sweet like that you had to go with it right away, you had to do or say something, or else they'd really see you cry. So Cynthia said, "I want to play poker."

"Poker?" April said, wrinkling her nose for comic effect. She'd seen some mischief in her mother's face, something that promised a return to form, and she tried to draw it out. "How do you play?"

"Well, there's a bunch of different ways, but I'll teach you an easy one. Go get that big bowl of change off Daddy's dresser." She began shuffling and bridging, which the kids loved. Counting out equal stacks of pennies, dimes, nickels, and quarters killed a good amount of time, long enough for Cynthia to feel herself out of danger.

She taught them to play five-card draw, and when they had the hang of it – one pair, two pair, three of a kind – she introduced the betting. She dealt out a hand, and Jonas, fanning out his cards, put his fist in the air and yelled "Yes!"

"Fold," Cynthia said automatically, and then, more gently, "now we're going to learn what's called the poker face. You want to have the exact same face all the time, like a statue. That way you're keeping the secret of what cards you have, until the end when it's time to show."

But it ran against their nature. They scowled and groaned when the draw didn't give them what they were hoping for, and they wiggled and widened their eyes when they found themselves with something good. Cynthia had so taken to heart the children's generosity in suggesting that today they should all play what Mommy wanted to play that she couldn't bring herself to just throw them the game. She wanted to even things out between them, not lose on purpose to keep them happy, or allow herself to win a few just to teach them another lame lesson about being a good sport. It wasn't as though she was really taking their money. They were excited, and as long as the spell was unbroken the hours would keep marching smartly by and maybe tonight for once she wouldn't already be staring at the front door when it opened and her husband came home.

So she sent April back to Adam's dresser, to the top drawer this time, and April came back holding two red bandannas. Cynthia knew they were there because she'd used them to tie Adam's wrists to the headboard, though that seemed like an awfully long time ago now. She called the kids in front of her chair and tied the bandannas around their faces so that everything below their eyes was draped like a bank robber. Then she sent them back to her bedroom to look at themselves in the full-length mirror, whence she soon heard screams of delight. Jonas ran back into the kitchen, pretending to shoot her.

"Stick 'em up!" he said.

"Back in your seat, there, pardner," Cynthia told him. "If you want my money you'll have to win it off me fair and square. Now, the name of the game," she said, dealing, "is Jacks or Better."

She ordered out for an early dinner – turkey sandwiches, chips, a bag of Milanos, even one small glass each of regular Coke, which they weren't normally allowed to have. Anything to keep them at the table. The bandannas weren't enough, because the kids' expressive eyes still gave their hands away, so she went into the bedroom herself and came back with two pairs of sunglasses, her own and Adam's, and balanced them on the children's ears. They looked like little Unabombers, but at least now the playing field was somewhat level. They would never, ever fold, even after the principle had been explained to them more than once;

but even so, at one point in the afternoon Cynthia was thrilled to discover that she was down three bucks to her children.

Then their attention began to waver. Jonas said he was bored, the word itself billowing out his red bandanna. April's desire to keep her mother happy was much stronger, but she had started putting her head down on the table between hands.

"Can we go to the playground?" Jonas asked.

Cynthia glanced quickly at the air-shaft windows to confirm that it was still raining; then something made her look again, and she saw one of their neighbors – some old woman, she didn't know who – standing at her own kitchen window, staring brazenly in at Cynthia and her incognito children, and scowling. What was worse, Cynthia saw, was that she was on the phone.

"Hey!" Cynthia said. She stood right up from the table and pulled open the kitchen window as far as it would go, which wasn't very far owing to the child-safety guards. She bent from the waist and shouted sideways out the window. "Hey! What are you looking at?"

Emboldened by his mother's high spirits, eager to jump to her defense whether he knew the source of the attack or not, Jonas ran up beside her, lifted the corner of his bandanna, and yelled out the window, "Yeah! What are you looking at?"

Cynthia turned; they stared at each other, and for a few seconds, in the wake of what would normally be considered a serious transgression, it was not apparent which way things would go. Finally she offered him a high five. "Darn right!" she said. "Nobody stares at our family!"

The woman in the window's eyebrows seemed to jump, and she moved quickly out of their sight line. There were two windows in the kitchen: Cynthia opened the other one and both kids took up a position there.

"Go stare at somebody else, you old bat!" Cynthia shouted across the air shaft.

"Go stare at somebody else, you old bat!" the kids echoed, beside themselves.

"Mind your own beeswax!"

"Mind your own beeswax!"

Then Cynthia stood up on the windowsill and braced her hands against the frame. It wasn't dangerous, she felt, though there wasn't much between her and the air shaft now. April, too caught up in her mother's euphoria to be scared herself, pulled Jonas up on the other sill and they stood there with their arms around each other's waists.

"Our family rules!" Cynthia yelled, her breath fogging the glass.

"Our family rules!"

Then something flickered in the reflected light on the pane her nose was nearly touching; she turned her head and there, in the kitchen doorway, was Adam. He still had his dripping raincoat on. There was no telling how much he'd heard but his head was cocked warily, like a dog's. Cynthia hopped down to the floor, a little out of breath. The kids did the same and came and leaned against her on either side, still wearing their bandannas and sunglasses. Her nostrils flared with the effort not to laugh. She put her hands on their shoulders.

"Hello, dear," she said in a bright voice. "The children and I have been gambling."

After four years at Morgan Stanley, an operation so vast that Adam's true bosses existed mostly on the level of gossip and rumor, a feeling of toxic stasis had begun to provoke him in the mornings when he arrived at work. It wasn't all in his head; lately a number of his colleagues had been promoted over and around him, and when he asked about it at his review, the thing that kept coming up was that they may have been dullards and yes-men but they all had their MBAs. · Why this should have impressed anybody was beyond him. In theory he could have taken a leave of absence and gone back to business school himself – lots of the firm's junior employees did it at his age – but those people didn't have children to support, and anyway Adam lacked the tolerance for the one step back that might or might not set up the proverbial two steps forward. He'd worked hard to get where he was and he couldn't see giving up that ground voluntarily. The momentum of the business world was one-way only, a principle that should not be rationalized. He and Cynthia had a vivid faith in their own future, not as a variable but as a destination; all the glimpses New York afforded of the lives led by the truly successful, the arcane range of their experiences, aroused in the two of them less envy than impatience.

So he called a guy named Parker he'd met a few times

playing pickup basketball at Chelsea Piers, and took him out to lunch, and two weeks later Parker had brought him on at a private equity firm called Perini Capital, an outfit with a shitload of money behind it but so few people working there that Adam knew everyone's name by the end of his first day. The money, pre-bonus at least, was actually a little less than he'd been making at Morgan, but it wasn't about that. It was about potential upside, and also about his vision of what a man's work should be: a tight group of friends pushing themselves to make one another rich. No hierarchies or job descriptions; there was the boss and then there was everyone else, and the boss, Barry Sanford, loved Adam from day one. Sanford was a white-haired libertine who was on his fourth wife and had named the company after his boat. It was obvious to everyone that he saw something of his young self in Adam, and though Adam didn't personally see the resemblance, he was unoffended by it. The job's only drawback was that it required some travel – the occasional overnight to Iowa City or the equivalent, to sound out some handful of guys who thought their business deserved to be bigger than it was. And strippers: for some reason these aspirants always had the idea that strippers were the lingua franca of serious money men. In truth Adam considered few things in life a grimmer bore than an evening at Podunk's finest strip club, but he went along with it, because his job was to make these people admire him, a job at which he excelled.

His Perini colleagues, Parker included, were all still single; he'd go out for a few drinks with them after work but then the evening would start to turn into another kind of evening and he'd excuse himself and go home. Still, the new environment – the informality and irreverence, the clubby decor, the foosball table, the sense that they were bound not by any sort of dull corporate ethos but only by the limits of their own creativity – fit him perfectly; he felt he belonged there. Its best amenity, though he wouldn't have said so to anyone but Cynthia, was that in the basement of the building, which was on Ninth Avenue, there was a swimming pool. Whenever he didn't have a lunch, Adam would take the elevator all the way down, hang his suit in the changing room, and swim laps until he wore himself out. Sometimes there was a group of kids wearing floaties in the shallow end – one of the other, bigger companies in the building had its own day care – but most days he had the water completely to himself, his every stroke echoing off the walls, his heartbeat loud in his ears. It felt like stealing. Then he'd shower, put his suit on, and go back upstairs to his desk. Sometimes he'd have Liz the receptionist order him something to eat, or sometimes he'd just skip it and let the adrenaline carry him through until dinner. He was in the best shape of his life, and it was a boon to his job performance too, because he always thought more clearly when he was a little exhausted.

At school April's first task was to esteem herself. They began with self-portraits, huge-headed, in which the bodies were an afterthought, apportioned roughly the same space on the page as a nose or an ear. The portraits smiled widely with crooked teeth, not because the children's teeth were crooked but because teeth were hard to draw. They made lists of the reasons they liked themselves, lists of the things they were good at and the things at which they were determined to improve. They named the comforts of their homes – pets, siblings, favorite toys, or favorite places. One girl said her favorite place was Paris, but April took this to mean the imaginary Paris of the Madeline books. Her own favorite place was her parents' bed, with her parents not in it, just her and a few stuffed animals and a juice box and a Disney movie on TV. She dreamed of this situation often, though in practice she usually had to be sick to attain it. Something told her, though, that it would be seen as babyish, and so she said the Central Park Carousel instead.

Less auspicious was the name project. A name, the students were told, had a secret history; it might connect you to the country from which your family had first emigrated, or to the language or the religion of that country, or even just to the family itself and the loved ones who had gone before. It let you know that you were not just some one-time phenomenon but an outcome, a culmination, the top branch of a majestic tree. Told to go home and conduct some research on why she was named April Morey, she saw her parents exchange a quick look before her mother answered.

"Well," Cynthia said, muting the TV, "Dad and I talked about a lot of different names. We would sit on the couch in our old apartment and try them out on each other back when I was pregnant with you, say them out loud to see

51

how they sounded. And there were a few we liked, but we kept coming back to April. April Morey. It just sounded the most beautiful to us."

Her dad smiled, and patted her mom's leg.

"That's it?" April said.

They looked as confused as she was. "Also," her father said, sitting forward on the couch, "it's a pretty unusual name. Not a lot of other Aprils in the world. We wanted a name as special as you are."

They'd given her her name not because somebody else had had it, but because nobody had? "Was there ever another April in our family?" she asked. They looked at each other again, and shook their heads. "Why didn't you name me after a loved one?"

"A loved one?" Adam said.

April nodded. "A dead loved one. That's what a lot of people do. Or somebody from the old country." Her mother punched her father in the thigh, and that, it shocked April to realize, was because he had been about to laugh.

"Where do we come from?" she demanded of them. "What country?"

Stunningly, they seemed less than sure. Adam knew his father's family had come from England, but he didn't know where in England specifically, nor how many generations ago that had been; his mother's family was part German and part Dutch. Cynthia knew her father's ancestors were Russian, unless he'd been lying about that too, and as for her maternal grandparents, her mother had always refused to discuss them.

"Was there something special about the *month* of April?" April asked. There wasn't. No historic event had taken place then, no anniversary or birthday, though they did offer that if April's birthday had actually fallen in April, they would have named her something else.

"What would you have named me instead?" she persisted. The revelation that she, April, might just as plausibly have been Samantha or Josephine or Emma, that only chance was behind the whole solemn question of her identity, made her feel worse than ever. She could see that her parents were now upset, but she was angry at them and didn't care. They kept coming back to beauty, but it was a beauty she couldn't comprehend and that she wasn't at all sure her teacher would consider a satisfactory completion of the assignment.

Ms Diaz was nice about it, of course, but there was nothing to be done about the jealousy engendered by the other, longer name-essays that went up on the walls above their lockers, stories of honored relatives and cool languages and religious rituals tended through the generations. April felt as if her family came from nowhere, and, more puzzlingly, that this suited her parents just fine.

The next unit was family traditions. The teacher took pains to define this idea as broadly as possible; still, what traditions did April's family have? They hardly ever did the same thing even twice. They had no ancestral home they returned to, no church they attended (her mom had gone to church as a child but April had heard her say that she hated it and was glad she never had to go again), no special place they liked to travel to – indeed, having been someplace on vacation once, like Nantucket or Vail or Disney World, even if they'd had a good time there, was usually cited as a reason not to go there again. Even their Christmas tree wasn't in the same spot every year. April knew her own grandparents so little that she sometimes mixed them up in her head and was shy about talking to them on the phone. She had one uncle and no aunts, just something her mother called a step-aunt, whom she'd only ever seen in a photo in her parents' wedding album.

Soon the whole temper of the assignment had changed, in April's mind, from an exercise in self-discovery to an indiscriminate hunt for what Ms. Diaz, for whom she would have died in any case, wanted to admire in her. It seemed perfectly defensible to start making things up. She wrote down that her family went to Saint Patrick's Cathedral every Sunday, and that they were considering a trip to Jerusalem for Christmas. Her grandmother on her mother's side, who was named May, had lost her parents as a girl but had gamely made her way from Holland to America by boat. Every summer April and her cousins gathered for a reunion at the family estate on a mountain in New Hampshire. It was so big that some of her distant pioneer relatives were buried in a small graveyard right there on the place.

Adam and Cynthia read these notions on the wall beneath their daughter's self-portrait on Parents' Night, mute with amazement. April's teacher couldn't really believe this stuff, could she? Yet she had posted it right there with all the other handwritten, dubiously spelled histories of perseverance and hardship. They already felt conspicuous, as they always did at these school functions, as the youngest couple in the classroom; at twenty-nine they were still strikingly young, by Manhattan standards at least, to be parents at all. Jonas's best friend in kindergarten had once slept over for a whole weekend while his father took his mother to London for her fiftieth birthday. Every Parents' Night Adam and Cynthia were a kind of generation unto themselves, and it didn't take much, in that context, to awaken a vestigial unease about being in some sort of trouble they didn't even understand. When Ms Diaz, deep in conversation with some kid's father who was surely old enough to be their father too, smiled at them from across the room as if to say that she would be with them in just a moment, they smiled back warmly until she turned away and then Cynthia squeezed his arm and they got the hell out of there.

When she'd first stopped working outside the home, as the expression went, the kids were toddlers with unsynchronized nap schedules and so Cynthia's brain was pretty much indentured to them; even apart from the physical exhaustion, it was a struggle just to find a little interior space for herself, a little space in which to *be* herself, when they were so present and so vulnerable and so demanding every minute of the day. The only time that truly felt like her own was late at night when everyone else was asleep, when she would stay up and watch movies and savor the day's one cigarette, blowing the smoke out the window; but even that came at a price, since the sleep she lost made the next day's selflessness harder to maintain.

But now they were older, the school day was longer, and she determined that she could pick up where she left off and start working again. She took this idea more literally than she would have if she'd thought about it more. Her first and only job in New York, from the summer after college until after Jonas was born, had been as an editorial assistant at a glossy, ad-heavy magazine called *Beauty,* and in the absence of any other sort of work she particularly burned to do, she thought she might go back there. It was a painful miscalculation. Her best memories of *Beauty* were mostly memories of the kind of euphoric bitching that took place over drinks after work with her fellow assistants; most of those smart young women and gay men were now, like Cynthia, long gone, but a couple had stuck it out and managed to rise up the masthead. That was the only way to get anything decent out of a career in magazines – become a lifer. The current features editor was someone she used to eat cheap lunches with back when they were happy to get through the day without getting screamed at by someone important. Her name was Danielle. Cynthia left a message with Danielle's assistant, got a call back from a different assistant asking her to come in the following Monday at eleven-thirty, and arrived to find Danielle standing up behind her desk with a look of awkward condescension on her narrow face that said everything there was to say.

Still, they had to go through with it. Cynthia, angry and humiliated and eager to leave before Danielle had even sat down again, produced pictures of April and Jonas. Danielle told the story of her own broken engagement. They recalled some of the people they had worked with back in the day. Cynthia had no idea what had happened to any of them; Danielle knew what had happened to all of them. It was possible to connect the overbearing power chick she was now to the emotionally manipulable peon she had been back then, but just barely. Finally they came with mutual reluctance to the subject at hand.

"Come on," Cynthia found herself saying. "I'm smart and I work hard and I can tell a good idea from a shitty one. If that was true three years ago it can't be untrue now. Children don't actually make you stupid – you do know that, right? Or maybe that would make a good investigative piece for you."

What kept her there past the point of good sense was her imagination of the dismayed, relieved, pitying expression into which Danielle's face would resolve the moment her office door closed between them. She postponed that moment as long as she could, even when doing so came off as begging. "You don't want what I can offer you," Danielle kept saying, and she was right, Cynthia didn't want it, but even less did she want to be spoken to like a child by someone who used to be her peer and now presumed to tell her what she did or did not want. In the end, in a thoroughly bridge-burning mood, she wrote "eat me" across the top of the résumé she'd brought, slid it across Danielle's desk, and walked out.

On the street she had a sudden memory, useless now, of a night out after work six or seven years ago when Danielle had gotten so drunk – Cynthia, pregnant by then, was stone sober – that she'd started hitting on the troll of a bartender and Cynthia was deputed to take her home in a cab. The bed in her York Avenue studio, which Cynthia had never visited before, was covered with stuffed dogs. But it wasn't surprising that Danielle should have changed. There was a fast-moving mainstream in life, and once you'd dropped out of it, as Cynthia had, you weren't going to be hailed by everybody when you tried to step into it again.

That was what had happened to her: she had fallen into the underworld of women with nothing special to do. Like those moms she despised, the ones you made small talk with while you waited for your kid to find his shoes after a playdate at their Versailles-like apartments, who had live-in help and no real responsibilities and yet all they did was complain about how they never had a moment to themselves. But what filled Cynthia's days? She was at the gym five mornings a week now; Adam kept telling her she looked hotter than she ever had in her life, which was probably true, but maybe the whole routine there wasn't even about that, maybe it was about something else entirely. She had volunteered, again, to head the silent-auction committee for April's grade and for Jonas's too, even though she took no pleasure in it because of the proximity it forced her into with women whom she imagined were nothing like her. She had a rule about not drinking before five. She never broke it, but why was it there at all?

She and Adam joked all the time about the social purgatory to which they'd condemned themselves by having kids so young: some of their old friends were still hooking up in bars and setting up Hamptons shares, while the people who actually lived the same sort of domesticated life the Moreys lived tended to be a dozen years older, boring as hell, and too covetous of their youth to befriend them in any case. They'd go to some school function and after a couple of drinks all the middle-aged Wall Street husbands would be macking on her; she thought it was hilarious, and Adam did too, and then the next day their fat-ass wives would make a point of not talking to her, as if that was supposed to be some sort of punishment. Still, her own charisma had become latent in her; who were her friends now?

Her erstwhile maid of honor, Marietta, was one of those with whom Cynthia had lost touch, all the more disgracefully since she lived right there in Tribeca – more than a hundred blocks away, but still. She was married now, to some Viacom executive she had met through some online personal ad – you had to hand it to her, she embraced all that stuff, the newer it was the more unintimidated she felt – but married or not it was hard to stay in contact with her because she worked ten or twelve hours a day as vice president of a media-relations company, one of those places that orchestrated the public rehabilitation of the disgraced: drunk starlets, politicians who turned up in sex videos, clients like that. "It's a lot like being a lawyer," was how Marietta had explained it to her. "Or a lot like advertising. It's a lot like most things, actually." As if to prove their bond, just when Cynthia was missing her most Marietta called one night out of nowhere and begged Cynthia to meet her for a drink the next afternoon: there was something she needed to ask her. Cynthia said that, since she had to pick up the kids from school at three-thirty, maybe coffee was better. "Fuck that," Marietta said. "We'll have drinks at two, then. It's not like it's unprecedented. Remember that time at Head of the Charles when we made martinis at nine in the morning?"

"Less than distinctly," Cynthia said, smiling.

She actually wondered whether Marietta was going to offer her a job, weird as that would be, but instead it turned out that she was trying to get pregnant. She and Mr. Viacom had only been at it for six months but Marietta, who at thirty was a less patient person than she used to be, was getting ready to start on clomiphene. "How did it happen with you?" she asked Cynthia. "When it happened, I mean like the moment it happened, did you just know?"

"Don't you remember?" Cynthia said. "It was a total fucking shock. I was on my honeymoon. I'm still not sure how it happened."

"What about with Jonas?" she said, biting a cuticle. "Were you trying there?"

"Nope."

She scowled. "Fertile bitch. Well, you're still the only friend I can talk to about any of this who wouldn't try to talk me out of it. If they got wind of it at work, forget about it."

They sat at an outdoor table at a café across from the entrance to the Met, drinking lemon-drop martinis. There was no one else in the place at that hour but their waiter, and even he was barely in evidence.

"Here's the big discovery," Marietta said. "Here's the one aspect of this subject about which I know more than you. Sex where you're *trying* to get pregnant is the absolute worst sex known to man. Another six weeks of this and I swear to God if I'm not knocked up we're going to get divorced."

"Come off it," said Cynthia. Her new martini was too full to lift without spilling, so she was hunched over in her chair trying to sip from it.

"They always tell you that this is the true calling of sex, right? The higher purpose. It should be beautiful. Two people in love trying to create a new life. And let me tell you, it is easily the most joyless humping I've ever been a part of in my entire life. Remember Tom Billings?"

Cynthia thought for a moment. "From freshman orientation?" she said.

Marietta nodded ominously. "*That* was better than this," she said. "I just want him to come already and get out of the room so I can lie there like an idiot holding my knees up in the air like I'm supposed to. You'd think it's a guy's dream, right? Just blow your load and get out. But no: he wants to act like he's in some kind of weird Christian porno, going really slowly, stroking my hair, telling me that he loves me. Jesus!" She looked at Cynthia for a frozen moment, her mouth open in amazement, and then she started to laugh. "And he knows what I'm thinking, and I do feel sorry for him, but at the same time if this is all too hard on his fucking *ego*, well boo hoo. The last time we did it we didn't even say a word to each other until the next day. Speaking of which," she said, pulling her phone out of her purse, "I should give him a call. Today is supposed to be one of our prime fertility days. He has to come straight home from work and inseminate me, and if he's forgotten, I'll kill him. Excuse me a minute. Two more?" she said to the waiter.

They were both laughing so hard by now that they had to steal napkins from the empty tables around them to wipe away tears, drawing stares from the pedestrians who passed in the sunlight just beyond the awning. Half an hour later they had hugged goodbye three times and vowed to see each other more often and Cynthia, drunk and paranoid, was on her way to Dalton to pick up the kids. She'd have to avoid conversation with the other mothers, but since they didn't like her anyway, there wasn't much trick to that. As for the kids, they weren't old enough, she reassured herself, to be able to tell; besides, this being Tuesday, April had dance and Jonas had tee ball so it was just a matter of rushing them into a cab and racing around the East Side anyway. No worries about making conversation. The kids hated it when they were late for things.

She remembered walking up this same stretch of Fifth Avenue years ago, when Jonas was still an infant, and as she waited for the light to change, one of those overly sunny old ladies who felt free to accost you whenever you were pushing a stroller had started pointing and cooing at him. When she was done she gazed up at Cynthia and said, "Enjoy this time. It goes by so fast," and Cynthia said, "Well then either my watch has stopped or one of us is nuts." Or maybe she hadn't actually said that out loud. She couldn't remember anymore.

That had been a tough time, with both kids still in diapers. Still, even now, probably her dirtiest secret was that impatience for these years to be over: for them to be teenagers, at least, where they started to fend for themselves a little bit and where she wouldn't have to spend so much time wondering whether she would prove equal to whatever bad thing might befall them. Most days were fine, but then once in a while she would feel herself caught in an afternoon that just seemed to refuse to pass. On the bright side, they were way ahead of most children their age, and part of that had to be that she made more than just a cameo appearance in their daytime lives, that unlike so many of their friends they weren't being raised by nannies who ferried them dispassionately from place to place like they were especially valuable packages. She didn't care whether or not they appreciated that now but some part of her was counting on their appreciating it later. And she hated it when people handed you that Norman Rockwell shit about kids growing up too fast; on the contrary, she looked forward to being able to talk to them almost as peers, maybe ask their advice once in a while instead of feeling like she had to have all the answers all the time. Anyway, when you considered the whole bazaar of damage that childhood exposed you to, was there even any such thing as growing up too fast?

She checked her watch again; she'd checked it just a few seconds ago, but somehow five minutes had gone by, and she quickened her pace. She didn't want to get there after the bell. Walking in the bright sunlight gave her a piercing headache, sort of like being drunk and hungover at the same time. As she searched her bag again for the sunglasses she already knew she'd left on the hall table at home, she heard a voice through the uncomfortable buzz inside her head, a voice that whispered *too late. Too late.*

Which was ridiculous. She was barely thirty. At Adam's old job there was a broker who used to be a professional dog walker, who graduated from business school at age thirty-five. Too late for what, exactly? It might have made a difference if there were some type of work she felt passionate about, or some particular skill she might cultivate into excellence, something a little more marketable than just above-average intelligence and fear of idleness. Marietta loved to make fun of her dissolute clients, but if you got her drunk enough she would start talking in dead earnest about her job in terms of second chances and the desire to repent. Well, if you got Cynthia drunk enough, Cynthia thought, she would cop to wanting to do some good in the world, or at least to feel like her presence in it was value-added. How, though? Without some framework, some resources, even your secret aspirations just curdled into sentimental bullshit.

A lot of time seemed to have gone by very suddenly. The injustice of it, the knowledge that one could never go back to where one had started, to the old advantages, didn't subside that day or the next. She knew that, every day, some woman somewhere did exactly what now seemed so impossible to her. Nevertheless she persisted in feeling that some sort of privilege had been stolen from her, not by the children, of course, but by someone.

Private equity was considered old-school in some ways, because it still had one foot in the real: IPOs, profits on actual goods sold, even the occasional start-up, compared to which the ethereal instruments hedge funds dealt in were like some branch of astrophysics that generated money. It even called upon some old-fashioned people skills, which Adam turned out to possess in precocious abundance. You had to sit down with a guy, to listen to his pitch or to listen to whatever it was he talked about when he thought the pitch was over, in order to gauge whether he himself was the key to his own company's prospects or whether, at some point down the line, extracting a worthwhile profit was going to require taking the whole thing out of his hands.

Still, the ethereal was where the real money was, and everybody knew it. Parker in particular loved to bitch about how working at Perini was like driving some financial horse and buggy and how he couldn't wait for the old man to loosen his grip a little bit so they could start making themselves into real players. He was eaten up by envy of guys he'd gone to Wharton with who were worth fifty million in these high-flying VCs they'd started maybe three years ago. At least once a week he tried to draw Adam into some conversation about how the two of them should walk out and start their own fund. It might even have been worth listening to, Adam thought, if it wasn't for the fact that Parker sucked so bad at his job. He'd played football at Cornell and it was easy to see what Sanford had once liked about him, but lately the old man seemed to have soured on him completely. The more Parker worried about his own job security, the more contempt he showed privately for the whole operation, and the stupider high-risk shit he proposed in the hopes of proving his indispensability to the place once and for all.

He came over to Adam's desk one morning holding a manila folder and said, "Dude, can I run something by you?" He'd gone to Los Angeles for the weekend, to some decadent birthday party one of his B-school classmates had thrown for himself, and he'd returned to New York with the notion that Perini should get into the movie business. Commercial credit was tight enough now, apparently, that rather than scuttle existing projects, the smaller studios would take financing from anywhere. "Here's the thing," Parker whispered. "It's kind of an outside-the-box idea, and if I go in there alone with it, he'll hand my balls to me before he's even heard what I have to say. But if you go in there with me, he'll give it a chance. He fucking loves you. So will you just go in there with me? You don't even have to say anything."

Adam was pretty sure that even five minutes' thought would reveal the idea as a terrible one. But he felt both pity and fascination when it came to Parker, who seemed more and more capable of some kind of epic crash and burn; and he knew Sanford would recognize that he was there only as a favor. Plus it was such a lunatic idea that he hated the thought of not being in the room when Sanford heard it. "When?" he said.

Parker beamed. "No time like the present," he said.

The rear wall of Sanford's office was floor-to-ceiling glass that looked out over the Hudson. It was all dark wood and leather and had so much nautical crap in it that he might have stood by the window and imagined he was in some sort of high-tech crow's nest. It was pouring rain out there and much darker than it should have been. Parker nervously laid it out for him, and with a glance at Adam the old man gestured for the manila folder to be handed to him. He pored over Parker's analysis, not impatiently. At one point he looked up and said, "But who is Joe Levy?"

"Production head," Parker said.

"Yes, I see that, but who is he? What's he done? What sort of track record does he have in terms of, you know, actually making money?"

Parker shifted in his seat. "Well, he's produced numerous films as an independent," he said. "*Boathook* was one that did pretty well, in a box-office sense. But really what's intriguing about him is mostly a matter of pedigree. He's the son of Charles Levy, who was the head of UA back in the glory days. A legendary guy. Something like five or six Oscars. Joe grew up surrounded by all the great minds in the business."

Sanford made a snorting noise. "That's it?" he said, and leaned back in his chair. "His father? What is it, some sort of feudal system out there?"

"Kind of, actually," Parker said.

But Sanford was getting on a roll. "Were more chilling words ever spoken," he said, putting the folder down, "from the investor's point of view, than 'he's the son of the founder'? He figures the old man made it look so easy, how hard can it be? I mean, don't get me wrong, I'm sure he's a lovely guy. I'm sure the parties are amazing. But I'm always leery of guys who do that, who step into their fathers' shoes. You know why? Because usually they're Pete Rose Junior. I mean, my father was a tailor. Should I have gone into that business? Do you suppose I had some kind of genetic affinity for it? What about you? What does your father do?"

Parker was nodding now, trying to get out in front of the idea that the whole proposal had been a lark to begin with. "He's a tax attorney," he said.

"Well then maybe you missed your calling. Maybe you should be a tax attorney too. Adam, how about you? What's your father's trade?"

Adam smiled. "Pipe fitter," he said.

The eyes of the other two men met for a silent moment, and then they burst into laughter. "I can just see it!" Sanford said. "So maybe you're considering going into business with him?"

"Not likely," Adam said. "He's dead."

He'd meant it as what it was, a fact, but it came out all wrong. He could tell from their faces. One thing he did not like was for people to feel sorry for him. When the sympathy faded, they would remember the weakness, and then one day they would turn around and shank you.

The rain made for an odd effect forty floors up, because you didn't get to see it hit anything on the way down, it was just a kind of static in the gray air.

"Jesus Christ," Sanford said. His voice was very different. He had a sentimental streak in him – everybody knew about

68

it, and some weren't above playing on it, but Adam really hadn't been trying to do that. "I didn't know."

"Did he die like when you were a kid or something?" Parker said.

Adam thought for a moment. "A little less than a year ago," he said.

"What?" Sanford said. "You don't mean when you were working here."

"Just before."

"I had no idea. Was he sick?"

"No," Adam said. "Well, yes and no. He died of a coronary, but it was his third one."

"How old was he?"

"Sixty-two."

Sanford turned white. "I had no idea," he said.

"Well, that's okay," Adam said. He waited for the conversation to resume. Sanford was looking right into his face like he wasn't even there, like he was some portrait of himself. Finally he tapped the folder with his forefinger. "Why don't I look this over," he said. Adam and Parker nodded and got up to leave, and they didn't really speak for the rest of the day, though Parker must have been talking to others there; Adam could tell by the way they stared at him when they thought he wasn't looking. At the end of the day he felt hyper and irritable and wanted nothing more than to get out for a run, but the rain was so heavy now you almost couldn't see the river anymore. Then he had a brainstorm: he grabbed his gym bag and went down to the basement, but the pool was already locked, even though it was just a few minutes after six. By the time he got back up to the fortieth floor the office had cleared out completely. He went and looked out Sanford's window for a while, and then he went back to his desk and picked up the phone.

"Nice weather we're having," Cynthia said. "I thought you might be on your way already."

"What are you doing right now?" Adam said.

"Doing? What am I doing?"

"Can you call that Barnard girl? Do you think we could get her to come over and babysit right now?"

"I'm sure we could not," Cynthia said. "Why?"

"Because here's what I want to do," he said, watching the lights flicker on the phones in the silent office. "I want to check into a hotel with you for a couple of hours. I want to go to the nicest place we can think of and have a good dinner and some wine and then I want to take you to bed. I want you to think of something you've never asked me to do before and then I'll do it. I want to amaze you. I want complaints from the front desk. I want to get kicked out of there. Seriously, I am as hard as a rock right now just thinking about you."

She laughed delightedly. "I believe I'm getting the vapors," she said. "You better hope this phone's not tapped, pervert. Maybe you need to call that number for when you experience an erection lasting more than four hours."

"I'm not kidding, though," Adam said. "I love you. Seriously, the kids are old enough to be by themselves for a couple of hours, right?"

"No," she said indulgently, "they are not. They do go to bed early, though. So here's my counterproposal." He could hear her walking with the phone into another room. "After they're asleep, you sit down on the couch, and I will bring you a Scotch, and then I will kneel in front of that couch, and whatever happened to you today, I'm betting that between me and the Scotch we will make it all better. Okay? I love you too, by the way. And I do like the way you think. But this way we won't have any visits from Child Protective Services. Okay?"

"Okay," he said.

"We will call that Plan B," Cynthia said. "Now come home."

He hung up. It was almost dark now, and the rain on the windows made for a beautiful effect on the opposite wall, like a bleeding shadow. He called the car service and fifteen minutes later he was in the back seat of a limo that sat motionless in the rain on 57th Street, in traffic that was so bad he felt like time had stopped.

Isn't your father dead, Barry? he had wanted to say. Doesn't everybody's father die? Isn't that what happens? But he'd figured the less he said, the sooner they'd move on. For a long time Adam had known his father mostly as a short-fused bastard, but then in his teenage years something had shifted, and he'd felt like both his parents were a little afraid of him. It wasn't such a bad feeling, actually.

Even when he wiped the windows with the back of his hand he couldn't see outside. It didn't feel like they were moving at all. He thought about laying into the driver for

71

taking 57th in the first place, but that wouldn't make him feel any better. He just needed for a new day to start.

Sanford owned several secondary homes, but the one his current wife was most enamored of was in Cornwall, Connecticut, two hours and then some outside the city. The following Thursday at lunch he decided aloud that Adam should visit them there that very weekend, and should bring his wife and kids; initially Adam wasn't sure how seriously to take him, especially since this was a lunch at Gramercy Tavern that featured lots of wine, but when Sanford's secretary faxed him driving directions the next day, he phoned Cynthia and gave her the news. She was a sport about it. She asked if the kids should pack their bathing suits, and he answered that he didn't have the slightest idea.

"I owe you one," he said. He was actually thinking about Sanford's wife, whom he had met but Cynthia had not. He didn't see that going particularly well.

He spent Friday laughing off the mostly good-natured stink eye from everyone else at Perini, none of whom had ever been graced with such an invitation before, though they'd all been employed there longer than he had. The drive upstate the next morning opened gradually into the kind of calendar-art New England hillscape Adam had grown up in – stone walls, church spires, village greens – but Sanford's house, down at the end of a dirt road they passed twice before finding, was a white Regency-style mansion so gigantic and out of place it looked like a theme park. It sprawled across an expensively produced clearing as if it had been dropped there from the air. Adam turned off the car and the four of them got out and stared. In its inappropriateness the house was so self-absorbed that it could have sprung fully formed from the head of Sanford's awful wife; still, the sheer ballsiness of it, the arrogance required to raze whatever must have been there before in order to erect this monstrosity precisely where it didn't belong, was kind of impressive. He knew Sanford had a lot of money but sometimes even someone in Adam's job had to be reminded what the phrase "a lot of money" really meant.

"This," Jonas said, "is the coolest house I have ever seen."

No one came outside to greet them; he wasn't sure how to let their hosts know they had arrived. Honking felt wrong on multiple levels. "So what time is the next tour?" Cynthia said, but just then Mrs. Sanford #4 – she introduced herself to Cyn as Victoria, thank God, because Adam had blanked on her name – came gaily through some side door that they hadn't even noticed was there.

Sanford himself was waiting in the foyer to shake hands with Cynthia and the children, in whom he took no pains to seem interested, and then he and his wife did something that struck Adam as truly old-school: they segregated their guests immediately by gender, with Victoria taking Cynthia and the kids upstairs and Sanford leading Adam down some steps, through a media room, and onto what turned out to be a screened back porch that faced directly, with only a few feet of mowed grass intervening, into the dense woods. The porch was crowded with dozens of large potted and hanging plants, creating for a moment the effect that the spanking-new house was actually a sort of ruin the birches and pines were intent on reclaiming; but in there among the fauna were two large and very softly upholstered rattan chairs, and in between them was a table that held a pitcher of Bloody Marys. The porch was cool and dark, despite which Sanford wore a pair of sunglasses on a cord around his neck. His own glass was already three-quarters empty – he must have been sitting out here before the Moreys arrived – and he filled Adam's with a stately flourish. "You have a beautiful family," he said as he sank back into his chair.

"Thank you," Adam said. "Where have they been taken?"

"Not much to do out here," was Sanford's answer. "You're at least a hundred miles from the ocean, is what I don't like about it. Still, it is quiet." He took the celery stalk out of his drink and stuck it in his mouth.

Victoria had launched without prelude into a house tour, recounting the difficulties she'd had getting the various painters and decorators and contractors to adhere to her clearly expressed vision, a separate haughty narrative for every room in the mansion. By the fourth or fifth room Cynthia had a powerful urge to burn the whole place to the ground with this Botoxed stick figure inside it. There was no way they could have been more than ten years apart in age – unless she was a mummy, Cynthia reflected while watching the jaw move in her eerily smooth face, or possibly a vampire, preserved for centuries by the blood of her social inferiors – and yet she spoke as if from some great experiential height, as if, at the end of her remarks, there might be time for a few questions.

"Three times, we painted this room," she was saying, as if she would even know which end of a paintbrush to hold. "And I had a chip from Barry's house in Stowe for the painter to match. Hello? Is that so hard? But you know how it is up here in these small towns, you just have to make the best of what you're given, in terms of contractors and such I mean."

"Sounds rough," Cynthia said.

"Are you from New York originally?" Victoria said.

Cynthia, who had turned around to make sure the children hadn't fallen too far behind, or maybe been snatched by silent ninja domestics, said, "What? No. Near Chicago."

"And what line is your family in?"

Cynthia repeated the question in her head to be sure she had heard it right. "They're small-town contractors," she said.

That she had put her foot in her mouth seemed more plausible to Victoria than the idea of being openly mocked; embarrassed, she looked away, and in avoiding Cynthia's eyes she seemed to remind herself of the presence of the two children, who, though of course they could have cared less about paint shades and window treatments, were awestruck by the house itself, the scale and gadgetry of it. There were environmental-control panels in every room, touch screens that not only calibrated light and temperature and music but also gave you access to security-camera views of the garage, the grounds, the driveway, and even the other rooms inside the house. It had taken Jonas about ten seconds to figure it out. "There's Dad!" he said. Cynthia kept throwing him doomsday looks over her shoulder, but having solved the puzzle of the touch screens he couldn't keep his hands off them, and anyway she was half rooting for him to figure out how to make it rain in there. Soon he had left a trail of images of his father and Sanford flickering in every empty room through which they passed.

Victoria hadn't noticed that, but she picked up on the kids' general enchantment and felt gratified again. April was walking a few steps ahead of her brother now, embarrassed by his youthful enthusiasm, trying to blend in with the women, mimicking their facial expressions like someone trying to sneak into the second act of a play. She loved it when new people thought she was older than she was. She was leaning toward Victoria like some kind of thirsty plant, but Victoria seemed disinclined to engage her too directly. "God, these are gorgeous children," she said to Cynthia. "How old did you say they were?"

"Seven and six," Cynthia said, ignoring a scowl from April, who felt ages should be rounded up.

"They could model. They look like a Ralph Lauren catalogue. They go to school?"

"Why, yes," Cynthia said. "We thought that would be wise."

"Where, though?"

"Dalton," April offered.

"Very nice," Victoria said. "And you were smart to have them so young. Easier to bounce back." And she reached out and casually patted Cynthia just below her waistline, approvingly, a touch so condescendingly intimate that Cynthia was speechless. She tried to remind herself that this was the wife of her husband's boss and so she would just have to suck it up for the weekend, and when that didn't work she tried to drum up some sympathetic revulsion at the thought of what old Vicky here must have had to deliver sexually in exchange for this life of high-end vision realizing. But that didn't really work either, because Sanford, even in his late sixties or whatever he was, was a ridiculously handsome guy.

It was apparently his intent to sit there on the porch drinking Bloody Marys for the duration of his guests' stay. He was talking now about the upcoming Newport-to-Bermuda yacht race. The Bloody Marys were excellent; Adam was starting to recall the pleasures of getting drunk before lunchtime but this seemed like an odd setting for it, like a myth or a fairy tale in which he might drink the proscribed drink and never find his way back to the surface of the earth. Not that he was nervous around the boss – they'd been drunk together many times – or felt he needed to keep up appearances of any sort. On the contrary: the more he was himself, the more the old man seemed to like him.

He looked abruptly at Adam, struck by an idea. "You could crew," he said. "The crew I had last year was hopeless. Interested? We'd be out anywhere from four to six days."

"Sadly," Adam said, "I know fuck all about sailing." Sanford's disappointment lasted only an instant. "You could pick it up," he said. "I know a sailor when I see one. I see great things in you, you know."

Adam pretended he hadn't heard, which was his nearest approach to modesty.

"Those others, they'll do fine," Sanford went on. "But they're lieutenants. You give them a job to do and they'll get it done – any business needs that. But I see bigger things for you. God knows I won't be around forever."

Rather than allow Sanford to stray any farther down this path, Adam said, "So I'm meeting your pal Guy in Milwaukee on Monday morning. I have to fly out there tomorrow night." "Your pal" was said with some levity; Sanford scowled at the mention of Guy's name.

"The man is an animal," he said. "I think there's money to be made there, but I'm not sure I can spend another hour in the same room with him. Last time we met he threw a pen at my head. I'm sorry to sacrifice you to this lunatic. Maybe you can get it done, though. People like you. You know that? That's a gift. You can't teach it. I'm hungry," he said suddenly.

"Can I ask you something? Is there a pool here?"

"Good Lord," Sanford said, "you and the swimming."

"No," Adam said, "I was thinking of the kids. They brought their suits. Throw them in the water and they're good all day. It might give them something to do while we're sitting here getting loaded."

Sanford folded his hands on his chest. He had sunk quite low in his chair. "Helicopter," he said. "That's the term, right? These days? Helicopter parents, helicopter parenting."

"Sorry?"

"You're close to them, aren't you? I think that's great."

"You have children yourself, sir?"

The old man loved to be called sir. "Oh God yes," he said. "Of course. Anyway, no, there's no swimming pool here, but we do belong to this little club in town where they can swim all they like. Maybe we can even get some goddamn lunch there, since no lunch appears to be forthcoming here."

They followed the Sanfords in their car, in a silence generated by the fear that anything they wanted to say might later be innocently repeated in front of their hosts by one of the kids. It also required all of Adam's concentration not to lose sight of Sanford's Boxster, which he drove through the narrow roads at aristocratic speed. Adam thought the word "club" betokened a simple swimming pool, and had told the kids so; the family made a collective gasping sound when they came instead upon a clean, still lake hidden improbably high up in the Berkshire foothills. A wooden sign at the gate told them the place was called Cream Hill Pond. The quiet was overwhelming: "No power boats," Sanford pointed out. "Sunfish city." White sails dotted the water. There were two tennis courts, but no one was on them. The kids were vibrating with impatience to get into the lake; Cynthia asked Sanford's wife where the changing rooms were, but Victoria, who looked unhappy and even somewhat baffled to be there at what seemed like the children's behest, didn't know and had to ask someone else.

The dark pines, the sun on the water, the shimmer of the

triangular sails, it was all so postcard-beautiful that you felt a little stupid giving in to it; but April's and Jonas's uncomplicated pleasure was infectious. Cynthia watched them organizing some game in the water with a group of kids they'd met five minutes ago. Rarely did you see the two of them get along so well for so long a stretch and you had to think that the relationship between that and the sheer sense of space out here wasn't coincidental. She lifted her head to admire the green bowl of the hills. Wide open yet secure. Maybe she'd been looking at this place, this life, through the wrong eyes. All you wanted was for your children to become their best selves, but how were you supposed to know if this was not happening? Victoria was right: they were beautiful, so beautiful you almost felt like you should apologize for it, like something fundamental had been rigged in their favor. Maybe you were denying them something they needed without even knowing it, just because you weren't thinking big enough, or far enough outside the box of what your own childhood was like.

But as she watched them play she admitted to herself that sometimes this anxiety over whether your kids' lives were perfectly realized could reach the point where it wasn't a lot different from Victoria's trying to match a paint chip: you had to justify the day, and your existence in it, somehow. It was impressive, in a way, that a woman Victoria's age not only didn't want children but didn't really even pretend to like them. Certainly such a life was possible. Certainly there were other things one might do. According to Adam, she sat on the boards of about ten different national charities, where she no doubt made herself a pain in the ass, but what did that really matter when she had the assets and the social position to actually do some good in the world? What did it matter that the money wasn't hers, as long as it was hers to give away? Cynthia already lived better than anyone in her family ever had, at least until Ruth remarried; still, there was rich and there was rich. She glanced over at Victoria, who wore a huge straw hat that she clamped down on her head with one palm even though there was no wind onshore at all. Cynthia was sorely tempted to ask her how old she was. It wasn't impossible that they were actually the same age.

"You have a beautiful home," she said. Victoria was staring back in the direction of the parking lot and didn't seem to hear.

Sanford, though, nodded graciously. "Shame you all can't spend the night," he said. "Next time." Adam's shocked expression was luckily hidden behind his sunglasses; they had their overnight bags in the car. "That's very kind of you," Cynthia said; she didn't know how she would keep the kids from howling, though, so she went down to the dock to give them the news out of their hosts' earshot. Adam saw her put her finger to her lips and give them the universal five-more-minutes signal as they stomped their feet in the water and complained. She knew how to be gracious. Even after ten years together, his more complex desires for her wound up translating themselves into the simpler language of arousal; and as he watched her walk back up the lawn toward the umbrella table where the adults sat, he experienced an untimely urge to pull her back to the parking lot and do her right there up against some old Brahmin's car. Victoria went off to use the bathroom, and Sanford went off to take a phone call, and Adam was able to give his wife at last the private eye-roll he had wanted to give her all day.

"I am so sorry to put you through this," he said.

But she just smiled. "Actually, I'm really glad we came," she said. "If you want to know the truth, it all makes me kind of jealous."

He was so surprised by that, he couldn't think of another word to say until their hosts returned. The kids had such a meltdown when the time came to get them out of the water that Adam and Cynthia wound up deciding to leave for New York straight from the club. Once again the men were cleaved from the women, the old man walking Adam in the direction of his own car, with his arm around him.

"So what do you think of all this?" Sanford said, and it sounded astonishingly heartfelt, even if he was drunk. His life, Adam supposed he meant. The thought of being asked to pass judgment on it, even just as a matter of etiquette, made him almost resentful.

"Green with envy," he said finally. "You have a beautiful home. I mean, I'm sure you have several. But this is a great part of the world. And frankly," he said, tapping the hood of the Boxster, "this gets me a little hard too."

Sanford laughed enchantedly. Then he laid his hand on Adam's cheek. "Patience, my son," he said. "One day, all this will be yours."

While they searched for Route 22 signs, Adam noticed

his fingers were white around the wheel. "Pretty quiet back there," he said. "Did you guys have fun today?"

"It was awesome," April said. "I thought they would have kids, though."

"Not everybody does, you know," Cynthia said.

"Dad?" Jonas said meekly. "Can we have a country house?"

Cynthia laughed. "Yeah, Dad," she said. "How about it?" Adam said nothing, and after half a minute Cynthia turned around in her seat. "One day," she said to the kids. "One day soon. We'll have all that stuff. It just takes time. You have to remember that Mr. Sanford is almost two hundred years old."

Actually, Adam thought, there was no reason why they couldn't buy some sort of weekend home now, although having gotten a load of Sanford's place Jonas would no doubt feel let down by anything Adam could afford. But there was something in Adam that stiffened against that idea – more so after today than ever before. Some manor in the country to return to over and over again, in which to sit and drink among the plants and do nothing in particular: was that what he was supposed to want? All day long he had felt like the house, the car, the club, the view, that whole life was being conspicuously shown to him, held out in front of him. *Patience, my son.* Why didn't he want it, then? Maybe he just wanted to determine his own rewards, and the pace at which they would come. Or maybe it was the presumption that all this privilege, no matter how touching it was that Sanford wanted him to have it, was Sanford's to give him in the first place. Patrimony, even the sentimental kind, had nothing to do with it. Something in Adam bristled at the thought of inheriting anything from anybody.

The next night they had an early dinner together so that Adam could make his flight to Milwaukee. Guy – whose last name was Farbar but whose abusive phone manner had earned him monomial status in the Perini office – ran a company that made cryogenic rubber; he wanted financing to take it global. Adam didn't have a perfect understanding of what cryogenic rubber was or what it was used for, but one of the beauties of his job was that he didn't really have to. Sanford was high on the numbers, and with good reason, even though as a man of business Guy himself was essentially everything Sanford was not – loud, confrontational, impetuous, undisguised. His staff turnover was incredible, a fact that his seeming compulsion to fuck every single one of his female employees did nothing to diminish. In fact, probably the biggest red flag about getting into business with Guy at all was that there were already two pending lawsuits against him, one of which involved a temp who had been nineteen at the time.

He turned out to be even more of a character in person. He had bushy hair and a retro mustache and had taken this cryogenic rubber company from receivership to eleven million in profit in less than three years. His office had one of those topless gas-station calendars on the wall. "We were up thirty-one percent last year," he shouted at Adam. "In fucking Wisconsin! What is taking you people so long? Where's the money already? Fucking tight-ass Ivy League

Wall Streeters. None of you have ever run an actual business in your lives – I mean, a business that *makes* things. Calling me up and asking for this form and that prospectus. Get your heads out of your asses! I talk to that Sanford guy and it's like talking to one of those animatronic Disney things. The Hall of WASPs. You, on the other hand, seem almost like an actual person. Why can't I just deal with you? Just write me a fucking check already!"

"It's not my money," Adam said, amused.

Guy scowled. "Whatever," he said. "If it was your money we could shake hands and get rich. But you're still young and you still have a boss to jerk off, I get it. When do you fly back? Do I have your cell?"

"Tomorrow first thing. Here, let me write it down for you again."

"Then by Wednesday morning latest I need sixteen million for starters or I go elsewhere."

"Understood," Adam said, meaning that he understood that Guy delivered this same ultimatum every time. Secretly he had an intuition that there was no way this maniac would not succeed, no matter what he was selling. Still, it wasn't Adam's money.

"Whatever way it works," Guy said, and turned around to make a phone call.

And that was it: no lavish dinner to woo him, no junior executives, no strip club. Back at the hotel Adam tried to book a flight home that same night, but there was nothing – some kind of storm was coming in, and flights were being canceled in bunches. A hotel room these days was basically like a mausoleum with a big TV in it: he couldn't just sit there. But the health club in the basement was closed for renovations; and there was a Journey tribute band playing in the bar. It was like a nightmare. He hadn't even brought any work with him. Rain battered the windows, and in the lobby the staff ran around putting wastebaskets under new leaks in the ceiling. He went back upstairs to his room and called Cynthia.

"So what have you been up to?" he asked, drumming his fingers on the bedspread.

"Math homework. April's class started talking about geometry this week. Not exactly my strong suit. She gets a little stressed if she doesn't pick up something immediately."

Her voice flattened out in the evenings, once the kids were in bed – he'd noticed that lately, but never as distinctly as he did now, when her voice was all he had of her.

"There's acute angles," he said, "and also some other kind."

"Okay," she said. "Home schooling probably not an option, then."

"Why so early, anyway? Didn't we start geometry in like ninth grade?"

"I can't remember," Cynthia said.

"Well, you have to talk to me about something," he said. "I'm in some kind of black Midwestern hole here. What have you got?"

She sighed. "Okay," she said. "Marietta has this shrink she used to see, and I called him up today and made an appointment."

He said nothing.

"Discuss," she said.

"An appointment for yourself?"

She laughed. "Yes of course for myself, genius. At least it's not like he's some stranger. I mean he's a stranger to me, but Marietta vetted him for like three years. It's just something I've been thinking about a little bit and I decided to see what it's all about."

He could feel that she needed him to say something, but something was preventing him, something that felt, at least a little, like panic.

"Adam, of course I won't do it if it's going to freak you out," she said. "I mean it. I know it's probably not something you approve of in general."

"Of course it's okay with me," he said. "Of course I approve of it. I mean it's not for me to approve or disapprove. It's just I guess I didn't know you were unhappy."

"Not unhappy," she said thoughtfully. "More like stuck. Anyway, Christ, it's like going to the gym, everyone does it. You know that, right?"

He tried to say the right things, and then he heard April come in with another homework question and he had to let her go. The truth was that he did disapprove, at least a little – not in general, not for other people; but the two of them were different. One of the things that made the two of them so great together, he'd always felt, was that shared talent for leaving all their baggage behind. Why would you want to go back and pick that up again? Everybody's got their own; just walk the fuck away from yours and don't turn around. He saw it borne out every day in the world of finance: the most highly evolved people were the ones for whom even yesterday did not exist.

Still, she was unhappy; she was unhappy, and that had to be his responsibility. He opened up the minibar, sat on the edge of the vast bed with his feet on the windowsill, his back to the empty room behind him, and watched the lightning over black Lake Michigan. A few mini-bottles later he felt less agitated; but he hated doing nothing, and these were hours he was never going to get back.

The first thing Jonas ever collected was Duplo animals. He was too young at the time to remember it now, but his mother liked to tell him stories about himself. The different Duplo sets had different animal-shaped blocks, and he would take them out of their sets and line them up on the coffee table in the living room, or on the rim of the bathtub, or on the floor under his parents' bed, always in the same mysterious order determined somehow, as best she could tell, by their color. Cynthia would find them arrayed like that, in different places around the apartment, two or three times a week.

Next it was pennies: he would arrange them by year, once he'd learned his numbers, and then he'd arrange them by color, really by gradations of dirtiness, from the bright polish of the new ones to the murky greenish-bronze that made the man on the penny look like he was sitting and thinking about something on a bench inside a cave. Then his mother was talking to another mother in the playground and after that she showed him how to bring the shine out of all the pennies by soaking them in lemon juice. That was a lot of fun – like leading the penny man outside where it was light – though it was also the sort of fun that could only be had once and then it was done. This was often the case when grownups got involved.

There was one morning when Jonas walked into the living room to ask his mother for Oreos before dinner even though he knew he wasn't going to get them; he saw her sitting on the window seat, holding onto her knees, looking out the window, like she was sad about something she couldn't find. Think, she often said to him. Where did you have it last?

He loved it when she played with him, but when it came to the collecting she had a way of getting too involved. Like when Grandma Ruth sent him one of those state-quarter sets. His mother would go through her own quarters before he'd even seen them; she knew the ones he was still missing and she'd just walk into his room and hand them to him. Or later when he started reading the Nate the Great books. She saw he liked the first three and so she went out and bought the entire rest of the series, numbers four through sixteen. When it was almost more fun not to have them yet – to know they existed out there somewhere and waited patiently to be found. He didn't know how to tell her this.

Of course she didn't only bring him things he'd asked for. Once in a while she'd buy a few CDs and they'd sit on the living room floor and listen, and if there were one or two he didn't show any interest in, they probably wouldn't play those again. There was one called *Flight of the Bumblebee* – as soon as that one was over he asked if he could hear it again, and his mother's face softened, like that was what she'd been waiting for. Pretty soon she told him that he didn't need to ask permission every time. He knew how to operate the stereo himself though he wasn't supposed to fiddle with the volume knob.

April said one day that if she heard *Flight of the Bumblebee* one more time she'd go postal. He didn't know what that meant but it made him self-conscious so he didn't play it again for the rest of that day.

"He's got an unusual attention span," he heard his mother telling someone else in Zabar's one day. "For a kid his age, a boy especially, he can focus on one thing for a long time."

He finally found a way to pursue his interests without having to worry about others spoiling it with their own enthusiasm or else getting their feelings hurt: he started a secret collection, which, given his limited freedom of movement in the outside world, pretty much restricted him to collecting things from inside the apartment. Also, in order to maintain the collection's integrity as a secret, it had to consist of items people had forgotten about or would eventually be willing to forget about. He knew that this was pretty close to what people called stealing but he chose not to dwell on that. So far he had one of his mother's lipsticks, a combination lock from his father's gym bag, April's hairband with the sunflowers on it, four different wine corks, his father's empty money clip (this he had found serendipitously under a couch cushion), an electricity bill, one photo from his parents' wedding album, April's preschool report card that said she had a "quick temper," two mismatched earrings from the bottom of his mother's purse, a tiny wooden carving of a cat from Dad's boss's house in Connecticut, and a book-light that clipped onto the top of the book you were reading in bed. That last one almost undid the whole project, because his mother had searched for it with unusual thoroughness before giving up.

No one ever looked in the old Lego box that was inside a drawstring bag that was at the bottom of the toy chest that he sat on to read or to draw. He didn't need to look inside the box to remind himself what was in there – he could tick off its contents in his head at any moment of the day, or while lying in bed at night – but once in a while he liked to open it up anyway. It made each item seem even more valuable to know that everyone else had given up on it, because he was the only one in the family who knew the secret, which was that things might disappear but, thanks to him, rarely was anything ever really lost. He held each object between his fingers for a while, recommitting it to memory; then he packed them all away and opened the door of his room and walked past his mother at the kitchen table and into the living room to hear *Flight of the Bumblebee* again.

For Christmas break they were going to a resort in Costa Rica; some guy from Morgan Stanley Adam still played basketball with had said the beaches there were the most beautiful beaches on earth. To the kids, one resort was the same as another, which was to say a kind of paradise where all strangers were nice to you and your parents never said no to anything or asked how much it cost and all you had to do to get anything you wanted was to pick up the phone. April was also mindful, though she knew she shouldn't be, of the jealousy these trips engendered in some of her school friends, who maybe got to go skiing for a couple of days or spent the break in Florida in the hot, featureless homes of their grandparents.

Just a week or so before they were due to leave, the most recent hire at Perini – a guy named Bill Brennan, just barely out of college, whose junior status was unfortunately cemented by the fact that he was only about five feet six – strode around the office tossing postcard-style invitations on everyone's desk. "Some buddies of mine are opening a bar," he said. "Grand opening tonight. Actually, I have a piece of it too. You have to come. All of you are comped. They have to get some buzz going. Every hot woman I know will be there. Adam, dude, it's on 89th and Second, right in your backyard. You have to come. I know it's not your thing anymore."

"Fuck you it's not my thing anymore," Adam said, laughing. He called Cynthia and told her to get the sitter they used, or some other sitter, it didn't matter. They hadn't been to a real meat-market bar like that in a long time, long enough that everything about it seemed hysterical now. The men – if you could even use that word, since despite their suits and loosened ties they all looked about twenty years old – nodded meaningfully to the pounding music and generally stood around hoping for disinhibited women to fall on them like some humanitarian airdrop. Parker and the rest of them were in heaven. Brennan comped all their drinks, but it was so crowded that it took Adam almost fifteen minutes to complete the round trip to the bar from the spot they'd staked out against the wall. By the time he made it back from his third go-round with a Scotch for himself and a vodka and soda for Cynthia, she was holding a different, brand-new drink someone else had bought for her; she was visibly smashed, and encircled by strange, hyena-like guys.

"This, losers, is my husband," she shouted when she saw him, because you had to shout in there to say anything at all. Even so, they smiled and nodded and were likely only pretending to have caught, or cared, what she was saying. A beautiful drunk woman standing alone, even for five minutes, drew these guys like touts at a racetrack; they were too young and callow even to check for a wedding ring. "He is more of a man than any of you will ever be. Especially you, fatso," she yelled, gesturing to one guy, who just smiled.

"Hey now," Adam said.

"You have lost a step, though," Cynthia said in his ear. "I mean, these bottom-feeders bought me three drinks while I was waiting for you to come back with this one." She took one glass out of his hand, took a sip from it, and then with drinks in both hands put her arms around his neck and started making out with him. He felt a little vodka splash on the back of his neck. He wasn't sure whether or not this was hilarious. The circle of guys may not have been able to hear anything she'd been saying to them, but this kind of display they understood, and with no hard feelings they turned away to see what else was available.

Cyn stopped kissing him for a moment and screamed after them, "His dick is bigger than yours too!" That they heard. In fact, a number of people seemed to hear it. "Okay," Adam said, putting his hand gently on the small of her back, "I'm thinking it's time to call it a night."

When they were out on the sidewalk she turned around toward the bar's façade and made the sign of the cross. It was only about ten blocks home but under the circumstances he thought they'd be better off in a cab. He watched her as they rode, eyes closed, head against the window. He hadn't seen her this drunk in years; or maybe he had, but the difference was that he'd been that drunk too. She held her liquor like a champion, so if she was this far gone – and without him – it could only be because she wanted it that way. They got off the elevator and she went straight to the bathroom; Adam waited by the front door while the sitter, Gina, a round girl from Barnard about whom he knew absolutely nothing other than that she was from Minnesota, found her jacket and her shoes and wedged her textbooks back into her backpack. He counted out her money, including a twenty for cab fare. "Is it okay if I don't walk you out tonight?" he said.

"No problem," she said. "It's not like it's a rough neighborhood."

He waited until the elevator door closed. Walking back

through the foyer he saw that Gina had written on a pad underneath the phone, "Cynthia – Your mother called," and then underneath that, "2x." He went to the bathroom to make sure she was okay, but the door was open again and she wasn't in there. She wasn't in their bedroom either. He found her in the kids' room, sitting on the floor against the wall between their beds. Her eyes were wide open.

"We need a bigger apartment," she whispered. "They can't keep sharing a room forever."

He nodded and reached out his hands to help her to her feet. When she was on the bed in their room he took her shoes off and brought her a couple of Advil and a glass of water. The room was lit only from outside but she lay back on the pillow with her forearm over her eyes.

"You okay?" Adam asked her. She nodded. Then, because her unguardedness was contagious, as drunk people's often is, he said, "Hey, Cyn, can I ask you something?"

Without moving her arm from her eyes she gestured grandly with her hand, like, knock yourself out.

"When you go to that shrink," he said, "what do you talk about?"

She grinned. "Not supposed to ask that," she said.

He nodded, though she couldn't see him, and kept lightly stroking her hip with his fingertips. The radiator hissed softly.

"Now," she said, lifting her arm from her face. "Time to show me what you've got. Come on, stud. I knew you'd be good when I saw you in that bar."

She started struggling with her jeans. He stood up beside

the bed to help her, and by the time he had them off, she was asleep.

The next morning he took the kids to school and let her stay in bed; he put the note about her mother's phone calls next to the coffeemaker where she'd see it. She scowled; okay, two more Advil and something to eat before I start to deal with that, she thought, but no such luck, at about five minutes to eight the phone rang again. Ruth sounded tense and offended, though that was pretty much par for the course.

"I called three times last night," she said.

"We were out late. Which is why a stranger answered the phone. We got home way past your bedtime."

"Well, anyway, I'm calling because I have a favor to ask you, and as I thought you might have gathered, it's urgent. It's about your sister."

"I'm sorry?"

"Your stepsister, Deborah." Before Cynthia could even think of what to say, Ruth pressed on: "You know she's living in New York—"

"No, I did not know that. I thought she lived in Boston. How would I know where she lives?"

Ruth made a sound of exasperation with which Cynthia was very familiar. "Well, I don't know how you manage not to know these things. Yes, she's been living right there in the same city as you for two years. She's been getting her PhD in art history at NYU."

"That's super for her," Cynthia said, holding the phone with her shoulder as she poured water into the coffeemaker. "So why—"

"She has been," Ruth said, and here her voice slowed down a bit as if she'd hit an obstacle, "she has been having some difficulties. Apparently. I mean we just found out about it. Apparently it involves a man, or anyway that's where it started. A professor of hers."

"How original," Cynthia said. She sat on the windowsill, feeling the metal safety guards against the small of her back.

"But it goes beyond that. She has – there have been – well, she ended up in the hospital, more or less against her will, there were some sort of pills involved, she says it was an accident but apparently some doctor there refuses to see it that way."

"Some doctor where?"

"In Bellevue," Ruth said.

"In *Bellevue*?"

"It's not as bad as it sounds. The way it was explained to me, it's just a formality. Warren says it's a liability issue for them. They need to release her to someone, a family member, and so I need you to go down there and get her. The admitting doctor's name is—"

"Whoa," Cynthia said. "Whoa. I am not a part of this. Bellevue? Are you fucking kidding me?"

"She's your *sister!*" Ruth wailed.

"She is not my sister. Jesus. We are leaving for Costa Rica in less than a week. Why the hell don't you and Warren come get her?"

"Warren is in San Francisco. He'll come get her if he has to, but it would mean another night in that place for her. Who knows what goes on? Even the doctor said

97

she obviously didn't really belong in there. He seemed so nice." The thought of institutional niceness in such circumstances undid Ruth, and she started crying. "Please, Cynthia. Please. It's his only child. Maybe you don't care about her but surely you won't just let someone you know keep suffering if you can stop it. You're not that kind of person."

Her head was pounding. She really needed to eat something soon. An egg sandwich, maybe. "God damn it," she said. "God damn it. All right. Where the fuck is Bellevue exactly, anyway?"

Ruth gave her the address. "Just a night or two with you," she said, "and she'll be better, maybe well enough to go back to her own place, though they told us she shouldn't try—"

"No way is that happening. She's your problem. And don't hand me that family shit. This is not some sanitarium. I have children here." In the cab down to 27th Street she called Delta and booked Deborah on a flight to Pittsburgh that night. Some two hours later, after she'd filled out every form and then waited in the lobby, which was lit like an autopsy room, for somebody to find somebody else who would sign off on the discharge, the steel door to the ward clicked open and her stepsister walked through. They hadn't seen each other in eight years, but Cynthia, remembering the old hostility in Deborah's eyes, was surprised to see it gone, and nothing else in its place. Probably just the drugs, Cynthia thought. They've got to have some designer shit up in here.

She was thin and pale, and looked very much like some-one who had just spent a lot of time throwing up. Like a much more intense version of the hangover Cynthia herself was still fighting down. Her hair was in knots. The great unlikeliness of this moment was actually kind of compelling, but Cynthia tried not to let it show. "So you're on a 7:32 flight to Pittsburgh," she said, but Deborah didn't even break stride, she was in such a hurry to get out of there. Cynthia fell into step alongside her. "They probably won't even let you on the plane looking like this, though. You can come back to our apartment and clean up and borrow something to wear. Do you have to go back to your place for any reason?"

Deborah licked her lips and said hoarsely, "No."

"Good. I don't think there's time, anyway."

She sat in the kitchen while Deborah took a shower that lasted a good thirty minutes. Cynthia was torn between irritation – the kids had to be picked up at school at three-fifteen – and nervousness about whatever might be going on in there. Finally Deborah exited in a huge cloud of steam, looking flushed and a little more like herself, though still woefully skinny. Cynthia's jeans barely stayed on her hips; she had a smaller pair but there was no way she was giving those up. "I can't believe you live like this," Deborah said. "That is the nicest shower I've ever been in. You should see my place."

Cynthia looked her over, not listening to what she said. She didn't trust her. In her state she might do anything, and if it happened here, it would become Cynthia's problem. "Come on," she said. "We have to go pick up my kids."

Dalton's lower-school building was a double-wide town-house just a few blocks away; the early-arriving mothers went into the lobby, where there was a fireplace, to keep warm, but Cynthia and Deborah waited outside at the bottom of the steps for April and Jonas to emerge. Deborah seemed to have some awareness of herself as out of place; she stayed a step behind Cynthia's shoulder and cringed a bit as if trying not to be seen, not just by the kids (whom she wouldn't have recognized anyway) but by anyone. More than half the women out on the sidewalk were nannies, substantial and mostly dark-skinned and sober-looking, talking to one another with their eyes on the door and occasionally laughing without smiling. When April and Jonas appeared on the landing, wrapped tightly in their coats, and walked smiling down the steps toward their mother, Cynthia heard from behind her, softly but unmistakably, a gasp.

"Kids," Cynthia said; and then, just because it was the shortest available explanation, "this is your aunt Deborah."

Their mouths fell open, but they also remembered their manners and held out their hands for Deborah to shake. "I've seen pictures of you," April said, and for a moment Cynthia was surprised. "At Mom and Dad's wedding. You were one of the bridesmaids."

"That would be correct," Deborah said. Cynthia rolled her eyes. Some people had no talent for talking to children at all.

At home the kids watched TV and had a snack, as usual; and Deborah, after sitting silently under the kitchen clock with Cynthia for a few minutes, stood up from the table and went into the living room to join them. Cynthia phoned her mother with Deborah's flight information. "Yes, Mom, she's fine," she said, watching warily through the kitchen doorway. "Perfectly normal. I mean, if a grown woman sitting on the floor eating Goldfish and watching the Disney Channel is normal. Just be there when her flight gets in so she doesn't go AWOL or whatever." When Adam walked through the door, Cynthia stood up, kissed him, and grabbed her keys. "They've eaten," she said to him. "Let me just get my coat and we're out of here." He went into the TV room, and the kids jumped all over him. "Daddy," they yelled, "have you met Aunt Deborah?"

Deborah stood up, brushing crumbs off her shirt. She and Adam nodded to each other awkwardly. Jonas, holding both his father's hands, walked up his thighs and flipped himself over.

"How's your brother doing?" Deborah said.

Adam's eyebrows went up. "Good," he said. "He's in Los Angeles. I guess I'd forgotten you knew each other. You want me to tell him you said hi?"

"No," she said, as Cynthia reappeared in the doorway behind him and beckoned with one finger.

They hit traffic getting on the FDR at that hour and again once they were over the Triborough. Cynthia started looking nervously at her watch. No way in hell they were missing this flight. Suddenly she felt a kind of shudder go through the seat beneath her, and when she turned she saw that Deborah was crying, and shaking with the effort not to make any noise while doing it.

"Oh please," Cynthia said – not to Deborah, exactly, but that was how she took it.

"Please what?" Deborah said angrily, wiping her eyes on her borrowed shirt. "I'm sorry that unhappiness doesn't fit in with your lifestyle. I know you don't give a shit about me but I'd think I'd merit the sympathy a total stranger would, at least. Of course maybe the total stranger would get nothing from you either. I'd forgotten how easy everything's always been for you. I just didn't expect I'd ever feel so jealous of it."

"As I understand it," Cynthia said, "you banged some married professor and what do you know, it turns out he's a liar. Wow, I'm sure you're the first person that's ever happened to. So you forget about it and you move forward. The rest of it is just drama, which should really be your middle name, by the way. You may not respect me but at least I'd respect myself enough not to wind up in the batshit ward."

"What do you know about it? What do you know about anything? You have never suffered a day in your life. You've never not gotten anything you wanted. And now those kids of yours are growing up the same way. Like a little ruling class. It's terrifying."

"What did you say to them?" Cynthia said.

"Everything given to them. No idea how fortunate they are. Sweet and content and well bred. Everything as it should be and they have no idea how the other ninety-nine percent lives."

"Hey, you're right," Cynthia said. "I really should try to ennoble them with some early suffering. I really should go back home and take some things away from them. Boy, it's a mystery to me how someone as smart as you has never had a kid of her own."

And when she said that, Deborah stiffened as if she'd been hit; she stopped talking and turned to look out the window; and just like that Cynthia had a pretty good idea what had really happened. They rode the rest of the way to LaGuardia in silence.

"Keep the meter running," Cynthia said to the driver. Deborah, her hand on the door, turned to face her. "I know you only did this because you had to," she said, "but thank you anyway."

"I didn't have to do it," Cynthia said. "Why would I have to do it?"

"Because we're quote-unquote family," Deborah said.

But that's what's so fucked up about it, Cynthia thought when she was back in the city-bound traffic on the L.I.E. Everyone thought they could keep playing this family card with her to get her to do what they wanted; the irony was that they had no idea how deeply she bought into the idea they were so cynical about. She believed in it more than any of them. But you didn't get to screw around with definitions, your own or anyone else's. Just because Ruth found some rich guy to get old with, it didn't follow that Cynthia was no longer an only child. And she hadn't heard from her father in the last three years, but that didn't mean he wasn't still her father, or that anybody else was. That was how you kept the whole idea meaningful, and powerful. You kept it small.

But the whole blowup stayed with her, particularly the indictment of her children, or at least of the way she was raising them. That was beyond the pale. Even if you'd spent the previous night in Bellevue, she thought, you should know better than to go there. It wasn't the first time she'd reached the conclusion that, on the subject of children, most people were full of shit. What was supposed to be the point of denying them anything? Who decided that not having things that your parents hadn't had either was character-building somehow? Narcissistic bullshit. Your children's lives were supposed to be better than yours: that was the whole idea. And what was the point of getting hung up on how much things cost? You were expected to complain when things were, or seemed, more expensive than they should be: braces, for instance, which their dentist said both kids were eventually going to need. Fifteen grand, probably, before that was all over. But the fact was they could afford it. They spent sixty thousand dollars a year just to send their kids to school and they could afford that too. They knew or observed plenty of people – in their neighborhood, in their own building – richer than they were; still, they already had much more money than Cynthia had ever seen as a kid, even during the flush times. In fact the very notion of "flush times" was one that Cynthia did not care to revisit.

And as far as the kids' characters being shaped by money, it was clearly untrue because money itself was one area where you saw the fundamental differences between them. The two of them fought less and less as time went on; there was little ground for competition or envy because they just didn't want the same things. April was a thoroughly social animal, obsessed with preteen perks and downright lawyerly when it came to the question of their early acquisition. She'd been given her own cell phone this year, because that was a safety issue; but just last week Cynthia had bought her a pair of Tory Burch shoes for Christmas – to be honest, it thrilled her somewhat, just on the level of pride in her daughter's precociousness, that April had even asked for them – and before that there'd been a kind of mini-scandal at school when some kids she knew in the grade ahead of hers were caught trying to pay for lunch at Serendipity with a parent's credit card. You could hold them off for a while, but any parent knew that it wasn't about possessing all these things so much as it was about asking to be trusted, to be let into the world a little more, and in that light Cynthia couldn't see the argument for saying no to very much. That the lines should stay open, that she should always be the first person April would come to about anything and everything – that was the important consideration, and she wasn't going to risk losing her daughter's confidence over something as stupid as other people's bitchy judgments of her privileges. She knew April already had a bit of a mean-girl rep at school, but as far as Cynthia was concerned, wailing over that kind of natural social stratification was more about the mothers' egos than the kids'. April could handle herself just fine. In truth

Cynthia couldn't help but be a little impressed by the fantastic amount of ingenuity April put into appearing two or three years older than she was. The great irony, of course, was that Jonas's complete lack of interest in whatever his own peers were doing or buying or watching made him seem like he was about forty years old.

But there was no getting out of certain forms of sibling togetherness; she had to take them to see that dentist again before they left for Costa Rica, for instance, and even though April was furious about having to miss ballet, Cynthia had made this appointment six months ago and if they missed it this huckster was booked until summer. She picked them up at school, and even though they were running late they had to take the subway instead of a cab, because for the past three weeks Jonas's homeroom teacher had been doing a unit about conservation and air pollution and if Cynthia had to hear another word about the fucking ozone layer she was going to scream. They crossed 87th and at the storefront gap that led to the subway entrance they found themselves converging with a guy pushing a baby in a stroller – actually not a baby at all, Cynthia saw, more like three years old, a kid who, by virtue of still being strollered around at that age, was clearly running the show. Beautiful boy, though. The father was a good-looking guy too, very expensively tousled. All four of them did that little no-you-go-first dance at the top step, and even though it only took a second, Cynthia was suddenly conscious of impatient people mustering behind them.

"Sorry," she said to the dad, "you go ahead," and she smiled before she realized that he was not even looking at her but instead, uncertainly, down the steps themselves. She had a vestigial memory of pissing off rude strangers while pushing April around in one of those strollers, and also a mother's instinctive assumption that men are overmatched by small children. "Guys, go on downstairs," she said to April and Jonas. "Not through the turnstile." She turned back to the father with her most prim smile as other commuters swirled into the open lane created by the kids' departure and said, "Can I give you a hand carrying the pasha here?" Suddenly his eyes seemed to focus on her, and he gave her a very winning smile, though without nodding or shrugging or otherwise acknowledging that she'd spoken. He did not even seem to notice the swarm of hostile strangers struggling to get past him, which was an admirable quality, Cynthia thought. Or maybe there was something wrong with him.

"Yes, thanks," he said at last. "That's really nice of you."

He didn't move and so she went around to the front of the stroller and picked up the strap between the front wheels, even though that meant she would be the one backing down the stairs. He lifted his end by the handles and they started down slowly.

"So you've obviously been in my position before," he said. "Beautiful kids."

She smiled, looking down at her feet for the next step. In front of her, the little boy's eyes opened slightly.

"Easy to see where they get it from," the father said.

"Thanks. Well, you too. He's a knockout."

"So, I guess this is like the meet-cute," he said, and she laughed, even if she didn't quite know what he meant. People flowed all around them. She tried to find April and Jonas but couldn't turn her head far enough to see them. "My name's Eric, by the way," he said.

"Cynthia."

"Hey Cynthia?" he said. He bent from the waist, and so she knew she was almost at the bottom step. She had to lean forward suddenly just to hear him. "This was so nice of you. Look, this is going to sound bizarre, but do you live in this neighborhood? I would hate to think that I'll never see you again. You are a really beautiful woman."

"I'm sorry?" Cynthia said.

"I can't believe I said that," Eric said, and it seemed exactly like he was telling the truth. He was probably an unemployed actor. His wife was probably some corporate lawyer who felt guilty for not spending more time with her son, while her husband spent his afternoons in the playground collecting phone numbers from au pairs.

They were now both standing on the cement floor inside the station, still holding the stroller between them, a couple of feet off the ground. People hustling down the stairs brushed past them as if they weren't even there. She knew that the longer she just stood there, the more emboldened he would become. She could feel herself turning red.

"Do you do this a lot, Eric?" she said.

He knew how to stare into a woman's eyes, that was for sure. "I know I'm being insanely forward," he said, "but

I'm not sorry, because two more seconds and I was never going to see you again. I know you're married. I'm married too. It doesn't have to be about that."

What? she kept saying to herself, as if she were deaf to whatever she was thinking. *What?* His son's eyes were half open and on her, as expressionless as if he had just sentenced her to death. It made Eric himself seem like some sort of superman to know that on some level he'd forgotten that the boy was even there.

She put her end of the stroller gently on the floor and turned and walked away as fast as she could. Jonas and April were standing by the nearest turnstile with that look of infinite sarcastic indulgence kids always wore when they had to wait for you. Cynthia panicked for a moment, thinking that they would surely ask her what all that was about and knowing she was still too rattled to make up an answer; but they didn't say a word, they couldn't have cared less. They turned and ran their MetroCards through the slot and walked ahead of her down the steps to the express track.

Cynthia was neither offended nor flattered, really – mostly she just thought it was hilarious. She couldn't wait to tell Adam about it. It did bother her a little bit to think that this kind of unsanctioned activity went on without her, that she was not a part of it, even though she had no desire to *be* part of it – married strangers hooking up in earshot of their kids. Who knew? Maybe this sort of decadence went on all the time. There was a time when she might have at least led the guy on a little bit just to shock herself, when anything that new to her would have presented itself in the form of a hypothetical dare.

"Earth to Mom," Jonas said. A train was already there at the express platform, its doors just sliding open, and the kids had quickened their steps to catch it. She ushered them along in front of her, where she could see them; when the doors opened, they stepped inside, and then a voice from on board the train roared, "Hold the door!" She heard a ticking sound; it was the cane of a blind man, white-haired, wearing an old blue blazer, a baseball cap, and enormous wraparound sunglasses. He seemed angry about something, or at someone. "Hold the *door!*" he yelled again, though someone, not Cynthia, was already holding it. His cane swung incautiously at about ankle level, swatting the base of the seats, the pole at the center of the car, the door frame, and people's legs. She couldn't tell whether he was actually orienting himself this way or just panicking. She took another step back, to avoid the cane's arc – not because she feared it would hurt, but because she didn't want to send the man any kind of false information – and then it happened: the doors closed with their two-note chime, and she was on the platform and they were on the train, and as it pulled out she saw the look of terror on Jonas's face, though he might well have been terrified mostly of her, banging her hands on the glass and screaming *Wait*.

Even before she'd reached the end of the platform the train was moving too fast for her, and there she was, watching the train lights shrinking away from her down the tunnel. She couldn't turn away from it. She could feel that the strangers behind her had stopped moving too: nothing was moving anymore but that train. "You got kids on that train?" a voice said behind her, a young voice, a man's voice. Misfortune made everyone familiar with you. "How old are they?"

Cynthia turned around and tried to answer but could not. She could actually see a black circle forming at the edges of her own vision.

"Go to the booth and ask for a transit cop," the young man said – he was wearing a huge Knicks jersey. "*You* go," someone else said to him contemptuously. "You're going to send this woman up the stairs? You can't see she's about to pass out as it is?" Over their heads she heard a gathering roar, and she thought at first she was fainting but it was a real roar, there was another express train pulling in beside them. Two people were holding her gently by the elbows. The children had disappeared into a tunnel: it didn't seem real. "What's your name?" an older woman's voice said.

Cynthia got on the first car of the train and groped her way to the locked front door that faced forward into the darkness. She understood it was a stupid idea but the logic of the situation was all dream logic now and she didn't feel there was anything to discuss. The children's fear filled every cell of her. She had to go find them. She had to put her face flat against the glass in order to see past her own reflection, even though there was nothing to see for a long time but the track and the steelwork that held open the tunnel and the ghostly local stations they sped through without stopping. Finally she felt the train slowing down beneath her feet and

111

the lights of the platform at 59th Street floated toward her. She burst out onto the platform and only then did it occur to her that there was no real reason to think that the kids had gotten off here at all, maybe they were still crying on the train as it continued on its long loop beneath the city, but then she saw a cop farther down the platform and the cop had his hands on two children's shoulders and the two children were April and Jonas.

"You're *here?*" the cop said, not very sympathetically. "I just radioed 86th Street to look for you there. That wasn't real smart, getting on another train." The kids were staring at her with the blank expression of kids overhearing their parents fight. Even an hour later Cynthia couldn't remember much about how she got them back up the stairs and into the bright street and into a cab and back home, but she didn't recall any of them saying a word the entire way.

She made Adam sleep in the kids' room that night, so they could both stay in the big bed with her. The next day she kept them both home from school. Adam was a little surprised but put it down to erring on the side of caution: they were quieter than usual, it was true, but it was hard to tell – even for April and Jonas themselves – how much of their anxiety was still their own and how much of it came from being treated so solicitously, as if something terrible had happened to them. He told them both how proud of them he was for being so brave and for being smart enough to ask for help from a police officer, just like they should have. He said that anytime they wanted to talk about yesterday, he was there for them; but that was not Cynthia's approach. She sat the kids down together and asked them what questions they had, about what had happened yesterday, and about why Mommy hadn't gotten on the train with them, and when they came up with nothing, she took that as evidence of how traumatized they were, how quickly you had to act before what was in them buried itself so deeply you were never going to get it out again. She let them return to school the next day but was so worried for them that she sat them down to talk again as soon as they got home, just to compensate in case she'd made a mistake. That night April woke up sobbing from a nightmare. Ten minutes later both kids were sleeping beside their mother and Adam was curled up in Jonas's short bed watching the shadows, awake but too tired to get up and turn the nightlight off.

By the weekend, they seemed to have gotten past it; they were a little less clingy, and that uncharacteristic wide-eyed silence in which Adam or Cynthia would sometimes come upon them diminished and then was gone. They went to the Radio City Christmas show and packed for the trip to Costa Rica and ate at 3 Guys and it all seemed behind them.

But Cynthia was unconvinced. Every night she postponed Adam's sleep demanding to know what more he thought they should do about it. He tried his best to say all the properly sympathetic things; he was pretty sure that the suffering she ascribed to them was really her own, but the great thing about Cynthia was that no matter how stressed she might get, she always returned to her own center, somehow, if you had the patience to just let it happen. But when she told him Wednesday night that she had called Dalton to ask if they could recommend a psychiatrist who specialized in treating children with PTSD – and that not only was there such a person but she had already made an appointment with him – Adam started to wonder whether the whole thing was getting out of hand.

"In a few days," he said soothingly, "we'll all be sitting on the beach, and we'll have a new perspective on everything. Them too."

They were whispering because though the kids had been put to bed down the hall hours ago, you never knew.

"Not so much," Cynthia said. "I called the resort tonight and canceled our reservation."

He struggled up onto his elbows and stared at her.

"The plane tickets weren't refundable. Sorry about that. But I told the kids and they're fine with it. We'll have Christmas at home for once. It won't kill us. I just don't feel like being in a strange place right now." She started crying. "But something has to change around here," she said. "Something has to start getting better. You can't just do nothing."

"It will. Things are going great." It was true, and yet even as he said it he could feel himself starting to panic. "Bonuses are this week, you know. It's only going to get better for us."

"I know it. But time doesn't mean the same thing to you

and me anymore, you know? You're all like, in ten years we'll have everything we want, and in the meantime I feel like I need binoculars just to be able to see to the end of the fucking day."

"Look," he said pleadingly, "I don't blame you for being upset about what happened, but isn't there another way of looking at it? I mean, April and Jonas knew what to do. They did exactly the right thing. In a way it should make you worry less. Plus, I don't want to make light of it or anything, but it's New York. You can't protect them from everything."

"Well, maybe we shouldn't live here, then," she said.

"What the hell are you talking about?"

"Maybe we should live somewhere else. Maybe we should be living a different kind of life. Who says it has to be this way? You think this is the best life we could be living? There's so little space here. There's so little room to move. It should feel safe but it just feels exposed. There's got to be somewhere else for us to go."

He was nervous about touching her all of a sudden. "I thought you said you wanted to stay here, though," he said tentatively.

She shook her head, wiping her eyes. "Don't you get it?" she said. "This is the only thing there is for me to be good at. And I suck at it. In fact I'm terrified I'm getting worse at it instead of better."

"Cyn, it was one bad hour out of their lives. You seriously think, as good as our lives are, that that's what they're going to remember?"

"Don't be an idiot," she said. "You think you're born knowing how to forget shit like that?"

Each December Sanford took them out to lunch one by one and gave them their bonus checks, along with a kind of performance review, known among the staff as the State of the Career Address, that helped explain the amount. The business itself was his whim, and while they all knew that it had been a profitable year, there was no expectation that the relative size of the bonuses reflected anything more precise than Sanford's own fondness for them.

They were good enough friends to joke about their fear. The whole operation was so mercurial that it wouldn't have been outside the realm of possibility for one of them to be fired at his or her bonus lunch, or for all of them to be handed a severance check and told that Sanford had decided to shut the place down. Adam, whose lunch was scheduled for the Friday before Christmas, was on a roll. He'd put together the first round of financing for a generic-drug start-up that was poised to get huge in a way few people other than Adam had foreseen; and he'd set up a friendly takeover of Wisconsin Cryogenics, friendly enough to keep the volatile Guy from Milwaukee in teenagers and blow for the rest of his life. The hardest part about putting that together was getting Guy to keep his mouth shut about it, so the stock wouldn't overreact and screw the deal.

Sanford took Adam to Bouley, where they split two bottles of wine before the boss produced a check in a glassine envelope. "Open it," he said immodestly, as if there were a ring inside.

Adam opened it and saw it was for three hundred and fifty thousand dollars. It was much more than he was expecting, or had received in previous years, and he'd heard enough to know that none of his colleagues had gotten anything close to it.

"This is between you and me," Sanford said unnecessarily. In his old age he cried more easily. "This is not about the past year. This is about the future. I need to make sure you aren't going anywhere. I need to be sure you know how you're valued. I'm getting to the point where I need to think about the legacy that I leave in this world."

Like a lot of his peers, Sanford maintained his social profile through lavish entertainments tied to charities; it wasn't long after bonus season, when presumably they were all feeling flush, that his employees were dunned to buy tickets to that spring's annual benefit for an organization close to his heart, the Boys and Girls Clubs of New York, to be held on the deck of the *Intrepid,* the decommissioned aircraft carrier that served as a floating naval museum at one of the Hudson River piers. A thousand dollars a head. For those who worked at Perini it was not an invitation there was any question of refusing. Adam bought a ticket for Cynthia as well. Normally he wouldn't have forced her hand like that, but he needed to see a little of the old Cynthia, radiant at a party, for her sake but also for his own. She was so down these days, and though for the life of him he couldn't see what there was to be down about, he was so used to being grounded by her that he had a real fear that, wherever she was drifting, he'd end up drifting right out there along with her. He couldn't figure out what to try other than maybe to re-enact an evening when she was happier.

It wasn't much of a plan, but for that night, at least, it seemed to work. Cynthia was beaming as she shivered in a black dress in the hangar-like space below the deck of the ship, drinking some kind of themed martini, the center of attention among Adam's colleagues from Perini, none of whom had sprung for the extra grand for a date. They took turns asking her to dance. He could see how smitten they were with her, with the idea of her, proof of life after marriage. Even when they got a little drunk and their gaze became a little more direct, it did not occur to him to feel jealous, because she deserved their attention. They ate rack of lamb. They saw Tiki Barber. Sanford and his wife came magnanimously by their table, everyone happily drunk.

"One of these things is not like the other," Sanford said, smiling rakishly at Cynthia. "What are you doing at this table full of empty tuxedos?" He held out his hand to her, and when she held out hers, he kissed it. Victoria smiled into the middle distance.

"So nice to see you again, Barry," Cynthia said.

"Please. The pleasure is all mine. You are the absolute jewel of this sorry gathering. Let me ask you something. Do you dance?"

"Not really."

"Splendid. Son," he said to Adam, "you don't mind if I

make off with your wife for a while, do you? Adam may not have told you this but I am a dance instructor par excellence. Among my many talents." He held out his elbow; Cynthia, with a mock-frightened glance at her husband, put down her martini and glided off on Sanford's arm toward the dance floor. Victoria saw a friend a few tables away, or pretended to, and she waved and chirped and left the table without a word.

"Unbelievable," Parker said, not without a little envy in his voice. "Fucking old goat. And with his wife right there too. Amazing what that guy gets away with."

Parker's bonus, Adam knew, was so insultingly small that he had skipped right over resentment and moved straight to terror. He emptied another martini, and beckoned to the waitress with the empty glass. "There's no buzz," he said to Adam, "like that good-cause buzz."

"True dat," Adam said. In fact, though, the drunker he got, the more restless and vaguely surly he began to feel, which was unusual for him. He could feel himself smiling, so he stopped. There was a bar up on deck as well, and he headed outside to visit it, just to get away from the table for a few minutes. On the stairs he turned and was able to pick out his boss and his wife on the crowded dance floor. It was a field of tuxedos but his eyes were drawn right to them. He watched Sanford turn her around and around in that small space; he said something that made her laugh. It made Adam nostalgic. All the energy and heedlessness and faith in herself that he had always adored had lost its outlet and so that faith had backed up, as it were, into the lives of the children. What was worst was that the life of maximized potential they had always believed in for themselves was still right there in front of them, closer than ever really, but she had stopped looking forward to it, she wouldn't even lift her head to see it. When he told her about the bonus, she had mustered a polite smile and whistled, like, How nice for you. It was both thrilling and a little sad to see her out there dancing like her old self, drunk and luminous, because it took a crazy setting like this, a fantasy almost, to bring it out of her again. Maybe life needed to better resemble the fantasy. Not that there was some thousand-dollar gala to go to every night. But whatever it was that had to be done, it was his turn to bail her out; she'd bailed him out in more ways than he could count. He couldn't picture what he might have become without her.

He knew his boss well enough to have no doubt that seducing Cynthia was the one and only thing on his mind right now. It didn't bother him. Not just because he knew it would never happen: it was right, somehow, that that was what Sanford should try to do, regardless of the fact that his wife was standing right there, or his love for Adam, or the presence of hundreds of onlookers. That was the point of a life like Sanford's. You pursued what you wanted.

Up on the deck there was some kind of disturbance in the line for drinks: a frat-boy type in front of Adam was complaining to his friends that the kid at the front of the line, who looked about nineteen years old, was chatting up the bartender. "Mack on your own time, Junior," he said. "Some of us are thirsty here."

The kid turned around. He had a huge nose, one of those noses that starts practically on the forehead, but on him it looked sort of Roman and oddly handsome. "Take it easy there, Bluto," he said, and Adam's eyes widened gleefully at the audacity of it. "She's my sister."

"What?" Bluto said.

"I'm not shitting you," the kid said. "I think we're twins." Though he had his drink in hand, he turned back and started murmuring to the bartender again.

Another Wall Street tyke, Adam thought, another kid blowing his bonus money on a party where he thinks he'll network with people who don't even know he's alive. The whole bonus thing got to him, actually, in a way it hadn't before. He'd been given a big bonus this year. What did that even mean? Maybe he should buy himself a sailboat, or find more expensive hotels to stay in during the few weeks a year he was allowed to travel where he wanted instead of Charlotte or Omaha, or see if he could find an even more overpriced school to send his kids to? He felt like a sap. Everybody acted like the amount mattered, when what mattered was the notion of getting a bonus at all, of being outside that small circle wherein it was decided how much a man's work was worth, how close you had come to some goal somebody else had set for you. Sanford could have given him two million and the principle would still be the same. Meanwhile time was going by, and the life around you started to calcify while the Barry Sanfords of the world paid you to wait to be told what would happen next.

His relationship to drinking had grown complicated. The more he felt he wanted one, the more he tried not to have it: it was a self-control exercise, of course, but also he was working out more and more lately, and drinking and especially hangovers were incommensurate with the plan to get into perfect shape. He weighed less and could lift more now than ten years ago. One day off from his routine, though, and he could feel the backslide beginning. Even now, standing in the bar line in a tuxedo, he had a restless urge to descend through the loud metal innards of this impotent ship and, once out on the thin path that ran between the Hudson and the West Side Highway, go for a run.

When Bluto got to the front of the line, he pushed the kid aside – just a nudge, really, but the kid was so much smaller that he stumbled and lost about half his drink on the floor. He put the glass down on the bar and for a moment Adam thought the kid was drunk enough to do something seriously stupid. Instead, though, he stuck out his hand. "No hard feelings, bro," he said to Bluto, and when Bluto scowled and shook his hand, the kid reached up with his other hand and clapped Bluto on the shoulder. Then he wandered off, not toward the tables but in the direction of the moribund planes, some of them spotlit, welded onto the deck as exhibits. Adam continued to stare after him, not so much intently as distractedly, and then suddenly the kid turned around and caught him at it. A few strange seconds passed, strange in that it seemed less awkward than it probably should have. The kid raised his eyebrows, and then – Adam was absolutely sure of it – as he started to walk away again he held up his right hand, opened it up by raising his fingers as one might open up a book of matches, and there, facing out from his palm, looped around a couple of his fingers, was a wristwatch.

No way. Bluto turned away from the bar again to head back into the crowd, holding three beers by their necks in one hand. "Have a good night, G," he said to Adam.

"You too. Hey, do you have the time?"

Bluto shook his thick wrist out of his sleeve and held it up in front of his face. It was bare. "Holy fuck," he said.

Adam left him there pushing everyone backward while he searched the deck for his expensive watch. He got about halfway back to his own table before he stopped. It took a second in that sea of tuxes but he could pick out his colleagues sitting at the Perini table with their heads close together, probably in some timid bitchfest about something. They didn't see him. Cynthia must still have been dancing. Adam turned around and walked back into the darkness punctuated by the hulks of old Mustangs and helicopters and fighter jets. He found his man lighting a cigarette, way up by the bow, looking across the water to New Jersey, as if the boat were on its way there.

He looked a little nervous at Adam's approach. "Cheese it, the cops," he said.

"Why did you show me the watch?" Adam asked him. "How did you know I wasn't some friend of that guy's?"

He shrugged. "He was laughing," he said. "Whereas you looked pissed just to be here."

"Where did you learn to do that? What are you, like

some child of the streets or something? Did you even pay to get in here?"

Once he realized Adam wasn't there to bust him, the kid relaxed a bit. "Somebody gave me his ticket," he said. "His boss paid for it because he believes in Giving Back. I'd love to tell you some Oliver Twist bullshit but the truth is a whole lot geekier. I used to do magic. Right through high school. I can get wallets too. Want to see?"

"Where do you work?" Say I'm a broker, Adam thought.

"I'm a broker at Merrill Lynch. What about you?"

Adam didn't answer. You could never, ever go back to this moment in time, he was thinking, to this one permutation of the random. It wasn't about fate – fate was bullshit. It was about a moment's potential and what you did with it. Unrealized potential was a tragic thing.

"Do you know how perfect this is?" he said out loud. "There's no connection between us at all. We don't know each other, we don't work together, we didn't go to the same school. I don't even know your name. Your name isn't even on the guest list here."

"Wait," the kid said. "Don't tell me. *Strangers on a Train*."

"You're not going to give that asshole back his watch, are you?" Adam said.

A little smirk that Adam hadn't even realized was there suddenly faded from the kid's face. The inchoate patter of the bandleader beneath them and the tidal rush of the Hudson below them were like one sound. He looked at Adam and swallowed. "No," he said.

"Why not?"

"Because fuck him. That's why not."

The adrenaline was pounding through him now. He hadn't felt like this since he proposed. Without turning he gestured over his shoulder toward the party, which they could hear but not see.

"They're all like him," Adam said. "They wear a uniform to make it easier to tell. They give us gifts, like tickets to benefits, to make us forget that life is short. We can't just wait around. We don't have that kind of time."

"We who?" the kid said.

"We happy few," he said. "You and me. It's time to bum-rush the show. It's time to change the terms. It's going to require some bravery on your part."

What was scary was how immediately all this came to him, when he hadn't even really known it was there: an urge for vengeance, sure, but vengeance against what? He used to be a leader. He'd never done what others his age were doing, he was always in too much of a hurry, and yet somehow that hurry, instead of bringing him the life he wanted, had marginalized him. Now all of a sudden the margin seemed like the only place to be. As for the kid, Adam could tell from the look of terror on his face that he was not wrong about him.

"I don't know what you're talking about," the kid said, which was the right thing to say.

"Yes you do," Adam said. "I'm going to tell you something now. You don't need to do anything but hear it. Wisconsin Cryogenics. Can you remember that without writing it down?"

He nodded.

"Now, you can do with that what you will. If you like, it can just be my little gift to you. And that can be the end. But it doesn't have to be the end."

They froze and watched a man and a woman, both holding martini glasses, stoop to walk under the stilled blades of a helicopter. Drunkenly they climbed inside. Music started up again within the ship.

"Give me a number," Adam said. "Not a work number, or a home number. Maybe like a girlfriend's cell. I'm going to contact you in about three weeks, okay? Three weeks. Then we'll either talk about the future or you can just hang up on me. My name is Adam."

The kid was right with him. He whispered a number, and Adam recited it back. Once he had a number in his head he didn't forget it. "One more thing," Adam said. "Give me the watch."

The kid was confused but handed it over. Adam had a quick look at it: a gold Patek Philippe. He wasn't much into watches himself but he appreciated value. He pursed his lips respectfully, and then he threw it over the side.

Back at the table he found Cynthia sitting with Parker and Brennan and one or two of the others, all of whom were too drunk and needed to go home. Cynthia, still glowing from all the dancing, glared teasingly at him. "Leave a lady hanging, why don't you," she said. "Where've you been, anyway?"

He told her he'd run into some old friends from Morgan. It was the easiest lie he'd ever told. Parker staggered around the table to say goodbye to her; he bent over with drunken gravitas and kissed her hand, and she laughed, and Adam thought how right she was: you couldn't just do nothing. It wasn't enough to trust in your future, you had to seize your future, pull it up out of the stream of time, and in doing so you separated yourself from the legions of pathetic, sullen yes-men who had faith in the world as a patrimony. That kind of meek belief in the ultimate justice of things was not in Adam's makeup. He'd give their children everything too, risk anything for them. He knew what he was risking. But it was all a test of your fitness anyway. The noblest risks were the secret ones. *Fortuna favet fortibus.*

Sanford talked a good game but he wasn't about to give up what was his except maybe in his will, just like all the other bloated old satyrs capering around on this big docked ship. As for Adam, when he was lying speechless in some hospital bed after his third coronary, everybody would think he was thinking about one thing, but he would be thinking about something else.

They finally found a new apartment, on East End, a long way from Dalton but bigger and better in so many other respects – not only would April and Jonas finally have their own rooms, there was a guest room also, and a patio and access to a pool – that even the kids gave in to the idea of uprooting pretty quickly. But the renovations Cynthia wanted took months longer than expected, and in the end they had to knock fifty thousand off the selling price of their own place in return for the buyer's agreement to delay the closing. It was a strange period, with about half their stuff packed away, calling the contractors for updates every afternoon, living like subletters in their own home. The kids lost their enthusiasm and started to complain remorsefully about having to move at all. They'd act out, Cynthia would get frustrated with them, and after one particularly trying weekend in this short-tempered limbo, Adam proposed to his wife that they go away somewhere for a few days, just the two of them. Couples they knew did that all the time, but when they stopped to think about it, they hadn't really done it themselves since April was born. He even offered to take Cynthia to Paris; he knew he probably wouldn't enjoy it that much himself, two flights across the Atlantic in three days, but he made the offer just to show her he was serious. Sitting on a beach someplace in the Caribbean was more their style, but in the end it didn't matter because there was no one to leave the kids with for that long. Cynthia couldn't think of anyone she knew or trusted well enough for that. Who, that little Barnard girl they hired, from Minnesota? It was a wonder she could survive a weekend in the city herself. It was true that the two of them didn't have parents who lived nearby, or whom you'd necessarily trust your kids with even if they were nearby. When Adam was a kid, his parents thought nothing of stashing him and Conrad at some neighbor's place if they had plans, sometimes on the shortest of notice. But when Cyn asked him if he had any bright ideas for April and Jonas, he had to admit that he did not. As a family they were a little more of an island, for better or for worse, than he'd realized.

So they compromised: he got her to agree to spend one night in a hotel with him right there in Manhattan. Gina, the Barnard girl, who despite being in college never seemed to have weekend plans, consented to sleep over at their apartment. They told the kids they were going to Atlantic City, where it was very boring and there was gambling and children were not allowed. Then on Friday afternoon they checked into the Parker Meridien and called room service for oysters and a bottle of Absolut Citron and some ice. Adam had her out of her clothes almost before the waiter had left the room. She couldn't believe how much energy he brought to it. You might have thought he hadn't gotten laid in months, but God knew that wasn't true. For a couple with two young kids, they were at it pretty often. But she could see, if not quite understand, how badly he needed this particular encounter to be great. When he wasn't bending her legs back over her head, he was pulling her to the side of the bed so that her palms were on the floor. It was like some sexual epic, like it was important that they outfuck everyone else in the hotel. Two hours later she was very sure that they had. She didn't have to fake it with him, mercifully, but seeing the way he was acting – how much he wanted to please her – she would have faked it for him if she had to.

He took a break and pulled a ten-dollar bottle of water out of the minibar. He drank it in front of the dark window, his chest still heaving; my God, Cynthia thought, he is so fucking gorgeous. She rolled over on to her stomach on the oversize bed. It was a long way from their wedding night,

129

passed out from fatigue in that kitschy little B and B in Pittsburgh; she surprised herself by even remembering it. But when you did remember it you had a hard time not feeling optimistic. Things had been getting better the last few months. Adam was doing really well. He'd started trading on the side, he said, and suddenly there was money for everything. They were going to Vail in February, and to the Caribbean in the spring. The new apartment was going to be amazing. Sanford's wife had asked her to join the Coalition for Public Schools. That had to be Adam's doing too, of course. And what he kept telling her all these months was absolutely right: you just needed to get out into the world a little more. She felt his fingers on her calf and turned around to see him smiling sweetly at her. "Okay, shorty," he said. "Break time's over."

He kept telling her how much he loved her, and she would turn her face away when he said it for fear she would start crying. He came again and went directly to the bathroom: "Just checking for a defibrillator," he said. The door closed. Cynthia lay staring at the ceiling; after a minute she rolled to the edge of the bed and walked somewhat stiffly to the chair by the window where she'd dropped her bag. The room was huge, with a stunning view from the foot of Central Park. Cynthia thought she might even be able to see their apartment from there, but they weren't quite high up enough. No voicemail on her phone, but in her bag she found three tightly folded pieces of lined paper – notes to her that Jonas must have slipped in there just before they left the apartment. The first two said "Love U" and "Miss U," and the third one said, "R U winning?"

She was still looking at them when Adam came up behind her. She was worried he'd be angry at her, but of course he wasn't. He was perfect. "Maybe," he said, and kissed her neck, "we should just head home."

They called Gina from the sidewalk outside the hotel so she wouldn't panic when she heard their key in the door. Adam took her downstairs to put her in a cab; Cynthia slipped off her shoes and went into the kids' bedroom. Jonas was sleeping on his stomach as he always did, the covers kicked off, one palm flat against the mattress as if it were a pane of glass. She sat on the floor, against the wall across from his bed. In the dark the room was a comforting weave of long shadows, from the dresser, from the window frame, from the rolling backpack full of April's schoolbooks that sat beside the door. She held her breath for a moment until she made out their own.

It made sense, she supposed, that the kids were a little nervous about moving into a new place, and a little nostalgic too. Everything that had ever happened to them had happened here. But she was flat faking it when she pretended to share their feelings about saying goodbye to this apartment. She never thought this was going to be their last home. To tell the truth she didn't think the next one would be their last either. It was a vaguely shameful thing to admit. But there was always that moment when you fell out of love with a place, when you looked it over and asked yourself if it was so unimprovable that you wouldn't mind if you died there. Once that thought lodged itself in your head, forget it, it was over.

Not the kind of reasoning you could share with kids that age, obviously. Jonas had already gone through a brief obsession with death, when he was just three. Cynthia was never sure what triggered it – probably some story she'd read to him, though she couldn't think which one – but one day he was just aware of death, and he had trouble grasping some of its basic tenets. To him it amounted to being paralyzed, eyes open, inside a coffin, forever. The absence of consciousness was literally unimaginable. He believed the dead could still see, for instance – it was just too dark for them to see anything. Distinctions like that were not anything Cynthia wanted to get into with him.

She tried what she could think of. She had him pull out his toy cash register. "How many days until your birthday?" she said.

"Fifty-six," Jonas said, who knew this because he asked about it every day.

"And is that a little or a lot?"

"A *lot*!"

She thought a moment, then punched some figures into the beeping cash register. "This is how many days until you're Grandma Morey's age," she said. "And even Grandma isn't dying anytime soon." Her own mother was older than Adam's, but she didn't use Grandma Ruth as an example because Jonas hadn't seen her in so long Cynthia thought she might not seem sufficiently real. She turned the numbers toward him.

"Wow!" he said. But she should have known that wouldn't work: at that age, any number over one hundred was the same in his mind, and anyway to tell a child that he shouldn't be afraid of something *yet* was no kind of advice at all.

"It's all a part of nature," she said another time. "Every living thing is born, and grows, and dies. Every single animal and plant and bird and flower and tree. It's what's called," she said, hating herself, "the circle of life."

"So you'll die? And Daddy? And April? When?"

"No," she said, panicking. "Mommy and Daddy are not going to die. You don't even need to worry about that. Just put that thought right out of your head." She pantomimed plucking a bad thought out of her own head and sniffing it and throwing it away, which made him laugh, and then she let him watch TV.

"He'll move on," Adam had said. "He's three. Something else interesting will come along and bump it right out of his head. I remember going through a phase like that when I was around his age."

"You did? What did your mother tell you?"

He thought. "I have absolutely no memory of it."

"So you recall asking the question. It's just that your mother said nothing worth remembering."

He nodded.

"Well, there you have it," Cynthia said.

Then one day the preschool called; they had her come pick Jonas up early because after snack time he had just started crying. He wouldn't discuss what was bothering him.

Probably just tired, the teacher said with that slightly lunatic patience you wanted in a preschool teacher, but all the same maybe she ought to come and get him.

She took him home in a cab, stroking his hair and kissing the top of his head, not asking any questions. She was trying to soothe herself as much as him. Who is this boy? she said to herself. Why is there no one to help me? How am I supposed to know what to do?

When they walked in the front door, she said, "We have to go get April in about an hour. You want a snack and I'll read to you?"

"Mommy?" he said. "I don't want to die because when you're dead you can't talk or get up and I'll miss you."

And here she learned a lesson about desperation and the ways in which a parent could sometimes rely on it. "Come here," she said. He sat on her lap. She told him that he was a big boy and it was time for the truth. The truth was that no one knows what happens after we die, because we can't talk to dead people and dead people can't talk to us. But some people have some ideas about what might happen. Some people believe in an idea called reincarnation, where when one life ends there's a little rest time and then you get to come back and live again; not the same exact life, though, and maybe not even the same kind of life – maybe you came back as an eagle, or a dog. In fact, maybe this life, right now, wasn't even his first one: maybe he'd been a dinosaur, so long ago that he'd forgotten. (She could feel his little arms relaxing.) Another idea, which a whole lot of people believed in, was called heaven. Heaven was a place that depended on your wishes: the place in life when you'd felt safest and happiest and most comfortable, heaven was that place for you all the time, forever.

"A nice warm house," Jonas said, "with you and Daddy."

He left his sister out of it, Cynthia noticed, but she had let that go. It was a little rite of passage for her, a confidence builder, a lesson in love's resources even when there was nothing in particular you yourself believed in.

3

JONAS WOKE UP FIRST – HE could tell by listening – with the shutters open facing the sea. No sound but the rain turning to mist on the stones of the patio. It often rained in the first hour of the morning, as if considerately, to get it out of the way early in case the Moreys or the rest of the island's inhabitants might have had anything planned. Not that there was much to plan, even if you were so inclined. Another walk on the beach, maybe, or another ride across the harbor to Scilly Cay to eat a lobster. That was the genius of the place, as far as Jonas was concerned: wasted time. You needed that in order to properly value, and to gauge the insanity of, your regimented life back home, where sometimes that first minute of brain activity after waking generated so much anxiety that you'd have to get out of bed just to stop thinking. Then again, Anguilla itself was starting to feel a bit like home by now. Twice a year – Christmas break and spring break – for four years. That kind of fidelity was unprecedented. His father must have found something he liked here, since it was the only place they'd ever visited that he had expressed any desire to go back to. Maybe when Jonas was his father's age, and someone used the word "home" in his hearing, Anguilla would be one place he'd think of. Probably not, though. They rented the same Greek-style villa here every time, even though his parents surely could have afforded to buy it. At least Jonas thought so. It wasn't always easy to tell what they couldn't afford anymore.

April was in the bedroom right behind his head, with her friend Robin from school, and the very thought of Robin lent Jonas's thoughts an instant and somewhat humiliating focus. He put his ear to the wall even though the two girls would not be awake for a couple of hours. They were sleeping in the same king-size bed, because they liked it that way, and this provoked Jonas in ways he almost resented. His mom had urged him to invite a friend on this trip too, but he didn't really have any friendships that intense; there were the guys in his band, but frankly they were better off taking a little break from one another. Robin was tall and thin and long-haired, like all of April's nasty school friends really, but she was also on the lacrosse team and knew who Gram Parsons was and turned red when she laughed and was nice to him, and not just when his parents were in the room either. He sublimated a lot of his feelings toward her into a sentimental appreciation of her as a tragic figure, because her own home life was so bad. Her father was a partner at White & Case and they were over-the-top rich – plenty rich enough to take their own family trip to Anguilla for Christmas, or anywhere else in the world, if they could stand being around one another that long – but the mother was bipolar, or so he'd heard his own mother say, and Robin's father either couldn't acknowledge that kind of defect or else just chose not to make the requisite sacrifices to deal with it. Robin had been spending a lot of nights with the Moreys back in New York lately, sometimes on short notice. When she was with them and the phone rang, Jonas had been instructed not to answer it until April or their mom had a chance to screen the incoming number. Robin had an older brother who didn't always come home at night anymore either, though nobody knew where he went instead.

The sadness of it all did nothing to diminish his urge to masturbate, and this was a perfect opportunity, but then Jonas's eye fell on the Gibson electric guitar he had received two days ago for Christmas, on its stand in the corner of the bedroom. His feelings for it were as passionate as for any object he had ever owned. Indian rosewood neck, humbucker pickups; he'd coveted it for so long that he was in the weird position, Christmas-gift-wise, of knowing exactly how much it had cost. His amp was back in New York but the guitar came with a pair of wireless headphones, so he could jam away without bothering anyone else. He got out of bed, put on a T-shirt, and sat on the couch by the glass doors with the guitar in his lap. The rain was already letting up, and the sky was brightening in great slabs of blue and white. He heard a door open downstairs and footsteps on the patio, but at this hour it could only be Simon laying the table. He decided he'd work on mastering the opening lick from "One Way Out" until his dad appeared on the beach for his morning swim. He clapped the headphones on; an hour later, when he saw Adam winding his way down the whitewashed steps toward the calm ocean below the house, he unplugged and went downstairs to tell Simon what he wanted for breakfast.

Adam walked into the mild surf until the dropoff came, and then he turned and floated, with his toes sticking out of the water, and stared up at the villa. The water on the island's bay end was impossibly warm. A cargo ship was passing to the north of him, toward the open Atlantic, and he watched it for a while but there was no way to track its progress. Even the plume of smoke trailing behind it was as still as a painting. He swam back and forth for a while, but when he paused the salt water held him up easily and so he closed his eyes. When he opened them again, female figures were moving back and forth on the patio, and he walked out of the surf, grabbed the towel that Simon had hung on the beach chair for him, and headed back up the stairs.

"You might put on a shirt there, nature boy," Cynthia said to him, rolling her eyes at the girls, and so he stood up again and went to the bedroom to get one. Simon, having dried off the chairs and opened the umbrella that shaded the table, was pouring coffee and taking omelet orders. He was one of the house's amenities; in the hot off-season, he went to college in Atlanta, and in the winter he saw to the needs of the villa's guests and went home to his parents' place at night. Cynthia caught April and Robin nudging each other from time to time when Simon was entering the room, or leaving it, but that was okay. Let them. She prided herself on not talking to her daughter about sex or men in the censorious way most mothers would.

"Robin," she said, "that skirt is so cute on you." They'd given it to her for Christmas, and Cynthia was proud of the rightness of it for her. She was fascinated with Robin, who had both everything and nothing. She just loved it that you could have such bitter fuckups for parents and still somehow foil them by turning out so sweet and poised and confident at age fifteen.

Robin paused before she sat down and gave a modest little comic twirl. "It's really beautiful, Cynthia," she said. "Thank you again. So, what's on the agenda today?"

"Hmm," April said. "Tanning by the pool for a few hours and then eating again?"

"That's what I love about you," Robin said. "Always willing to think inside the box."

"Adam," Cynthia said as he sat down again, "you're golfing this morning, right? What time?"

"Nine forty-two," he said.

"So precise," Cynthia said. "That's what I admire about golfing." Turning toward her son, she caught him artlessly checking out Robin's breasts again; Jesus, it must suck to be a boy, she thought. Completely pathetic and condemned to know it. "When are you going to initiate young Jonas into the golfing mysteries, anyway?"

Jonas dropped his fork and waved his hands in front of him. "Please, God, no," he said.

"Maybe someday when he's done something really horrible," Adam said. They fell silent as their plates arrived. The shadow of the villa receded over them as the sun rode a little farther up the sky. Adam drained his coffee and held his hand over the cup as Simon moved to fill it again; he excused himself and went to the bedroom to change into shorts and a collared shirt and a baseball cap. He threw his clubs in the back seat of their rental car and drove north on the island's one highway, past the overgrown lots and the discreet high-end resort entrances and the bright pastel exteriors of houses no one was living in anymore. At one point he waited patiently for some goats to develop the urge to get out of the road. He drove past the golf course and all the way to the little business district in Shoal Bay East, at the island's northern end. There was a bar there that was open even at ten in the morning; he parked in the shade behind it and walked across the street to the Royal National Bank of Anguilla.

It wasn't really much of a bank; it looked more like a doctor's office, with a heavy-lidded fat woman in a tight pink dress sitting at a receptionist's desk and a closed door behind her with a security camera above it. The woman was not someone Adam had seen before.

"Mr. Bryant?" he asked her. Regally she looked him over

and then stood and passed through the door behind her without a word. Adam looked up at the camera. In a few seconds she reappeared and beckoned him through, smiling now as she closed the door behind him.

Mr. Bryant rose from behind an old metal desk and shook Adam's hand; behind him were two low metal filing cabinets, the paneled wall, and, through a narrow window, the blue marina. "Merry Christmas to you, Mr. Adam," he said. "You have everything you need?" He meant at the villa. He had absolutely nothing to do with the villa or its operation, but he liked to ask. "You are enjoying yourself?"

"As always," Adam said.

"Your family is well?"

"Very well. And yours?"

Mr. Bryant nodded in answer, or maybe he was just nodding approvingly at the question. They would never meet each other's families, but the civilities could not be bypassed, as Adam had learned, when you dealt with Mr. Bryant. Now he unfolded his long-fingered hands, opened his desk drawer, and took out a collection of five checks, all for different amounts, all payable to cash, held together by a paper clip. He removed the paper clip and handed the checks to Adam. Adam looked them over, though not carefully; he folded them in half, put them in the pocket of his shorts, and rose to shake hands a second time.

"My friend says to expect him next around Easter," Adam said.

"At your service. When do you fly home?"

"Tomorrow."

Mr. Bryant clucked regretfully. "You'll miss the regatta," he said. "Oh well. Duty calls, I am sure." They shook hands yet again, warmly. Adam never understood why it was so important to Mr. Bryant to treat this like a friendship, but would not have dreamt of offending him either.

He drove back along a different route, taking his time, less for clandestinity's sake than to catch one last view of the hills of Saint Martin across the water before it got too hazy. It was still only about quarter to eleven, though, and a plausible round of golf had to last three hours at least. So he drove back to the course, went into the pro shop, and bought two large buckets of balls for the driving range. He took the checks out of his pocket and zippered them into one of the compartments of the golf bag before he got started. It was so hot by now that he was the only one out on the range, but he didn't care. The heat rarely got to him, and the scolding a slight sunburn would earn him would only help cement the question of his whereabouts.

Half an hour later, sweat was pouring off him, but he was absolutely striping the ball, better than he'd hit it in months. He had the driver going a good 280 yards. He was so locked in, he wound up sorry there wasn't enough time to get out on the course after all.

There was a lunchtime board meeting of the Coalition for Public Schools at some restaurant down in Soho, which by any reasonable standard should have been over by three; but it wasn't, and when Cynthia couldn't stand it anymore she rose to excuse herself early, telling everyone she had a doctor's appointment uptown. She couldn't make it out the door without ten women stopping her to express the bogus hope that it was nothing serious. On days like this she just had to take a deep breath and remind herself that it was all for a good cause, namely the separation of these aimless gossips from some of their millions, so that those millions could start to do some good in the world. It took up a lot of time. You could just stay at home and write checks, of course, and when Adam had started making serious money that's all she initially thought she would do; but a big check was wasted on these halfwit dowagers with no idea how to do anything more substantial than send out invitations to a benefit, and before you knew it you were involved. Not just the CPS either; she'd become involved to various degrees with the Riverside Park Fund, the Coalition for the Homeless, and Big Brothers Big Sisters. She did have a rule about staying away from disease charities: there was something about them that just struck her as especially haughty, a blithe tossing of money at the ineffable, like Won't You Please Join Us in the Fight Against Death. She knew on some level she was wrong about this but obeyed the feeling anyway. She preferred causes that dealt with what might actually be improved, not the hard-to-fathom world of genes and viruses but just the generally fucked-up way in which human institutions worked – homelessness, public schools, Habitat for Humanity, things like that. Anything that improved the lot of children got her money in a heartbeat.

"You're sweet," Cynthia said, smiling and backing away, "but no, it's nothing major, just something I scheduled months ago, and you know how hard it is to get in to see these guys." Which probably left them all thinking that she was going in to get her ass lifted or something, but so what. In truth all she had to do was make a phone call, but it was a private one that had to be made before close of business and she had lost faith that they could wrap up this meeting in time. It was a kind of universal truth in the nonprofit world that everything took at least twice as long as it needed to. She used to have to schedule her shrink appointments for five in the afternoon, because her commitments had grown to the point where that was the only window; but if she had an evening event, as she often did, there were days when seeing the shrink meant not seeing the kids at all, and so she'd finally just quit therapy altogether. No room in her day for it anymore, which was probably the best circumstance for terminating, she thought, and probably why doing so had turned out easier than she'd expected.

Despite the accursed narrowness of those Soho streets, her driver was idling right there in front of the restaurant. They inched toward the West Side Highway and she started to open up her phone right then, but she didn't want to make the call in front of the driver either. He was totally trustworthy but it had nothing to do with that. Half an hour later she was home. They'd been in the new apartment on Columbus for almost two years now, after a restless few years in the place on East End she'd loved so much when they bought it. Almost as soon as the renovations were done she'd started glancing adulterously at the real estate section. But the priceless thing about Adam was that he didn't really give her much more than one night's shit about it, because the truth was, he understood. He got why she didn't mind packing up again, why there was such romance in the new, why it was so hard to stay in a place that had maxed out its own potential. Plus they'd made a fortune each time they sold. This was Manhattan, after all; everyone wanted a foothold, and they weren't making any more of it.

Still, the place on Columbus was so wonderfully eccentric that Cynthia couldn't imagine ever growing tired of it: a penthouse duplex that looked directly down onto the planetarium behind the Museum of Natural History. At night the spheres glowed blue through the planetarium's glass walls, and from the wrap-around windows thirty stories up it seemed to Cynthia almost like their home was returning to the planet after a day's journey into space. The kids had the downstairs floor mostly to themselves; it had a separate entrance, which meant she had less of a sense of their comings and goings than she used to. They were too old to want or need an escort back and forth to school, and they had so much else going on in their lives, socially and otherwise, that it wasn't always possible to know exactly when she'd see them next. Or Adam, for that matter.

Which could sometimes give rise to a sort of loneliness; but today Cynthia was just as glad to come home and find nobody else there. It was still well before five, so she called their accountant; she knew he would have taken a call from her no matter the time, but she liked to be considerate about it. She asked if he would please handle a wire transfer for her, a small one, just ten thousand, but it was important that it be done right away.

"Charles Sikes," she said.

She heard him typing; he wore one of those phone headsets, like only receptionists used to wear. "Same account as before?"

"Same bank, different city," she said, and dug a folded, typed letter out of her pocket and read him the number. He took it down, and then as he always did he asked after her kids, whom he'd never met but knew in his way, and then they said goodbye.

Still no one home. The winter sky outside the living room was just beginning to gray. She opened up a bottle of wine, took one cigarette out of the pack she kept hidden behind the leather-bound volume of wedding photos on the bookshelf, put her coat back on, and stood outside on the balcony that overlooked the planetarium. She spent maybe twenty minutes that way, looking down on the still planets, listening to the symphony of faint sounds that passed for silence. Then, in a spirit of beneficence, she opened up the cell phone again and called her mother.

Ruth seemed almost miffed to hear from her, though no more miffed than she was by anything that rose up unexpectedly in her day without giving her adequate time to prepare. "We are doing as well as can be expected," she said. "Warren's health is not good, as you know."

She didn't know; or maybe she did – in her mother's conversations it was hard to separate fact from dire prediction. "Well, tell him I hope he feels better."

"How are the children?"

"They're great. So busy I hardly see them anymore. The amount of schoolwork they have is just brutal." There was a pause, and somehow Cynthia knew what was supposed to go there. "I'm sorry we haven't been able to get out there to visit."

"Probably not the best time for a visit anyway," Ruth said.

"You're right," Cynthia said, misunderstanding her. "It's impossible to get away. Sometimes I wonder why they have to work so hard. But then just last week I was in this public school in East Harlem—"

"Good Lord, why?"

"This charity I work with. We were dedicating a computer lab. Anyway, you wouldn't believe—"

"Your education was always very important to me," Ruth said. "That came first."

Cynthia laughed affrontedly and took another quick drag. "Are you joking?" she said, exhaling. "Dirksen? That place was like a drug bazaar. There was an English teacher there who killed herself over Christmas break. Remember that? It's a miracle I learned a fucking thing at that place."

Ruth closed her eyes. She was trying to get some dinner ready, even though Warren probably wouldn't eat any of it; he was so sick he hadn't been out of the living room chair all day except to go to the bathroom, and even for that he had to call out to her. She missed part of what Cynthia was saying because when he got a coughing jag it was so heart-wrenching that she couldn't hear anything else. "I don't know what you expected me to do about it," she said. "There certainly wasn't money for private school. It was hard enough to hold on to the house those years."

"There are ways," Cynthia said, tossing her cigarette over the edge of the patio railing, hearing a key turn in the front door inside. "It's just a matter of where your priorities are."

"Well, anyway," Ruth said. "You certainly managed to land on your feet."

Me: SWM, 27 – Big Mets fan, good income, not afraid of adventure. Willing to think long term, or, if you prefer, NSA. You: athletic, 19–24, long hair. Not afraid to act if the moment seems right. Send photo, plz.

He left out, of course, any references to his face, specifically his nose, because while some women were into it, most, he found, were not. But that seemed fair, since he hadn't mentioned anything about what he liked or didn't like in a face either – those faint mustaches, for instance, which were a total dealbreaker. He hit Send and switched back to the streaming video of Kasey in her apartment in California. Maybe it was California. The windows were always covered, so she might have been in Bayside for all any of her subscribers really knew. Right now she was in the kitchen making herself some kind of smoothie. There was a laptop on the kitchen counter near the blender, as there was in every room of Kasey's house, and so she could see, as he saw, the requests typed in by feverish guys: Take off your top. Mmm how's that taste? It was pretty embarrassing. He'd stopped communicating with Kasey himself months ago, but he still watched her, and the meter still ran on his credit card.

Would like blowjob without paying for it is what his personal ad should have read, that is if there were any such thing as an honest personal ad. People said that there were women out there, maybe not a lot but some, who thought the way guys did, but that had to be a myth. The truth was, he had zero interest in thinking long term – that was just one of those things you had to say if you wanted to get any responses at all. He was just so on edge all the time, but that tension could, if you willed it, channel itself into the sexual and thus could be relieved. It always worked, and it never worked for long. He had a lot of stress in his life to fight off.

And as if to punish him for letting that thought into his head, the cell phone rang in his bedroom. He had three cells, actually – they were lined up on top of his dresser – but he could tell from the ring that it was the disposable.

"Devon, what's up," Adam said, but it didn't sound like a question. "So we have some Bantex, right? Financial services? Start shorting it. We can take our time, though. We have a couple of months. So go slowly. Spread it out."

That was always his mantra: spread it out. No more than a certain number of shares in one transaction, because anything over that number supposedly tripped SEC radar.

"Huh," Devon said. "How about that. I was just reading that they were doing really well."

A silence.

"I know, I know," Devon said. "The less I know, the better." Adam sounded like he was in a taxi. "So what shall we talk about, then? How's the family?"

Adam laughed, not unkindly. "They're good, thanks. Listen, you know we shouldn't stay on any longer than we have to. I'm sure a single guy like you has got plans, anyway."

"Mos def. I have a date."

"My man," Adam said. "Enjoy." He hung up. He was so fucking cool all the time. In one way it would have made Devon feel better to hear, even just once, a little panic in his voice, but in other ways it would have made him feel infinitely worse. It was like high school all over again with that guy. He was one of those alphas, master of every situation, receiver of every gift, one of those guys you made merciless fun of until the day he actually brought you inside the circle and then you turned into a simpering little bitch. They saw each other very rarely – maybe three or four times in the last year – but in the aftermath Devon always felt humiliated by how slavishly he had said yes to everything.

He put the phone down on the dresser and went back to the screen, but Kasey was in the bathroom; there were cameras in there too, of course, but he scowled and went to the kitchen to see if there was anything to eat. Some people were into some perverse shit.

They'd brought in a couple of other people – they'd had to, to keep things sufficiently spread out – friends of his from the old boiler-room days on Long Island who now worked at more legit houses. They'd set up accounts for one another's aunts, cousins, whatever they could get documentation for, and siphoned the trades through there. To most of these guys Devon himself was the ringleader, the mastermind, though without a tip to act on, of course, they were all nothing but a group of enlisted men with a willingness to get ahead. His stomach felt like shit again. Maybe because he hadn't eaten anything, but that, he was reminded as he opened and closed the freezer a couple more times, was only because there was fuck all to eat around here. He took the bottle of pear vodka out of the freezer instead, and in the cabinet it turned out there was still half a bag of salt-and-vinegar potato chips. Presto. Dinner.

He poured himself some vodka and sat down in front of the computer. Kasey was sitting at the kitchen table writing something – paying bills, maybe? – but at least she had her pants off now, which was promising. His own apartment had a pretty spartan look to it, which was to say that it had a couch and a flat-screen TV that were both huge and expensive, and a rug that was huge and not expensive, and that was it. Nothing on the walls. He'd bought some kind of print of the Golden Gate Bridge and hung it on the wall over the couch, but he just felt stupid and pretentious looking at it – like, do I actually give a fuck about the Golden Gate Bridge? – and he took it down. In the bedroom was a bed and a dresser and a closet, and underneath a ceiling panel in the closet was a gym bag with about a hundred and sixty thousand dollars in it. This, Devon felt, was the true source of his stomach problems, though he also wondered if that was just dramatic nonsense, if his stomach would quiet down if he ate the occasional well-balanced meal and generally just took a little better care of himself.

He went back to the kitchen to throw out the chip bag and returned with the pear-vodka bottle. The stuff tasted like Jolly Ranchers after a while. Why did he have to get stuck with all the grunt work? The money was pretty much its own answer, even though the more he made, the harder it got to figure out how to spend it, or even where to put it, without attracting attention. Jesus, just one good blowjob would go such a long way right now, he thought. There was an outcall service just a few blocks away; he had it on speed dial. He called them up and asked if Teresa was available tonight, just so he could clear his mind of the whole thing. Fuck Bantex, until tomorrow anyway. It was all that paranoia about being watched that was making him feel sick all the time. He bet the rest of them felt sick too. But no one is watching, he thought as he logged off of Kasey and put the bottle back in the freezer and picked some laundry up off the floor. He was the one doing all the watching. That's what you paid for. I see you, but you don't see me.

Titles were considered unimportant at Perini but a natural hierarchy evolved and was respected. Sanford's reliance on Adam made him the de facto number two; he spent more of his time out of the office now wooing investors in the fund, drinking with them, charming them, impressing them, seducing them into confidence even after the rare misstep or during the always-brief lean times. Precisely the kind of thing Sanford himself used to do all day long – and still did, though he had less of a taste for it now, and also seemed to recognize that youth itself was part of the package that investors wanted to be sold. Sanford himself didn't really look any older, just more dissolute, a little puffier and less put together.

No one else there begrudged Adam the boss's favor; it was a measure of their comfort with it that they made jokes about Sanford's obvious late-stage conversion to homosexuality at every opportunity. Every job but Adam's and Bill Brennan's had turned over at least once since Adam had arrived there; Parker had finally been belittled into quitting almost three years ago, and since he'd stopped coming to basketball, Adam had no idea what had become of him. The office's basic fraternal atmosphere was unchanged. Most of them were younger than Adam now, but he could still outrun them and outlift them and outdrink them and while they honored his status as their superior, in every important way he fit right in. Still, there was of course something momentous about his very presence in that office that none of them even suspected, and their not knowing sharpened the borderline Adam prized between his own character and theirs.

Friday afternoons at work tended to devolve into a head start on the younger employees' bachelor weekends, with beer and foosball tournaments and a general disengagement from their adrenalized professional selves; usually the last hour of work was turned over to discussions of why the bar they went to last Friday sucked and which one they should try tonight instead, but on one particular spring afternoon they managed to talk Adam into coming with them to

154

some catered event they knew about that was taking place inside the Delacorte Theater in Central Park. A fund-raiser for something or other. Brennan had tickets and they all wanted Adam's company so badly that they even offered to pay for him. "I cannot get too hammered," Adam said. "Tomorrow's my son's birthday." Something else to drink to. They took over one of the round tables on the bare stage and there they met their waitress, whose name was Gretchen. Gretchen was provocatively tattooed and reluctantly conceded that she was an actress and would not tell them her age, which led to a general consensus that she was no more than twenty-two.

"God, I love me some of that hipster pussy," Brennan said.

"Because they hate you. That's why."

"Yes," he said. "Yes. Because she hates me. That is precisely why."

They kept ordering more drinks so that Gretchen would have to return to their table, and each time she stopped there they did a clumsier job of chatting her up. They thought their own artlessness was hilarious. Gretchen knew better than to flirt back, but she was enough of a pro, Adam saw, not to let her contempt for these guys show either. The tips were becoming outrageous.

Somehow a serious betting pool took shape around the question of whether Gretchen's tongue was pierced. She came back with a round of Maker's for everyone but Adam. It impressed him that she wasn't a little frightened of them by now. "Gretchen," Brennan said earnestly, "I don't want this to come out wrong, but if you open wide and say Aaah, you will make me a rich man."

"You gentlemen have a good night," Gretchen said, smiling. She cleared the last of their glasses and walked away. A few minutes later Adam stood up to go home, prompting a wave of questions about the staunchness of his heterosexuality. Instead of heading out the theater gate, though, he turned and went underneath the grandstand, where the kitchen and bar setups were, and when he found her, she rolled her eyes and smiled.

"Pay no attention to me," he said. "I'm counting your tattoos."

"Well, you won't get an accurate count," she said.

"I'm a very busy man. I have to get back to the table soon because I'm in charge of the centerpieces. We're planting them in the Sheep Meadow. So I just need your phone number and I'll be on my way."

She turned and looked at him, her head at an inquisitive angle, and he could tell she was amused not by anything he'd said but by something else about him. "How drunk are you?" she said.

"Not at all. I just have to see you again. I don't want to live in a world where women like you are never seen again."

She stared at him as the bartender loaded up her tray. "Oh, this," he said, grabbing his ring finger, "this comes right off."

She laughed. "Leave it on," she said. "I like married guys. Keeps things on a basic level. You're happily married, am I right?"

"Extremely," he said.

She pulled his hand toward her and wrote a phone number on it. "Wow," Adam said. "What a world."

The sun set in front of him as he walked west out of the park, the long shadows behind him gradually merging into nothing. He took his time; it was probably one of the five most beautiful nights of the year. In the rare moments when he stepped back and thought about it at all, it was vital to Adam's conception of his professional life that he wasn't stealing from anybody. There was nothing zero-sum about the world of capital investment: you created wealth where there was no wealth before, and if you did it well enough there was no end to it. What Adam did was just an initiative based on that idea, an unusually bold manifestation of it. Why should he be restricted – or, worse, restrict himself – from finding a way to act on what he was enterprising enough to know and to synthesize? It took leadership skills as well, because you couldn't pull off something like this by yourself even if you wanted to. In order to minimize the risk he had to command the total trust and loyalty of Devon and the handful of his friends he'd brought in on it from brokerages around the city. And that he had done. Devon had turned out to be a young man prone to anxiety but whenever he seemed close to the point of bailing, five minutes together was enough for Adam to reassure him they still had the whole thing safely in hand.

It wasn't even his chief source of income, at least not any-more. His compensation at Perini had soared, and deservedly so. This was more in the nature of a self-administered bonus.

In the course of his work he learned some things about a given company, things not of a public nature; based on this information he gave Devon an instruction on the buying or the selling of that company's stock, spread out through about thirty small accounts with dummy names managed by Devon and the others; each account transferred its profits to different offshore banks, all of which then sent the money, in slow increments, to the Royal National Bank of Anguilla, where oversight policies were business-friendly. Adam's share in the last year was less than half a million. It was a nice margin to have, certainly, and every little bit added to the range of possibilities in his family's lives. But they didn't depend on it. He could have ended the whole scheme at any time and, in terms of their daily lives, they very likely wouldn't feel the money's absence at all.

But it wasn't just about the money, in any case. More than the money, which had to be spent with some care, it was about exercising that ability to repurpose information those around him were too timid or shortsighted to know what to do with: the night two weeks ago, for instance, when he and Brennan had sat there in the office having a Scotch after working late and had shared a laugh about Brennan's former frat brother who worked at Bantex, who had just called him up scared shitless because his entire office had just been served with grand jury subpoenas. That was what kept the whole scheme fresh at this point, that was its engine and its reward: the sense of living in two realms at once, one that was visible to others and one that was not. Every day he looked right into Sanford's face and confirmed with wonder that the old man was so blinded by affection that he didn't even see him.

Inside an empty playground Adam found a water fountain and washed the ink off his hands. He made no effort to memorize the phone number first; he hadn't even glanced at it. It wasn't the first time he'd done something like this. He'd never cheated on Cynthia and never would, because that would be weak and stupid, and the risk so much greater than the reward. But sometimes there was a thrill in walking right up to that line, and in charming the other person into stepping over it. He figured it was probably all downhill after that moment anyway.

He turned left at 77th and from that angle he could see the windows of their home high above him as he approached; the only ones lit were downstairs on the kids' floor. He took the elevator all the way up and walked into the moonlit living room. There was no note for him anywhere but he was pretty sure Cyn had told him where she had to be tonight and he'd just forgotten. The curtains blew toward him where the patio door had been left open. There was always TV but right now Adam just felt like talking to somebody; if he'd known he was returning to an empty home, he might have stayed out. He dropped his jacket on the couch and took the interior staircase, which was behind the kitchen, down to the second floor. All the doors were closed, as always, but there was some kind of noise escaping from Jonas's room. He knocked; no answer came, but the noise didn't stop either, so he knocked again and walked in. There were boxes and packing material all over the floor, and on top of Jonas's dresser, incredibly, was a turntable with a vinyl record spinning on it. Adam couldn't remember the last time he'd even seen one. Jonas, who had his headphones on, swung his feet down from his desk and smiled.

Adam pointed at the record player and then held his palms up to mime confusion. Jonas took the headphones off. "Mom and I decided to celebrate my birthday early," he said. "Isn't it beautiful? Thanks, by the way."

Adam, laughing, shook his head. There were two chairs in his son's room and they were both filled with LPs in their covers, probably forty or fifty of them, none of which had been there the day before.

"The sound just doesn't compare," Jonas said. "It's so warm. I can never go back to digital after this."

Adam walked over to the still-spinning turntable and saw what was playing: the Buzzcocks. "April home?" he said. "I saw her lights on."

"Her lights are always on. She's out somewhere. She's the Queen of the Night."

Adam flipped through the record pile. There was a fair amount of music he recognized, which was itself a little perplexing. The greatness of The Clash was indisputable, he supposed, but were kids Jonas's age really still listening to it? Wasn't that the whole point of music – that you had your own? For Adam, music was tied to time: most ineffably it served as the soundtrack to high school and college. Beyond that he had never given it a lot of thought. The names in the pile began to get even older and more obscure: Television, Fairport Convention, Phil Ochs, the Stanley Brothers.

"And how about you?" he said. "It being a Friday night. Any plans? A date, maybe?"

Jonas rolled his eyes. "Yeah, we've all got big dates," he said. "And then there's the church social, and then we're all going to the soda fountain for a cherry phosphate."

Cynthia worried lately that Adam and Jonas weren't as close as they used to be, and while Adam didn't know about that – was it even healthy for a teenage son to be all that close to his father? – it was true that they were growing conspicuously unlike each other. At the same time, there was a kind of spartan streak in his son that Adam recognized and respected. He'd gone vegan, for instance, which, even though it was not something Adam would have done in a million years, was certainly a form of discipline in the interests of the body. Still, having spent his own high school years as a virtual president of the mainstream, he couldn't help but find Jonas's taste for exile a little hard to understand.

He moved one pile of records from a chair to the floor and sat down. "So, punk," he said. "That was before my time, even. I didn't know you were interested in that." His son nodded, like some sort of scholar, less a nod of agreement than a nod to indicate that it was a worthy question. "That was probably the last really genuine thing to happen in pop music," Jonas said. "It was exciting while it lasted, though, which was about five minutes."

"But people your age still listen to it?"

"People my age," Jonas said, "are mostly morons."

"Wait a minute, though. Aren't you in a band? The band is still together, right? I assume you're not playing old Sex Pistols songs?"

"That is kind of a sore subject right now," Jonas said.

Adam held up his hand to indicate that they would speak of it no more. He picked up an album by Flatt & Scruggs; he didn't know the first thing about them but for some reason, gazing at their suits and crew cuts and formal smiles, he was struck by a kind of pity for them, because they were so dead. "There wasn't a lot of music in our house growing up," he said. "The stereo was like a battlefield. Your uncle Conrad and I kept breaking the rules – mostly about volume; I think the rule was no higher than four – and then the ban would come, no more music in the house for a day, a week, two weeks. We couldn't help it. We'd hear something on the radio, and when it got to the point where you couldn't stand waiting a few hours for it to come on again, we'd go out and buy it at Walgreens or someplace, and if it was any good obviously we'd turn it up. Then we'd forget to turn it back down, and a day later Dad would flip on the radio to hear Paul Harvey, and it would come on at ear-splitting volume."

Jonas nodded as if this story served to confirm something he'd known all along. "Music sucks now," he said. "It all comes out of a factory. It's not about anything except wanting to be famous. How people can even listen to it is beyond me."

Adolescence was all about overstatement; still, it made

Adam sad to hear his son talking this way. "Well, cheer up," he said. "Maybe punk is poised for a comeback."

Jonas shook his head. "No way," he said. "That world is gone for good."

In the winter Robin had started showing up at the Moreys a lot more often. Not always with April either, or even preceded by a phone call; one night she showed up at their front door so drunk you could barely understand her, and Cynthia, after whispering to her for a few seconds, let her right in. There was a while where she was basically living there. April's feelings about this kept turning out to be the wrong ones: when she wondered aloud why Robin continued to get away with murder in a way that April never could, her mother took her out on the balcony and told her that Robin was being physically abused at home, that one night at the Moreys' Robin had taken Cynthia into the bathroom and shut the door and showed her a series of cuts and red marks on her stomach and chest that had been left there by the power cord from a laptop. April acted totally shocked when the shameful truth was that she had heard that rumor before and thought that it was bullshit, that that kind of thing didn't really happen to anyone she knew. In her least generous moments she had even wondered if maybe Robin was amping up all these stories about how bad things were at her home, not just for drama's sake but because life at the Moreys' was like some kind of spa for her: she came and went as she pleased, ate what she wanted, either studied or didn't according to her whim. So April had to deal with her guilt over that. On top of which she felt disappointed and confused that Robin, who was her friend after all, had been moved to confess all this to her mother but not to her.

There was even one night when Robin's father had shown up at their door, unannounced, to take his daughter back home. That was some drama. The doorman called upstairs and said that he was down there in the lobby, demanding to come up. Cynthia said no. Two minutes later the doorman called again. By this time all five of them, the Moreys and Robin, were gathered in the foyer staring at the video from the security camera. Robin's father was just standing there in an overcoat, his hands in his pockets. "He says he isn't going anywhere," the doorman murmured into the phone. He seemed torn between excitement and fear that some sort of incident might imperil his job. "Ask if there's anyone else down there with him," Cynthia said to Adam, and when the answer came back no, Cynthia said to let him up.

They told Robin to go downstairs to April's room but she wouldn't; instead she withdrew into the living room, as far as she could get from the front door with her sight line unimpeded, as if her father's reach were impossibly long. He was a good twenty years older than Adam and Cynthia and that seemed to sharpen his contempt for them. "May I come in?" he said on the threshold, and April's jaw fell when her mother answered no.

When he made out Robin in the room beyond the foyer, standing behind one of the couches, he sighed. "This is ridiculous," he said. "You are fifteen years old. You do not have our permission to be here. Get your things."

Robin didn't reply. "She has our permission to be here," Cynthia said. "You might ask yourself why she feels safer here than she does in her own home."

At first he ignored her, his eyes still on his daughter. Eventually he turned on Cynthia his most withering look. It was interesting to April that her father didn't even try to come between them. Most husbands probably would have, even if they weren't sure why. But her dad obviously felt, as she did, that if anybody needed protecting in this scenario, it was the older man, with his combed-back silver hair and his steel glasses.

"I recognize you," he said to Cynthia. "All the parents talk about you. You like to play at being one of the girls. You're the youngest mother there and yet the one least able to deal with getting old. I don't know what kind of fantasy this is for you, but it couldn't be of less interest to me."

"You can see how eager your child is to have anything to do with you," Cynthia said. "Kudos. As long as she feels like she's in danger, she is welcome here. Her choice. Period."

Even if you knew that parents sometimes talked to one another that way, it still seemed incredibly transgressive to overhear it. April turned and caught Jonas's eye.

"She is fifteen," Robin's father repeated. "It's a legal matter. If you won't let her go, the police will have to get involved. I've lived in New York a long time and I know a lot of people."

"Oh, you've said the magic word," Cynthia said, smiling. She took a step closer to him. "Police. If you want to go there, we'll go there. I took pictures of what she looked like last time she came over here."

Something changed then, not on his face so much as behind it, but still April could see it. He knew he couldn't intimidate Cynthia so he took one more shot at intimidating his daughter, calling to her over Cynthia's shoulder to say that she had been forgiven for a lot of things, but she would not be forgiven for this. After he was gone the five of them stayed up almost all night, just watching TV in the media room, waiting for whatever would happen next without quite knowing what that would be. But nothing else happened at all.

The story was all over Dalton the next day. Robin and Jonas weren't talking about it, but April had probably mentioned it to a few people. It bolstered the already considerable perception that April's parents were the coolest parents on earth. And Robin's misfortune, as misfortune will do, lent her an aura of respect, even a sort of celebrity.

But eventually Robin did go back home. Either the situation cooled down there or she agreed to pretend it had. That was the thing about families: once they decided to close ranks, for whatever reason, you really had no way of knowing anymore. In school she was just like always, laughing and way into sports and usually surrounded by guys – a little needy for April's taste, maybe, but nothing that seemed like a red flag. If it was an act, she was fooling herself with it at least as effectively as she was fooling anybody else.

The only one who really had trouble getting over the whole thing, April recognized, was her mother. Robin had all but stopped returning Cynthia's texts, and when she did her tone was disappointingly chirpy and distant. It wasn't just that Cynthia didn't believe everything was now all right; she didn't seem to *want* to believe it. More than once April came home from school and found her mother sitting at the dining room table with a cup of coffee, crying.

April was proud that her home had such a rep as a stable place that it would actually occur to her friends to go there if they were in trouble. There was always somebody staying over at the apartment, not necessarily because they needed a place but just for the hell of it. Other kids' mothers would try to gain their trust by acting young, like they understood everything, and it was just pathetic. But April could tell that her friends really did consider her mother to be one of them – older, but just enough for her superior knowledge to seem attractive, like an RA in college. They confessed to her, they asked her advice, they shopped with her (though part of that was surely mercenary, since any time Cynthia thought something looked cute on them she would buy it). They would even talk about guys with her, which should have seemed creepy and out of bounds and yet somehow it did not. The fact that all the other Dalton mothers hated and mocked her only bolstered Cynthia's cred.

April's own circle had contracted a bit after eighth grade when a dozen or so kids went off to boarding school. Just like that they were gone from your social life, though occasionally in between classes some kid would immodestly flash a text or a camera-phone photo from a departed peer. The move didn't always work out for them; there was always some story circulating about someone who had gotten himself expelled from one of these places and been forced to return home, not to Dalton but to the kind of second-tier private school that still had openings mid-year. Still, an air of sophistication attached itself even to those of them who failed. April had no desire to go live in a regimented compound in some picturesque New England village where there was nothing to do at night and you weren't allowed out anyway, but she felt a touch of envy all the same. They were her age but, just by virtue of leaving, they seemed older.

Of course they did come back in relative triumph for a few days at Thanksgiving and then for longer at Christmas. Their homecoming for any vacation was pretext enough for a series of parties. On one of the first really warm nights of the spring, April went to one at a townhouse in the East Fifties, thrown by some girl they didn't even know – she'd been at Spence and was now home from St. Paul's – but dotted with enough Dalton kids to make her presence there plausible. She even ran into Robin on the street outside. The townhouse itself was phenomenal, a real old-money museum, and its trashing had a terrible inevitability. It was like the reign of Pol Pot, when legions of ten-year-olds were handed carbines and put in charge of national security. On the first floor was the kitchen and living room, speakers hidden somewhere in the walls blasting Jay-Z, every surface already sticky to the touch. April saw a Matisse on the wall, one of those paintings where figures danced in a circle, and she almost asked someone if it was real but then realized what a stupid question that was. It was hot inside, even with all the windows thrown wide open, and bodies were everywhere. A girl named Julie from April's Spanish class was lying on her back on top of the piano. She opened her mouth, and a guy in a hockey jersey poured streams of lime juice and vodka from two bottles he held up about a foot above her head. He put the bottles down, placed his hands on either side of Julie's head, and shook it. When he was done, Julie sat up and opened her mouth to show she'd swallowed it all. She bowed in triumph, but no one was looking.

April thought she'd just stick to beer for now. Robin was scanning the crowd for some guy named Calvin who was probably home from Andover and whom she'd hooked up with one night over Thanksgiving break. She staked out a spot halfway up the front-hall steps and said she'd promise to wait there if April would bring her a beer. April asked some strange girl where the keg was (you never asked a strange guy a question like that unless you were hitting on him, because that's how he'd interpret it anyway) and found it in the bathtub off the maid's room, behind the kitchen. She saw that some people had opened up the drawers in there and were trying on some clothes that belonged to the maid or the cook or whoever had been given the night off. Unreal. But low-rent shit like that went on at every party, though usually not this early. People continued to throw parties even though they always went bad in this way, every single time. Strangers showed up, fights broke out, cops came, shit got ruined. They were allowed to do whatever they wanted.

Naturally by the time April made it back to the front hall, struggling not to let the two beers she was carrying get dumped all over her, Robin was gone. There was no way April was going back through that mob again, so she kept going, out to the stoop, where some guys were smoking and where it was at least not so sweltering – a little chilly, in fact. She didn't recognize any of them, but one was wearing an Andover sweatshirt. She asked him if he knew a guy named Calvin. He nodded, and smiled broadly, apparently at the very thought of Calvin. He was either stoned or else just one of those guys who always appeared stoned.

"Haven't seen him, though," he said. "Want to get high?"

She did want to get high, being at this stupid party where she didn't really know anybody made it seem imperative to get high, but she didn't like the looks of the guy: his interest in her, for all his glazed affect, was too obvious. Her cell phone started buzzing in the back pocket of her jeans. She saw the caller ID and scowled and smiled at the same time. "Where the fuck are you?" she said.

"I'm at this party," Robin said. "Where the fuck are *you?*"

"Outside on the stoop," April said, taking a couple of steps away from the stoner, who shrugged. "I looked everywhere for you."

"I think not," Robin said, giggling. She was already

wasted and April felt a flash of resentment. "We're up on the third floor."

"There's a third floor?" April said, looking up.

She got there eventually, picking her way past a group of boys who had found a silver tea tray and were trying to surf down the stairs. Robin, red-eyed, hugged her for a good thirty seconds, which told April that it was X. But the X was now all gone, supposedly. They were all in some kind of den or study or something; this house was a trip, one of those houses that even this crowd couldn't quite believe somebody they knew lived in. The room itself, as a place to hang out, was tolerable – only about ten of them, the music reaching them as a kind of modulating throb – but the downside was that they were now so far away from the beer that there was no question of convincing anyone to make the trip. Someone passed April a warm bottle of Grey Goose and she did the best she could with it.

Two guys sitting about ten feet apart were texting each other and collapsing in laughter, and someone else was making a big show of checking out all the books on the shelves. Robin was talking with her eyes closed. Not the best sign. April was sitting in a club chair that was so comfortable she could have slept in it, even though it smelled like beer. Who would invite strangers in here, she thought? Who was this chick from St. Paul's, and where had her parents gone without her? April didn't understand some families. Most families, actually. Just then, as if on cue, her cell phone vibrated in her pocket again; it was Cynthia. April tried to think quickly. She was a little fucked up, but if she didn't answer now her mother would just keep calling, and she wasn't likely to get any less fucked up as the evening progressed. She walked out to the landing and answered. She was able to keep it short on account of the noise. A minute later she returned and they were all staring at her.

"Your mom, right?" Robin said. Her eyes were like little mail slots.

"And you answered?" one of the guys said.

"Shut up," Robin said. "Her mom is so cool. April, I think it's so cool that your mom is so cool."

"Ah," the guy said. "The Cool Mom."

"Also totally smoking hot," Robin said. "Seriously. Have you ever seen her?"

"I have!" said some random guy. "I saw her in some magazine! A total babe. She looks like, what the fuck is the name of that actress, the one who plays the mom—"

It should have made her feel weird, April thought, that they were all on the borderline of getting crude about her mom, but it didn't. She wasn't even sure they were all talking about the same person anyway. Besides, her mom was gorgeous, she'd been onto that long before any of them. "Hey," she said to the guy who was still struggling to remember the name of the actress, "are you Calvin?"

"No," he said irritably, as if his chain of thought had been broken. "I'm Tom. Calvin who? Calvin fucking Klein?"

A while later Robin said she wasn't feeling well, and next thing they knew she was asleep in the chair, with Tom's jacket over her.

"You think she's all right?" April asked.

"Sure," Tom said. "Not like we've never seen this before."

"I just love her so much," April said, and to demonstrate how much, she tried to look very hard into Tom's eyes.

"Don't worry," Tom said. When you were drunk there was something so impressive about people who held it together better than you. April had the sense that the other people in the room were now gone. "We won't let anything happen to her. We care about her."

"Do you think we should find a phone?" she said. What the fuck was she talking about? She didn't know. There was a phone right there in her ass pocket, for one thing.

"Yes, let's," Tom was saying very seriously. "By all means. Let's go look for a phone."

He walked behind her up to the darkened fourth floor, and when she turned around on the landing they were kissing. She felt cold and realized he already had her shirt up around her armpits and she at least had the presence of mind to walk backward a few more steps before anybody downstairs saw them. She wasn't going to be one of those skanks who got wasted and put on a show for everybody. She pulled him along by his jacket. She was trying to communicate without talking because she knew she had been slurring. Off the hallway were two closed doors. Tom tried them but they were locked. No telling what was going on in there. At the end of the hall, impossibly, was another, narrower flight of stairs.

"Jesus Christ," Tom said, "this place is massive."

At the top of the final staircase was a room with the door ajar and some light seeping through. Tom pushed the door open and they both stopped short: it was an attic that had been converted into a study or office of some kind, with a long desk and a computer, and there was a man sitting there. He spun slowly in his swivel chair, like the mother's corpse in *Psycho,* April thought, only this guy was wearing a cardigan and reading *The Wall Street Journal.*

"Hello," he said.

April was too freaked out to speak. "Hi, sir," Tom said. "Sorry to disturb you. We were looking for the bathroom."

"There isn't one on this floor," the man said amiably. Oh my God, April thought, you live here! She had an urge to go up and poke at him like he was a ghost. "There's one right underneath us." He had to be the father of the girl throwing the party. This had to be his own home that they were tearing apart downstairs. He was staring at her and she realized she was laughing.

"Sorry to disturb you," Tom said a second time, and pulled April outside and shut the door behind them.

Downstairs they found the bathroom; they went in and shut the door and kissed for a while longer, and then April went down on him. It was the quickest way to bring the whole thing to a close – ridiculously quick, in fact – and it was also the best way to keep his hands and mouth from going anywhere she didn't want them to go. Amazing how passive guys got, and how quickly, once you took over that way. It was all so predictable. She kept going even when she felt the cell vibrating in her pocket again.

On her way downstairs she peeked into the study but Robin, as April pretty much knew she would be, was gone. April had the cab let her off at 72nd and walked the rest of the way home to straighten out a little, and on the way she checked the phone and found a text from her mom: Where R U? She bought a pack of Juicy Fruit at a newsstand to clean up her breath. She came in through the downstairs door but went up to the kitchen for a bottle of water and saw the lights, like lights from a swimming pool, flickering on the walls of the darkened media room. Her mom was curled up against the arm of the couch. She smiled. "Everything okay?" she whispered.

April nodded.

"How was the party? Who'd you hang out with?"

"Robin was there, actually," April said.

"Oh yeah? How'd she seem?"

"Pretty good. She maybe had a little too much to drink."

"She got home okay?"

April nodded. "I put her in a cab myself." She blew her mother a kiss and started back toward the kitchen, but then she stopped.

"What's on?" she said.

"*A River Runs Through It*. Ever seen it?"

She had, but it didn't really matter; she went down to her room, put on some pajamas, and came back to lie down on the couch with her head in her mother's lap. Cynthia stroked her hair for a minute and then took her hand away. On the screen were these still, mountainous landscapes and endless skies, so dreamy that the hot guys in their fetishy western garb just seemed like figures in a painting, and after a few minutes of that she couldn't keep her eyes from closing, but whenever they did, what she kept seeing was the man in the attic. April reached up, grabbed Cynthia's hand and placed it on her head again, just like she'd done when she was little – just like she'd never stopped doing, really. Some people were in such a hurry to pretend they didn't need their mothers anymore, like they couldn't wait to leave behind the things that were great about being a kid in the first place, the things they still liked but for some reason thought it was important to feel ashamed of liking. She didn't understand those people at all.

In his office one May afternoon Adam got a call from his brother saying that he and his wife, Paige, were coming to New York for something called the upfronts; he didn't want to take Adam up on his offer to stay with them – writers, he said, got few enough perks in this world and he wanted to soak his employers for every room-service amenity he could think of – but they agreed to come over for dinner on their first night in town. Conrad had never been to the apartment on Columbus before. The brothers were less a part of each other's lives than they would have liked, mostly on account of geography and work schedules but also because of Paige. Twelve years younger than Conrad, she felt intimidated and rudely excluded by any conversation that referenced the years before he met her, when she was just a child; she also had a suspicion that Cynthia did not like her, which was entirely correct.

"What the hell does your brother see in her?" she would ask Adam after every encounter; Adam would shrug supportively, but he knew the answer to the question. Conrad made a tidy living in Los Angeles writing movie scripts even though nothing he'd written had ever risen high enough on the developmental scale to be acted out by performers in front of cameras. One of his screenplays, though, had led to a staff job on an hour-long TV drama called *The Lotus Eaters,* about a group of high-school students who lived in Hawaii. Conrad traveled there twice a year, along with the entire production staff, for research purposes, and on one of these trips he had become better acquainted with Paige, a production designer who worked just two offices down from him back in LA. There was something about those Hawaiian junkets that accelerated intimacy. Adam knew his little brother well enough to know that the point was not so much that Paige was attractive but that she was attractive in a certain sterile, classic way – blonde, very thin, small-featured, always put together – that Conrad had long ago convinced himself was out of his league. It made perfect sense that the first woman who proved him wrong on this score would be the one he wound up asking to marry him. Now they spent their off-hours at clubs and concerts and bars trying to absorb osmotically, for scriptwriting purposes, the rituals and value systems of privileged eighteen-year-olds. Paige was an enormous help in this regard.

After dinner the kids disappeared downstairs and Adam brought four glasses filled with whiskey out onto the patio, where Conrad was pointing out various New York landmarks, not always correctly, to his wife. The moon hung over the park and the blue-lit planetarium, low enough to be scored every few minutes by the silhouette of a plane. "This is quite something," Conrad said. "Who knew there was such good money in being a master of the universe?"

Paige sniffed her glass, made a face, and put it down on the table. "Maybe it's not too late for you," she said, in a kind of musical voice intended to suggest she was teasing. "Maybe you could still get into the family business."

"I would," Conrad said, "if I could even figure out what the hell it is he does."

"Not a problem," Adam said. "Always room for you, Fredo."

They all laughed, Paige a little less heartily, because she didn't know who Fredo was. In an effort to keep the conversation from escaping her completely, she said, "You know who would totally lose it over this apartment, Con? Tracy."

Conrad nodded vigorously as if he'd been thinking the same thing. "Who's Tracy?" Cynthia asked. "Tracy Cepeda is our show's chief location scout," Conrad said. "She would collapse if she saw this place. She'd offer you a mint to shoot in here. Even though we'd probably need to CGI some sand and palm trees out these windows."

Adam felt his cell phone vibrate; he ignored it. It was hard for your eye not to be drawn to Paige because she was, in a way that was compelling without being at all sexual, so flawless. When she opened her mouth she became Paige but when she was silent, and still, there were no idiosyncracies in her face at all. Adam knew from Conrad that she had started out as an actress but did not like to talk about how badly that had gone.

"You better be careful he doesn't write you all into the show," Paige said, elbowing him. Conrad winced. "Please," he said. "But it's true that this place looks like a set. And so do the people in it. I mean, no joke, we spend weeks in casting trying to find kids who look exactly like April and Jonas. Adam, this is bourbon? What kind is it?"

"It's rye, actually."

"Wow," Conrad said. He held up his empty glass and stared into it.

"Oh, Connie, you'll have beautiful children too," Cynthia said. "Provided Paige can find a way to reproduce without you, that is. What is that called again? Reproduction without sex? Paige, what's the word I'm looking for?" Adam shot her a look intended to signal that she was close to the borderline.

"If you're ever hard up for money, just fly the family to LA, and both kids will have agents before you're out of baggage claim," Conrad said. "Parthenogenesis, by the way, is what it's called. Seriously, though, I can't quite believe I'm related to them." He stared at Adam. "You either," he said, swiping at his older brother's stomach. "Seriously, what kind of Faustian shit is going on around here? You literally do not look a day older than you did in college. It's annoying as hell. What is the secret?"

Adam smiled. "Commitment, *mon frère,*" he said. "Commitment to the body. You should try it."

179

"Commitment my ass. You're a fucking vampire."

The cell phone buzzed in Adam's pocket. The incoming number was Devon's, which was not something that was supposed to happen. "Excuse me a second?" he said, and went inside.

The three of them stood silently in front of the moon for a while, arms crossed on the patio railing. Conrad started. "Jesus, I just almost dropped my glass over the side," he said. "Parthenogenesis. There, I can still say it. Cyn, where's the bathroom?"

"There's one off the kitchen," she said, "and one just to the right of the front door as you came in."

When he was gone, Paige and Cynthia exchanged a quick and awkward smile, and then went back to gazing over the railing, into the pocket of darkness that was Central Park.

"I'm sorry I said that about having children," Cynthia said. "I mean, it's really none of my business. I was just giving him shit. We've known each other forever."

Paige tipped her head to indicate it was nothing. "You have a beautiful family," she said. It was just one of those polite expressions people used when they couldn't, or didn't want to, come up with anything else to say; but for some reason it got to Cynthia this time. She felt a little sting at the corners of her eyes.

"Yeah, well," she said, trying to stop herself but failing, "that's what people start saying to you when you get a little older yourself. You have a beautiful family. It's like, yeah, we can tell you were hot once. You notice I don't get any of those remarks about how I don't look any different than I did twenty years ago."

Paige, for once, looked quite thoughtful.

"Time is different for us," she said.

Adam walked back onto the patio, stuffing his cell phone in his pocket. He looked back and forth between the two women. "What?" he said.

It was an old story, how time favored men over women, but in Adam's case, Cynthia thought, it was just as Conrad had said: he wasn't growing more distinguished as he aged – it was more like he wasn't aging at all. His waist size hadn't changed since they got married, which was freaky but at least explicable, considering what a fanatic he was about it. But he wouldn't even have known how to do anything to his face except wash it and shave it and yet that looked the same as it always had too. It wasn't the first time someone else had confirmed it for her. True, he didn't have too many vices, unless working out too hard counted as a vice, which she thought it probably did. He spent too much time in the office, he didn't sleep enough, but whatever toll all this might have been exacting, none of it showed in his face. And if you pointed this out to him, he didn't even understand what you were talking about.

She couldn't compete with that. She still went to the gym three or four times a week, but she had long since come to consider it a chore and, in an effort to at least make it diverting, had gone through fickle infatuations with every bit of technology in there, every new fad and philosophy. The two of them belonged to different gyms – she would never have dreamed of working out with him, he was far too humorless about it. Still, like him, she was interested in hanging on to her physical prime for as long as possible – indefinitely, really. Together they did quite a good job of it. And there was one respect in which Cynthia – though she'd never discussed it with him – was prepared to go further in this effort than he was. They had three friends who'd had work done already; she told Adam about the first two, and then when Marietta had her eyelids and neck done Cynthia had said nothing and waited to see if he'd notice, which he never did. It wasn't like Marietta's tits had gotten bigger or something; she was only confirming Adam's sense of what she was supposed to look like anyway. Aging would have been more conspicuous. Cynthia still looked fantastic – everyone said so, and she knew they were serious – but it was so hard to look at yourself with fresh eyes. That was the insidious thing about time and its effects: how incremental they were. So far, so good, was her thought, but whenever the moment came, there was no resource she wouldn't call upon.

In the cold morning overcast, wearing shorts and a T-shirt and a lightweight ski hat and a pair of fingerless gloves, Adam put his palms flat against the façade of his building and pushed, until the tightness left his calves. He shifted his hips forward and slowly lowered one heel to the sidewalk, then the other, and when his Achilles tendons felt loose as well, he was good to go. He bounced on his toes a couple of times, exhaled once forcefully through his mouth as if preparing for an entrance onstage, put one finger to his watch, and started running.

Though he kept to the south side of 81st Street, where the sidewalks were wider on the perimeter of the museum grounds, it was still stop and go; he had to work his way around or through the knots of tourists and the pairs of strollers advancing in unison as their nannies chatted behind them. There was nothing to be done until he crossed the transverse exit at Central Park West and passed through the low stone gate into the park, and then he found his rhythm. He glided around the softball fields, passing everyone else on the path – the fat guys with headbands and hair leaking up from the collars of their shirts, the women in Lycra tights with sweatshirts tied self-consciously around their waists, the serious rope-muscled runners with the perfect strides and fixed stares – feeling the familiar warmth and pulse of his blood radiating from his core until there was no part of his body uninvolved in it. He'd never been to the Conservatory Garden before, but he knew roughly where it was – not far from their old apartment, the one where April and Jonas had shared a room. He could have shortened his time by cutting across the North Meadow but it was blocked by that temporary soft-orange fencing that signaled a reseeding; so he passed all the way out of the park again on the east side and turned north along Fifth Avenue until he saw the theatrical flight of stone steps that led down into the garden. It was laid out in the dimensions of a cross, with trellised roses and reflecting pools on the right and left of him; at the far end, at the foot of a flagstone path, another flight of steps led up to a long, curved, and colonnaded stone arch, and there, sitting on the top step with his arms around his knees, wearing a khaki suit, was Devon.

He stood up slowly and bemusedly as Adam sprinted up the steps, touched his watch again, and stood gazing around the garden with his hands clasped on top of his head, waiting for his heart rate to slow. "Multitasking," Devon said, a little bitterly. "Nice. No reason meeting me should interfere with your regimen. Won't you have to go home and change now, though, before work, or is it Casual Tuesday or something?"

Adam shook his head. "Not going in this morning," he said. "The boss and I are flying to Minneapolis in a few hours."

They stood beneath the arch, facing back toward Fifth Avenue across the top of the sunken gardens. In the unseasonable cold the paths were almost empty, but not quite; the incongruous country-squire layout made it a popular spot for wedding photos, and so there was a full bridal party standing by one of the reflecting pools, blowing on their hands to keep warm, while a couple of boys in suits who couldn't have been older than six chased each other around the still water. In fact, Adam was the only one in the whole garden not dressed formally. Still, Devon felt like the conspicuous one.

"So?" Adam said. "Shall we go talk amongst the roses?"

"Why not," Devon said. "I'm sure everybody thinks we're fags anyway."

They descended the steps and turned left on the flagstones

toward the unoccupied reflecting pool. "Miguel is out," Devon said.

"No names, please."

"Whatever. One of my associates has told me he's out. The one who works at Schwab. He's getting married. He says he's made enough and doesn't want this hanging over his head anymore."

"Okay," Adam said. "You think he's telling the truth? There's nothing else going on there, no trouble he's in, no debts or anything like that?"

"Why?" Devon said. He meant to sound sarcastic but it just came out petulant. "You thinking of having him killed?"

Adam rolled his eyes. "I'm just wondering why you considered it some kind of emergency. It's happened before. I mean, you know this isn't a good idea, our meeting like this. Not that I don't enjoy your company."

As they finished their first circuit Devon looked up and saw a strange bald man in a tuxedo struggling to fix an expensive camera onto a tripod. He was all the way across the garden, where the bridal party was, but the camera looked like it was pointing right at him. He fought down a taste of panic in his throat. "That's kind of my point, that this same thing happened two months ago. It's not like we can take out an ad to replace these guys. Pretty soon it will be down to you and me, and that would not be tenable. We couldn't disguise it well enough."

"Well," Adam said, "you know a lot more guys in the trenches than I do. Can you think of anyone else you might bring in?"

Devon grimaced. "Yes, probably," he said, "but that's not the point. We can't keep piling risk upon risk, right, and expect to stay lucky forever. I don't know. Honestly I'm wondering if it's time to get out. I want to be smart about this. I mean, am I the only one? Don't you think about this stuff? Aren't you fucking freezing, by the way?"

Of course Adam thought about it, not because he was prone to fear or paranoia but just as a matter of risk management. He saw perfectly clearly that the whole arrangement was held together at this point only by own his ability to lead, to inspire faith in himself even among people he met only briefly, if ever. Any one of these brokers, Devon included, who slipped up and got caught could always save himself by giving up the top of the chain, and the top of the chain was Adam. So he wasn't sure what there was for Devon to get so stressed about. He had to admit that his initial assessment of the kid, aboard the *Intrepid* all those years ago, had turned out to be wrong in some respects, though not, of course, in the important one.

"You say you want to be smart about it," he said, looking into Devon's eyes. "But to say that we can't be successful today because we were successful yesterday – that's not smart, that's just superstitious. You start giving in to ideas about luck or fate or karma or whatever and you're fucked. There's no fate. Everything that you and I have made happen in these last however many years? It never happened. It's gone. It doesn't exist. The only thing that exists, the only risk to be analyzed, is what's in front of us today."

"I know," Devon said sulkily. He looked down. Adam knew he had him.

"We are hypercareful. We always have been. We don't give every piece of information to everybody in the chain. And I'm sure you figured out a long time ago that some of the information I give you is bogus, so it never looks to anyone like some unbroken winning streak."

"I'm not questioning anything like that. It's just – the whole thing isn't like I thought it would be. The money is almost like a burden because I'm so paranoid about spending it. And how can you not look back? I don't get that. Which is probably why I'll never be a billionaire. I'm just not a stone killer like you are. See, that's another thing I don't get: as little as I know about you, I know that you are one of those guys, those guys who are like missing a part of their brain or something. No conscience. No memory for losses. So you don't need this. You'd be a player anyway. Why are you doing it still? Don't you think about stopping?"

The bridesmaids had run off to the car to get warm and the wedding photographer was packing his gear into a couple of canvas bags. No conscience? Adam thought. It's not as though I can't remember; it's just that there's nothing constructive about remembering. Still, when he did consider the life his family was living now, a life in which literally anything was possible, every desire was in reach, no potential was allowed to wither, and they had all seen so much of the world; when he thought back to the moment he had gone for it, to his own fearlessness when threatened with the unhappiness of those he loved, and how readily, in the face of that, he had cleared the hurdle that most men would never have the fortitude to clear; and how all this was accomplished by his taking all the risk onto himself, so much so that they would never even have a clue that there was any risk involved; the only reasonable conclusion, he felt, was that it was the noblest thing he had ever done in his life. It was humility, really, that made him so uncomfortable reminiscing about it.

But it was also true that that particular hurdle had been cleared a long time ago, and that there were other reasons he was loath to terminate the life of secret risk, the world inside the world. "Devon," he said, "you're going in to work today, right?"

He fingered his suit. "Some of us have to," he said.

"Well when you do, just take a minute and look around you at everyone else in that office, everyone you work for, everyone who works for you. All of them with their fingers crossed, all of them so afraid that if getting some kind of inside information meant never seeing you again they would make that trade in a heartbeat. I think I know what you think of those people. But you are not one of them. You are Superman. You are a fucking gangster. The day we go back to feeling safe from risk is the day you can no longer look at them and say to yourself that there's any difference between them and you. Are you really ready to go back to that? Are you really ready to go back to reading bullshit quarterly reports and trying to use those to figure out how the world works? It's no kind of life, leaving your future in the hands of forces that have nothing to do with you and calling them fate or luck or whatever. And there is only this life, dude. I don't want to get all mystical on you, but this is the only life we get, and either you leave your mark on it or it's like you were never here." They had stopped walking. The garden was now abandoned. Devon, head down, nodded sullenly, like a child. Adam put his hands on the younger man's shoulders.

"No one else," Adam said gently, "knows the things that you and I know. Now. Speaking of being careful. It's time for new cell numbers, right? Did you memorize yours?" Devon nodded, and recited it. "Done," Adam said, and began bouncing on the balls of his feet again. "Now relax a little. Have some fun. Wait to hear from me." He ran up the garden steps, headed south until he could breach the low stone wall again, and twenty minutes later he was home. He showered, put on a suit, grabbed his briefcase, hailed a cab, and met Sanford inside the first-class lounge in the Delta terminal at LaGuardia. Sanford was sitting in a too-low club chair in front of a muted TV, holding a glass of wine and looking miserable.

"I can't tell you how much I hate flying these days," he said. "Commercial especially. It's so degraded. Look at what passes for first class now." His face was tired and florid, even though the glass of wine was his first. They were on their way to Minneapolis to close a deal with the state's teachers union, which had agreed to let Perini grow their pension fund.

"I almost wonder why we have to go at all," Sanford said to him as they boarded the plane, a few drinks later. "It's all in the bag. But they just need a little face time, before they hand over the pension money to a couple of sharks from New York City. Maybe they just want to make sure we're not Nigerian princes." Adam had the aisle seat and thus took the brunt of the resentful glances from those who boarded after them and had to stand waiting while others tried to smash their carry-ons into the tiny overhead bins in coach. "You know," Sanford said once they were in the air, "I spent a lot of time talking you up with them, and then one of them asked me an odd question. 'If this guy's such a star,' he asked me, 'how do we know he won't bolt and start his own hedge fund or something?' "

Adam smiled. "And you said, 'Hey, you're right, I'd better go and give that guy a massive midyear bonus right away'?"

Sanford slapped him affectionately on the knee. "Good one," he said. "No, I told him that you were still a young man. And that the best thing about you is that with all the ego in this business, you're not one of those guys obsessed with having a high profile. Honestly, if you'd asked me ten years ago, I would have bet I'd have lost you by now. But you're an old-school guy, a throwback in a lot of ways. Put your head down, do your job, respect the traditions, and everybody gets rich enough in the end. Lazard was like that when I worked there, a hundred years ago. Anyway, I can't tell you what a comfort it is to me now."

He looked out the window at the ground far below, the lit veins of the empty streets, the bright ballfields and parking lots. "It's funny how much I've grown to hate this," he said.

"I used to take it for granted. Airplanes and airports. But lately I just want to be out on the water. It's almost all I think about."

A few minutes later he was asleep, his cheek sunk against his shoulder, his lower lip drooping. Not a flattering look, Adam thought, and closed his eyes.

There was a template for everything somewhere, an overgrown headwater of the original and unprecedented, and you might hack away in search of it your whole life long and never find it. Or, on the other hand, you might. Jonas hated having his ignorance exposed. On the M79 bus coming home from school some fat guy wearing board shorts even though it was about forty degrees out tried to peek over his shoulder to see what he was listening to on his iPod. Jonas showed him the screen. The guy made a condescending face: "Reheated Joy Division," he said, and Jonas nodded in agreement, like what-can-you-do, but then he couldn't wait to get home and get on the computer and find out who Joy Division was. And a couple of hours later he had to conclude that the fat guy was right. Mostly just by virtue of being older, but still. The more you learned about something you thought was good, the more holes like this you fell into. His own obsessions tended to bear Jonas backward in time, and eventually they led him to the sad but empirical conclusion that the popular music of his own day and age sucked ass.

In tenth grade this was not a mainstream view. If you wanted to be a music snob, fine, but you were expected to do so by raving obnoxiously about some band no one else had ever heard of because they'd only formed three weeks ago and played one gig. Jonas knew guys like that, older guys who ran the high-school radio station nobody listened to and who were flunking English because they spent so much time commenting on one another's blogs, and even though he wanted nothing to do with them he had to cop to their being kindred spirits, because really they were jonesing for the same thing he was: the unspoiled, the uncorrupted, the pure of intent. They were just looking for it in the wrong place. Then of course there were all the kids in the happy mainstream, the kids whose moms drove them out to Nassau Coliseum to see some dancing boy-band lip-synch songs of longing vetted by a focus group of ten-year-old girls. That shit was beyond the pale. It was too hard to believe that there was such a thing as not even caring, not bothering to distinguish in terms of value between the simulated and the real.

There was something sort of priestly about him when it came to music, and as with most priests, some people respected his outlook and some people just found the whole attitude a bit much. Certainly it put him outside the realm of anything girls might be interested in. And there was another big downside to having such an exacting ear, which was that it tortured Jonas to know how mediocre and ordinary his own band sounded, himself not excepted. They were never going to be good. Still, he practiced and practiced. The others were blissfully optimistic, which was, he thought, a lovely thing to be able to be. They did a decent "Sweet Jane", because really if you couldn't get that down what hope was there for you? They played together once or twice a week in an old boathouse near the FDR Drive, a property that their lead singer's father had bought up but hadn't yet gotten a zoning abeyance to convert. It was hard to find places in the city to rehearse – probably easier to find places to perform, which was unfortunately where the fantasies of Jonas's bandmates tended to drift anyway.

Girls did sometimes come to their rehearsals, though. Even senior girls like the completely unattainable Tori Barbosa. It proved once and for all the tremendous magical properties of rock and roll, Jonas thought, that even a band that sucked as bad as they did still attracted girls. He was the youngest among them and had the reputation of being the best musician as well, but that was because he was the only one who bothered to practice outside of rehearsal. One of the most depressing manifestations of their lameness was how much time they spent naming themselves. Haskell, their singer, thought some preemptive irony was in order and wanted them to call themselves The Privileged, or The Privileges. The notion of preemptive irony made Jonas want to kill himself; since he was always trying to interest them in a more rootsy direction anyway, he kept suggesting The Headwaters, like a kind of quest for the source rather than just some bar-band-style aping of that month's Top 40. But every time they wrote it down and looked at it, somebody would say, "The Headwaiters?" Every time. Then Alex, the drummer, had a revelation while watching a film in twentieth-century US history and so their name, at least until the next time they decided to argue about it, was Run Bobby Run.

With the cars roaring by on the FDR outside the boathouse door, they summoned the attention span for a passable version of "People Who Died". Everyone was impressed with Jonas's solo, and a couple of the spectators even came over afterward to tell him so, but at the end of the evening of course all the girls went off with the older guys and Jonas called the car service to come take him home. He needed to study, and he needed to sleep, but surplus adrenaline wouldn't really permit him to do either; instead he turned on the record player and put on his headphones. Lately he was on a serious bluegrass kick. There was no end to that stuff – you were always stumbling on these amazing old 78s or field recordings that, the first time you played them, went off in your head like little bombs. He'd think so-and-so was a discovery of his and then learn later that, to real aficionados of the music, so-and-so was like Shakespeare or Tolstoy. His ignorance, he sometimes felt, was boundless.

He saw a shadow fall across the line of light that came in from the hallway, under his bedroom door. It was his mom, he knew, just checking to make sure he was back home. He didn't even need to take the headphones off; he shifted around in his chair so it squeaked a little, and the foot shadows moved off again. Someone was always awake in that apartment. He opened up his cell and checked the time: 1:52. Then he turned back toward the blue lights of the planetarium outside his window.

I used to think my daddy was a black man
With scrip enough to buy the company store
Now he goes downtown with empty pockets
And his face as white as February snow

What the hell ever happened to country music, anyway? It used to be so fucking dark it took your breath away. Just a few more weary days and then I'll fly away. Now it was a museum of itself, a pander-factory full of Vegas-style reactionaries in thousand-dollar hats. What was good about it was never coming back. Jonas slid the volume up and put his feet on the windowsill and listened until he saw the sun starting to brighten the planets below him.

This world is not my home, I'm
just a-passing through
My treasures are laid up somewhere beyond the blue
The angels beckon me to heaven's open door
And I can't feel at home in this world anymore

In the morning he came upstairs to breakfast feeling temporarily okay after a shower and drank the remnants of some kind of smoothie April had left in the fridge the night before. She passed him on her way out the door. She was part of that universe at school, the Tori Barbosa universe, and friends of his – total strangers, for that matter, kids from other schools sometimes – would come up to him and ask about her in ways that were pathetic and stalkerish. His sister was sort of a stranger to him but not enough of one that he could see her in the way everybody else apparently saw her.

"You look like shit," she said, and patted him on the head.

Adam came in through the front door drenched in sweat from a run. Jonas liked running too – he hated sports in general but there was something ascetic about running, something monkish – but there was no way he could hang with his father, who kept a chart of his own split times and was talking about entering next year's marathon. Adam sat down across from him and asked him how everything was going, and by the time that conversation was over Jonas had gotten permission to go down to Sam Ash and buy himself a banjo. Cynthia was still asleep and would be until after everyone else was out of the house.

It sounded hypocritical, he knew, to be so hung up on originality and authenticity when he was playing in a cover band; but that choice had been dictated less by aesthetics than by the discovery that songwriting was brutally hard. They all gave it a try at some point and the results were uniformly atrocious, with hurt feelings to contend with on top of that. So they went back to covers, but Jonas kept thinking that they could at least aspire to cover some material their audience didn't already know by heart. That way at least you could argue you were maybe doing the music a service. He came to rehearsal one night with the banjo and a CD he'd burned of Jimmy Martin's "You Don't Know My Mind", which was one of the scariest songs he'd ever heard in his life. He'd even found sheet music for it online, though only he and Alex knew how to read music anyway. He played the CD for them and was pierced by the looks on their faces even though on some level it was exactly the reaction he'd expected.

"It's interesting," Haskell said, "but I don't think we can pull off that whole blues thing. You least of all, actually."

"It's not blues," Jonas said. He felt exposed now, in the way one does when one confesses to a crush, and he didn't want to make things worse by getting into an argument. Still, he couldn't help it. "At least know what you're talking about before you dismiss it. This guy was a poor drunk from the Tennessee mountains. He wasn't trying to get on MTV or get his shit in a Verizon commercial. He had nothing but what came out of him. And you guys get all excited about The Strokes or whatever when it's all just prepackaged bullshit."

They looked at each other in a way that reminded him horribly of how young he was. "Look," Haskell said gently, "you want to talk authentic, how authentic would it look for me to be singing about being a Tennessee dirt farmer or whatever? That's not who I am."

"Who are you?" Jonas said.

There must have been some expression on his face he wasn't aware of, because Alex said, "Who needs a beer?" But it was past that point already. "I can tell you who I'm not," Haskell said. "I'm not some self-hating son of a zillionaire. I'm not some condescending hypocrite poser. So you and your banjo fuck off. Grab your fucking Gibson and back me up on some songs about getting drunk and laid

197

because when we are through here I am going to get both of those things. Authentic enough for you?"

Tori Barbosa was right there listening to the whole thing. It seemed too humiliating to walk out. Red-faced, he strapped on his guitar and looked at Alex, who tapped his fist to his heart a couple of times and then counted off "Sweet Emotion".

For Christmas, as usual, Jonas's parents asked him what he wanted; he said he wanted all twelve volumes of the Alan Lomax Library of Congress recordings, on vinyl, and since they didn't have the first idea how to acquire such a thing, he bought it himself online and put it on their credit card. Over the winter he got the flu and had to miss a few rehearsals, and when he found out they'd had some kid from Collegiate sitting in for him, he texted Haskell and said he was out of the band. He spent evenings in his room with the headphones on, reading liner notes about Lomax and how he literally tromped through fields with a microphone in his hand and a huge reel-to-reel slung over his shoulder, recording things no one had ever recorded before. The guitars and the banjo sat on their stands in the corner. The forties, the thirties, the twenties: that, he kept thinking, was the time to be alive.

In May, just a week before the end of the school year, Ruth's husband Warren died. He'd had a lung removed two weeks earlier but never made it home from the hospital. Even though his cancer had been diagnosed two years ago, Cynthia was almost as surprised as if the news had come out of nowhere; her mother's peerless flair for pessimism had her convinced, right up until the final hysterical phone call, that Ruth was probably making too big a deal out of it.

The four of them flew to Pittsburgh the next morning. Adam asked Cynthia if she planned to stay on for a few days after the funeral to "help out" and Cynthia said she didn't know, it hadn't occurred to her. Indeed there was a whole barrage of quotidian death-consequences that somehow had never occurred to her. Ruth came to the door to greet them in what for her might have passed as high spirits; she exclaimed, as well she might have, over the changes in her tall and comely grandchildren, who had not seen her in years and who were not entirely sure how to act but instinctively determined to err on the side of restraint. "It'll be so nice for you to see your cousins," Ruth said to them, and at the word "cousins" Cynthia saw them indiscreetly catch each other's startled eyes.

The funeral was still three days away. Ruth kept stressing how much she would require Cynthia's help with various decisions but then it would turn out that she had already made those decisions anyway, some of them so far in advance as to border on the ghoulish. Cynthia had little advice to offer in any case. She had no experience with funerals but beyond that she could bring only a generic approach to the question of how Warren's life ought to be celebrated. He was a sort of machine of dependability. He was also a former managing partner at Reed Smith and a surprising amount of ceremony was dictated by that, which was helpful if also a little perverse, as if the law firm were a branch of the armed services with attendant arcane, unquestioned rituals. Ruth wanted a closed casket because toward the end he'd looked too little like himself. They could put a lot of makeup on him but they couldn't put the weight back on. She went instead for a large framed photo to be placed on top of the casket itself, a formal portrait commissioned when he'd been made managing partner: round-faced, smiling appropriately, projecting, with his glasses and his silver hair, a kind of well-fed competence.

The house was too small for all of them to sleep in; they spent the day there, battling their own restlessness as an assortment of Tupperware-bearing geriatric strangers consoled them on their loss, and then at night they escaped to the Hilton downtown, where they splurged on every silly, expensive amenity as a way of getting the hours of toxic solemnity out of their systems. The tips Adam doled out had the bell staff literally fighting for his attention. He'd never really liked Ruth: he didn't do well with negative people. This time was different, obviously, and he was more than willing to make allowances; still, he wasn't sure how to take it whenever she acted as if she and Adam were as close as mother and son, not just when others were around but even in the rare minutes when the two of them were alone together. She didn't seem to be performing, either, as she often did. When he smiled and stood aside in her kitchen doorway just to let her pass, she put her forehead on his shoulder and closed her eyes, and Adam felt as he might have if a woman in a strange city had mistaken him for someone else.

He wasn't sure what to tell the kids to do in that house of mourning, so he settled for telling them what not to do: no texting from inside Grandma's house, no earphones in their ears for any reason. Save it all for the hotel. He and Cynthia took them to the church where they were married and the four of them even had dinner in the Athletic Club dining room, which was the site of their reception; Jonas and April were indulgent about it at best. Nor were they especially diverted by the introduction of their "cousins", a term that turned out to refer to the twin sons of Cynthia's stepsister, Deborah. The two women hadn't had occasion to speak to each other in years; April heard her mother cooing about some recent Christmas-card photo of the twins but it was not any Christmas card that she and Jonas had ever seen. The boys were five years old and, April couldn't stop herself from thinking, really unfortunate-looking. Virtually the only way to get them to stop talking was to feed them something. Somehow they'd gotten to know their grandpa Warren much better than she and Jonas ever had, and they turned cutely somber when discussing the loss of him.

Deborah was much altered. She was fat, for starters, with no vestiges of the goth edge, faint to begin with, she had cultivated as a grad student, to say nothing of her one night at Bellevue; she taught twentieth-century art history at Boston University, as did her husband, who was a good deal older than her and had been, Cynthia was amused to learn, the chair of the search committee that hired her. When Deborah cried at the funeral, not at all showily, Cynthia found herself struggling not to stare at her, without quite knowing why. She had written a eulogy for her father but had arranged for her husband to read it for her, as she doubted her ability to get through it. And when the last mourner had gone through the receiving line in the room at the back of the church after the service, Cynthia and Deborah hugged.

But that feeling of kinship was short-lived. After the last guest left Ruth's house that evening, Cynthia heard two more voices out on the deck, and when she went out to investigate she found Deborah and Jonas leaning against the railing, deep in conversation. She tried to conceal her surprise, but could not, and when they both noticed her standing there in the doorway, they laughed. "We're arguing about Andy Warhol," Deborah said. "Pittsburgh's own. I feel like I'm defending my thesis again." Unless Andy Warhol played the fucking banjo, Cynthia thought, she would not have guessed that Jonas knew or cared who he was; but before she could say anything else, Jonas said, "Mom, what time is our flight tomorrow?"

"I'm actually not leaving tomorrow after all," Cynthia said. "Your flight is at something like three-thirty."

Jonas pumped his fist, and Deborah said, "Well, would you mind then if I took Jonas out to the Warhol Museum? One of the curators there is an old classmate of mine. It's a pretty great museum, actually. Maybe you want to come too."

She did not miss the look that crossed her son's face when Deborah made that last suggestion. "No," she said, "I'm sure it's a real life-changer and all that, but there's things to take care of around here. You go. Knock yourselves out. Just be back at the hotel by, I don't know, one." Smiling as tightly as her mother might have, she stepped back inside the house and slid the door shut. Back in the kitchen there were a thousand dishes to wash, and she briefly entertained the pros and cons of just throwing them all in the garbage. It's not like there'd ever be a crowd this size here again. Andy Warhol, she thought suddenly. It's one thing to fall for that bullshit as a high-school student, but imagine devoting your whole life to it.

Adam and the kids flew home the next day, and so, as it turned out, did Deborah's family; but Deborah stuck around. Cynthia supposed she should be happy that the burden of the next few days – all those hours maintaining one's patience on the phone with the insurance company or the idiots at Social Security – wasn't all going to fall on her, only child or not. Still, it was a little confounding to see how close Deborah and Ruth seemed to have become over the past few years, outside of Cynthia's awareness. At some point, she thought, Deborah must have really bought into that whole extended-family thing, because she certainly hadn't been buying into it when they first met each other, more than fifteen years ago now.

As for Ruth, having both girls in the house helped her maintain the bizarre equanimity that had characterized her all week. She'd wept a little during the service but otherwise there had been no great outpouring of grief. Cynthia believed this was some kind of denial. Or maybe it was relief. Or maybe it was just that she was old and alone and so there was no longer any need for her customary exaggeration of how hopeless things were. She puttered and took naps and answered condolence cards and fought good-naturedly with them when they tried to cook for her. She was sixty-seven and there was nothing to suggest that she couldn't go on like this for another twenty or thirty years.

She was easily exhausted, though, and went to bed early, and a few minutes later Cynthia was sitting numbly in the kitchen staring at a light-switch cover shaped like a rooster when Deborah walked in happily waving a bottle of Knob Creek bourbon she'd found in the liquor cabinet. Hallelujah, Cynthia thought.

"So when are you heading back?" Deborah said, after the first one.

"The day after tomorrow, I think. I've got a board meeting, and then we have this place down in Anguilla we go to sometimes, so we'll go there when school's out, which is in . . . What is today? Anyway, it's next week."

Deborah nodded but was unable to suppress an ambivalent laugh. "You guys have really been successful," was what she said.

Cynthia wasn't sure how to reply to that one. "It's all Adam," she said finally. "Some people just have a talent for investing."

"Well, you two always did seem to have that kind of penumbra around you. And now your kids have got it too."

"Your boys are adorable," Cynthia said, reaching for the bottle.

"Thank you. And the weird thing is, I have two more. Sort of. Sebastian has two daughters from his first marriage. Both in college now. So after all these years, I'm the stepmother."

"Ironic would be the word there, I guess," Cynthia said.

"Say this for my dad," Deborah said, holding up the bottle. "He knew that life was too short to settle for cheap liquor."

"So I'm curious," Cynthia said. She could see already that Deborah was something of a lightweight, and who knew but that this might be the last time they ever talked. "What's happened to you? I mean the one thing I always thought we had in common was thinking that the whole blended-family thing or whatever people call it was bullshit. You always seemed to hate it worse than I did. And now you're all Aunty Deborah with Jonas, and you're treating Ruth like she's your own mom. Is your own mom even still alive? That seems like something I should know, I guess, but I have no idea."

Deborah looked at her slyly. "She lives with us," she said. "Back in Boston."

"Get the fuck out of here."

She nodded, amused by herself. "I don't know when it happened exactly, but somehow the older I got the more exposed I felt, and the whole family idea got real meaningful to me. I developed this need for it. I had a theory that it had to do with being an only child, like the fear of being alone that comes with that, but I guess not. It didn't happen to you."

"So is this it for you, in terms of coming out here to visit or to help Ruth or whatever? I've always kind of wondered about the step-thing. Does it end when you're an adult? Does it end when the marriage that made it happen ends?"

Deborah considered it. She put her chin down on the kitchen table and stared at the bottle. "Time will kick your ass," she said. "I used to be so angry about how fake the whole thing was. I was pissed about having to be in your wedding, even. But you wait around long enough and these bogus connections harden into something real, whether you like it or not. I really think of Ruth as one of my parents now. I don't think Dad's death can undo that."

"What will happen to her?" Cynthia said suddenly. "You know there's going to be a huge crash once we're gone. It must fucking suck to be old. It must suck to have your husband die. But I mean what can we do about it? The only way to hold it off is to stay here forever. And there's no way she's coming to live with us, I mean, hats off to you and all that, but I could never do it."

"She'd never come live with you anyway, even if you asked her. Or with me. No way Ruth could ever open herself up enough to depend on one of us like that. I think she'll actually do okay living alone. Better than most people. The thing to worry about, if you want to worry about something, is what if her health goes south, like Dad's did. Then you're looking at some hard choices."

Did she mean "you" as in "one", or "you" as in "Cynthia"? But there was no way to ask for a clarification because she felt craven and selfish just for wondering. Anyway, those decisions were still a long way off. "She's never been sick a day in her life," Cynthia said.

There was some kind of noise from the direction of the living room, and they both cocked their heads in case Ruth was up, but only silence followed. The muted TV still flickered on the walls beyond the kitchen door.

"You know," Deborah said, "my dad was really a great guy. He had his limits in terms of expressiveness, but he was really loving. And he always had a soft spot for you. I think because you were certain things I wasn't. It hurt him that you didn't think of him as a parent. You never really gave him a chance."

Her eyes were drunk. Either she hadn't done this in a long time or she did it a lot. Cynthia suddenly lost interest in the answer. You started taking on other people's grievances and there was no end to it. She was nobody's sister, and neither was Deborah. It was one thing to conspire about the future but there was no way she was going back into the past.

"I already have a father," she said.

Juniors and seniors from Dalton still came and went at the Moreys' apartment like it was some kind of after-school program; but months after April's friend Robin had stopped living there, gone back to reassume her place inside her own much more opaque home, April still missed having her around. Which was ironic, she thought, because toward the end of Robin's time there, the girl's behavior had actually started to offend her a little, less on her own behalf than on her mother's. Robin brought drugs into the house, she used her key to sneak out at night and flirted with the doorman so he wouldn't bust her, she even brought guys into the downstairs half of the apartment in secret, and even though April had done just about all of these things herself at one time or another, her thought this time was: My mother takes you in and gives you every freedom and this is how you pay her back?

When it got around Dalton that she was essentially a runaway, and that her mom had beaten her (April herself may have been the one who let that slip), Robin's school persona had undergone a sea change. She went from a carefully cultivated normality to a kind of exalted strangeness. She started playing up to her new persona by mouthing off to teachers (who, like Cynthia, basically let her get away with anything), to other kids, to the people who worked at the Starbucks near school where they hung out during free periods. Friday afternoons sometimes she'd be so drunk she'd fall asleep in class. To others it might have looked like acting out but April saw it as pure performance. Only she knew how good the chances were that this supposedly damaged badass would end the day lying in her pajamas on April's couch with her head in April's mother's lap while the three of them watched movies and shared a bag of red licorice. But now that was over and Robin and she, though still friends, didn't share anything like that at all.

Once in a while, when Robin was still living there, when the two of them were up late and couldn't get to sleep, they used to lie side by side on April's bed with their laptops and go into these chat rooms that were obviously full of older guys. It was hilarious, because you could say absolutely anything to them with no repercussions because they could have been anywhere in the world, and so, for that matter, could the girls themselves. The guys were just glad you weren't cops, probably. They would masturbate pathetically while April and Robin, lying on their backs with their laptops on their stomachs, typed the most ridiculous porn and then tilted their screens toward each other to read, trying to outdo themselves until they both laughed so hard they hurt. It would always end with the loser asking to meet you. He didn't care where you were; he'd travel anywhere to meet Bobbi or Sammi or whatever name they'd given each other that night. They were safe because they lied about everything. Though it wasn't the same, April still did it sometimes by herself when she was bored.

Now on most weekends it was just the four of them. One Friday April's mother announced that they were all going to the Hamptons the next morning to look at houses. This was a bit of a surprise; though they visited people out there all the time, her dad in particular had resisted joining the general migration for years, saying that it never changed and there had to be some more interesting place in the world to see. They would spend the next several weekends on the East End looking if they needed to, Cynthia said, but the kids exchanged an eye-roll at that one because once their mother had made up her mind to purchase something, she usually got what she wanted in the first hour. Their dad drove them out to Amagansett in the morning and, sure

209

enough, maybe the third place they saw had their mom hooked. It was really nice, April had to admit – about a hundred feet from the beach – and just being out here at all would bring her closer to a lot of her friends on the weekends. Another home to fill up with stuff. Her mom would be in heaven for the next few months.

Back in the city a few nights later she was in her room alone writing to one of the deviants in the chat room and, when he asked her her name, she thoughtlessly typed April. She had a moment of total panic until she remembered that there were a million Aprils in the world. But after that night, whenever she would log on, amid all the lying and the fake porn-star affect there would be this one voice on the screen that would sometimes pop up and say, April? Is that you? His name, or so he said, was Neil, and he lived in Connecticut. Far from the city? she wrote, and he said, Not far at all. Why? He asked for a picture, and she said no way. He sent her one of himself. A little old, maybe, but not a complete gimp, that is if it was really a picture of him at all. There was no way to know, or rather there was only one way to know. That's all the Internet was, lies gone wild, and it only made you dizzy if you tried to sort it out.

He was really clever about it. He didn't say, Do you want to meet? Do you want to meet? He said, I will be at the Starbucks on 41st and Seventh at 2:00 PM on Wednesday June 18th. I really hope you'll be brave enough to be there too. You'll recognize me from the photo.

She didn't breathe a word to Robin about it, nor to anyone else. On the other hand, even though it was a secret, there was no question she was doing it for an audience, even if that audience was, in a strange way, made up. People would be in awe of her if they knew: even if they said they thought it was an incredibly stupid thing to do, they would be in awe of her fearlessness, whether it turned out there was something to fear there or not. She would be the badass, the damaged one. If, in a given activity, there was a next step to be taken – a taller cliff to dive from, purer drugs to try, something bigger and more difficult to steal – someone, at some point, was going to take that step, it was like a law of nature, and so let the record reflect that that someone was her.

She saw him right away, and he smiled at her, but she made a big show of getting a Venti Americano first before joining him. "I cannot believe," he said first thing, "how beautiful you are," and she realized then how the very same thing that might sound desperate and pathetic when you saw it in type on your laptop screen might be, in other, more direct circumstances, a very powerful thing to hear. She didn't give away any details, not her last name or the name of her school or her address, or what her parents did; he seemed to understand, though, what was difficult about all this for her, even to anticipate it sometimes, and so he helped her relax by talking a lot about himself. He was, he said, a private investor ("So's my dad," she wanted to say but didn't) who worked at home but had managed to make a lot of money – "not as much money as you have, though, I bet," he said. She wondered how he could tell that about her, how it showed. He'd grown up in Greenwich and had inherited his own house after his parents died. Living in your hometown was cool, but it was hard to meet new people. She really wanted to ask him how old he was – she couldn't tell the difference between thirty and fifty, it all looked the same to her at her age – but she was afraid of appearing too interested in him. She hardly moved except to lift the coffee to her mouth.

"So I won't ask you where you live, April," he said, smiling, like it was some kind of coyness that kept her silent, "but how did you get down here today? Subway?"

She'd taken a cab, but she nodded yes. Any lie, even a pointless one, seemed like a good idea. Then, clearing her throat first, she said, "You? Do you take the train in or what?"

His smile broadened. "I drove," he said. "It's really a short drive. You'd love my car. It's a convertible. But then if you get stuck in traffic or the rain or whatever, you put up the top and I've got a killer sound system in there – you just plug your iPod in and blast it. You've got an iPod, right? Everyone does these days. I'd even let you drive it if you wanted. Or maybe you're not old enough for a permit yet?"

She stared at him. She wondered why they weren't drawing more attention from everyone else in there, an older guy and a high-school girl in a Starbucks in the middle of the day. But maybe it didn't seem that unusual to people.

"Well," Neil said, "even if you aren't old enough to drive, that could be our little secret."

She realized then that, whatever outcome she had been pointing this toward – one-upping Robin, getting her mother's attention again, whatever subconscious wish some shrink would probably say she was acting on right now – it was all contingent on the idea that someone would see her, that she would get caught. The idea that she would not get caught had never really hit her before now.

"Do you want to go outside and see it?" Neil said.

In the end she got as far as the car itself but she didn't get inside it. He wasn't angry with her at all. He knew how to be patient. He wrote down his cell number for her, said he looked forward to seeing her again, and he gave her a long hug.

Nine days later, the phone rang at the Moreys; it was Robin, and she asked, for some reason, for Cynthia. Cynthia held the phone to her ear and didn't say anything for half a minute; her expression was perfectly flat. Then she hung up and stood and walked straight into her bedroom and shut the door, but when she brushed past April in the hallway she was already crying. Robin's mother had cut her wrists in the bathtub the night before last and was dead. Adam was out of the country on business, and Cynthia, disappointingly, wasn't even able to pull herself together and at least make a show of strength for Robin's sake; so April wound up being the one Morey to go to the funeral. The whole class went. They sat together in the back pews from which they could easily see Robin and her father up front, but what difference did that make, April realized – Robin was a million miles away. They might as well have been watching her on TV. The gulf between them was so terrible that they were all too scared to say or do anything to try to traverse it.

Robin wasn't back at Dalton in the fall, but the dean of the upper school said he was still hopeful she'd be back in January. April threw out Neil's cell number, and never went back into those chat rooms again, though it was not exactly reassuring to know that he was very likely still out there somewhere himself, calling out her real name.

Dalton had a fathers' basketball league that Adam still played in a couple of times a month. It wasn't your standard pickup game. You could tell which ones were the lawyers from the way they stopped the game for two minutes to argue every time somebody called a foul. And some of them, the financial guys especially, were competitive to the point where you'd be breaking up fights once in a while – not often, but often enough that years ago they'd voted not to let faculty members play, because the idea of losing your temper and throwing an elbow at your kid's history teacher was a little too fraught. The level of competition was obviously spotty, but there were some decent athletes in there. And as his own kids grew older and the fathers of new kinder-gartners joined the league, Adam even found himself on occasion guarded by guys who were actually his age. One night he went up for a rebound and got knocked off balance by someone's shoulder against his hip, and as he landed on one foot he could feel his knee come apart. He remembered standing up again, his arms over the shoulders of two of his teammates, and watching the lower half of his right leg swing from side to side like a pendulum. After three days in the hospital and a week working while bedridden at home, he made his return to Perini on crutches, locked into a kind of massive splint that ran from his ankle almost to his hip and kept his right leg as straight as a pencil at all times.

They mocked him about it relentlessly at the office, hiding his crutches, making pirate noises when he stumped by, emailing him videos of famous sports knee blowouts. It was a survival-of-the-fittest kind of humor, where they laughed at his weakness more or less in lieu of killing and eating him, but he didn't mind it, he would have expected no less. His great fear in the months that followed was getting fat. He set his recovery back a couple of weeks, or so his doctor told him, by trying to double up on the exercises his physical therapist had given him.

The analysts in the office were almost all guys in their twenties, and though they loved hanging out with Adam and were in awe of his excellence at what he did – he saw a company's future almost instantly, an instinct that his lack of a business-school degree elevated to the level of the mystical and heroic – they couldn't figure out what he was still doing there. Over and over they would sidle up to him, usually in some bar, and let him know that when the time came for him to bolt Perini and start his own fund, he could count on their total loyalty. To a man they felt that Sanford was too risk-averse and that if it weren't for Adam's presence there, his clients' money wouldn't be doing much better than it would in a savings account.

"Someday it will be the right time," was Adam's usual line. "I won't forget we talked."

The truth was that leaving and starting his own shop

215

would bring into play questions of proprietary information, and other forms of unwelcome attention. Part of what insulated him from suspicion is that he himself never appeared, to anyone outside Perini at least, to be the one making the decisions. No one looking at the books would have any way of knowing that Barry, at this point, did literally everything that Adam advised him to. Adam didn't want anyone looking too hard at some of the deals he'd been involved in over the last eight or ten years, because while they might not have known exactly what they were looking for, there was always a chance they would find it anyway. From his point of view the most promising scenario was for things to stay just as they were.

Perini was still at the same address, the same layout as ever. Sanford came in less and less but talked to Adam four or five times a day wherever he was. Adam had his own office but the rest of them worked in a kind of open-floor plan and he spent most of his time out there anyway. He hadn't been beaten on the office foosball table in four years.

Usually if Sanford wanted to make a big personal display about something, he took you out to lunch. But one morning in February, just about the time Adam was walking normally again, a few weeks after the removal of the accursed splint, the boss came in at ten – early, by his standards – called Adam into his office behind him, and told him that he had decided to retire, effective in two weeks, and to turn his executive partnership position in Perini Capital, minus only some deferred compensation, over to Adam.

"It's largely a tax thing," the old man said. "I had to redraw my will and there are certain things they advised me to make clear." But his eyes were watering when he said it.

Adam was profoundly unprepared. He never saw it coming; for all the old man's sentimentality, Adam never imagined he'd let go voluntarily of anything truly estimable without dying first.

"Barry," he said. "You don't need to do this now."

"What should I wait for?" Sanford said. "You have to look forward. This is a beautiful institution and I want it to continue."

"Don't you – I mean, I know you have children of your own?"

"They'll be provided for," he said, "according to their merits. This is a separate thing."

Adam fought down an alien panic. "This place could never exist without you," he said. "It's a monument to you."

"Well, that does remind me, there is one condition to all this, and that is that the fund keeps its name. Even after I'm gone. One does want to leave a legacy, you know. One does want to be remembered. Why that should make a damn bit of difference I'm not really sure, but it does. Anyway, that will be a provision of the ten thousand things we will both have to sign."

Adam wound up saying that it was something he would need to talk over with his wife. Sanford took that to mean that he was too moved to say yes on the spot and decorously

217

granted his request. Adam went home that night and in the margins of a newspaper added up all the money he had offshore. It was rare for him to write anything down; he kept accounts in his head. There was enough for them to live on for the rest of their lives; but what did that even mean? It was unsettling to think of money in terms other than those of growth, of how it might be used to make more money. Something about it smelled of death to him but he didn't know why.

He went in the next day and told Sanford that he was going to decline the offer. He felt it was premature, he said, because Sanford was still a titan in the world of private equity and would be for years to come; anyway, Perini Capital was literally unthinkable without its founder at the helm and he was sure everyone else in the office would say the same thing. Then he said he was going to use a week of vacation time. It didn't take even an hour for Sanford's hurt and astonishment to turn into anger. It was a strangely joyous sort of anger, though, as if he'd found out that his doctors had made some terrible diagnostic error and in fact he was going to live forever. He stormed out without a word to anyone at about three o'clock and when the others turned to Adam to ask what the fuck was going on between the two of them, he said, in a tone that terrified them, that it was nothing for them to worry about.

He probably should have gone to Anguilla right away, but instead, that night at dinner, he told Jonas and April that he was taking them out of school for a week so they could all go to London. They looked at him like he was nuts, as did Cynthia, but they had always been raised to respect spontaneity and it was much too good an offer to turn down. On short notice, in the high season, everything was outrageously expensive, but even though they kept referring to that, it didn't really mean anything to them. They found a place in Mayfair and when April found out a former school friend of hers was on a modeling job in Surrey, Adam took them all to Battersea and chartered a helicopter to take them out there for a visit.

The model friend wound up asking April and Jonas if they wanted to come with her to see The Strokes that night at Hammersmith Palais; she was meeting some people there, and she herself was so freakishly hot that the mere prospect of her friends was enough to overcome Jonas's disdain for the band. Cynthia and Adam went out to dinner in Kensington and had two bottles of wine. There he told her that a few days ago Sanford had offered to retire and basically bequeath him the whole fund, but that he had turned the offer down. "Jesus," Cynthia said. "He must have been crushed. What did he say when you told him?"

Instead of answering that question, Adam said, "I was worried you'd be disappointed in me," and he was surprised to feel a little catch in his throat when he said it.

She took his hand, which was a pretty good indicator that she was drunk. "Listen," she said. "You're a fucking genius. Every single move you've made has worked out for us. Look where we are. Everything has happened for us just the way you said it would. What kind of an idiot would I have to be to second-guess you?"

He held her fingers to his lips and closed his eyes. Other diners were starting to turn in their direction.

"Go ahead and stare," Cynthia said softly, without taking her eyes off him. "Fucking old skanks wish they were me."

By their last night, Adam was saying to Cynthia that they ought to just buy the flat they were staying in so they could come and go as they pleased. "I had a good year," he said. She looked at him as if he were a little mad, but then she caught something exciting in his eyes and threw up her hands and said, "Why not?" That was it: everything was open to them. What was life's object if not that? Adam knew on some level that he had to get as much money out of those Anguillian accounts as possible and shut them down, but more than that he wanted to just spend it all on the three of them, as orgiastically as possible, challenge his family to come up with desires they hadn't even thought of yet and then make those desires real. There was, after all, no life but this life. The days were swallowed up behind you. He'd had a little too much gin. He wanted to be more like Sanford, actually, and just give it all away: he wanted to self-immolate in the name of the love he felt for his wife and children, a love for which no conventional outlet was close to sufficient.

By the time they returned to New York he'd come down a little bit. He went back in to work on Monday morning, and before he had his coat off Sanford called him into his office and fired him. It was not a cordial scene. "You haven't looked this young in years," Adam told him. Sanford gave him until nine-fifteen to clean out his desk. "I don't know what you're planning," Sanford said, trembling, "but I will find out. You will learn the hard way that you cannot fuck with me. I made you." Which was funny not just in the sense that Adam had been fucking with him for years with great success but also because the elaborate plan Sanford believed was behind this decision – a plan to start his own fund, a plan to force him out of this one, whatever – didn't exist, not in any form. Adam had no clue what came next.

When he got back home it was still only about eleven o'clock in the morning and no one else was in the apartment. He sat in the media room and watched TV, scrolling through the channels without stopping. He'd been careful for so long that he felt like doing something especially stupid, something that would finish him off once and for all. But he didn't. He reminded himself that there were other people involved, people he was bound to protect. Sanford was angry enough to do anything, to look anywhere. He went to the bedroom closet and got the disposable cell phone out of its hiding place inside one of his sneakers.

"I thought we said never during business hours," Devon said.

"It's over," Adam said. "We have to shut it down."

"What?"

"It's over starting now. Okay? Nothing for you to worry about."

"Nothing for me to *worry* about?" he said, in a kind of strangled whisper. "What the fuck are you talking about? Has somebody found out?"

There was something in his voice. It should have been

simple, Adam thought – yesterday is done, it never happened, tomorrow you start over – but he could hear the give in Devon's voice and knew that his thoughts were turning in a bad direction.

"Listen to me," Adam said. "It's just time. Nothing has happened. No one knows anything. We will be fine. And I will take care of you. I will not forget what you and I have put on the line for each other. Understand? Now, you will not hear from me for a while, maybe a long while, but that's just about being cautious. You have my word that I will not leave you hanging. Our future is still together. We could take each other down, but it's way preferable for neither of us to go down at all. Preferable and honorable. We've done something amazing together. I would never, ever give you up for any reason. And I know that I can count on your loyalty too. Right?"

Even in the silence that wasn't silence – there was too much noise in the background, phones beeping and keyboards clicking and salesmen screaming and purring – Adam could hear him coming around.

"Right," Devon said, to himself as much as to Adam. "No snitching. If you say we'll be fine, we'll be fine."

"We will be better than fine. The future is brilliant and I promise you you have a place in it. I won't leave you hanging. In the meantime get rid of the phone, get rid of everything. Just to be safe. Just don't look back and when the time is right you will hear from me again. Okay? Eyes forward. Trust me."

So that was taken care of, he thought. Still, though he

had always known how to act boldly in the moment, as the day passed in idleness the idea of his own past opened up in front of him as something threatening and, amazingly, ineradicable. You couldn't undo it, it didn't belong to you anymore, and yet it was still there. This was a new one on him. It was just as real – more real, in fact, as each day of unaccustomed inaction went by – as the present, but in another sense it was inviolate, behind glass, where even if you wanted to get rid of it you could not.

He had three different job offers in the first week, as word spread of his firing, but he declined all three and the offers stopped coming, no doubt because people assumed, as Sanford did, that Adam had some plan that had yet to be revealed. He didn't want to go to work for anyone else. Yet the solitude of sitting at home – even in his bright, high-ceilinged home office, the sky over Central Park like a frame around his computer monitor – wasn't good for him either. Eventually he figured out that there was one thing that did return him at least temporarily to himself, and that was risk. He took flyers in the market on companies that might turn out to be way undervalued and then watched with a gambler's intensity to see whether his instincts were correct. There was one memorable afternoon when Cyn went off to a Children's Aid Society board meeting and by the time she returned and said "How was your day?" he had lost two hundred and thirty thousand dollars of their own money. It was all their own money now. He told her he'd been to the gym, and that was answer enough for her. He felt, as he hadn't in years, what it was to be loved. He had a strong intuition that he would die without her, that just as any slacking off in his workout routine would surely lead to a rapid and shocking physical decline, so would time spent outside the field of her total belief in him eventually unmoor him from his status as a civilized man.

He saw that *Barron's* had a strong sell recommendation on a pharmaceutical stock called Amity. He'd long thought *Barron's* fatally unimaginative and decided it would be fun to prove them wrong. He bought ten thousand shares, and a week later sold them again at a net loss of four hundred and eight thousand dollars.

Cynthia had no idea about any of this, and if she had, her concern would have been disproportionate because she had no idea how much money Adam had managed to put away in accounts she knew nothing about. He couldn't think of a way to justify a solo trip to Anguilla when spring break was less than a month away and so he just had to bite the bullet and wait. He did float the idea that maybe this would be their last trip. He said he was bored with it and had heard about other places he wanted to try, maybe the South Pacific. She believed him. The whole scheme, he reminded himself, had been for her benefit, and in fact it had worked out just the way he hoped it would: he had seen her stuck and unhappy and the thought of it had been too much for him; he had an image of the life he was going to make for all of them and it wasn't coming fast enough and so he had done what he'd had to do to speed things up, to get them all intact to that place of limitlessness that she so deserved and that he had always had faith they would occupy. It wasn't about being rich per se. It was about living a big life, a life that was larger than life. Money was just the instrument. He thought about calling someone at Perini just to ask what was new, like say a visit from the SEC, but he decided that was a bad idea.

It was hard, some days, to keep himself stimulated. He shorted Wisconsin Cryogenics International, his old stomping ground, thinking that maybe irony would protect him now. Guy Farbar was long gone: the deal Adam had put together for him had made him a millionaire many times over but then he was fired by his own board for impregnating his secretary. The stock started soaring as soon as Adam picked it up, almost as if it had been waiting for him. He told himself that taking the loss was a smart move in this case because if anyone was looking into his past then this kind of miscalculation was bound to throw them off the trail.

Cynthia said she had something important to talk to him about. After the kids were home and fed and had disappeared downstairs for the evening, she came into his office and sat across the desk from him. Incredibly, what she wanted to discuss was his fortieth birthday – something that was completely off his radar, not because he was in any sort of denial about it but because he had turned forty ten months ago.

"We didn't do enough to celebrate," she said, "but that's okay, it's not too late, it's technically still the Jubilee Year. I want us to go somewhere. Somewhere amazing, somewhere we've never been. I thought about surprising you, but I decided that what I really want is for you to surprise me. Where would you go if you could just go anywhere?"

She was so excited. She looked older than she used to, that was true, and the unfairness of that made him a little sad. He opened his mouth to speak but he felt the catch in his throat and had to close it again. He smiled apologetically. He hoped she'd figure he was too choked up by her thoughtfulness to speak. He hoped she'd figure he was taking a moment to think about it, about where he would go if he could go anywhere. Or that he was sitting there thinking about how much he loved her.

But he watched her get up and shut his office door. "What's going on?" she said.

He told her everything. Even as he was talking he couldn't make himself stop trying to think of some way out of saying it, some way to keep her in the dark. Her eyes got very big. When he'd said everything he could think of to say, she started to cry.

"Are they going to find out?" she said. "Are they going to arrest you or something?"

He said that a lot of people liked him on Wall Street and so if someone were looking into him, someone from the SEC or the US Attorney's office or even just some investigator hired by Sanford, he had to believe he would have heard something about it by now. But it was a possibility, and maybe it would always be. And she should know that if he was ever even charged with anything, their powers were very broad. They might arrest him or they might just seize the money, which in some ways was worse, because

226

they could seize everything they figured the money might have been spent on, including the apartment in which all four of them were sitting right now. She shook her head. "I don't give a shit about the money," she said.

"You don't?"

"I don't. I want to ask you something else. It might seem off topic. Have you ever been unfaithful to me?"

And the amazing part was that he understood right away how she had gotten there, how it was part of what they were discussing. He stood up from his chair but kept the desk between them. "No," he said as gravely as he could. His heart was beating dangerously hard; he put his hand on it. "I never have, and I never would. If I lose you, it's all over for me. I don't care if they take everything else away. I honestly don't."

She walked around his desk and fit herself against him with her arms around his neck. He was shaking.

"Thank you for not telling me," she said. "All this time, I mean. What a burden that must have been for you. I know why you did it. I know you did it for us. I'm fucking proud of you, if you want to know the truth. You are a man, Adam. You are a man among men. Let them come after us. They can't touch us."

They stood like that until they were in the dark. He felt invincible, like a martyr, like a holy warrior. Why hadn't he understood it before now? No wrong for him but whatever was wrong in her eyes.

4

THERE WAS THIS CAFETERIA-STYLE restaurant on South Woodlawn called Mandel's; in the window underneath the awning hung a small square neon sign that read, see your food! Jonas couldn't get over it. Like only a sucker would agree to pay for food without seeing it first. He added it to a sort of honor roll he kept in his head of ill-advised, unappetizing restaurant names: Hot and Crusty, Something Fishy, A Taste of Greece, a Chinese restaurant he'd once seen from a moving car called Lung Fat, though he wasn't sure that counted because it was obviously more a translation issue than a case of simple cluelessness. It was a list kept for his own amusement, though whenever he found a new one he couldn't help mentioning it to Nikki, who understood why Lung Fat was funny but not why it was still just as funny the twentieth time you said it. He just had this strange, campy affection for people and places that tried hard to sell themselves but couldn't get it right. He even ate at Mandel's a few times during his first exam week, and thereafter as a kind of exam-week tradition, wanting to do his part to keep them going despite their entrepreneurial tin ear. The food wasn't terrible. Filling, for damn sure. And you did, in fact, get to see it there on the steam table before you ordered it.

Mandel's was dirt cheap and near campus and so it wasn't like other UChicago students didn't eat there too, but Jonas never told any of his friends about it or invited anyone along with him because he thought it would probably come off as slumming, even though it wasn't. As if he should have been eating at Morton's every night, as an undergraduate, just because he could afford to. People had weird ideas about money. Like not spending it was condescending somehow. Like being rich meant acting rich, whatever that entailed, and if you didn't live the way you could live every moment of the day, you were displaying a kind of reverse pretension. Or trying to pass as normal when you weren't. He wasn't trying to pass as anything. It was probably true that he'd been naïve about the degree to which he could reinvent himself by leaving home and going away to school. It wasn't like he'd changed his name or anything. People started to figure out who he was within about the first week; after that, it wasn't so much that they treated him differently, it was that they made a great point of not treating him differently. Occasionally someone would want to pick some sort of

Marxist fight with him, but it didn't interest him because he wasn't even involved enough to feel guilty about it. He and his father had never in their lives had one single conversation about, say, derivatives. It was unthinkable. No one could help what they were born into. You just had to start from zero and not let it determine who you were.

He lived off campus, but not in any great splendor or anything. A lot of undergrads lived off campus, just because the on-campus options were so dismal. When Nikki's parents came to see the place for the first time, you could tell they were a little puzzled that it wasn't nicer. Kind of mercenary of them, he mused later – out loud, unfortunately; he and Nikki had a fight over that remark that nearly undid the whole arrangement. She was four years older than Jonas – already in grad school – and he supposed that in the absence of any obvious gold-digging motive, her folks couldn't figure out what she saw in him. It was pretty disgusting, actually. Not least because they were so pleased to refer to themselves as a couple of old hippies.

He and Nikki had met at the Art Institute, though it wasn't quite as cute as it sounded, since Jonas was there on a field trip. Actually, it was more like an anti-field trip, for a course on Art Brut taught by Lawrence Agnew, a famously charismatic lunatic at UChicago whose intensity Jonas at that point still considered mostly laughable, but with whom he'd since taken three other courses – every undergraduate course Agnew offered. Nikki was a TA in that Art Brut course; he'd seen her before, in the darkened lecture hall where Agnew worked himself into a frenzy over slide projections (the informal record between slide changes was thirty-two minutes), but he'd never spoken to her until that day. She was the subject of a lot of male speculation in that class, with a face made up of perfectly harmonized eccentricities: freckles, an overbite, a mannish brow, long black hair that was never held back in any way, so that whenever she leaned forward to take a note, her face disappeared from view. That day at the Institute was freezing, and her strategy in response was to wear two sweaters and three shirts and a gigantic scarf and no coat. Jonas knew it was fashion at work rather than modesty but still liked to imagine the magnificence of the body that had to be buried under so many layers in order for her to be taken seriously and not incite a museum or lecture hall full of undergraduate boys. Agnew, who was only about five feet six, was lecturing invisibly from the center of a circle of about forty students, in front of a roomful of Monets.

"Was this shit *ever* good?" Agnew said. Not for him the reverent whisper one usually slipped into in museum galleries; where he went, the dynamics of the lecture hall went with him. "Well, it had to have something going on, because believe it or not, Monet offended people mightily in his day, at least for five minutes or so, but believe me, offending people even for five minutes is pretty damn hard to do. Harder today than it was then, but still. They literally wouldn't let his work *into* the museum. And now if you go over to the gift shop which is the raison d'être of ridiculous graveyards like this one, his work is on every desk calendar and coffee mug and golf-club-head cover you see. So what is the lesson there? I'll give you a hint: it's not a lesson about Monet. It's a lesson about what happens to the new in this world."

Jonas saw Nikki standing by herself on the edge of the circle, holding a notebook but not writing in it; from where she was positioned, she could see through the doorway to the next gallery, and something in there had caught her eye. Without giving it enough thought to lose his nerve, he walked quietly over to where she stood and looked straight over her shoulder, his face quite close to her hair, to see what she saw. It was a little girl, maybe three or four, who had somehow slipped under the rope and was reaching out with her fingertips toward one of the Seurats. She didn't touch it, though she was close enough. Some part of her was sensing the trouble she would get into. She was torturing herself. Her hand was held out in front of her in a position almost as if she were painting the picture. Jonas could feel Nikki holding her breath. Finally the girl's mother, or teacher, or nanny, grabbed her by the collar of her coat and yanked her back outside the ropes. Far from being upset, the little girl looked almost relieved. Jonas, who'd had a fair amount of success with women in his young life even though he never really knew what to say, felt the touch of inspiration.

"I bet that was you," he said. Startled, Nikki turned around, and then fought unsuccessfully to keep the smile off her face before finally turning back toward the invisible Agnew and pretending she had been listening to him all along.

"The Impressionists were outsiders," Agnew said, "but they wanted in. They wanted in more than anything. This is what drove Dubuffet crazy, that kind of aspiration. He didn't want the self-conscious new, the ambitious new. He wanted the untouched, the uninfluenced. He wanted to go back. He wanted the outsider who didn't care – who didn't even *know* – that he was an outsider. Was this a vain hope? In his own case, probably. But art history is in a lot of ways the history of failure. It takes a genius to find something truly worth failing at."

She appeared to be paying attention, but she did not move away from Jonas, not even when the group shuffled into the next gallery and Agnew began laying into Picasso. There were probably fifteen fewer students in the group than they'd started out with; nobody cared about that, though – this wasn't high school, you could cut whatever you felt like cutting, it was presumed to be your loss. Other than the Art Brut class, it was mostly old people in the Institute on a Tuesday morning. They glared menacingly at the point from which Agnew's heedlessly loud opinions seemed to emanate, but they couldn't make eye contact with him, because he was too short.

The Institute had a few Dubuffets, and they went and stared dutifully at them. Jonas didn't find them all that convincing, but that was the really electric thing about this class: the professor was so rough on the defenseless dead artists that you wound up feeling a little sorry for them and would look more actively for some aspect of their work to like. "You can feel the effort in his effortlessness," Agnew said, "the technique in the absence of technique. And though he's trying to chasten or alienate or ignore his audience, he still *has* an audience, which is to say an anticipated reaction, and that makes all the difference. You cannot, as the expression goes, get the toothpaste back into the tube. That state of pristine ignorance Dubuffet wants to go back to? Forget it, you can never go back to it. But does that mean it doesn't exist?"

They spent ten minutes max in the room full of Dubuffets, and then came the moment that turned Jonas from a student into an acolyte. "Now follow me," Agnew said, and he walked back through the museum the way they had come, into the entrance gallery, and, incredibly, out the front door onto the sidewalk. The group of students and TAs, now down to about twenty in total, followed him wide-eyed into the freezing sunshine and instead of turning left toward their chartered bus, followed Agnew to the right, in the direction of a group of artists who sold their work to tourists from card tables on the sidewalk. Mostly it was cheaply framed photos or pen-and-ink sketches of Chicago landmarks, including the Institute itself. There were some Seurat knockoffs that were pretty good too. Agnew stopped in front of one particular table where a young man sat drawing on a sketch pad held down on his crossed knees. A group of pages evidently ripped from that pad was held face down on the table by a rock; their frayed edges rustled in the breeze off the lake. Agnew leaned over and rapped with his knuckles on the table; the artist looked up at him, nodded just slightly in recognition, and went back to his drawing.

"Ladies and gentlemen," Agnew said, "this is Martin Strauss. Martin lives on the South Side with his parents, and he comes here every day unless it's raining."

Strauss stopped drawing, but not at the mention of his name. He looked at the pad in front of him for no more than a second or two, tore the page off from the spiral binding, lifted the rock, put the page face down on top of the pile, and placed the rock on top again.

"Though Martin has no particular notion of privacy," Agnew said, "I will honor his privacy by not discussing the specific ways in which he has been diagnosed by society as outside its norms. As a human being, we have marginalized him, but as an artist, he has no sense of himself as an outsider, or an insider for that matter, because he has no sense of what these categories mean. He has no sense of an audience at all, critical or otherwise. He simply needs to express something. Compulsion without ambition. Not only can this not be faked, it cannot be willed either. He could not stop what he is doing, or change it, or tailor it to someone else's expectations, if he wanted to. If you are enticed by the Art Brut ideal, you have to be willing to follow it where it takes you. This is not as simple as it may sound."

By now Jonas had made his way to the front of the pack and could see the sketches, which someone – Strauss's mother? – had stuck in cardboard matte frames and wrapped in cellophane to protect them from the elements, that were pinned to an easel behind Strauss's card table. They were fantastically detailed black–and–white cityscapes, but the city was not Chicago. Every inch of every sheet was filled. The details, particularly the repetitive arcs of imaginary Art Deco-style masonry on the buildings, were so hypnotic that Jonas felt, before he figured out, what was missing from each picture as a whole: a sense of perspective. There was no shade or depth to it, no vanishing point of the sort even a grade-school art class would have taught him. But it wasn't just some technique that Strauss didn't know. It wasn't a picture *of* something, Jonas realized with a kind of shiver. It was just a picture.

Raindrops started to fall. "Nikki?" Jonas heard Agnew say, and he looked up. "How much time?"

Nikki pushed up her many sleeves to look at her watch. "None," she said.

"Okay then," said Agnew, "take a good look, everyone, and then meet back at the bus, please, in five minutes." Nearly everyone headed back to the bus immediately. Other than a haircut that looked as if maybe he had done it himself in front of a mirror, and a somewhat intimidating focus, nothing about Strauss appeared all that unusual. Jonas saw Agnew fishing for his wallet in his jacket pocket. He took out a twenty and put it in a shoebox full of pens that sat on the card table not far from Strauss's elbow. Then he lifted the rock, took the entire sheaf of face-down drawings without looking at them, and headed back to the bus. Strauss didn't even raise his head; he just kept working.

On the bus Jonas realized that since Nikki was a TA she must already have her campus email somewhere; when he got back to his apartment he found it on the syllabus and emailed her to ask her out. Almost twenty-four hours later

– which meant either a certain reluctance to cross that boundary or just that she didn't check her email that often – she wrote back yes. It didn't take too long before someone spotted them having lunch together somewhere, and then it was all over campus like wildfire. Undergrads who dated TAs were like rock stars, at least if the TA was as beautiful as Nikki was. It made things awkward for her in Agnew's class, all those bold eyes on her, but by then the semester was nearly over anyway.

As the spring wound down, and the coffee shops and libraries emptied, and station wagons full of sagging boxes and laundry bags started crawling around campus, Jonas, who was falling in love a little with Nikki, or at least thought he might be, found himself resisting the idea of going back to New York that summer at all. For what? Everyone he knew would be somewhere else anyway, and if he went out to Amagansett instead, where he'd find a decent sampling of them, there was nothing there but decadence and narcissism, drugs and money and entitlement and waiting petulantly for the night. Worst of all was when people like his mother referred to it as "the country," as in, "We can't see you Friday night, we're driving out to the country." It wasn't the fucking country. It was a game preserve for rich people. But no one would acknowledge that: they all wanted to talk about this great farmstand they'd found, or how the guy who fixed their gutters came from an old whaling family. As for his parents, Jonas had nothing against seeing them, but the reality was that he probably wouldn't see them that much anyway: ever since they'd set up the foundation, the seam between the business day and the rest of their time had become pretty much undetectable. Evenings and weekends were always taken up with some kind of dinner or fundraiser or ribbon cutting or whatever. Which, you know, bully for them. He just didn't want it to turn into another summer where he watched movies all day. That was for kids; and now he had a kind of life within his reach that promised something more adult and substantial, while his peers were still mired in the habits of adolescence, mastering video games and illegally downloading movies and trying to figure out where drunk women were likely to congregate.

What he would really have liked, actually, was to keep studying. One of the things he envied about Nikki was that while he was still fulfilling various diploma requirements, she had worked hard to narrow her interests down to the point where she got to spend her whole day thinking about one thing. She'd have her master's by the end of the upcoming year, and she was already gathering herself, psychologically at least, for the big push of her doctoral thesis, which would be about Donald Judd. During evenings spent in restaurants – nicer ones, now that school was out and Nikki was less uptight about being seen and he was more eager to impress her – Jonas learned more about boxes than he ever would have thought possible. It could get pretty rarefied, to the point of absurdity sometimes, but that only made it more admirable, like she was some sort of nun with no choice but to accept her own estrangement from the world. Also he knew that her excitement – about the art, about her work on it, about the future that work might bring – would generalize into an excitement that she would want to work off sexually once they got back home. When she really got going she would start telling him what to do to her, which aroused him almost past the point where he could stand it. He didn't know it was possible to feel so well suited to another person, no matter how odd a match they might have looked like to others. The future, as his dad liked to say, was now.

Nikki had a research fellowship with Agnew that defrayed the cost of her tuition, and the terms of that fellowship, which were basically those of Agnew's cheerfully expressed but iron whims, were what kept her in Chicago over the summer. Her lease, though, like a lot of student leases, ran only through June. One morning at his place Jonas inexpertly scrambled some eggs and, as he watched her eat them in the summertime light with his bedsheet wrapped around her shoulders, he suggested, a little less blithely than he meant to, that she should move in with him.

He tried to hold on to this feeling of precocious maturity when his mother took the news that he wasn't coming home that summer rather harder than he'd expected. She even sounded like she might have been crying a little bit. Jonas wound up agreeing to let her send the jet for him so he could at least spend a week at home. It was a little jarring to be reminded how much bigger the townhouse was than the apartment where he and Nikki now chose to live. He said he was tired of going out so he and his mother sat at the dining-room table and the cook, whom Jonas hadn't met before, brought them skate in a kind of clam broth that was probably the best meal he'd had in a year. "Home cooking," he said, and Cynthia laughed. There was something different about her appearance. At first he thought maybe she'd had some work done, but it wasn't anything as radical as that. Probably just Botox or whatever was the equivalent du jour. He didn't know why she thought she needed it, but he didn't say so. She liked to say that he could talk about anything with her, but it was an expression of his love for her that he would treat a subject like growing older as off-limits. She had a lot of questions for him about Nikki, which Jonas did his best to answer without answering.

His father came in when they were eating dessert. "Look, darling, it's our son, home from college," she said, as she'd been saying all week every time Adam walked into a room. "You saw the OneWorld Health people today?"

"I did. For about two minutes. I really prefer it when they don't try to be charming, actually. They're like, we're busy saving lives around here, just leave the money on the table and let us get back to it."

"Really," she said, standing up and putting her arms around him. "Personally I'm a sucker for a well-planned charm offensive." They kissed.

"Nick and Nora up in here," Jonas said.

April wasn't home; she was spending the week out at the beach. Not surprising. Her boredom threshold was very low these days. He noticed that his mother would get a call on the cell every evening that wasn't from April but seemed to be about her. Maybe a driver or one of the other

Amagansett staff charged with making sure that his sister wasn't letting anything get out of hand. He was disappointed to miss her; but it didn't last long, because the week after he got back to Chicago she called and surprised him with the news that she was coming out there to visit.

He didn't meet her at the airport – it hadn't been that long since they'd seen each other, Christmas probably, though it felt like longer than that – but he waited by the window with a cup of coffee for her car to arrive. He'd called the service himself and given the driver his address, so he didn't have to worry that she wouldn't be able to find the place; but there was an element of uncertainty that accompanied April whenever other agendas, like airline schedules, intersected with hers. It was not unheard of for her to express her disdain for flying commercial by skipping the flight entirely in favor of another few hours in the first-class lounge. Jonas and their parents actually preferred it when she went to the lounges, though, not because they wanted to encourage her to fly drunk but because at least there were paid employees there who might help ensure that April actually boarded the plane.

When the town car rolled to a stop in front of their building's awning a few minutes later, he was a little shocked at how she looked: almost junkie-skinny, though her eyes and her skin were pretty clear and he had warned himself not to exaggerate or over-react. She set down her bag and you could tell right away, from the gimlet eye she passed around the apartment, what she was thinking.

"Be it ever so humble," he said.

241

April shrugged. "Whatever you're into, Gandhi," she said. "So where's the wife?"

Jonas scowled at her as Nikki emerged from the kitchen. Nikki was blushing and her voice was pitched unnaturally high; in truth she was a little intimidated by the image of Jonas's family and though she had professed to look forward to April's visit, at the last moment she seemed to have lost her nerve. She carried April's bag into the study that had been temporarily cleaned out to serve as a guest room. When she returned, she apologized for having to leave but she had a departmental conference with Agnew that started in half an hour. Jonas didn't recall her having mentioned it before. He and April watched the door close behind her.

"I am not at all sure," April said, "that chick likes me."

"I think," said Jonas, on whom this was just dawning, "she's a little anxious that you not get the wrong idea about her."

"What idea is that?"

"About why she's dating me."

"Ah. Well," April said, leaping onto the couch, "it's true that she's a little young to be doing the cougar thing. Also a little hot for you. Nerd–hot, I mean. No offense."

"You've never really understood that expression," Jonas said.

"But hey, one look around this garret is enough to quell any suspicions that she's a gold digger. Or else she's into the long con. I'll sit her down and ask her what her intentions are when she comes back."

She needed a nap, she said, and then she wanted to go exploring, which he knew meant shopping; they made a plan whereby he would meet her at Roberto Cavalli at six and then take her to Frontera Grill for dinner. It was the trendiest place he could think of and he imagined Nikki might even be pleased about that but instead she texted him to say that she was feeling sick and would skip it.

"Maybe she's afraid I'll carry her over to the Dark Side," April said.

"The dark side of what?"

She shrugged. "The dark side where people have fun and act their age. I've never in my life seen a chick as ready to get married as that one is."

"You're wrong," Jonas said, blushing. "You really think she'd be dating a junior in college if she was looking for a husband?"

"Well, not your average junior. But a forty-year-old junior like yourself? Perfect. She's in on the ground floor." She saw the look of grim defensiveness on his face and laughed. "Dude, you remain an enigma to me. For instance that apartment. What is up with that?"

"What do you mean?"

She put her drink down disgustedly but still carefully. "Come on," she said. "Knock it off. You know what I mean."

She was really the only one he could talk about this with, but somehow that only made him more uncomfortable talking about it. "Why is it necessary," he said, "to make a show of it? It's not like I've taken a vow of poverty. I live a lot better than most of my friends here do. Just because I have the means to live in some penthouse, does that mean I should do it?"

"Well, yeah, it does mean that, if the alternative is pretending, even to someone you're supposedly in love with, that you're somebody you're not. What, you don't think she would like it? Don't kid yourself."

"Mom and Dad's money," he said, "is not who I am."

"Except why shouldn't it be? In the sense that you are one of a handful of people to whom certain experiences are open, and not taking advantage of that isn't noble, it's just a pose. And anyway, who are you being modest for? Who is impressed by you? It's crazy. For instance, you're into art now, I understand. Why don't I see any art hanging on the walls at your place? Can't afford it?"

"Excuse me," he said, "if I'm trying to live a life that's more authentic than just buying whatever catches my eye, hanging out in clubs and getting high and showing up on Page Six."

"Please, let's not exaggerate, I have never been on Page Six. But that's your problem, right there, what you said. Who told you you were inauthentic? Where do you think this authenticity is waiting to be found, exactly?"

He rolled his eyes and said nothing.

"So come out with me tonight. Fuck eight hours of sleep for once in your life. Life has given you the gift of possibility, and the real arrogance is wasting it so that you can condescend to everyone else by calling them authentic. Do you even know where people go out in this so-called city?"

"No," he said, "actually, I don't. I have no idea. Can we talk about something else, please? How do Mom and Dad seem to you?"

She sighed; then she reached across the table and took his unfinished martini. "Mom is all up in my shit, as usual," she said. "To be honest, they seem really happy with the whole Robin Hood gig they have going. Totally uninhibited about it. Let me tell you, there are two people with no guilt. None. I don't know where you got it from, is my point. Maybe Dad is not your real father. Maybe Mom was having an affair with Che Guevara or something." She pushed some food around on her plate. "Who eats dinner this early?" she said.

She was supposed to stay a week, but the next morning she was on the cell with friends in New York trying unsuccessfully to get them to come to Chicago and hang out with her, and that night she called their mother for the jet and flew home. She was very friendly and apologetic about it, and she and Nikki were actually quite sweet with each other by the time it was all over. The next morning, a delivery van buzzed them from downstairs: it turned out that before she left, April had gone to a gallery on Michigan Avenue and bought them a Picasso. It was a simple sketch of a bull's head; when Nikki was out of earshot, Jonas idly asked one of the delivery guys if he had a receipt for it, and the amount on the receipt was sixteen thousand dollars. When they were alone again, Jonas hammered a nail into the wall above their couch and they hung the frame there and gazed at it. Nikki shook her head. "I don't get it," she said. "I really thought she hated me."

The research Nikki was doing for Agnew lost what little structure it had when summer came; by the end of August their scheduled conferences in his office had devolved into meetings for lunch or coffee or even just a standing invitation to show up at his apartment on South Blackstone and have a glass of wine. It was all well above board, though; Agnew was one of the few cult professors who had no reputation for trying to get over on his grad students, and in any case Nikki never once knocked on his apartment door without finding at least two or three others, usually more – grad students, faculty colleagues, friends of mysterious art-world provenance – already lounging inside. Jonas was curious about these salons but also too self-conscious about his own youth and ignorance to want to go with her. But before long Agnew himself made a point of asking Nikki where her boyfriend – "child bride", actually, was the expression he used – spent these afternoons and evenings while his paramour drank cheap wine and talked about art. Surely not home alone? When the teasing got to be too much for her, Nikki asked Jonas again if he would please reconsider, just for her sake, and he said yes.

The apartment itself was scruffy but large with, as Agnew said, a great view of the lake if you were willing to let someone hang you out the living-room window by your ankles. Nikki came bearing a CD full of images Agnew needed to copy for one reason or another and so the two of them went straight into his study. Jonas felt like people were smirking at him a little bit and so rather than try to horn in on a conversation he acted as if he were in a museum, touring the perimeter of each room, on whose walls hung dozens of small-scale artworks in cheap stationery-store frames. He didn't recognize any of it. Many of the drawings and paintings (anyone who'd taken Agnew's Intro to Seeing knew his dismissive views on photography) were unsigned. In the kitchen, an odorous thicket of old wine bottles and impromptu ashtrays, Jonas got to staring at one particular sketch, framed so that the frayed edge from the spiral notebook binding was still visible, of some kind of industrial landscape that kept yielding details that made less and less sense. The sky was filled with numbers, written very carefully as if in a sequence. Just a few feet from the walls of a mysterious factory or plant – which had no doors or windows, only smokestacks – there was a scaled-down forest about the size of a traffic island, with a lake or pond in it in which birds flew underwater.

"Recognize it?" a voice said; Jonas turned, embarrassed by how close his face was to the drawing itself, and saw Agnew. And though he hadn't recognized anything until that moment, now he did.

"It's the guy from outside the Institute," he said.

Agnew clapped him on the shoulder. "Good eye," he said. "Actually, I have to ask you not to mention to any of your art-world friends that you saw this here. I am in serious Dutch with Mr. Strauss's gallery over having this piece."

"I have no art-world friends," Jonas said. "What do you mean, his gallery? He has a gallery?"

Agnew explained to him, while opening another bottle of wine, that Martin Strauss, far from being Agnew's secret, was actually quite a name in outsider-art circles, a phrase that was accompanied by a roll of Agnew's eyes. Strauss was showing in New York and in Miami; though he was somewhere in his thirties, money from the sales of his work, which Agnew guessed might have been as much as thirty or forty thousand dollars a year, went straight to his elderly parents in their capacity as his guardians. Strauss himself had certain needs that had to be met but beyond that he had no use for the money at all. Agnew technically had given him money in exchange for this drawing – "I give him something every time I see him" – but the gallery owner considered this thievery because, he said, the artist had no way of properly valuing his own work. "You can imagine," Agnew said, "how provocative I find that idea. So I torture this guy a little by maintaining the friendship with his client, even though I am, I suppose, legally speaking, in the wrong."

Jonas was conscious that he was actually hunched over a little in order not to look down on his host. So-called outsider art, Agnew went on, was nowadays pretty much the sole focus of his own research, and for that matter of his interest in art, period. "And not 'outsider' as in 'self-taught', either," he said. "That's one of the many problems with the influx of people like this schmuck with his gallery – in an effort to maximize their own exploitation, they broaden the definition until it becomes meaningless. So no, none of that condescending Grandma Moses folk-art bullshit. I'm interested only in the artistic expression of those whose mental or psychological circumstances lie outside what society has defined as acceptable."

"The insane?" Jonas asked.

Agnew frowned. "I try not to romanticize them," he said, "for good or bad. Whatever they may have done to marginalize themselves is immaterial. As artists, they sit down to engage their art with absolutely no sense of a viewer, of history, of an outside world. Does that make them insane? You look at what they produce and the only proper answer to that question becomes, What's the difference?"

Jonas had many more questions, but just then Nikki walked in and stopped short in surprise. "There you are," she said uncertainly.

"Ah," Agnew said, "the power couple. Listen, Nikki, there's one of those – God, it makes my mouth hurt just having to say it – 'outsider art fair' fiascoes in town next month, and I was going to ask if you'd go. Larry Masters will have a little booth there – Larry, that's the dealer I was telling you about, Jonas, the one who accuses me of devaluing Martin Strauss – and so I can't go, he hates me, he probably has some kind of court order waiting for me, actually. But why don't the two of you go? There should actually be some great stuff there, some Wölfli, I think, some Ramirez, some Dadd. You'll do it?"

They glanced wide-eyed at each other; then Jonas turned back to Agnew and nodded.

"Excellent. About time we got young Mr. Morey here on the payroll. Just an expression, Jonas, don't look like that.

Not that you need it, like most of these indigents. In fact, maybe you can put us on the payroll, right?"

Jonas smiled nervously. He was surprised to learn that Agnew knew who he was.

"Seriously," Agnew said, "you'd be doing me a real favor if you'd return this. I love it, but I don't feel like getting sued over it. Tell him who it's from." He took the framed Strauss down from the kitchen wall and handed it to Jonas.

"You can't," Jonas said without thinking. It was too extraordinary; he didn't want to be the one to hand it over. "It's like – I don't know. It's like putting a kid into foster care. There has to be some other way."

Agnew's eyebrows were up, though not, it seemed, in a bad way. "Well, I'm glad you like it," he said. "But, like it or not, it is in the world, and has been assigned a value in that world, quite independent of what you or I or the artist think about that. Or can do to stop it, for that matter. Outsider art is very hot right now. I've been happy to hang this piece here but now it's time for it to go, as they say, into the system."

Jonas looked at it again. He was flushed with the awareness of Agnew's interest in him, in what he was going to do; he wasn't courting that interest, but still, he could feel it. Something about the drawing was too compelling to just let go of like that. It wasn't like it spoke to him or anything. It resisted all that – you could admire it, but you had no real hope of interpreting it. It was an artifact of an unimaginable state of mind. There was no dialogue going on there, no puzzle to solve, no meaning to extract. Or, if it hada meaning, it was a meaning he had no hope of understanding.

"How much do you think he wants for it?" Jonas said.

Clubs were over, there weren't any good ones anymore, and anyway a key component of the usual club high – getting in when you weren't supposed to, when it was technically illegal for them to serve you, but they would serve you anyway and for free because of how you looked and because they knew who you were – was gone now that April was of age. Yet at a certain point the night always took a certain turn and the next thing you knew you were sitting in some VIP room with a bunch of people who said they were with you, paying five hundred bucks for a bottle of Ketel One while the bass throb reached you through the walls. The reason this was a bad development was that the disgust and contempt it engendered in her, directed at those around her but at herself too, left her open to longing for stronger intoxicants. And little men, older men, would pop up in her field of vision at the very moment this desire started making itself felt in her mind – as if she were tripping already, as if the world itself were some sort of Second Life dreamscape programmed to tempt her with her own wants – and once you reached that point, bitch, you were finished.

When the speed kicked in, the music dropped out of the mix for a moment and she heard as clear as a bell the voice of her friend Katie, her best friend Katie whose last name April couldn't remember but whom she'd known and hung out with when they were in middle school. Katie went to

Spence. The two girls made eye contact and screamed. "You went to Spence!" April shouted over the music, which was loud again, as if Katie might have forgotten. "Yes!" Katie said. "Yes! Six years ago!" Her math seemed wrong, but her eyes were like pinpricks and she was so happy to see April that she was crying. Where had she come from? The world got so small when you were out at night. In the shadows over Katie's shoulder, as they hugged again, April could make out two very sketchy-looking guys sitting on the arms of Katie's vacated chair, older guys, though they were hard to reckon in the way of shaven-headed men. The world was full of these guys, who were waiting, always waiting. Waiting for what? Well, she wasn't an idiot, they were waiting to fuck Katie, Katie and her; they were pathetic and old and degenerate but April liked having them around for a couple of reasons, one being that the nauseating prospect of one of them being there to catch you when you fell was the only thing that kept you vigilant, and the other was that their gaze reminded you where you were, which was basically at the exact center of the fucking universe, young, hot women of privilege at the very peak of everything that was desirable, the very apex of all in life that was worth coveting. And who the hell wanted to sleep through that?

"Katie," she said to Katie, who was talking at the same time, "that guy over there, his head looks like a fucking turtle. Who is that guy?"

"I don't know," Katie said. "He's not American, though. He wants to fuck me."

"Well we cannot let that happen!"

"I know." Katie turned and looked right at him. "He has the best drugs, though. He likes my tattoos. He has his uses." The guy's stare was reptilian. He would sit there for thirty years if he had to. "Look," April said. "Look look look. He is a goblin. I was sent here to earth to save you from him, you fucking stoned bitch." They hugged again. "How are we going to throw these guys off the trail?"

The answer was to pile into April's car and have the driver take them to Scores. She called ahead for a room and set them up with lap dance after lap dance. While this one completely amazing Amazon was rubbing her tits on the turtle's head, April and Katie motioned that they were going to the bathroom, and once they were out of there they ran stumbling out the door and piled back into April's limo and told the driver to hit it.

They laughed and got up on their knees in the back seat to look out the rear window but then it was just the two of them in the car, and they realized they didn't know each other particularly well and the speed was wearing off. The driver hadn't even asked them where they were going, because he was waiting for them to figure it out. Waiting while driving. April couldn't remember his name, but he was the best. Katie said she knew where she could get some Adderall; probably from her own bathroom cabinet, April thought, and anyway, Adderall seemed a little low-stakes right now. "I know a guy we can call," she said. "And he owes me a favor." If you made a lot of friends when you went out then there was always somebody who owed you a favor. The guy's name was Dmitri and when he called back he was, where else, in a club, so she told the nice driver to take Canal almost all the way over to the highway, and he nodded without turning around.

That was where they started in on the meth. Then it was some time later and they were on the sidewalk in the hostile sunlight and "they" no longer included Katie, whom April hadn't seen in a while. Dmitri was there, and three other sketchy guys with accents, and two women whose job, it seemed, was to make out with each other once an hour or so to keep the others from losing interest in everything. That may not have been a joke; it wouldn't be unlike Dmitri to have actually paid them to do it. They found a diner and ate without tasting anything, while the sketchy guys glared menacingly, to zero effect, at the disgusted cashier. April felt ashamed to be with these people she didn't know, but they were like vampires, she was one of them now, she couldn't just go back to the living. She looked out the window and there at the curb, unbelievably, was her driver, leaning against the side of his car, looking exhausted. She had to let him go. She wanted to tip him a few hundred bucks, but when she looked in her bag she saw that she had like thirty dollars in there, which was fucked up but true. So she called him on her cell, watching his angry face through the window, and sent him home.

Her cell had a bunch of voicemails on it but she didn't bother with them. Some were from her mother, but she was out of town herself, so there was no stress there. Everyone was arguing over the check like a bunch of losers, not because they particularly cared but just as a symptom of their panic over coming down. "Where can we go, my love?" Dmitri said to her. One of the chicks was trying to reapply her makeup.

"Your place?" April said. "I mean, you must live somewhere, right?"

He shook his head. "Not with these pigs," he said. "If we go there, it is just you and me. Is that what you want?"

No, it was not. "I want the festivities to go on," she said.

"Brava. Well, in that case we need someplace big. Big and empty. Private."

And then April had what she knew right away was a terrible idea.

"Hey," she said loudly to the group. They were like rats, red-eyed and squabbling. "Does one of you lowlifes have a car?"

One of the lowlifes did indeed have a car; it was in Queens, though, so he and Dmitri went to get it. The others went somewhere to steal cigarettes and take a shower. April waited more than an hour for them in a Starbucks on Varick Street. Dmitri texted her every few minutes. She didn't know what time it was, or what day it was, but the Starbucks was packed. And the strange thing, even though she wasn't high anymore, was that the people in this fake space exhibited the most terrible intimacies – yelling into their cell phones, popping zits, putting on makeup, talking to themselves like maniacs – six inches from your face. Their conviction that you could not see or hear them was so strong that, in fact, you usually did not see or hear them.

Sitting across the tiny table from April, picking at some kind of muffin, was a woman about April's mother's age who had unmistakably, some time in the last day or two, been punched in the eye.

They all got high in the car again and two hours later they were in Amagansett. April hit the security code and they were in. The streets were empty and when the sky darkened they didn't see lights coming on in any of the neighboring houses.

There was a lot of alcohol in the house, which helped them avoid peaking too drastically. Their only foray outside was down to the beach at night, just to listen to the receding water and watch the stars. April felt very happy. Like being a kid: finding a hiding place in your own home. They all got briefly excited when they saw, way way down the beach, a bonfire burning in the sand; but it was freezing and they weren't really dressed right so they didn't go check it out. At one point April and one of the Russians – they were Russian, she'd decided – were alone in the pool house, and they decided to try to have sex, but it was pretty much a nonstarter.

When they left to drive back to the city, the last few bottles in hand, April turned to look at the place one last time and consoled herself that not a lot had gotten damaged or broken, though the whole first floor just looked vaguely grimy. Even the walls. Someone would come and clean it, though. Dmitri drove while the others tried not to fall asleep; they were still on Route 15 when Dmitri, who was trying to text someone with one hand while passing another car, hit a van traveling in the other direction. The van managed to turn a little so they didn't hit head-on; it skidded over to the shoulder and then fell lazily and loudly onto its side.

None of them was wearing a seat belt, but Dmitri was the one who was truly fucked up. Somehow the rest of them were standing outside the ruined car now – the two chicks were wailing – and looking curiously through the driver's-side window at Dmitri, whose head rested on the steering wheel and was turned so that you couldn't see his face, which was probably just as well. No sirens yet. Where were they? April started to get scared. She had lots of shameful thoughts in succession: Thank God it wasn't her car. Thank God she wasn't driving. Still, this was not going to be good. It was all going to fall on her, because they'd all been at her place, and because who were these people, really? Hers was the only name that was going to give anybody anything to latch on to. She looked again at the door to the van, which had not moved. It said Sagaponack Nursery on it. Nursery like trees, she told herself. Not like nursery school. Suddenly she wanted so badly to be ten years old again. No more pretending now. Her own phone had been dead for days. "Who has a phone?" she asked the others, but they were like statues, like garden gnomes. "A *phone!*" Finally, desperate and shaking, she took two steps forward and, holding her breath, reached through the shattered window, pulled the cell phone out of Dmitri's clenched hand, wiped it on her jacket, and called her mother.

The fair was held in the McCormick Place convention center just off Lake Shore Drive; Jonas and Nikki had to pay thirty-five bucks each just to get in. A number of galleries from all over the Midwest, and four or five from New York, had paid for and staked out square footage inside. Little pamphlets on draped card tables held one-page biographies of the artists, like trading cards for mental illness; Jonas picked up as many of them as he could find. The rule of thumb seemed to be that the farther a particular artist's own mind had pushed him toward society's border, the more you could charge for his work. It was somehow revolting and thrilling at the same time. A few dead outsiders had become stars, like Henry Darger or Martin Ramirez. Maybe this was no different, Jonas thought, from the way the art establishment had processed, say, Van Gogh. But everyone moving through the building's vast warren of temporary drywall seemed so loathsome to him that it was hard to judge. He was surprised how old they were, ten or twenty years older than him at least, if you discounted the occasional baby in a stroller – smug bohemian speculators, praising everything noisily in overcompensation for the fact that they were no match for the magnificent strangeness of what hung right in front of their eyes.

He and Nikki caught a break when they stopped at Larry Masters's booth and found that Masters himself had gone to lunch; they left the framed Strauss sketch with an indifferent gallery assistant and hurried away. Nikki had a list on an index card of particular artists Agnew wanted her to look for; he wanted to know what their work was selling for and also, more problematically, camera-phone shots of the work itself, but there were security guards here and there and Nikki, who was afraid of cops even of the rental variety, could sneak a shot only occasionally. She took copious notes, though, and collected all the pamphlets and price lists. It wasn't really a two-person job, so Jonas just walked around following whatever caught his eye. He squeezed through a pack of reverent yuppies for a look at those great iconic deer in the work of Martin Ramirez, who had lived on the streets of LA apparently incapable of so much as a conversation and whose asylum warders at first tried to stop him from drawing on the grounds that it was unhealthy. That stuff was going for tens of thousands now. There were diagrams of nonexistent machines, maps of nonexistent places, ferociously detailed charts filled with dates and numbers in an order that you were never, ever going to divine. There was a grown man named Morton Bartlett who had spent decades photographing his own doll collection. Jonas was just about to start looking for Nikki again when he saw a group of charcoal portraits, if you could call them portraits, of people screaming. Were they screaming, though? Their mouths were open. Maybe they were just trying to speak. Their eyes were always neutral, and their necks were thin and cylindrical, like plant stalks almost. Sometimes there was a background, slight variations on what Jonas ultimately decided was a gas station, or at least looked like one; there were also some simply drawn dogs, and box-like forms that may have been televisions, though, if so, they were never turned on. But it was the faces, the upturned open mouths, that were most ambiguous and obsessive.

The number written on a sticker beside the portraits was 12; Jonas checked the gallery pamphlet and saw prices listed but no biography of the artist, who was named Joseph Novak. When he asked the stout, short-haired woman at the card table if she could tell him anything more, she sized him up and smiled with a touch too much patience, probably, he realized, because his youth and appearance didn't suggest that he was in a position to buy anything.

"Joseph is new to us," said the woman; she didn't introduce herself, but she seemed to Jonas like the gallery owner, in which case her name was Margo. "He – well, I don't want to get into specifics, but he was in an institution for several years, in the wake of a crime he admitted to committing as a minor; like a lot of artists he really only began drawing when his freedom was taken away, but he has kept up the pace since his release."

"So he's still working on this series?" Jonas asked.

Margo considered how to answer. "Presumably," she said. "I mean, 'series' is a word you could use. I've only met Joseph one time myself. These drawings came to me via a brother of his in Kenosha who had a suspicion they might be worth something. Joseph himself is – well, communication is difficult, let's say that."

Jonas stared at the drawings for a while longer. They had a broken, smudged line, like if you extracted the lead from a pencil and just tried to hold it in your hand. They were figurative and thus a little less grotesquely original than some of the other stuff there; still, the longer he stared at the faces, the more excitement he felt, like what he was seeing was something that had never even been looked at before. He tried to forget what little Margo had just told him about the artist himself, but that was difficult to do. A while later Nikki was walking past and spotted him. He asked her right away if the name Joseph Novak was on Agnew's list and felt a small thrill when the answer was no. "How about you?" he said. "See anything interesting?"

"Kind of," Nikki said. She beckoned him around the corner with one finger, to the exhibition stall right behind Margo's. There was a good crowd there. On the wall hung an array of large, photo-realistic oil portraits of an iconic-looking family, most often standing in front of what was probably their own house, staring right back at the viewer, happy and stiff – in fact, it was almost as if the paintings were portraits not of the people themselves but of photographs of them. It was easy to spot the dealer, who wore a tweed jacket and a name tag and kept touching everyone who spoke to him on the shoulder. And after a moment Jonas realized that the proud-looking family standing with their backs to the artwork, accepting the occasional congratulations – a father, a mother, and a boy who looked like he was maybe in eighth grade, wearing a DePaul University sweatshirt – was the same family represented in the paintings.

"No," Nikki said, taking his hand. "Over there."

Jonas looked to the right of the exhibition stall, where there was a little recessed area beneath a fire-door sign, and saw a man who looked just about his age, wearing a crewneck sweater with a name tag on it and jeans and unlaced snow boots, sitting lotus-style on the floor; beside him was a worn stack of khaki-colored loose-leaf notebooks that said DePaul University on them. He had his head down and his eyes closed, and his index fingers stuck inside his ears, and his lips pressed together, as he rocked very slightly but rhythmically forward and back. "Who is that?" Jonas asked, though he saw the family resemblance right away.

April was still sound asleep when Cynthia left the house to meet with their lawyers at Debevoise. From Debevoise she went straight downtown to Marietta's office; Adam couldn't get away to meet her there but they had him on speaker. It was chastening how long these meetings took – how much more there was to take into account than she'd even realized. She'd never seen Marietta so businesslike. By the time Cynthia got back home it was nearly three, and Dawn, her assistant, met her at the front door to let her know that April was still not up. God bless Dawn: even though she and April had barely met, she'd done what Edina, the housekeeper, was too scared to do and opened up April's bedroom door every twenty minutes or so just to make sure she was still breathing, because she knew that was going to be Cynthia's first question whether Cynthia actually asked it or not.

Her eyes adapted to the dark inside her daughter's room and she saw April's legs twitch in her sleep. There were snoring noises, sick-sounding but still reassuring. She closed the door again and went back to sit in the solarium. Her daughter had been sleeping for about fifteen straight hours but in a way it played into Cynthia's desire to be able to put off talking to her until Adam was home from work. Not that she wanted April to think it was some kind of intervention or something. Hard to get up on any kind of moral high horse when she'd spent the last thirty-six hours involuntarily remembering all the times she herself had been high and in a car, as a passenger or, God help her, behind the wheel, back when she was April's age. She wasn't about to deliver a lecture on the subject when the fact that she was here at all was nothing more than evidence of a charmed life.

Two hours with the lawyers this morning, two hours to go over the ways in which April's name could be kept out of any court papers and then, as a separate issue, out of the press as well. They didn't pretend it wasn't a crisis atmosphere; there were faces around that conference table she'd never even seen before. That was okay. That was why you kept them on retainer: for emergencies. She felt worse about all the lying she'd asked poor Dawn to do in the course of canceling all the appointments originally scheduled for today; probably some of those people hadn't bought it and were offended now. But family trumped all other considerations. All she dared to want from this day was for her daughter to end it in better shape than she'd started it. It was beyond Cynthia, and probably beyond Adam too, to express or even to feel privately any real disappointment in either of their children. But the hard fact to get used to – the thing that Marietta kept harping on – was that the Morey family existed now on a public plane as well as a private one, and in that light something had to happen to make sure this kind of incident never took place again.

"It's nice," Marietta had said to her, "to have done so many favors for people in influential positions, so that they will then do this favor for you. But I'm telling you, you can go back to that well only so many times before people start to feel taken advantage of. And then the dam bursts in terms of curiosity about the Morey family, in terms of the desire to see the high brought low; and then the foundation's work is hurt, and your name starts to get associated with things other than the good work you and Adam have started to do. People want that bubble popped, believe me. People would love nothing better than for you to turn out to be hypocrites and scumbags instead of the generous, caring family that you are. Far be it from me, as a friend or as someone technically on your payroll, to give you parenting advice. But just as a professional matter, this is something you and Adam need to get out in front of."

Then a frightened-looking Edina was in the doorway mouthing the words "She's up," and a few moments later April walked heavily into the living room, in a T-shirt and Adam's pajama bottoms, her hair everywhere, her face bloated, her eyes nearly closed. You had to see her looking her worst, Cynthia thought, in order to understand how irreducibly gorgeous she was. Cynthia didn't stand up. "My head is pounding," April said hoarsely. "Will you tell whats-herface to get me some Advil?" Cynthia leaned over and typed something onto the laptop on the coffee table in front of her; communication like that was all done wirelessly now. April made her way over to the couch and curled up against the arm farthest from her mother.

"Do you want anything to drink?" Cynthia said politely. "Or eat?"

"Oh my God no," April mumbled.

Maybe it was selfish of her, but what Cynthia most wanted to hear right now was the same note of pleading, childish belief in her that she'd heard in that first phone call from the shoulder of Route 15, just to reassure her that it hadn't all been an act, that it wasn't just a matter of April's knowing how to play her in order to get what she wanted: Mommy-I'm-scared, Mommy-I-need-your-help. "Dad will be home in a little while," Cynthia said. "I spent this morning with our lawyers and basically, as it concerns you at least, in legal terms, the whole thing never happened."

April's face was hidden behind her hair. "Of course it didn't," she said weakly. "Um, is there any word on Dmitri?" Before Cynthia could ask who the hell Dmitri was, April added, "And the guy driving the van?"

Cynthia sighed. "They're not dead," she said, which sounded harsh but was all she really knew. "Nobody's dead."

"Okay," April said.

She'd always been precocious, she'd always set herself apart. Sometime in the last couple of years she seemed to have run up against some kind of interior wall and now she spent her days and nights running into that same wall over and over again. Cynthia believed that there had to be a kind of key to the adult April somewhere, and that it was her fault for not having found it. If you were the mother it was always your fault. But it's not too late, Cynthia told herself. There's still time. She tried to be calm and unprovocative, but she couldn't help herself.

"How did we get here?" she said. "I mean, I try to sort of look back and find out where I made the mistake, but I can't." And then, frustratingly, she started to cry – like she was the daughter, like she was the one who had been through something and needed to be comforted. "I feel like I'm losing you. How can I keep that from happening?"

"Mom, you are not going to lose me," April said, not particularly kindly. "Please. Like there's not enough drama here already."

"I'm sorry, but you cannot just scare the shit out of me like that and expect me to be cool about it. I do not want that to happen again."

"I don't want it to happen again either," April said.

Edina came in with the Advil and a glass of water on a tray; she placed it on the far edge of the glass-topped table and withdrew.

"That's what gets me, actually," April said, in a voice that wasn't quite as sharp. "I'm pretty sure it will. Happen again. Even though I don't want it to. I can feel myself forgetting what it feels like to feel this way." She snorted. "Another few days and I'll be hanging out with the same people doing the same stupid shit even though I don't really want to. Why is that? I mean, what am I supposed to do with all my time?"

Cynthia reached out and tried to stroke April's tangled

hair, but April pulled her head away. Her kids' moods had
always had a way of swamping hers and so after ten minutes
of sitting at the opposite end of the couch staring at nothing,
she found herself feeling just as mad and hopeless as April
did, just as stonewalled and estranged, even though in truth,
outside the confines of this moment, she had never in her
life felt closer to the heart of things than she did right now.
She was chair of one of the top ten fastest growing charitable
foundations in New York. The foundation, at Adam's
insistence, had her name on it. People brought her anti-
poverty initiatives of all kinds and her interest made them
real, not just at home but overseas, in countries she had
never seen. No more intermediaries between her desire for
a better world and the world itself; all she had to do was
imagine it. But even these triumphs receded like moons into
a distant orbit of the fact of her child's unhappiness. She laid
her cheek on the arm of the couch and waited.

Adam found the two of them still in that position, like
listing bookends, when he came home half an hour later;
their expressions made it appear as if they'd fought more
than they actually had. He sat down across from them and
took a silent minute to try to focus. It was much harder than
it should have been to stop thinking about work. The
problem was that everything seemed rooted in work these
days. Day and night. Everywhere he went, people begged
him to take them on as investors in his hedge fund, which
over the four years of its existence had put up numbers that
pushed him into shamanistic territory, where people
earnestly believed that he was performing a kind of magic.

Old friends, total strangers — they treated even finding themselves in the same room with him as the portent of a lifetime, and some of them were the type who prided themselves on not taking no for an answer. They would lose their manners completely. Some of Adam's junior partners tried to tell him he was insane for not traveling with security just to keep the wannabes at a respectful distance from him, but he really did not want to go that route, especially not at what were nominally social occasions. Now the fund was filing for its own IPO and that meant the news was about to break that one of its non-voting stakeholders was the Chinese government. There was nothing wrong or underhanded about it; still, when it came to money, there was a certain threshold of size past which outsiders just reacted irrationally. But that particular freakout was still a few weeks away. He and Cyn had spoken at least ten times that day already, so there was nothing on which he needed to be brought up to date. They had a plan and now just needed to draw from each other the resolve to go through with it. He waited for April to meet his eyes.

"First of all," he said, "Mom and I want you to know that this isn't about the drugs. We are not going to be hypocrites about that."

"Is it the drugs, though?" Cynthia said. "I mean, I think it has to be asked. Are you an addict, do you think?"

"Jesus," April said. "If you had ever in your life seen an actual addict, you would know better than to ask that. I love how you guys always want to establish your street cred."

"Okay," Cynthia said. "It just had to be asked."

No one said anything. Adam's phone vibrated; after a second's deliberation, he looked at the screen and saw that it was a call from Devon. Six months ago he'd put Devon in charge of the fund's nascent commercial-realty specu-lation arm; it was the only aspect of the fund that might be said to be underperforming right now, but that would turn around. The more immediate problem was that in terms of decision-making Devon wasn't quite the self-starter Adam had hoped and so he was getting these phone calls seven times a day. He let this one bounce to voicemail. Some-where upstairs they heard a door open and close.

"It's true that I would like to do less drugs than I currently do," April said. "But that's not the same thing."

"I think even you have to admit," Cynthia said, "that this was a close one. You get that, right? I mean, you have to admit that yesterday could easily have ended in some way very much worse than you sitting on the couch in your own living room getting lectured by your parents. It's not exactly a big stretch to imagine it ending with you dead or in jail."

"Or dead and in jail," April said.

"Please don't be smart," Adam said. "There is a point to this conversation. We spent a lot of time today talking to Marietta, and what she kept stressing is that we all have to get used to a new way of thinking around here. Like it or not, this family has a name now, a profile. We have been fortunate enough to make a lot of money, which is fascinating to people, and we are in a position to use some of that money to try to do some good. Which, oddly enough, makes us all a target. There are a lot of people who do not want people like us to succeed, even when our success benefits them. Like the scorpion and the frog. They would rather see us brought down. But we are not going to be brought down. We've done what we can to keep the media in particular off the scent of what happened yesterday, but information like this is like water, if you're not ultra careful it's going to find a way out, and in order to protect both you and the good work that this family wants to continue to do, we have to take some steps. We have to be proactive."

April started to look worried. "If you say the word 'rehab'," she said, "I swear to God I am going to fucking lose it."

"Nope," Adam said. "Better. This was Marietta's idea, actually. I have to go to China for ten days or so, for business and also for a little foundation work, and we have moved up that trip so that it starts the day after tomorrow. You're coming with me. That'll be enough time for your buddies who trashed our country place to go through the system and for us to settle with the van driver on their behalf."

"What?" April said. "China? Wait. If you want to just stash me somewhere, can't I at least pick where?"

"Sorry, no. No St. Barts, no Chateau Marmont, none of your usual haunts. None of your usual friends. The whole point is to be somewhere where nobody has any idea who you are."

"I can't believe this," April said. She was struggling not to cry. "You're trying to disappear me."

"Au contraire," Adam said. "You will never be out of

my sight. It'll be a little father–daughter time." His phone vibrated again. "And I'm pretty sure you will see some things you've never seen before. Travel broadens the mind. Anyway, it is not negotiable. Cyn, could you maybe have Dawn help with calling the consulate and all that?"

"Already taken care of," Cynthia said.

"Mommy?" April said.

Cynthia put her palm gently underneath her daughter's chin. "Oh, my sweetheart," she said. "Ten days. It's not that long."

April stood up, stomped back into her bedroom, and slammed the door. Adam and Cynthia exchanged a look that made it permissible for them both to laugh, just for a second. "Déjà vu, or what?" Adam said.

"All of a sudden I feel ten years younger," Cynthia smiled. But then she lost herself in staring at the closed door, and when she looked back at him she was crying again. "Seriously," she said. "I don't understand it. What did I do wrong?"

His cell phone vibrated again; he stood to leave the room. "You didn't do anything wrong, my love," he said. "She'll figure it out. The way you grow up is you find your thing to struggle against, and, I mean, look around." He kissed her forehead on his way past the couch. "Whatever it is, we've hidden it pretty well."

The image of the presumably autistic young artist rocking on the floor with his fingers in his ears imprinted itself on Jonas, and when, a few days later, he and Nikki met Agnew in his office on campus to deliver their informal report on the fair, that, rather than the art, was the thing he found himself describing. Agnew had a way of leaning backward when he felt something interesting was being said – usually by himself – and so Jonas could tell he had not miscalculated in telling the story.

"So what do you imagine this guy was shutting out?" Agnew said.

"The whole condescending circus. The whole glorified Tupperware party they're basically making out of his attempts to communicate. The profiteers. The charlatans."

"Wrong," Agnew said. "He would have had his hands over his ears if it was Mother Teresa talking too loud for him, or Rembrandt, or Clement Greenberg. Or his family. You're the one making the value judgments for him. To him, noise is noise."

Jonas nodded submissively. He felt a little naïve for romanticizing it like that.

"And as far as charlatanism goes, you're right: outsider art is overrun by thieves and hacks and opportunists and corrupters. Which makes the difference between it and any other type of art exactly nil. Forget about them. They're not worth getting mad at. The difference here is that the artists themselves can't be corrupted by it. Nor can they be uncorrupted, for that matter. It's not in them. If they're really outsider, that is. There's a tremendous amount of bullshit involved."

"How do you tell what's real and what's not?"

"Well, anything can be forged in this world, but the total

absence of self-consciousness turns out to be pretty damn hard to fake." This for some reason made Agnew bark with laughter. "But often you just need to meet the artist. Simple as that. It's like being one of those psychiatrists for the prosecution. I spend a lot of my time doing that now."

On the walls of Agnew's dark office there was no art, nor any reproductions. Instead there hung framed photographs of artists: Duchamp, Pollock, Warhol, and many others whose faces Jonas didn't recognize. Nikki had told him about this. Apparently Agnew found actual works of art too distracting; he became so lost in staring at them, even in reproduction, that he couldn't get done whatever work he had shut himself in his office to do. So he displayed the artists themselves, because, he liked to say, they were much easier for him to ignore.

"You could make the case," Agnew said, "that the history of modern art is the history of artists trying to unlearn what they know. To them, the world that is made is really the only world that matters. You can work all your life to break all those connections to the known world and re-form them, but it's never the same as not having had those connections in the first place. So in that sense it's not hard to tell when someone's a true artist, whether or not he considers himself one at all."

"You have a budget," Jonas asked, "from the department for the research you're doing for your book? To pay for graduate assistants?" Nikki, still holding in her lap all the one-sheet artist bios from the fair she had assembled for Agnew, turned and looked at Jonas in budding surprise.

"Yes and no. The department basically lowers the tuition of the students I have working for me. It's not like I have actual cash to distribute. But, in any case, I've used up my allotment and then some."

"Would you be willing to take on another one? Off the books? I don't mean 'off the books', sorry, I just mean that no one would have to pay me anything. It's not necessary."

Agnew leaned back. "Well aren't you the young man on the go," he said.

"I could do some of this research for you. Check out some of these artists. Maybe even find new ones. I wouldn't presume to offer you my opinion or anything, like your grad students do, but just legwork. However, I could be useful to the project."

"Why?"

Jonas cursed his own blush, just at the moment he was trying to seem a little older than he was. He was trying not to look at Nikki, whose mouth was hanging open. "Why? I just . . . All my requirements are done, or just about, and I haven't found anything that interests me as much as this. It's like something I've been looking for, if that makes any sense. To be honest, I'm already thinking ahead to what I want to do after next year. I think I could get a jump on a thesis this way, not that it would intersect with your work at all, I'd keep that totally separate. But it is a huge field."

Agnew rocked in his desk chair and drummed his fingertips together in the air for what seemed to Jonas like a minute. "Can I ask you a personal question?" Agnew said. Jonas nodded.

"I read in the paper, a few months ago, about a guy named Morey, one of those hedge-fund guys, who threw a birthday party for his wife. Rented out the New York Public Library for it. Wyclef Jean played. Those are your parents, aren't they?"

Jonas nodded again, fidgeting a little.

"Did you go?"

"Sure. It was their anniversary, actually, not her birthday."

"Some big one, right? Like their twenty-fifth or something?"

"Twenty-third," Jonas said, and laughed grudgingly. "He does kind of jump the gun sometimes."

"I have to admit," Agnew said, "I read about how guys like that make their money, what they do all day, and I don't grasp it at all. Alternative assets or whatever they're called, it just bounces right off my brain. And I'm presumably not a dumb guy. But hey – people think what I do for a living is arcane."

Jonas didn't smile. "I know what people think about throwing a party like that," he said, "but the thing is, all the display wasn't for anybody else's benefit. It was for her. That's the way my dad thinks. They are just really in love with each other, in this kind of epic way. So I just try to focus on that. That's the real context of everything they do – each other. The other stuff is just kind of outside the walls. Every family is bizarre from the outside in some way, right?"

But Agnew shook his head. He looked at Nikki and pointed back at Jonas with his thumb. "That's some end-times shit, your boyfriend's family," he said. "That's okay, though. It's not possible to hold it against him, and anyway I wouldn't, because it just makes it more interesting that he's in here. Because this is some end-times shit too, what we're doing. I mean, what we're studying here, what comes after it? That desire to feed on every new expression of what it is to suffer and be human, that need to seek out what's unfamiliar and make it familiar, it's like a goddamn fox hunt, and over the centuries it has narrowed down to this. Should we call off the hunt? Probably, but the question is moot anyway, because the world is incapable of leaving art alone. And après nous, what? I don't know what comes after, what kind of art, what kind of artist. I really don't. But after all these years, you and I will be there at the end. It's kind of thrilling, isn't it?"

Cynthia had learned the hard way to be vigilant about giving out her cell number, but she wound up having to change it every six or eight months anyway. No matter how careful you were, inevitably you were going to start getting calls from total strangers – charities legit and otherwise, journalists, angry socialist crackpots – all of them wanting something, because when you were giving money away, people were terrifically inventive about finding you. At which point it was time to change phones again. Sometimes she'd find herself in the embarrassing position of not knowing her own contact information, but Dawn was always on top of it.

Dawn was in charge of the home phone as well. Though they'd unlisted it, that number had stayed the same for years;

Cynthia just never answered it anymore. At the end of the day Dawn gave her a typed list of whatever messages had been left. They were about 95 per cent junk, but Cynthia couldn't bring herself to just change the number or disconnect it; it was too much like telling people who used to know you that they didn't know you anymore. Adam wouldn't have minded. The cache of things capable of troubling Adam seemed to clear itself every week or so. She was shocked, sometimes, by the things she had to remind him of, the people they'd met and places they'd visited and times they'd had together that produced a blank, apologetic look on his face when she brought them up.

On Friday afternoon, with Adam and April still in the air on their way to Shanghai, Dawn handed Cynthia the day's list of home-phone calls and then, unusually, lingered in the door to her office while she read it. Dawn had come to work for her with the announced goal of saving up money to apply to business school; Cynthia had grown to depend on her to such a degree that she now paid her not just enough for business school but so much that business school itself would seem like too big a sacrifice. She was twenty-four, just a couple of years older than April, and scary-competent, and if she'd wanted to she could have found myriad ways to manipulate Cynthia's obvious affection for her, but she wasn't that type of person. Boundaries were never an issue. They talked about everything. The poor girl's taste in men was even worse than a twenty-four-year-old's should be, and with Dawn's mother living with a new boyfriend in Queens and functionally out of the picture, Cynthia suffered through

Dawn's non-working hours imagining all the mistakes a beautiful young girl like that might make.

"What?" Cynthia said quietly, looking over the list.

Dawn shook her head. "Nothing. Just wanted to see if you recognized that last name. I wasn't sure if it was on the level. But I guess not. Sorry not to catch it."

Cynthia's gaze hadn't actually made it all the way to the bottom of the page. She looked down again and saw the name Irene Ball.

"Nope," she said. "A name like that I'd remember. Why?"

Dawn shrugged. "She said she was calling on behalf of your father. She wouldn't say why, though. I kind of had a feeling it was bogus. She actually called three times."

Cynthia looked down at the name again.

"I mean, this is totally something I should know, but didn't you tell me that your father had passed away?"

"That was my stepfather."

Dawn blanched. "I'm sorry. Oh my God. Teach me to ask personal questions."

Cynthia glanced up at her, then reached out and squeezed her hand. "Please," she said. "It's me."

Saturday morning Cynthia sat in the dining room drinking a protein shake the weekend cook had made, languishing over the paper, and staring out the window at the boat traffic on the churning East River. It was a novelty to have the house all to herself. Not that she was completely alone; there was a housekeeper moving around audibly in the master bedroom above her head, and the cook was on until four, doing prep work for a cocktail reception Cynthia was hosting the next night. It would be strange to host anything without Adam there too, but that kind of thing was happening more and more, as they had to split up to accommodate the foundation's reach. She was about to go downstairs and read through a few grant proposals on the StairMaster when the home phone rang on the sideboard behind her. She turned to look at the caller ID, which read only, private name, private number. She pursed her lips. No one else was going to pick it up. Just before the fourth ring, which would send it to voicemail, she answered.

Irene Ball was a real person, all right. She had been keeping company – that was the expression she used – with Cynthia's father for the last four years. Her thin, formal voice suggested she'd be about his age, at least, even if her name sounded like that of a stripper.

"Irene Ball," Cynthia said. "And my father gave you this number?"

There was a pause. "Yes, of course," Irene Ball said. "I wouldn't just call out of the blue. I understand this is an awkward conversation for us to be having."

She had stayed with him even through his illness—

"Illness?" Cynthia said. There was another pause, either shocked or decorous, but either way Cynthia, who was becoming flushed, didn't have the patience for it. "Look, Irene," she said, "just please go on the assumption that I don't know what you're talking about, all right?"

Cynthia had last seen him more than a year ago, when, unusually, he'd turned up in New York. She knew he'd been living in Florida; once or twice a year she'd transfer some money to a bank account in Naples, and at some point he would thank her politely with a note. It was hard to know how much to send him. She could have made him a millionaire if she felt like it, but since he never asked her for anything, she didn't really know what he needed, nor what he might take offense at. When he called to say he was in the city she invited him to stay with them for a few days at least but he said he couldn't, he said he had business to attend to. So they wound up having him over for dinner. The kids sat at the table mute and amazed. He told them stories about her childhood, and hugged them all warmly, and left, and shortly afterward, Irene now said – or maybe, it occurred to Cynthia, shortly before – he was diagnosed with liver cancer. The chemo weakened his immune system, he got pneumonia, he had a heart attack while in the hospital, the cancer turned up in his pancreas as well . . . long story short (there's an expression, Cynthia thought), he had not been out of the hospital for the last month and felt quite sure he was never going to get out again at all, and in light of this, he had made a decision.

"He's asked his doctors to stop treating him," Irene said, "and they've agreed to honor that request. He's still lucid enough to know what he's doing, except when the pain medication kind of overwhelms him." She was weeping now, which was moving but also confusing and inappropriate, like weeping from a TV newscaster. "I don't think he should do it. I want him to keep fighting. He's a wonderful man. He talks about you all the time. When he sees your name in the paper he always cuts it out and shows it to me."

What was there to say to that? Instead of calling his child for help, he clipped her name out of the newspaper and showed it to people. "So he's in the hospital right now, or out of it, or what?"

"There's a hospice down here that has an opening. It's such a nice place. It's—"

"Where?"

"Sorry?"

"Where," Cynthia said, her face heating up, "is here? Where is my father? I mean, like on a map?"

"Oh. Oh, I'm sorry. I just assumed . . . My apologies. We're in Fort Myers, Florida. I have a—"

"Is he there with you right now?"

"No," Irene said. "He's still in the hospital. They can't move him until they have somewhere to move him to. I'm in our home."

Our home! She tried to keep her emotions moored in the practical. "What's the name of the hospital?" she asked.

"They probably won't let you talk to him, I'm afraid. Not on the phone. He's just awake too little of the time."

"Why is he still there, if he doesn't want to be there anymore?"

Irene cleared her throat. "This is a part," she said, "a very small part, of why I'm calling. This place, it's called Silverberg Hospice of South Florida, it's . . . it's an expensive facility."

"Aha," Cynthia said. She halted in her pacing and stared out the window past the Triborough, over the level expanse of Queens. When it was clear, you could stand at that window and count a dozen airplanes stratified in the sky. "Well, Irene Ball, you've come to the right place. It's called Silverberg?" The cook came in the door; Cynthia made a furious scribbling motion in the air and then snapped her fingers at her, which surprised the woman visibly. "And it's in Fort Myers. Well then. You've been a great help. Many thanks. Best of luck to you."

"I'm sorry?"

"I can take over from here," Cynthia said, leaning her forehead against the glass. "Thank you, Irene. I'm very grateful to you. I mean it."

More dead air. "I thought," Irene began. "I mean, maybe I didn't explain it right. You are coming down to see him, right?"

"Of course. It's just – well, look, I have no desire to hurt anybody's feelings here, but since my father has never mentioned you to me, I just didn't want to take anything for granted. I don't want you to think that I expect there's any obligation on your part. I'm happy to take care of whatever needs to be taken care of. That's all I meant."

The cook appeared with a pad and pen. Cynthia sat back down at the table and wrote the word "Silverberg," and closed her eyes.

"Your father and I," Irene said, sounding quite confused, "are in love with each other."

These long silences; was this how other people, people who didn't live in New York maybe, conducted themselves on the phone? It was harder to be polite now that there were all these arrangements to be made, so Cynthia said, "Well, I imagine we'll see each other soon, then. Goodbye," and hung up. Irene Ball, she thought. What a name. She was shaking so hard she had to light up a cigarette in the house. At least no one was around to scold her for it. She called Lee Memorial in Fort Myers and asked to speak to the head of the cardiac-care unit there, and while she was waiting for a call back she spoke to the director of the Silverberg Hospice, who told her that she was very sorry but there were no beds currently available. She ended the call politely but without ever quite accepting that answer, and then she ran into the living room, grabbed her laptop, found Silverberg's annual report online, and scrolled all the way to the end of it. It was run, as she'd guessed, as a charity, and though it was a local one, the board included a couple of names she knew. She called one of them – even though it was still early, even though it was Saturday – and said as plainly as she could that she needed a favor. There was always, when it came to getting things done, a level above your level. There was always that next level to acknowledge, and to aspire to.

By the end of the afternoon her father had been transferred to the hospice by ambulance. Since Adam and April had taken the jet, she left Dawn a voicemail asking her to book a charter to Florida Monday night; there was a foundation board meeting first thing Monday at which she had to present, and anyway, she figured, why not give him a chance to settle in a little bit, get comfortable, maybe give

Irene and her long silences a chance to say a private goodbye.

He was an exceptionally proud man. He'd never asked her for anything and he wasn't about to start now that he was at his weakest. She was proud of him for that and frustrated at the same time. Why would he risk having some need of his go unmet rather than ask her to meet it? Surely there was no question in his mind that she might say no. Maybe he felt guilty. Or maybe he thought it was more considerate to spare her the facts of his weakness.

She put off trying to reach Adam because she was worried that he would want to turn right around and fly home. Too grueling, and also pointless, since the cardiac-care doc she'd spoken to estimated that her father still had several weeks to go. Jonas was in Chicago and there didn't seem much point in pulling him away from his studies to sit at the deathbed of a man he hardly knew.

The next night was the cocktail reception, for a children's charity the foundation had just gotten involved with called Little Red Wagon. A small affair for a few influential donors, maybe twenty people altogether. She spent a lot of time apologizing for Adam's absence. It was depressing, working the room alone, even though this wasn't the first time she'd done it, even though the room in question was in her own home. She felt liberated and sad at the same time. Always the same faces at these events.

Toward the end of the evening, one of the cooks came all the way into the doorway of the solarium and discreetly caught Cynthia's eye. There was a phone call for her, which had for some reason been transferred to the kitchen; she took it in there, while all the servers turned their backs and acted soundlessly busy. Remarkably, it was Irene calling again; but before Cynthia could politely defer her, she interrupted to say that her father's health, now that he was comfortably installed in the hospice, had taken a precipitous turn, such that rather than wait until later in the week as planned, Cynthia had better fly down there as soon as she possibly could.

There was no way, not even after Jonas shamelessly dragged his parents' name into it, that Margo the gallery owner was going to give up any contact information for Joseph Novak. She kept telling Jonas that she had been in the business for thirty years, as if that explained anything. But then Jonas had a brainstorm: he recalled Margo's mention, at the art fair, of the brother in Kenosha. There were a lot of Novaks in Kenosha, as it turned out, but he finally dialed the one he was looking for, and after that it was a simple negotiation. Arthur Novak didn't care who the money came from. You could tell from the merriness in his voice that he just couldn't have been more tickled to have stumbled into this world of rich idiots who forever needed new things to waste their money on.

When Jonas asked for his brother's address, though, Arthur hesitated a moment. "You do know what he was locked up for, right?" he said.

The sudden caution in Arthur's voice spooked Jonas into

285

fearing that he might change his mind about the whole thing. "Sure," Jonas said, "I know all about that."

"Well then," Arthur said, and he gave Jonas the address. Jonas didn't mention the jail business to Nikki – she was freaked out enough as it was by his "infatuation" with Agnew and this whole notion of making him a gift, in effect, of an artist so far out on the margins that even Agnew had never heard of him.

"I'm thinking ahead," Jonas said. "I mean I'm genuinely interested in the subject, and I'm sort of in Agnew's favor right now for whatever reason and I want to capitalize on that. I can get a jump on a master's thesis this way."

"What the hell difference does it make," she said, "how fast you do it?"

He shrugged. Maybe it was a way of closing the gap between him and her. But in the end the impulse was so strong that it didn't really matter to him what the reason was. Two days later he rented a car and drove into Wisconsin. Nothing but brown fields and broken stalks surrounded the highway, until some strange concern would rear up out of nowhere – a liquor wholesaler, a John Deere dealership, a Church of Latter-day Saints – and then disappear in his mirror. When it got to be a reasonable hour he started dialing Novak's phone number, but Arthur Novak had told him not to expect his brother to answer necessarily, and he didn't. Jonas never let it go past five or six rings for fear of antagonizing him. He held the printed directions against the steering wheel with his thumb as he drove.

He was almost there – going too slowly, bent over the steering wheel to stare up at the street signs as he passed them – when his cell phone rang. "Who is this," the voice on the other end said, "why do you keep calling me and hanging up?" and Jonas felt a chill go through him. "Your brother gave me your number," he said. "I'm sorry to have called you so many times, I was just trying to get a hold of you. My name is—"

"Why don't you just leave a damn message?"

A perfectly sensible question, and it both relaxed Jonas and disappointed him a little to think that he was dealing with someone a little more reasonable than he'd imagined. "You're right," he said. "I'm sorry. Anyway, I called because" – he saw the sign for Novak's street out the window, but decided to circle the block a few times and keep talking – "I called because I'm, I'm someone who's interested in art, and I've seen some of your drawings and I think they're really great. And I just happen to be in town today – I live in Chicago – and I was hoping I could meet you and maybe see some more of your, of your work."

There was a very long pause.

"Joseph?" Jonas said finally. "Are you there?"

Nothing. No way the call could have been dropped – he was only circling the block. Jonas saw the number 236 on a tattered-looking row house and realized he was right outside Novak's door. He was starting to think he'd made a terrible mistake – not in seeking out Novak in the first place, but in the impetuous way he'd handled it. Strange to feel yourself the object of someone else's paranoia. And here he was, staring at the artist's windows.

"I'm hungry," Novak said.

"What? You're hungry? I'm kind of hungry too. Do you want to go out and eat something?"

Silence.

"Or do you want me to bring some food," Jonas said, "when I come over?"

"Arby's?" Novak said – a little softly, but sounding more interested now.

"Sure," Jonas said. "I'll get some stuff from Arby's and come over. Is there an Arby's near where you live?"

Novak hung up. Jonas rolled his window down, looking for someone on the street he could ask where the Arby's was. But the streets were pretty empty this time of day, unless maybe they were like this all day. He could sort of see it from Novak's point of view: if the voice knows where I live, then why wouldn't it know where the Arby's is?

Dawn chartered a plane from Teterboro and rode along in the limo; poor thing, she was constantly tearing up – mostly out of a kind of terrified remorse that she had almost screened out a call that had come from her boss's father's deathbed, but also because she had lost her own father to cancer when she was in high school. In the limo she asked, in a tone that was businesslike yet tinged with hope, whether Cynthia needed her to come to Florida. Cynthia put her hand on Dawn's discomposed face and told her that her only job, for the next day or two or however long it would be, was to apologize convincingly on her boss's behalf to the dozens of people whose appointments to see her would now have to be postponed indefinitely – an easy enough job if Dawn had been free to explain what it was that had called her away, but Cynthia, for privacy's sake, had asked her to please come up with a different story.

The plane was still being fueled when they got there, so the limo sat on the tarmac for a while. The horizon was just starting to lighten. Dawn fell asleep against her shoulder. Cynthia saw the pilot pass bleary-eyed in front of their windshield, trying to button down his collar with one hand while holding a Diet Coke.

It would have been nice to have her family around her now, but their pursuits were spread all over the world, and so she sat in the main cabin alone, save for an attendant who mostly tried to stay out of her sightline behind the bulkhead. Jonas wasn't answering his cell. Maybe he was in class; anyway, she could certainly send the plane up to Chicago for him if there was any need. She'd spoken to Adam while she was packing – too emotional to calculate the time difference – and just as she'd expected he offered to fly back right away, but there was no point. The work he was doing was too important. And it sounded like her father might be dead anyway by the time Adam could get to Fort Myers from Shanghai; but she knew that if she said that out loud she would burst into tears that would cause him to fly back immediately anyway, so she settled for telling him that she loved him and would keep him posted.

She hadn't brought anything to read, and there was too

much cloud cover even for a look out the window. She supposed that this was a time when one might naturally think about the past. Up to now she'd been able to keep herself moving and thus hover above whatever it was that she should be feeling. But going over her father's failings, their little moments of disconnected joy – this seemed too much like eulogizing him, hurrying him into the grave, and she resisted it. Instead she found herself wondering what was the last really great advance, in terms of speed, in human transportation. The jet engine? What was that, a hundred years ago? Why did it take just as long to get from New York to Florida now as it had before she was born? What kind of sense did that make? But if she was thinking of it now, chances were excellent others had already been thinking about it for a while: work was being done somewhere, somebody needed an angel.

Dawn had found her a decent hotel in Fort Myers, and Cynthia went there first to drop her bags and take a quick shower. She tried not to hurry, because hurrying seemed like bad luck somehow, or an absence of faith; her cell sat on the dresser as she changed, and she avoided staring at it just as she might have if someone were watching her. She called the concierge up to her room to tell him that she would need a car and driver on call at all times during her stay, which would be indefinite; but it turned out Dawn had called ahead and arranged for all that too. Cynthia's driver was a man as old as her father, a Cuban named Herman with a crewcut and a neck whose folds were unevenly browned. Herman was unfailingly polite but he had a real meanness in his eye. She thought he was probably ex-military. He never spoke first. He wore a suit jacket over a short-sleeved shirt, and she imagined that when he got home after work every day, the first thing he did was throw that jacket on the floor, and his wife would pick it up and hang it for him.

Florida. It really was a blight. Maybe that's why old people assembled here – having to leave it behind wouldn't seem like such a bad deal. She stared out the back of the limo at the six-lane roads and the shopping plazas, the endless construction, the high walls and dimly visible golf courses, as if life on a golf course were so desirable that too direct a look at it would sear your eyes somehow. They were still in the middle of the whole car-infested hellscape – somehow she'd imagined they wouldn't be – when she felt Herman slow down, and they turned left past a gas station with a Krispy Kreme inside it, and another two hundred yards past that was the Silverberg Hospice of South Florida.

She'd never had any reason to see the inside of a hospice before and had only a dim idea what went on in there. Partly in fear, partly out of a superstition that it was important to continue acting as if she had all the time in the world, she walked in a sort of dream languor down the long corridor to the nurses' desk, her heart banging, and from what she could observe it was basically a hospital that didn't smell like a hospital. Also it was quiet, and less crowded, and only one story high. Also it was staffed by people who were clearly angels of some sort, drably luminous avatars of selflessness. She was ambivalent about this. She could not be expected to integrate with these people. She was hoping that at least one of them would feel as scared and selfish and inadequate as she did, that maybe there was someone who was only working here as a condition of his community-service sentence and would form a bond with her and maybe give her a slug from the bottle he kept in his locker just to get through the day without freaking out completely. But no. Some stout woman in a nurse's outfit that could almost have been worn as a Hawaiian shirt actually came out from behind the desk to greet her before she'd even reached the end of the hallway. Somehow the woman's very informality was scary too, as if civility were one of the pretentious earthly comforts Cynthia was apparently supposed to have checked at the door.

"You're Charlie's daughter," she said. "I could see it a mile away. I'm Marilyn."

"Hello," Cynthia said. She wanted to turn and run back up the hallway to Herman, to jump in the back seat of his car and see, in the rearview mirror, his disappointed frown.

"Your dad's sleeping at the moment," Marilyn said, "but I'll take you in to see him. He is a charmer, that one."

She took Cynthia's hand and led her down the hallway; and Cynthia, a grown woman, a woman who ran a major philanthropic foundation, with a staff for both business and household, a woman who had dedicated her life to good causes all over the world, actually caught herself pulling backward slightly, like a child, on that hand as they walked through her father's door. It was like a fantasy hospital room, like the secret room deep within a normal hospital that only the man who'd endowed it would ever be allowed to use.

It was huge and well furnished, with a high, gabled ceiling where a large fan turned slowly and noiselessly. The lights were off, and the blinds were about three-quarters shut; the walls had a bluish tinge but it was too dark for her to tell whether they were actually painted blue or not. There was a dresser along one wall, on top of which was a portable stereo and a stack of CDs. At the room's far end, in the soothing gloom that was like the gloom not deep underwater but just a foot or two below the surface, there were some monitors on either side of the bed. All of them were turned off. The bed itself seemed gigantic, proportioned like a regular-size bed would be to a child. After a minute she could make out his head lying on the pillow. There were railings on either side, and a mountainous comforter that certainly didn't look like hospital-issue. It might have been something he'd brought from home. She wouldn't know. It was so quiet that suddenly it struck her, as in a dream, that everyone else was just waiting for her to realize what they knew, that her father had already died. She turned around but Marilyn had left the room.

In the darkness she would have to get quite close to his face to really see it and she wasn't prepared to do that yet. Through the blinds to the left of the bed she could just make out a small lake: plainly man-made and perfunctory-seeming, a kind of trope of serenity, in spite of which a few ducks had come to paddle in its shallows, and on a rock on its far bank a cormorant held its wings spread to dry them. The lake's symmetry was unlovely and it seemed squeezed into a space too small for it, like the fruit of some design compromise or maybe the sentimental whim of whoever endowed this place, which the contractors had no choice but to shrug their shoulders and carry out. Marilyn came back into the room behind her carrying a jar of moisturizer and a Snapple iced tea with a straw in it.

"So that's the last thing a lot of people see," Cynthia whispered to her, still looking out the window.

"Who knows what they see," she said kindly. "Anyway, your father's friend spends a lot of time looking at it."

And only then did Cynthia notice that to the left of the dresser there was a door – oversize, so that through it could pass a wheelchair or maybe even the great bed itself – that led to an enclosed veranda, where it would be possible, at least, to feel the breeze and the sun, and to hear something, even if it was very likely just the sound of traffic and construction. Sitting in one of the two chairs out there, smoking a cigarette, was Irene Ball. Cynthia couldn't see much more than the back of her head, which was coiffed and blond almost to the point of whiteness. Her legs were crossed, and a huarache hung as still as an icicle from her toes.

Beyond the lake was a strip of trees probably meant to hint at forestlike depths, even though the highway was just on the other side of it. Or maybe a golf course. She thought it was the highway, though. She'd lost her bearings a little bit when they turned into the driveway.

As quietly as possible – not wanting to wake him, she told herself – Cynthia sat down in one of the chairs that had been pulled up near the head of the huge bed. It was probably there because that's where Irene liked to sit. Her father's mouth hung open, and when she tilted her head forward a bit she could hear the arrhythmic catch of his breath. She started to cry when she saw how he looked: starving, thin-haired, his skin spotted. But she also felt she would be happy to stay like this for a while, if not indefinitely. She wasn't ready to let him go, but she didn't exactly want him to wake up either, because anyone as weak as this was very likely to need something, and how would she know what he needed? How would she know how to give it to him? She'd come all the way down here and all she was really good for was to ask for help from someone else. She wished the bed, or the room, or the place itself, was unsatisfactory in some way she could see, so that she could inquire nicely or pitch a fit or even just donate some money and cause it to be improved. But everything here seemed perfectly suited to its purpose. His old head was like some vandalized monument and she resisted the urge to reach out and stroke it. I'm here, she said silently to him. I made it in time. Outside, the smoke from Irene's cigarette rose and rose until it blunted itself on the roof of the veranda. She hadn't lifted it to her mouth in a while.

Holding the grease-spotted bags and balancing a stiff cardboard drink holder with several types of soda in it, Jonas rang the bell at 236 with his elbow, then rang it again, but no one came to the door and he couldn't hear anyone moving around inside. The street behind him was narrowed by two lines of parked cars but nothing anywhere seemed to be moving. When he walked around to the side of the house to see if there was a window he might discreetly look through, he noticed a flight of exterior stairs that led to an entrance on the second floor. That had to be it, he thought; he climbed the stairs and, rather than knock with his foot, called through the door that he had brought the Arby's. A second later the door opened inward and Jonas stepped inside.

No one was there in front of him, but he was aware of being peeked at through the wedge of space between the open door and its hinges. He took another step or two forward. Though he could see opposite him a tiny hallway that must have led to a bedroom and a bathroom, Novak's home was mostly one square living room, which would have been dark, since it faced alleys on two sides, were it not for the fact that there were at least twice as many lamps as were necessary for a room that size. All of them were turned on. The effect was compounded by the fact that the walls were freshly painted in a kind of skull-frying white. Pieces of paper were taped over the windows. The odor inside the room was such that Jonas had to make an effort not to flinch.

Novak closed the door behind him and grabbed the food out of his hands. There was a small, grimy-looking kitchenette off to their right and Novak emptied out the bag on the counter in there, unwrapping each item and checking carefully, in the case of the sandwiches, underneath the bun. He lifted the cover off each soda, stuck his finger in it, and then poured it down the sink. Jonas cleared his throat.

"Joseph?" he said. "I'm Jonas."

"That's going to be confusing," Novak said, and started eating a roast beef sandwich with some kind of cheese on it. Jonas felt his own surprise reflected in Novak's stare and realized that each was taken aback to see how young the other one was. Novak, though he was well on his way to baldness, still looked no older than about twenty-five.

"Why did you bring all this food?" Novak said. "This is way too much. Nobody else is coming, right?"

"Just me. I just wasn't sure what you liked, so I got a sampling."

"A what?" Novak said. He scowled. "You're here to steal from me."

"No. Absolutely not. Like I said on the phone, I'm kind of a fan of yours. I went to a fair in Chicago and some of your drawings were hanging on the wall there. I thought they were really beautiful. Did you know that people as far away as Chicago think you're a great artist?" He could hear himself talking as if Novak were a child, but how else was he supposed to handle it? How did you know what aspect of him you were speaking to?

"You don't know what you're talking about," Novak said.

"I will pay you a lot of money for your art, if you're willing to sell it. But I'm not going to steal anything from you. I promise. Why, do you think other people have been stealing from you?"

"Do you think other people have been stealing from you?" Novak repeated, licking his fingers.

"Like your brother, maybe?"

"Like your brother, maybe?"

He said these things that seemed sarcastic or childish or angry but the tone of his voice didn't really change significantly, nor did the look on his face. The sandwich got the lion's share of his attention. He wore glasses with clear plastic frames, and what hair he had was so fair as to be almost invisible, like a baby's hair; his pale skin was still touched by acne. Most remarkably, though Jonas was uncomfortable even noticing it, was that these features sat on a head that was so small he thought he could have palmed it like a cantaloupe. Novak put a handful of french fries in his mouth and then went over to the door and locked it.

"I don't like other people seeing my drawings," he said.

That's what makes them so worth seeing, Jonas thought, but instead he said, "I can understand that. It's private. What do you usually do with a drawing after you finish it?"

"I don't know."

"How often does your brother come to visit?"

"I don't know."

Jonas stopped trying to make eye contact with him; he felt the need to make his own presence less provocative somehow. As his eyes grew used to the overpowering lighting, he thought he picked something up from the walls themselves, something other than just the shocking white. He took a few steps forward and saw, or thought he saw, the ghost of a face.

"Do you draw on the walls sometimes?" he asked. Novak reacted as if he'd been poked, jumping up and walking toward the papered-over window, lacing his fingers on top of his head. "Only sometimes," he said. "Not that much. She just painted again. She was really mad. I only do it if I'm out of paper and can't go out, when I'm not feeling good."

"When you're *not* feeling good?" Jonas said. No reply. "Does drawing make you feel better?" No reply. He felt like he was burying himself deeper but he had to keep going until he hit on the right question to ask. "What makes you feel like doing it?" he said.

"I don't know," Novak said, pacing now.

The wall drawings were an interesting idea but Jonas's first thought was that of course there would be no way to get them out of the apartment itself. Unless he came back with a camera. But right now it was hard to imagine Novak ever letting him back in here again. "Joseph," he said, "you know, if you like, I would be happy to give you some more paper so you don't run out. I could buy a lot of it for you. Is that something you'd like?"

"I don't know," Novak said.

"You don't know? But then you could draw all you wanted, and you wouldn't have to worry about her" – he didn't know who he was referring to: Novak's landlord, he assumed, unless it was his mother – "getting mad about the walls."

"She said she'd throw me out," Novak said.

"Right, so this way you could keep drawing and not have to worry about that. What do you like to draw with most?"

"Sharpies," Novak said miserably. He stopped pacing in front of the papered-over window, with his back to Jonas.

"Sharpies cost money too, right? I could get you all of those you wanted. You could draw whenever you felt like it without getting into trouble. Wouldn't you like that?"

"I don't know," he said.

It could have been the "I don't know" of a three-year-old, just a conversation stopper; anyway, Jonas chose not to hear it. "Really?" he said. "Then why do you do it?"

"I don't know," Novak said, and turned around, and started walking forward; and Jonas, when he saw the expression on his face, took a step back toward where he thought the door was. "I don't know I don't know I don't know I don't know I don't know."

Their eyes met, and for one incredible moment he knew they were wishing the exact same thing at the same time, which was that Jonas had never come here; and then Jonas started a little too casually toward Novak's front door, but before he could figure which of the two locks to unlock, something hard, harder than a fist anyway, connected with the back of his head. He had never really been hit before, not ever, his whole life long. Everything went white, as if his eyes had rolled all the way around, and it couldn't have been more than a few seconds later that he opened his eyes and was looking up at Novak sitting on a stool in the kitchenette, eating another one of the cold Arby's sandwiches, and looking very worried.

Time, of course, would not stand still in the way Cynthia wished it to, and so eventually the door to the veranda opened and Irene came back squinting into the darkened room. The change in light was such that Irene didn't seem to see her right away. Cynthia didn't say anything for fear of waking her father, though she was unsure why, when she had rushed down here precisely because his death was imminent, she should now be placing such value on his sleep. Then Irene began gesturing with her thumb, like a hitchhiker, and Cynthia understood that she was suggesting the two of them go out into the hallway.

They shook hands. Cynthia put her age at about sixty; she appeared younger than that, but she had the look of a woman who was older than she looked. She smelled like cigarettes. Her hair had that sculpted sexagenarian appearance Cynthia had become familiar with through her time on the charity circuit. She was almost a head shorter too. Her skin was amazingly fair; how could you live in Florida, Cynthia wondered, and have skin that looked like that? Did she never go outside?

"Oh, I'm so excited to finally meet you," Irene said. "Charlie talks about you all the time. He's so proud of you and your husband, and all the success you've had." Cynthia, with no similar civility to offer in return because she had had no notion of this person's existence until a few days ago, smiled weakly. She could see already that Irene was the sort of woman who wore every emotion, no matter how fleeting, on her face, and so it became clear that she had been anticipating a more expansive Cynthia, as if there were already a bond there, as if this were a long-awaited reunion rather than a meeting of total strangers. "Anyway," she said, "part of the reason I wanted to talk to you out of the room

301

is that there are some things you may want to be prepared for before Charlie wakes up."

"What is that?" Cynthia said. There was something about this moment, about Irene's status as an intermediary between Cynthia and what was happening to her, about the spectacular presumption of her kindness, that was threatening to reveal itself as unbearable. Irene closed her big eyes, giving Cynthia a look at her horrifying blue eye shadow, and sighed.

"So at Charlie's request they've taken him off every type of medication except pain management. One of the side effects of that is that his blood pressure has dropped so low that it's affecting the blood flow to his brain, and so he's showing some signs of dementia. Nothing big – sometimes he doesn't know where he is, and sometimes he thinks he's somewhere else – but he's in and out of it, and it can be kind of scary, especially if you're not expecting it. He's been sick a long time but still, it's happened so fast. Part of it is going off the medication but really it's amazing how fast he slipped physically once he'd made the decision to let go. Amazing to me, at least. Marilyn says that it happens that way all the time."

She finally found the Kleenex she'd been fishing around for in her bag. Nurses and other personnel moved around them with perfect impassive grace as Irene stood there crying in the middle of the hallway. The fact that you never saw them look the least bit disconcerted or surprised should have been soothing but instead Cynthia felt a little undermined by it.

"Anyway," Irene went on, "I'm sorry to drop that on you first thing, but when I saw you sitting there beside the bed, I didn't want you to be too upset if it happened, or if he didn't know right away who you were. I'm sorry for the circumstances but it really is such a privilege to meet you. I'm really looking forward to us getting to know each other. It's never too late, right?"

"What have you signed?" Cynthia said. Her sudden curiosity about this surely could have waited, but Cynthia felt a strong, almost fearful impulse to keep things on a certain officious level. "Here at the hospice, I mean. If he's not sure where he is they must have needed somebody to sign some consent for this or that."

"Charlie signed everything. He was still perfectly lucid. They only stopped the medication after he was admitted."

"It's not that I don't take your word for all this," Cynthia said. "But are there any actual doctors here during the day? Or is it all just nurses and priests and whatnot? Because I wouldn't mind speaking to an actual medical professional at this—"

But then, she saw, or rather felt, that one of the nurses who slid so unobtrusively behind her back had gone into her father's room. "Good afternoon, Charlie," Cynthia heard her say. "You have some visitors here. Is it okay if I turn a light on?"

Cynthia spun and hurried back through the door, just as the nurse snapped on the lamp beside the bed. She had implored herself over and over not to let herself be shocked, for her own sake and for his, but it was no use. His face was like a skull. He was wearing some kind of nightshirt, much nicer than the standard-issue hospital gown but antiquated and ridiculous all the same. His neck throbbed perceptibly, like a frog's, and his mouth still hung open. His eyes seemed almost to protrude from his head, but then Cynthia caught on that, unlike the rest of his face, the eyes were actually expressing something; they were especially wide right now because he was trying to figure out where he was. He was staring right at her but he couldn't figure it out.

"Your daughter is here," the nurse said softly to him. She didn't make it into a question, like she was trying to reorient him; it wasn't condescending in that way. There was no more progress or recovery, in that sense, to be made. It was just about making him less terrified.

Incrementally, the light came back into his eyes. From that terrible leveling impersonality, he returned to occupy his own face, and where a minute ago he hadn't really seemed in the room at all, now he dominated it again. He struggled to raise himself up on the pillows, and his hand started vainly toward his hair before falling back on the comforter. He licked his lips. "Hello, Sinbad," he said hoarsely. "What do you make of all this?"

The nurse was already backing away discreetly from the head of the bed before Cynthia even realized she was moving toward it. She hadn't heard herself called Sinbad in about thirty-five years.

There was no getting around it: he felt like a total pussy for having been taken out and disoriented so completely by one blow to the head. One's head, he felt, should be tougher than that. He didn't see any blunt object around and so was thinking that maybe it was only Novak's fist after all. And Novak was a figure whom he would have naïvely estimated, as recently as a couple of hours ago, that he could take. Fear and heedlessness were all the guy was really armed with, and it turned out to be enough.

He was still a little in and out, maybe just from the shock of it all. He was sitting on Novak's rancid couch, at the end of the living room farthest from the door. He had to squint a bit against the blazing lights. He could see that a lot of the furniture in the room had been pushed around so that it was no longer in the configuration he remembered from when he first walked through the door. Most of it was now in front of him, and one wall, the wall directly across from him, was cleared away. Novak wasn't in the room but Jonas could hear him moving around somewhere – maybe around the corner in the kitchenette. Then he heard something else – a ringing phone – and he recognized the ring as his own, though it was coming not from his pocket where his cell phone belonged but from somewhere else in the apartment.

Novak came around the corner from the kitchenette, holding Jonas's cell phone in front of him like a compact mirror. "Stop it," he said. After the fourth ring it stopped. Novak put it back in his own pants pocket and left the room again.

What the fuck is happening? Jonas asked himself. He couldn't make sense of it. He wasn't restrained or tied down in any way. It was possible to get up, and yet he couldn't, and he realized that what was really going on was that he was frightened, almost to the point of paralysis. The series of events that had led to his being here in this room at all was so bizarre and arbitrary that it seemed to him like if he thought about it logically enough, he could actually undo it, like snapping himself out of a dream – prove to himself that he wasn't here, but somewhere else much more familiar.

He felt like he might throw up, but instead he went to sleep again, and when he woke up, a good portion of that blank white wall in front of him – the upper third of it or so – was covered with a picture. The whole place now smelled like Sharpies, which was sickening but still something of a blessing considering the other smells the Sharpies were masking. The picture itself was fantastically detailed, full of dogs and cats and televisions and those signature open-mouthed faces, like a Brueghel almost but without the technique, an unpatterned riot of primary industrial color, and it might have been beautiful, but Jonas really couldn't see it.

Cynthia asked Dawn to fax her whatever she could find on the Silverberg Hospice and learned that it was one of the most popular, high-profile charities in the city, well run and financed to the gills. She was secretly hoping for a different answer because she had conceived this fantasy that she would just buy the place. It's not like there was anything she could have improved about it. She would have given everyone there an immediate raise but she also just wanted to be able to succumb to the illusion that every single professional in the building was working for nobody else but her – the sort of selfish emotional fancy anyone with a sick parent or child might have had, the difference being that Cynthia had the resources to make such fancies real every once in a while. She wondered if her father was in the best-appointed room available and though she could have learned the answer to this question in five minutes just by walking up and down the hall – there were only about eight other rooms, and the apparent custom was for the doors to stand open – who knew what you were liable to see when you poked your head in one of them. She finally got up the nerve to ask one of the nurses; the answer was that the rooms differed only in whether or not they had the lake view. No one there ever looked at her strangely when she had a question like that.

The hospice really only employed one doctor. He made the rounds twice a day, and he did almost nothing, which Cynthia had to keep reminding herself was the goal. She overheard an exchange at the nurses' station between the doctor and Marilyn that suggested they both belonged to the same church: that explained a lot, she said to herself, though in truth she wasn't sure what it explained at all.

It was particularly hard to watch when they would change the sheets in her father's bed with him still in it, the gentle but practiced way they rolled the wisp of his body from side to side, the passivity outside the reach of shame with which he submitted to it. He was similarly receptive to being shaved, though it was easier for Cynthia to understand the sensual appeal involved there. Knowing him, he'd probably splurged on the occasional professional shave back in the day. She wished she could do it for him, but there was no way she could trust herself to stay calm enough; shaving someone's face with a razor would have been nerve-racking even under better circumstances. When watching this kind of upkeep got to be too much for her, she stood out on the veranda and stared at the artificial lake. It was easier to look at somehow when the birds were around; they didn't seem on any kind of schedule, though. Irene didn't join her out there, because Cynthia had told her she was allergic to cigarette smoke – a lie Irene likely recognized, but there were moments when Cynthia found she just couldn't bear anyone's company.

She would have brought him anything at all to eat, and they encouraged her to do that, within certain limits; his systems were closing down, and so anything too hard to digest might not bring him as much pleasure as she expected. But he had very little interest in food. Once he asked for ice cream, which was brought to him immediately, but after Cynthia fed him one spoonful, he declared himself full. He had always had a terrible sweet tooth, so maybe the whole ice cream thing was more memory than desire anyway.

"Would whipped cream help?" Irene asked him, too loudly, from over Cynthia's shoulder. "Do you remember how I used to put whipped cream on it for you?" She spoke to him in a tone of dramatic simplicity, like she was sitting at a Ouija board. It wasn't long before he was asleep again, his mouth open, his breaths arrhythmic. The two of them sat on opposite sides of the great bed and talked in hushed tones when they talked at all. The nurses brought them meals, after a fashion; Irene kept suggesting they give themselves a break and go out somewhere for a lunch or dinner where they could, she said earnestly, stop whispering, but Cynthia declined. Her excuse was that she was too afraid that her father would wake up and ask for her and she wouldn't be there, which was true though not comprehensively so; whatever it was that Irene was so eager to talk about, Cynthia felt pretty certain she did not want to talk about it. Disillusionment was too bitter a prospect.

It wasn't hard to outlast Irene: around dinnertime she would start to yawn, and a few minutes later she drove home to sleep in her own bed. Visiting hours were technically unlimited, but the nurses kept suggesting, in their seen-it-all way, that Cynthia go back to the hotel and get some real sleep too. She'd seen the nurses wheeling some kind of cot down to the far end of the corridor, for a guy she'd bumped into a few times at the nurses' station or the soda machine who was there waiting for his wife to die of leukemia. His eyes were always red. He looked about forty and had a bald spot that was so sunburned it was peeling. He gave off absolutely no vibe that suggested he wanted to talk to Cynthia about anything, which was great, because Cynthia had no desire to talk to him either. They scared each other a little bit. If your experience was too similar to someone else's then maybe it wasn't worth all that you felt it was.

When she was too tired to stay awake, or when she needed a change of clothes so badly she could smell herself, she would give in and call Herman and have him drive her back to the hotel. But she couldn't really sleep there either: it engendered despair even more quickly than the hospice, she found, because it was nowhere, and she had no one. She would turn the TV on, mute it, try to figure out what time it was in China, and then call Adam anyway.

"He's not dead yet," is how she would begin these calls.

"Is he comfortable?" Adam said. "I actually don't know what I even mean by that. What about you? How are you doing?"

"I don't know. It's rough. Sometimes he's fine, sometimes he's agitated and it's pretty hard to know what to say to him. I just want to be some kind of comfort to him but it's all so deep inside him at this point that you can't get at it."

"What about this Irene? Is she any help at all? I mean presumably she's been with him the whole time he was sick, so maybe she's more used to the signs or whatever?"

References to the past, even the recent past, made her instantly tense, or maybe it was just lack of sleep. "You'd think," she said. "But actually she tends to fall apart every time his condition slips the least little bit. It's almost like she expects me to help her get through this, which is so not what I signed on for."

"So what other—"

"I mean she's not exactly a complex figure," Cynthia said. "You can look at her and pretty much imagine what that whole relationship was like. You can see what a good audience she must have made. She's like a dog. One bit of kindness and she's so grateful she forgets about whatever happened a minute ago."

She squeezed her eyes shut to keep from crying.

"What about the nurses, though," Adam said. She loved him for changing the subject. "You're getting some help from them at least, right?"

"The nurses are basically unicorns," Cynthia said. "I feel like I should photograph them to prove that I'm not insane."

He laughed. There followed one of those silences the presumed awkwardness of which was the difference between a conversation on the telephone and a real one. "Listen," he said. "This may sound weird, but one thing I keep thinking about, which may or may not make you feel any better: you will not have to go through this yourself."

"I thought I was going through this myself," Cynthia said.

"No, I mean . . . I'm sorry I'm so far away. This isn't how it's supposed to go. But what I mean is that you and I pretty much had to start over in terms of family, and we did it. We succeeded. We're Year Zero. Those things can't ever be taken away from you again. Who knows why he chose to live like he did, but you will never be alone in that way. Just in case you were looking at him and wondering that."

That he would even try to articulate something like that meant more to her than whatever he was actually saying. "Baby, we didn't just succeed, we're a fucking multi-national," she laughed, wiping her eyes. "We've trademarked

311

ourselves. It doesn't get any more solid than us. Anyway, I am madly in love with you. Do you ever wonder what would have become of us if we hadn't found each other?"

"Never."

"Yeah, me neither. Listen, have you been able to get a hold of Jonas?"

"No. I left messages. You mean he doesn't even know you're down there?"

"Maybe not. I mean definitely not, or else he would have called. How about April? Is she right there?"

"Next door. Still sleeping. It's not quite six a.m. here. I'll send her your love."

Each day the dementia was a little more pronounced. You could always tell from his eyes when he didn't know where he was. Somehow he both recognized Cynthia and believed she was away at college; sometimes she seemed younger to him – "Do you want me to read to you?" he said to her once – but mostly he asked questions about classes, and about how soon she had to leave again, when the new semester began. Which was odd, since the two of them had never had a conversation like that for his memory to draw on. He was out of the house intermittently for as long as she could remember, and then gone for good by the time she was nine or ten; by the time she went away to school, whole years would go by where she would hear from him only via letter or the occasional, unpredictable phone call.

"So," he said to her, "any boyfriend at present? Or boyfriends? At your age, that's allowed, you know."

She smiled at him. Irene sat across the bed from her, though at the moment he didn't seem to know she was there, and Cynthia found it perversely satisfying that, for all the other woman knew, father and daughter were remembering something that had actually happened. His lips were cracked; she refilled a kind of sippy cup from the water pitcher that always sat by the bed and held it to his mouth. "A few," she said to him, a little coquettishly, imitating the self he thought she was. "Nothing exclusive."

"Well, you just have fun. That's what youth is for. You don't need me to tell you to be careful. You have your mother to do that."

She wanted only to be generous. Still, she was worried that she was going to start holding things against him. It did get to her a bit that the past into which he was receding wasn't what really took place, wasn't even the past at all – more like something new. Unless this was a fantasy he had kept to himself for a long time, and now he had been stripped of the ability to maneuver between what was in his head and what was outside of it.

Several times, over those first few days, he would suddenly try, apropos of nothing, to get out of bed; he would submit when she touched his shoulder, but he kept looking around him for something on the floor, like maybe something had fallen there. The third or fourth time it happened, late at night when the two of them were alone, he passed from a mild curiosity into a state more like anger.

"Dad," she said, "what – Dad, stop – what are you looking for?"

He looked up at her as if she were asking him to repeat something he'd already said ten times. "My shoes," he said. "Where the hell have I put them? Do you know where they are?"

When her own panic and reluctance to restrain him physically reached the point where she started to cry, she caved in and buzzed for the night nurse, Kay, who was there in two seconds. Part of the reason she didn't like relying on Kay was that her father seemed, in his deluded way, to be in love with her, and flirted with her ridiculously. Despite the fact that Kay was about sixty and fat as a house, Cynthia didn't blame him. Her wry competence in even the scariest situation was fucking hot.

"Charlie, what are you worried about?" Kay said calmly. He stopped fidgeting and stared at her with his mouth open, like a baby. Cynthia felt herself starting to lose it again and went out into the corridor. Kay joined her out there about two minutes later.

"Is he all right?" Cynthia said, her voice shaking a little. "Did you give him anything?"

"He's fine," Kay said. "Just a little worked up. That happens. We try not to overdo it with the drugs."

"It's just, I don't know what I did to set him off. He was looking for his shoes. It sounds so stupid. But that's like the tenth time it happened. He was always kind of vain about his appearance. Maybe it's you he wants to look all dapper for."

Kay shook her head. "That's not it," she said, smoothing the front of her festive-looking uniform. "Believe it or not,

314

that's kind of a common one, the shoes. Or the coat, or the purse if they're women. Had a lady in here just a few weeks ago who kept accusing me of stealing her hat."

Cynthia looked at her, confused.

"They know," Kay said. "On some level. They know they're about to go on a trip somewhere, and they need to get ready. Yeah," she said, nodding at Cynthia as she started to cry again, "I know, right? You think it's a metaphor or something until you've seen it a few times."

In Dongguan they stayed in a Western-style hotel where everyone spoke English and the food was badly cooked but still recognizable and you got a strange, xeroxed version of *The New York Times* slipped under your door; but in the morning when they drove out to someplace called Changan, nothing outside the bubble of the car was the least bit familiar anymore. The foundation had built a new dormitory for the people who worked at some factory – it even had the Moreys' name on it, supposedly – and so they were all going out to have a look. One of the bodyguards had told April this part of China was called the Pearl River Delta, but that had to be some kind of marketing term because it was the butt-ugliest place she'd ever seen in her life. Nothing but concrete and smoke and claustrophobia and a sky that had no hint of blue in it anywhere. The fact that every character on every sign she saw outside the hotel was completely incomprehensible to her made her feel like she was a baby. She kept trying to hold on to her contempt for all of it but in truth the sheer strangeness was so menacing that she sat with her arms folded the whole time just to keep from shaking. The driver offered three times to give her his coat.

Adam sat beside her in the back, reading that little photocopied *Times* from the hotel. Past his head she could see the bodyguard, whose motorcycle traveled with them everywhere. Why? Why did no one seem freaked out about that except her? Her father had had some kind of meeting that morning, he wouldn't say with whom. Business, he'd said. The fund, not the foundation. Whatever the hell that meant.

They hadn't spoken much. Fear made her clam up and she was still mad at him for making her come. She wondered when they were going to get out of this district they were crawling through, which was full of these gigantic, toxic-looking factories, and then, incredibly, the driver coasted to a stop in front of one of them and turned off the car.

"Do I have to go in?" April said. "Can I just wait out here?"

Her father and their driver, who was also their interpreter whenever they got out of the car anywhere, traded amused looks, like it was all just hilarious. "Absolutely not," her father said.

The first thing that happened was that they were given these huge headphones to wear, and she didn't get more than ten feet through the door before she understood why. Even with the headphones on it was deafening. But at least this way your ears wouldn't actually bleed. All the workers wore them too, and helmets and goggles and jumpsuit-like uniforms. It had to be more than a hundred degrees in there. The workers all stared at her as if she couldn't see them too. They were girls – not all of them, but most of them—April's own age or younger.

Some very nervous guy in a suit was giving them the tour, shouting at Adam and pointing to a clipboard, even though he must have known that there was no way to hear anything anybody said. Then a strange thing started to happen. Word began to get around the factory floor who the visitors were. April could see the workers talking to one another. One girl's mouth fell open, as Adam stood nearby still leaning into their guide and nodding as if they were actually conversing, and then she boldly left her place on the line and skipped over to him. April froze. The Chinese girl was speaking rapidly and smiling and lowering her head. She took both of Adam's hands in hers, and when he gave her a small smile in return and said *You're welcome,* that was like a signal to the others, many of whom broke from their place on the line and came to gather around him. It was all happening in front of April not silently, exactly, but like a movie whose soundtrack has been replaced by roaring industrial static. Adam took the women's hands and nodded courteously as if this were all the most natural thing in the world. When the wait to touch him got too long – at least one red-faced supervisor was screaming at them – another group broke away from the first and rapidly surrounded April herself. She was terrified. The girls lowered their heads and jabbered and took April's hands in theirs, and when she looked down at one pair of hands that seemed unusually fair, almost pink, she saw that those were burn scars, and that was the last thing she remembered.

Her father was sitting in the front seat this time, twisted around to face her, and she was lying across the back. "Good morning, Sunshine," he said. "I believe you fainted."

Her neck hurt. Two minutes later they were back at the hotel, unless she'd fallen asleep again and it was longer than that. He decided they would just have dinner in the room that night; as she lay on the bed he called room service and ordered her a Reuben, but when it came and he lifted the silver cover off the dish, she started crying.

Adam pulled a chair closer to the foot of the bed and sat with his feet up next to hers.

"I want to go home," April said. "I'm afraid of this place. I know I shouldn't be, but I am. I'm scared of poor people, basically. What kind of a hideous person does that make me?"

"Poverty is scary," Adam said. "The thought of not having what you need is terrifying. That's why people try so hard to avoid it."

"Okay, so, good, we avoided it. Why do you have to come here at all, then? Why isn't it enough just to be us?"

"Your mother and I are trying to make the world a better place," Adam said.

"Okay," April said. "But why?"

"Well, you can't just do nothing. Otherwise it's like you were never here."

He picked up half the Reuben and took a bite. "Wow,"

he said. "Pretty terrible." April took the pillow from behind her head and put it over her eyes. "But what if you *do* do nothing?" she said. "What if nothing is all there is for you to do? I try not to look forward but sometimes I do and it's all these days and I have no fucking idea what to fill them with. That's why sometimes I wonder if maybe what I'm really trying to do is, you know, shorten it."

He stopped chewing. "Do not say that," he said darkly. "I don't want to hear that kind of talk from you ever again. Understand me?"

She reached under the pillow to wipe her eyes. "I'm sorry I fainted," she said. "I'm sorry I embarrassed you. It's just that I couldn't handle it when they all started thanking me. Thanking me? For what? All I wanted was to be as far away from them as possible. I so don't deserve to be thanked."

"You are loved," Adam said. "Okay? And if you know you're loved then you might make a mistake once in a while but you are never in the wrong. I know this isn't a great time for you but I have total faith that things will get better, because that's what things do. They get better. This is something I know something about. It is, as they used to say, the American way. You may feel a little lost right now but you will know what to do. For now maybe just focus on what not to do. Like hang out with Eurotrash dealers with names like Dmitri."

"Fine," she said. "He's an asshole anyway. I'll never find someone like you and Mom did, though. You two are ridiculous."

319

"Sure you will. I know it will happen. It has to. Put it this way: there's always someone out there who can save you."

"So then you believe in fate or whatever?" April said.

He licked his fingers. "Maybe not for everybody," he said.

He tried to get her to eat but he couldn't really blame her for refusing; the Reuben, like most of the American-style food they'd seen in Dongguan, was like an approximation based on photographs. Even the ingredients seemed like a best guess guided mostly by color. Instead she closed her eyes, and he sat there at the foot of the bed and watched her, and when she was asleep he got up quietly and went back to his room, leaving ajar the connecting door of their suite.

He'd had to cancel one of his two meetings today in order to stay with her, but the other one had gone well, and everything else he could think of was as it should be; still, something made him uneasy as he stood there staring out the window, which could not be opened, at the gray sky fading unpicturesquely to black. It was the hotel room itself, he decided, the sense of restless distaste these rooms always engendered in him. They made him a little crazy; sometimes he'd wake up in one and it would seriously take him a minute to remember where he was and how he'd gotten there. Having come halfway around the world, you'd think it might feel different. But this room was the same everywhere: blank and haughtily self-sufficient as if it knew it would outlive you by a thousand years. It made you reflective, which was not a state he welcomed or thought highly of, in himself or others. The best thing would have been just to go to bed, but Adam knew his body well enough to know that there was no way he would fall asleep for another hour at least. Just lying there awake in the dark would be worse.

Cyn had told him to call her anytime, but when he tried her now he got bounced straight to voicemail. She might have left her charger back in New York. He left a message at her hotel saying that he hoped her dad was still comfortable and that he loved her.

End of an era, he thought: somehow the fact that his father-in-law had been such a ghost while he was alive made it harder to imagine he'd soon be gone for real. Here was a guy about to pass from the earth having left no trace of himself at all – having lived, in fact, in such a way as to take care that he wouldn't. It made no sense. Adam had never told Cynthia this but if that child Charlie Sikes had abandoned thirty-odd years ago had been him, the guy could have died alone in a ditch for all he cared. He would never have given him a nickel, he wouldn't have contacted him or spoken to him or even thought about him. But Cynthia had a bigger heart than he did, in all things. "Better half" was one of those expressions people used without thinking, but she was absolutely the better half of him, and without her he felt like he knew exactly the sort of abyss he would fall into. He'd probably see Charlie there. But family civilized a man. See, this is the kind of shit I hate thinking about, Adam said to himself, and he got up and turned on the TV; but the only thing he could find in English was Larry King and he wound up muting it anyway for fear of waking April.

Outside the window the whole panorama of squared-off rooftops was swallowed into the grimy dark. That morning he'd gone downstairs to the lobby in shorts and a T-shirt for a run but the concierge had literally sprinted to the door to block his path and said the air quality was too bad for such an activity. Which was plausible. Or maybe the concierge just didn't want Adam to get kidnapped or shot on his watch, or to see something an American wasn't supposed to see. This was a ruthlessly ugly city. It was the future, though. Everybody nodded when you said that but only a few people got off their asses and acted on it.

Even inside the fund there were a few people who felt that someone in Adam's position shouldn't be doing business in China at all. Most of his employees thought of him, for better or worse, as apolitical, but that wasn't really true. He was perfectly aware that what he was doing here affected many more fortunes than just his own. Money was its own system, its own language, its own governing principle. You introduced money into a situation and it released the potential in everybody. Maybe you got rich, maybe others around you got rich while you didn't, but either way it had to be better to learn the truth about your own nature.

The room was as silent as if he'd had earplugs in and so he jumped a little bit when he heard a noise at the door: someone from the front desk was trying to slide a thick stack of what looked like fax paper into his room. He didn't really feel up to going through it just now. He could feel himself starting to tire. Tomorrow first thing he would get out there and run through those toxic streets even if he had to lay out that concierge to do it. The more he thought about it, the more pissed he was that he'd let himself be turned back this morning. That was five days in a row now – ever since they'd left New York – with no exercise. He was in better shape than most men half his age but what people didn't appreciate was how fragile a state it was. You had to work so hard just to maintain it: let up even for a moment and that was where time took over. He pulled up his shirt as he sat there on the bed and was able to pinch a small roll of fat between his thumb and forefinger. That was no good. He made himself a solemn promise to double his workouts the moment he got back home.

Back to the hospice at dawn, but her father was already awake. He was staring at the slowly turning ceiling fan, in something like alarm. "What?" Cynthia said. "You want it off? Are you cold?" She switched it off, but the expression on his face stayed the same. She saw his lips moving and went to lean over him at the head of the bed.

"What is that?" he said. "That is, how far away is it?"

You'd answer a question like that, and he'd nod, as if you'd made perfect sense, but then half a minute later you'd see the same look in his eye and you'd know that the question was just more substantial than any answer you could provide. The detailed aspects of himself that would resurface from time to time – the wink that used to mean he was putting you on but couldn't possibly mean that now, or the particular clicking noise he made with his tongue when he understood something he hadn't previously been able to figure out – were, Cynthia realized, just vestiges, tics that no longer signified what they used to but that had somehow outlived the more essential parts of him, as if he were fading away from the inside out.

"Who are those idiots?" he said. He lifted his hand to shield his eyes from the sun even though the room was darkened almost completely. "Clear the green!" he said. "For Christ's sake!"

"Oh my God," Irene said nervously. "There's nothing there. You're seeing things." She took his hand; he jerked it away and started swinging his legs toward the side of the bed. The rails weren't up, and Cynthia didn't know how to operate them. The two women began trying to force him back into a prone position.

"Are you crazy?" he said to them. "It's a shotgun start. We have to get out there! Where are my shoes?"

"Ring for the nurse," Cynthia said to Irene, but Kay was already behind them. One look into his eyes was apparently enough to satisfy her that he was beyond the reach of her usual charms; she touched a button beside his bed, and another nurse came in holding aloft a needle.

"Oh shit," Cynthia said. She and Irene backed out into the corridor and tried not to listen. "Shit shit shit. It's not supposed to go like this. I mean, is it?"

"It's just a bad moment," Irene said, though she was

shaken too. "It's not his last. He won't go out struggling like that. He'll be ready."

God, it hadn't even occurred to her, until Irene mentioned it, that her father might be in the process of dying right now. One of the nurses came over and gently closed the door. Cynthia stared at it. "How do you know?" she said.

"The Lord won't allow it," Irene said. She smiled and laid her hand on Cynthia's arm. Her expression suggested that she was trying to convey something important and soothing. Cynthia wasn't sure whether Irene was choosing this moment to out herself as some kind of Jesus freak or whether she was just saying whatever came to mind to calm Cynthia as if they were mother and child, but either way, that hand on her arm sent a bolt through her that made her whole body stiff with revelation. Oh my God, Cynthia thought. There's no more time. She drew her arm away as cautiously as if she were pulling an arrow out of it.

"The Lord won't allow it?" she said. "The Lord won't allow it. Okay."

A few minutes later, Kay came out of her father's room and left the door open behind her. "He'll be sleeping for a while," she said, her eyes moving back and forth between the two women. "We really don't like to do that unless we have to, but as I guess you saw, he was getting very agitated. The only other option was restraining him. I'm sorry."

Cynthia turned to Irene. "Well," she said brightly, "it looks as if we have a few hours anyway. I'm hungry. Are you hungry?"

One of the orderlies directed them to a Cracker Barrel just across I-75. Cynthia rode shotgun in Irene's car. She didn't know what time of day it was anymore but she ordered a huge breakfast. "Breakfast served twenty-four hours is one of the things that makes America great," she said to Irene, who wasn't really sure what that meant but smiled delightedly. It was the opening Irene had been waiting for, and after they ordered she began by asking Cynthia some perfectly reasonable questions about her children: how old they were, whether she carried any pictures of them, the degree to which they looked like their mother and grandfather.

"I have three grandchildren," Irene offered. "The oldest is in the navy, living on a submarine, if you can believe that. I don't know how he does it. My two daughters are home-makers, one in Charlotte and one all the way out in California, in Silicon Valley. Jackie has a son who would be just about your son's age. Wouldn't it be something if they could meet?"

Cynthia waved to the waitress and mimed drinking a cup of coffee.

"You know," Irene said in a different tone, "I know that your father may not have been the most stable figure in your life. But some men just aren't made that way. For what it's worth, I know he had a lot of regrets along those lines. There are a lot of things he would have done differently."

"Irene?" Cynthia said.

Irene gave her the look of a patient receptionist as the

waitress set before them two plates so laden that food tilted over the sides.

"I do not want to talk about these things with you," Cynthia said.

"Why not?"

"It's past. There's no point."

"But it helps to talk about it. Right? I know it helps me to be able to talk about him with you."

"It does not help. You weren't there. You cannot insert yourself into it and honestly the thought of you talking about it at all seems kind of obscene to me."

Irene looked stricken.

"I'll tell you my thoughts about the past," Cynthia said, leaning back against the plush booth. "It's like a safe-deposit box: getting all dressed up and going downtown and having a look in there isn't going to change what's in it. I have very little time left with my father. The closer the end gets the more suspenseful it all is and to be honest I don't have the time to learn anything new about you or about anybody else he might have shacked up with. I don't have any interest in any kind of half-assed bonding experience with you, like you're going to be my stepmother or something. And if he'd wanted things to be like that between you and me, he would have mentioned you to me back when he still could have. You know, I've changed my mind. It actually does help to talk about it."

The corners of Irene's mouth were weakening. "May I ask, then," she said, straining to be dignified, "why we're here?"

"Because there's something I want to ask you, Irene, and I haven't really known how to ask it. But as I'm sitting here, I realize that it doesn't matter what you think of me. It doesn't matter. So what I've been wanting to ask you is this: what is your endgame here? Because I'll tell you something. I don't know you very well, obviously, but I know him well enough to guess what kind of relationship the two of you had. He was a man who got off on being admired, and when that feeling wore off he would move on, but since you had the good fortune to be there at the end you probably think it was a love that would have lasted forever. He didn't really live much of a life but if he had a woman in the room with him who thought he was just the shit, well, that's all he needed to feel good about himself. He could be a little cutting sometimes, right? Pumped himself up by teaching you things and making you tell him how smart he was? And I'll bet he had lots of good reasons not to get married whenever you brought that up. But the bottom line is you have no real legal connection to him, no obligation, and to be brutal not even an emotional relationship with him anymore, considering that he doesn't know who you are." She put some half-and-half in her coffee, because that was the only option on the table down here in fat country. "Do you see where I'm going with all this, Irene?"

Irene's lips were pursed, and her face moved irregularly like a bobblehead.

"I think our interests here actually coincide," Cynthia said. "I would imagine that you, an older woman with no visible means of support, as they used to say, are thinking

328

that your years of devotion to this fun guy with the rich daughter, if you can hang in there until the end, deserve some recompense."

"I beg your—"

"And I," Cynthia went on, "I would like you to go away and let me have this little bit of time alone with him. I would like that very much. I feel like I can see a way for these desires to dovetail nicely. Can you?"

Irene's face had gone bright red.

"It's not about you," Cynthia said. "You seem like a nice enough person."

"I don't understand."

"What don't you understand?"

"I mean, I don't want to be rude."

"If not now, when?" Cynthia said.

"He abandoned you," Irene said, and then put her hand over her mouth. "I know that he was a terrible, terrible father to you. He knows it too. And he took your money. All those years. He never asked for it, but he could have refused it. He should have."

"Au contraire. He could have had anything he asked me for."

"I wasn't even sure you'd come down here," Irene said. "I really wasn't. He said you would, but I thought that was just the way he wanted to see things. And yet you seem so in denial about it all—"

"You had fun with him, didn't you? I can tell. It's sad when the fun comes to an end. Somewhere in the world a woman learns that lesson every day."

329

Irene closed her eyes. "I'm just trying," she said, "to honor his wishes. I'm just trying to do what's right. Money has never even occurred to me."

"Well, I'm sure that's true. Let it occur to you now. You honored his wishes. That part is done. I'm asking you to honor my wishes now."

She began eating. It seemed as if even Irene's hair had started to come undone as they sat there at the table, as if she were riding in a convertible or sitting uncomfortably on a boat. Into her eyes came the glaze of the rest of her life. Cynthia knew her father well enough to know exactly what he had meant to this poor woman, all the high spirits, all the promise, all the purpose implicit in taking care of someone who expected to be taken care of. But now he was on his deathbed and there were no more high spirits for Irene. Abruptly her mouth fell open, and she emitted a laugh that was more like a bark; she shrugged, with her hands in the air, and shook her head as though denying that she was even the person saying what she was about to say.

"A hundred thousand dollars," she said.

"Done," Cynthia said. She reached for a napkin and pulled a pen out of her bag. "I'm going to give you a number to call. Call it tomorrow. There'll be something for you to sign as well."

"That won't be necessary."

Cynthia was about to insist, as she knew she should have, but something in Irene's face advocated for mercy. Instead she looked down at the table and spun the syrups meditatively. "God, this is decadent," she said. "Do people down here really eat like this? Boysenberry syrup? Well, okay, what the hell. When in Podunk."

"Do you," Irene said, and then closed her eyes and put her head in her hand. "Do you need a ride back to the hospice?"

"That is very kind of you," Cynthia said, reaching for her cell phone. "But no."

When Jonas's cell phone began ringing more insistently, Novak, who could not figure out how to turn it off, came up with a novel solution: he walked briskly into the bathroom and dropped it into the toilet. Jonas saw it when he went in there. He was allowed, it seemed, to get up from the couch – nothing but fear restrained him – though whenever he did, Novak would stop drawing and stare at him, inscrutably, like a cat, until he was back in his seat again. Jonas was left unsure whether his status was that of a prisoner or hostage of some kind or whether he was simply free to leave. Novak had already demonstrated how far he was willing to go to enforce his own sense of it, though, whatever that was, and Jonas didn't really feel up to the risk of testing him again. At least not yet.

One of the things that enervated him was the fact that he hadn't eaten in – well, he didn't know anymore how long he had been here. Along with the phone he had been relieved of his watch, though for some reason not his wallet or his car keys. The paper had been torn down from the windows but the shades were drawn. Novak had pulled a two-step ladder out of his bedroom, presumably for covering the parts of the wall too high for him to reach, and Jonas thought maybe that would be the time to break for the door, but he hadn't seen him use it yet. The food from Arby's had been sitting in the kitchen long enough to contribute to the rank, maddening airlessness, which was almost enough by itself to put you back to sleep.

Novak worked without stopping but he didn't work particularly fast. Jonas decided, maybe too dramatically, that whatever was going to happen to him would happen once the wall drawing was finished. Of course there were other walls to fill, though filling them would require moving the furniture again. There was no look of rapture or emotion on Novak's face as he drew; just concentration, that was all. As for what he was drawing, it was just another reconfiguration of the same shit he always drew; it was obsessive and incomprehensible and conveyed nothing, which would once have presented itself as a virtue but was frustrating now that there was something Jonas actually wanted to know. Novak's mural was no sort of key or portal to anything. And drawing pictures didn't seem to liberate him from his inner misery at all. If anything he looked grayer and more haggard than he had when Jonas first arrived. It was all one burden, a huge burden, but one for which Jonas had lost all capacity for empathy or even interest. It would not admit him. For the life of him he couldn't remember why he had been so excited about coming here.

Out of nowhere there were footsteps on the stairs outside Novak's door, and then a knock, not a friendly one. Jonas's head lifted up like a dog's, but Novak did not even react.

His fingertips were completely browned by Sharpie ink of all colors. "Joseph?" a woman's voice called. He went about his business, not responding but not making any effort to be silent either. "Joseph?" More knocking. "Joseph, if you are in there, I have warned you about taking garbage out. I know you don't like to do it but you have to. I can smell it from all the way down on the sidewalk. Do you hear me?"

Novak may or may not have needed glasses but he worked with his nose almost touching the surface on which he drew. He was working now, in green, on one of the square, blank-screened, rabbit-eared TVs he favored. This particular one sat on the roof of a gas station.

"By tonight," the woman said. "By tonight or I am calling your brother." The footsteps receded.

Use your key, Jonas yelled in his head, *use your fucking key, you idiot,* and then, cursing himself for his cowardice, he jumped up and ran for the door. Just as quickly, Novak dropped his pens on the floor and cut Jonas off, just by standing between him and the exit. Jonas stopped and put his hands up in front of him, his head pounding. Novak's leg started to shake. Tears came into his eyes. "Just please be still," he said. "Just be still. Unless you have to pee or something, and then just use the bathroom. This isn't my fault, you know. You think you're so smart but you're stupid. Do you have any idea how much trouble I'm in now?"

What exactly was she hoping might still happen? She was desperate that he not die, that was true, and she knew there was something shameful about that feeling because of its obvious defiance of what he wanted, back when he could want anything. She would never have admitted out loud to anyone how much she needed him to stay alive. But that wasn't because there was something she had to have from him before he went. It was more that she couldn't imagine herself in the world without him somewhere in it too. He was the living rebuke to whatever other people may have said or thought about his selfishness, his delinquency, his supposed mistreatment of her, because his adoration of her was no fake, no pose. He knew how to do it, and to make her feel it, from afar. He believed in her self-sufficiency. She adored him too. Everything was good between them, but she needed him alive in order to prove that.

So as bad off as he was, it was agony for her to watch him slip even farther. In his sleep his breathing degraded into a terrible sort of rasp: she'd heard the phrase "death rattle" before and at first assumed that this was it, but then maybe not, because he woke up again. He hadn't spoken in a day. She took over from the nurse the task of balming his lips, which were cracked all the time, because he no longer had the wherewithal even to lick them.

Still, when she would start awake in the chair by the head of his bed, or when she would rush in from the veranda overlooking the phony lake because she thought she'd heard a noise, she tortured herself with the thought that he had said something and she'd missed it.

She stopped going back to the hotel. She called the front desk to make sure Herman would continue on a 24/7 retainer, with whatever increase in pay that necessitated. It was silly but without Herman she was cut off from every-thing else she knew. She had no idea where the hell she was. On the other hand, maybe Marilyn the nurse could give her a ride somewhere if she needed it. Maybe they'd even have to stop off at Marilyn's home first, on their way to wherever they were going, so Cynthia might get a glimpse of how such people lived.

Time had shrunk down to the point where its only unit of measure was each irregular breath. One night, or day, she woke up in the chair and found him staring right at her. "Sinbad?" he said. His skin was drawn taut around his skull, but the film that seemed to lay across his eyes most of the time was gone.

She sat forward. He seemed a little sweaty; she dampened the washcloth and gently patted his forehead, his temples, his cheeks. "That's nice," he said clearly.

Bright institutional light slanted in from the open doorway; only by looking through the half-closed louvers could she see that it was dawn. Unless that was dusk. Either way, it cast the empty lake and the man-made berm beyond it in shades of the same blue.

"Don't cry," her father said. But she wasn't crying. She even put her fingers to her face to make sure. "I'm not crying, Dad," she said to him, and smiled.

"There, there," he said. He was looking right at her. "Take it easy. I'm right here."

Why should her first reaction, when he would stray like this, be to try to correct him, to bring him back into the moment? What difference did it make anymore, as long as he wasn't mad or agitated or looking for the goddamn shoes he was never going to put on again?

"Okay, Dad," she said. "Thanks. I feel better now."

"Good. We probably have to get to the church pretty soon. Don't we?"

Cynthia felt his delusion pulling at her like a drowning person might pull at your ankle from under the water. What was it? He couldn't possibly be talking about his own funeral?

"What time is it?" he asked her.

She shook her head, but she couldn't be sure he saw, so she cleared her throat and spoke. "I don't know," she said.

"Well," he said, with a bit of a rasp now, "I'm sure we have a few minutes. They can't very well start without us, can they?"

She held the cup to his mouth and he took a sip of water. Some of it ran down his cheek, and she reached out and stopped it with her fingers before it reached the pillow.

The way to stay with him, if you didn't understand exactly where he'd gone, was to eliminate the backdrop of time and place, forget about it, let it fade away, so that it was just the two of you standing against a blankness. So that there was only the present. This was what the two of them knew that no one else had ever understood. Everyone always wanted to know how she could forgive him, but forgiveness was a false premise. The whole idea of forgiveness presumed you were locked in the past and trying to let yourself out. She wasn't going to drag him back in that direction, to make him explain why he'd lived as he'd lived. That wasn't who they were. Each moment bore only on the next one and if you were going to be successful in this life, that was the plane on which you had to live. If you started going on your knees to the past, demanding something from it that it hadn't given you the first time around, you were dead. She asked for nothing from it. Neither did he. She was proud of his lifelong refusal to give in to the pathetic narcissism of depression or remorse. He had done what he had done and there was no changing it. There was no going back. She leaned over until her mouth was close to his ear.

"I'm so tired," she said. "Is it okay if I lie down with you here while we're waiting?"

He stared at her, every muscle in his face gone slack; his left hand spasmed a bit, and she recognized that what he was trying to do, or thought he was doing, was patting the bed beside him.

She still didn't know how those rails worked, so she had to climb over as if it were a fence and drop down beside him as gently as she could. She curled up with her back to him on top of the comforter, which didn't smell that great, and listened to his even, shallow breathing. She didn't move; he was so frail that she was afraid of hurting him. "This is your day," she heard him say. "It's all in front of you. What a gift to be young." Some hours later she felt a hand on her shoulder; it was a nurse, one she hadn't seen before, trying to wake her as gently as possible, and before she had even lifted her head she could tell from the look on the woman's face that her father, whose weight she could still feel on the bed behind her, was gone.

What had he come here looking for? It was all forgotten now. He had a vision of himself trying to explain all this to someone – what he was doing there in the first place, what he had expected to find, and not to Nikki or Agnew either but to a total stranger who didn't know who he was – and he felt nothing but that stranger's disgust for the folly of it. It was all so trumped up. He had invented it for himself. It was like there was no actual heart of darkness anymore and so he had to go and build one up out of nothing, and he had done such a good job of it that maybe now he was really going to die here and wind up as just another element of the overpowering stench in which Novak somehow managed to live.

And where was that Stockholm-syndrome thing you heard about? All he felt for Novak – whom he had romanticized into a figure who suffered for his art and for his noncompliance with the jaded world and its corrosive history – was an instinctive homicidal hatred, as he would for an animal that threatened him. The guy was balls-out insane and that was all there was to it: what difference did it make, to him or to anyone else, if his drawings hung in museums or if he just drew with his own shit on the walls of some madhouse?

Novak mumbled to himself as he worked. The wall was about eight feet by eleven feet. Like a giant piece of paper, was maybe how it presented itself to him. He covered every inch of it. *Horror vacui* – the phrase popped into Jonas's head, a phrase he'd once had to ID on the final in Agnew's Art Brut class. The wall was turning into a landscape of sorts, a flat, dimensionless one, full of those same gas stations and dead TVs: whatever it was he was trying to say with those few icons, he was apparently never going to get it said. A river ran across the picture, or maybe more of a canal, since it flowed straight as a board from one side of the wall to the other. A road made of water. All kinds of people and detritus were borne along in it, some aboard rafts or boats, some swimming or maybe drowning – the ambiguous open mouths of everyone in the picture made it impossible to tell. Novak worked the way a house painter might work, strictly in terms of space, from left to right; no figure seemed more important or more difficult to him than any other. It might have been his masterpiece; at the very least it was going to get him evicted. The strongest feeling Jonas could work up about it was fear of what would happen when it was finished.

A definite knot had formed on the back of his head, right where his skull met his neck. He had touched it so often he couldn't tell if it was still growing. Maybe it was life-threatening. He was quite sure he'd suffered a concussion at the very least: he felt like sleeping, he was not at all confident that he knew how long he'd been there, he had a headache like he'd never had before, which the blazing lights just made worse. He'd lived his whole life without ever being seriously hurt: that couldn't be right, it seemed to him, it was too ludicrous, and yet he tried in vain to think of another time in his childhood when anything like this had happened. And just like that, there it was: the Stockholm thing, the point of identification with your captor. His whole life is stunted, Jonas thought; it has not conditioned him to survive even one day outside his own front door. Neither has mine.

His mind drifted a bit and then suddenly he was aware that Novak was lying prone on the floor, working on the last bit of white space on the wall, the lower right corner. Except he didn't seem to be working at the moment. There was a green Sharpie still between his fingers, and Jonas waited and waited, trying to quiet his own breath, until finally the Sharpie rolled out of Novak's hand onto the floor.

"Joseph?" he said softly. Jonas couldn't see his face, but it made sense, certainly, that he might have been asleep. As far as Jonas knew, he hadn't slept the whole time they'd been together, however long that was. Nor had he seen Novak take any kind of pill. Pills must have been a significant part of his regular, solitary life. Who knew how that would affect him physically. "Joseph," he said again.

Is this really how it ends? Jonas thought. He felt like a coward and an idiot and still somehow closer to death than ever. As slowly as he could – in part because it turned out to be far more painful than he'd been ready for – he stood up from the couch. The glare from the lights was such that he cast no shadow anywhere. He took a step, and then another, at which point the floor cracked beneath him. Novak didn't budge. It was maybe ten more steps to the door; Jonas paused a second or two between each step, telling himself not to blow it by panicking, but poised to run for it if Novak so much as rolled over. Then he was sliding the deadbolt slowly, with two hands, and then he was outside on the landing, closing the door behind him to muffle the sound of him tiptoeing down the steps, holding both railings as he did so because he was so dizzy he thought he might pitch forward and descend the hard way.

His whole head was pulsing. The car was still parked right there, just a few steps away; somehow just by tailing the car in front of him he made it back onto the highway again. When he realized his cell phone was still in Novak's toilet, he was not all that displeased, because even though he knew Nikki would be out of her mind by now and had probably called the police, he wasn't ready to talk to her, or to anyone. Nikki herself didn't seem quite real to him yet. He supposed that feeling would come back, maybe when he saw her, but right now, when he tried to summon up anything more than just the image of her, he couldn't do it.

Maybe he could have left Novak's apartment hours ago and just didn't realize it. Maybe Novak had forgotten he was even there. A feeling of epic embarrassment began to press down on him. He hadn't eaten in so long he wasn't even all that hungry anymore; when he saw a McDonald's off the highway, he ordered a burger from the drive-thru, but a couple of miles later he pulled over to the shoulder, opened his door, and threw it up all over the side of the road.

It would have made a lot of sense to get off the highway and find a phone, or find a cop, or even just go to sleep; but he remembered hearing somewhere, maybe in a movie, that concussion victims weren't supposed to go to sleep, and anyway all he cared about was getting home. Cars were honking at him constantly, or flashing their lights, and he didn't know why, but they weren't helping. Somehow he got things turned around in his mind and he thought that the home at the end of this drive was not the one he shared with Nikki but the home he had grown up in, or one of them anyway, that penthouse that overlooked the planetarium, and he was pretty sure that his parents were expecting him there. He didn't want them to worry. He had something he needed to tell them, which was that he had finally figured them out. They had more money than anyone could ever spend – so much money that they had to hire people just to help them figure out how to give it away – and yet, rather than stop, his father worked harder than ever, making insane amounts of it, obscene amounts of it, out of thin air. It was like when people used to ask, do we really need all those nuclear missiles? How many is too many? The correct answer was that there was no such thing as too many, because it wasn't about need, it was about feeling safe in the world, and were you ever going to feel as safe as you needed to feel? No. No. Success was a fortress at which fear constantly ate away. Whatever you might have done yesterday meant nothing: the moment you stopped to assess what you'd built, the decay set in. What you wanted most of all, from a strictly evolutionary point of view, was a short memory. And Jonas was getting there: he had already pretty well forgotten everything other than his desire to recover his rightful place in that world that was deep inside the world – the more inaccessible the better. That was his real home. He couldn't wait. He planned on asking his parents for as much money as they would give him. The first thing he would do with it would be to get Nikki out of that dump they lived in and into some place that offered them all the advantages that were at his disposal, that had been at his disposal all along only he was too stupid and childish to appreciate it. But in order for that to work, he knew, he was first going to have to come up with some decent explanation, something more convincing than the humiliating truth, to offer Nikki when she demanded to know where the hell he had been.

I went looking for this artist but I never found him. I had the wrong address. I had an address for him but I waited and waited and he never came home. I decided to see some of the countryside. America's Dairyland. I drive so rarely. On the way home I got into an accident. Feel this knot on my head? On the way home I stopped in Joliet to see the house where my mother was born. On the way home I went to Pittsburgh to see my grandmother. You wouldn't like her. I didn't want you to feel obligated. I didn't particularly want to go myself, but family is family. On the way home I got into an accident and decided to check into a hotel. I got carjacked. I got kidnapped and my parents paid my ransom. I checked into one of those monasteries where they won't let you communicate with the outside world. Because I just needed some time to myself. On the way home I worried that we were getting too close. I'm leaving you. I left you but then I changed my mind and came back. Will you marry me? On the way home I drove into a ditch. I was mugged. I got lost. I went blind. I went to a bluegrass festival and shacked up with this woman I met but it was a huge mistake and I want you to forgive me. On the way home I was mugged and hit my head and got amnesia. I don't remember anything that happened before yesterday. I found your address in my wallet. I couldn't remember my name. I couldn't remember your name. I still can't. Let's go out and get new ones. My treat.